CLOUD GIRLS

CLOUD GIRLS

a novel

LISA HARDING

HARPERVIA
An Imprint of HarperCollins*Publishers*

Excerpt on page vii of "Advice to a Girl" by Sara Teasdale is reprinted with the permission of the Office for Resources, Wellesley College, Wellesley, Massachusetts.

This is a work of fiction. Names, characters, places, and incidents are products of the author's imagination or are used fictitiously and are not to be construed as real. Any resemblance to actual events, locales, organizations, or persons, living or dead, is entirely coincidental.

HarperCollins books may be purchased for educational, business, or sales promotional use. For information, please email the Special Markets Department at SPsales@harpercollins.com.

Originally published as *Harvesting* in Ireland in 2017 by New Island Books.

FIRST HARPERVIA EDITION PUBLISHED IN 2023

Designed by Janet Evans Scanlon

Library of Congress Cataloging-in-Publication Data has been applied for.

ISBN 978-0-06-327028-2

23 24 25 26 27 LBC 5 4 3 2 1

This book is dedicated to all those
whose lives have been stolen by traffickers.

No one worth possessing
Can be quite possessed;
Lay that on your heart,
My young angry dear;
This truth, this hard and precious stone,
Lay it on your hot cheek,
Let it hide your tear.
Hold it like a crystal
When you are alone
And gaze in the depths of the icy stone.
Long, look long and you will be blessed:
No one worth possessing
Can be quite possessed.

Sara Teasdale, "Advice to a Girl"

1

Nico

A cooling breeze creeps up my skirt, tickling my thighs, as I climb to the highest branch of the highest tree in the forest. Puffs of cloud, like God's breath, float all around. Some of the other fellows are yellowing and balding, but this old man holds on to his crown all year round. He smells of leather and Papa's pipe. Lying back on his wrinkled bark, blotched with freckles, I scout the sky for shapes. With a slight squinting and blurring, a galloping filly appears just beyond my reach. I swing both legs either side of the branch and ride like the cowboys ride in the films Maria's dad lets us watch.

"Would you like a man like that?" he'd say. "A man with bandy legs who spits on the ground?"

Maria would laugh, and I would think: but what about the gun packed so close to his thigh?

When we're alone, Maria says she dreams of those spitting men.

Luca has climbed up behind me and is shaking the branch I'm clinging to. "Hey, don't be such a dumbass! I could fall." He starts to laugh, sounding as cruel as Sergiu. The dog is running round and round the base, making strange grunting sounds.

"That stupid animal doesn't know it's a mutt," he says, and throws a baby-green fairy cap in its direction. He should know better. Mama says if they are pulled too soon, you can hear their cries on the wind.

Luca hits the dog on its head, and it yelps helplessly, looking towards the sky. It still hasn't worked out where we go when we climb up the trunk of the tree; as far as it can see, we disappear into the clouds. It's been around as long as I have, which must make it very old in dog years. "Senile old nutter," Sergiu would say, as he'd give it its tenth whack of the day with his pointed boot. We've never given the old hound a name. My brothers all laugh when I suggest it. "It's an animal, a creature, an "it," and that's that, silly sis." Mama reckons the boys were knocked on their heads when they were little, or jostled about too much when they were growing inside her. I think it's because they came out just like Papa, except for Luca, who is more like Mama and me, although he tries very hard not to be.

"Where is your little friend today, sis?" As if he doesn't know. He follows us to the river most days and hides behind a bush where he thinks we can't see him.

"Just who are you talking about, donkey?" I've arranged to meet Maria later at the watering hole, at the same time we meet every day during the summer holidays.

"Do you think she likes me?"

He's asking for it now. "She doesn't even know you exist."

He shakes the branch in a fury so I'm on the edge of falling.

"Stop, you castrated bull!"

He laughs. "Don't worry. I'll catch you on the way down." The dog's anxious grunting increases. "Stupid yoke," he says.

Of the three boys, Luca has the bluest eyes, the thickest hair, and the smoothest skin. Although he's the youngest, he's also the tallest, with wide shoulders, narrow hips, and a taut body. The girls in school giggle when he's around and wear high color on their cheeks. Maria's no different, although I'd never tell him this. "Come swimming with us today." The words are out of my mouth before I can pull them back. Maybe it's because I know there are only five more days left before school starts, or maybe it's because I want the shaking to stop.

"Okay," he says, as if he doesn't care.

An image of Maria and Luca alone together floats out of nowhere, gaining substance until it's hard and solid, hitting me in the chest, leaving me breathless.

"I can see up your skirt," he shouts, conceding nothing.

There is a silence, until I realize he has started climbing back down. I let go of the branch I was clinging to and spread my arms wide. Look: no hands! The sky is piebald blue and white, and I am trotting, cantering, galloping along the plains.

I would much rather *be* one of those men than meet one, as a girl.

"Are you coming down?" He's in a desperate hurry to get to the river.

"In a minute," I shout, as a strange and strong pain hits me in the stomach. It has been happening more often: this clutching feeling, which comes with no warning and leaves me with wet in my eyes. I lean forward and lay the length of my body down, pressing my stomach against the wood, resting my cheek on the rough bark. Waves of swimming lines float in the air.

"Come on, sis, Maria might think you're not coming."

I turn my head so the other cheek is rubbing against the old fellow's gnarled skin. I press and I breathe. Almost as soon as it arrived it's gone and I sit back up, swing my legs around and drop down into the center of the tree, using legs and arms to root and dangle until the last swing lands me on my feet.

"What took you so long?"

"Just thinking."

"You do too much of that already. Look, sis . . ." He holds out the palm of his hand and there's a giant centipede marching up towards the soft part of his arm.

I won't give him the satisfaction of hearing me scream. "Disgusting."

"It's what the stupid dog is snuffling around at." He points at the dog, its nose pressed deep into the earth, digging a frantic hole. "There must be some kind of a nest down there."

"Those things don't build nests."

"A hive then?"

The dog looks frantic. I don't want to see. "Come on. Maria will be waiting."

"Race you."

Without saying anything, I build up my speed inside, until I take the first step, pushing off the ball of my right foot. I run like the rabbits run when they know they are being hunted. Even though I'm smaller and my sandals are loose around my ankles, I'm still the fastest. "Swift as the foam bubbles dissolving on the river," Papa says. "Like a silver bullet," Luca says. The dog loves the speed of these bursts and the squeals that come from me as I push out past my brother. It runs ahead and then circles back, barking madly at the air.

When we arrive at the watering hole, Maria is already there, lying on her back in her white dress with the yellow flowers. She has two dresses this summer: the other is light blue and has longer sleeves and a longer hemline. I wish she was wearing that one now. Her legs are bent, feet lined up underneath her knees.

"Hello, you," she says. "What's *he* doing here?"

The veins on Luca's neck swell, and he starts to back away. "Just passing. I'll leave you two to it."

Maria rolls onto her elbow and sits upright. "Last one in is chickenhearted," she says, as she rips off her dress and wades into the cold, murky water in her bra and pants. I had forgotten about this part. I don't wear a bra and don't want Luca to see my naked body, so I run in in my cream cotton dress.

"What are you doing, you queer duck?" she says. "You're going to ruin your dress. It's filthy in here." We've been warned all summer about the dangers of this polluted river with its tongues of yellow foam lapping against the banks. Plenty of others swim here, and no one I know has been ill, although there have been whisperings about the Tcaci sisters from the next village. Something about them becoming so sick that there was nothing left inside them, that they'd surely be left barren. The water becomes clearer the deeper you go, and anyway, it's way too hot not to swim.

I stick my head under and push my body down to the silty floor. The silk-like liquid covers my sticky body with cool, the dress billowing around me as I swim low. I kick my legs and open my arms in big circles, holding my breath for sixty-one seconds, hoping they'll be impressed. When I come back up, the other two are splashing each other and Maria is pushing Luca's head beneath the surface. He's making a big show of spluttering and waving his arms about, even though he's one of the strongest swimmers in the school, and Maria knows this. The dog is running up and down along the banks of the river, howling.

"I was under for sixty-six seconds," I shout—hand in the air, clenched fist, victorious—thinking that number sounds more impressive. No one's listening. I lie on my back and try to float. Although I'm light, the river won't let me; my legs and feet keep sinking and then the rest of me goes down. Papa says it's because it has no salt in it, unlike the Black Sea. He says you could lie for hours on your back on the inky, salty water, floating in the night sky. Mama would bite on her cheek as he'd tell me these stories, only letting herself speak later when he was out of earshot. "Don't mind your father, Nico, he has never been to the sea."

I allow my feet to touch the bottom, which makes a sucking sound when you stand. My toes curl around the mud as I wade against the water, feeling strong as I press it away. The other two are shouting and laughing still. I shouldn't have told Luca to come. I swim until my arms and legs are burning and my heart's pounding in my ears, then I climb onto the bank, my wet dress sticking to me like another skin. The dog pushes its head against me, shaking, and I pat it between its eyes.

Maria comes out next and throws herself on the ground beside me. "You didn't tell me you were bringing your brother."

"You don't seem to mind."

She smiles at me and rolls onto her front. I wish she would put her clothes back on. "Are you cold?" she asks. I'm shaking and there are blue and yellow patches on my legs and arms.

"I'm fine, but you must be . . ."

She turns onto her back and stretches her arms long over her head, her toes pointing towards the ground, back arched. I see Luca staring over, and I cross my eyes and touch the tip of my tongue to my nose. He pokes his tongue through his teeth, narrowing it, before he too, touches his nose.

"Impressive," says Maria, deadpan.

"I bet you can't do it," I say.

"Nope, and I wouldn't even bother trying. It's a Zanesti thing."

I feel a small shiver of victory.

"The clouds are moving about fast up there," Maria says. We both look up at the shifting shapes in the sky. "I'd love to get on an airplane and fly away from here." I ask her where she thinks she'd go. She tells me her older sister Alina met a man in the village who said he could get her a job as a waitress in Greece, and she could earn more money in a month than she would working in a factory in Chişinău for a year.

"You're too young," I tell her.

"I heard Papa say I will make a good marriage, in time." We both lie on the ground silently, staring at the clouds as they skitter across the blue. I don't want her to go away from me. I don't want her knowing this.

"What do you wish for, dreamer?" I've never thought beyond this—beyond school terms and holidays and essay prizes and climbing trees and swimming in the river. "Are you writing in your notebook every day?" she asks, looking at me closely. "You're the best in school, everyone says so." That's just because everyone else is so lazy. "You'll win the essay competition again this year." I shrug, pretending that I don't care. "You should be a teacher, like Miss Iliescu." I like this idea, for then I might not have to marry at all. "Ms. Smith thought you were the cat's meow!"

My heart hurts thinking of her open face, always kind, even when the stupid boys fell asleep in her class, or pulled our ponytails, or wrote filthy notes and flew them as paper airplanes, aiming their pointy noses at the back of the girl's head in front. "You have a bright future, Nicoleta," she'd said on her last day, before she returned home to America after volunteering at our school for two whole years. "Students like you make doing what I do worthwhile." My face tingles recalling these words.

Luca climbs out, his body strong and wet. He goes for a run, to warm up, the dog running alongside him. Maria laughs. "That dog is in love," she says.

2

Sammy

Since it happened a year ago—I was a late developer, though I've wasted no time making up for lost time—the dog up the street won't stop humping me, Mother looks like she wants to devour me, Dad looks (and goes) away, Brian and the lads want to do me, and men are craning their necks everywhere I go. The other day a taxi driver sped through a red light and almost caused a massive pileup, horns honking furiously, as he kept his eyes fastened on me. That would be about right really, that I would be the cause of such commotion. "Havoc follows you wherever you go," Mother says. She seems to think I'm the reason she is the way she is—she wishes she'd pushed me back inside her the minute I slithered out, and demanded I be turned into a boy who would grow into a big strong man to worship the ground she walks on. Instead, she got this awful girl. Sometimes when I see her sitting on her fat ass, glugging her Chablis or her Sauvignon, or worst of all, her Chardonnay, I get the feeling she might open her greedy gob and suck me in, swallowing me whole. I can imagine Luce calling over and seeing my bony body pushing through her jelly belly, elbows and knees jutting through, my voice coming from far away. Luce would cut her open with a kitchen knife and free me.

I hear the doorbell ring: it is my savior. Mother answers the door, and I can imagine her laser-beaming Lucy with her yellow eyes, her gaze working upwards from Lucy's ankles to beneath the hem of her skirt. "Hello, Lucy," I hear her say. "Samantha is having a strop, locked herself in her bedroom, making an awful racket. I'm at my wit's end with that one." Even though she's not one to pray, Luce thanks God or the tooth fairy or whatever entity has decided not to land her in this house.

"Sam?" I pretend not to hear her, allowing her to suffer the pleasure of Mother's company a moment longer. Feel it, Luce? I'm hooked up to Eminem on my mobile, on a loop, over and over: *Oh, where's Mama? She's taking a little nap in the trunk.* Eminem is the king. He does it better than any of the new-bies out there. Mother hates the racket he makes: "Angry little man." Really, Mother. I imagine her going into the kitchen to light a cigarette and suck on a glass of chilled plonk; she's waving the cigarette towards the ceiling and the "strop." "What did I do to deserve this little hussy?" she says, all teary and bleary. Luce turns one of her special hate-filled stares on Mother, believing for a moment that maybe she possesses special powers and can turn the monster to stone. Instead, the full force of Mother's toxic gaze is turned back on her and she withers. Poor ole Luce wants to wee and wants to run. She's momentarily paralyzed, standing at the base of the stairs.

"Go on home now, and I'll deal with the trollop later on."

This is it. Some power she never knew she had pours through her. "Where do you think you're going, missy? I thought I told you to go home." Luce must hear the voice behind her: a voice that is full of swaying and malice, a voice that is saturated with booze. She gets to the top of the stairs and bangs on my door. "It's me, Lucy."

Mother is mounting the steps behind her and I imagine Luce willing herself not to look back, to hold her nerve, not to give up on her best friend. Louder now, "It's Luce," and the door opens a crack and my tearstained face—blotchy, bloated, and bright red, for full effect—peers around the gap. My arm pulls her in. Her breath is coming fast and shallow. Just from looking at me, she seems as if she might faint. Luce hates to see anyone upset, most of all me. Even though I try not to let it in and I'm old enough to know the score, last night's shenanigans were bad, even by this house's standards (although I can't be sure it really happened the way I think it happened; I was half asleep and I'm prone to nightmares and hyperimaginings and lying, even to myself). Thing is, I don't like her coming into my room in the middle of the night to stare, or whatever it is she's doing, and I told her as much. I told her to fuck off and she said, "How dare you speak to your mother like that?" in that haughty injured tone she has, and then I couldn't sleep and my airwaves closed down and my head sped up and I lay there, rigid and tumbling inside.

"Come on, Sam, let's get out of here," Luce says. "Dad gave me this . . . so pizza?" She holds out twenty quid. "Let's get a movie and some grub." She notices that I'm wearing new high, high wedges and a short, black leather mini with a tight T-shirt. A present from Brian. "Where are you going dressed like that?" she says.

"Maximum exposure," I say, winking. She knows this particular one—it's what I say when she asks me why I roll my uniform so high. "Don't you start anyway. You sound like the aul wan below. Come on, let's go."

"Aren't you going to put some clothes on? Seriously, it's not that warm out there." Her voice is high.

"Well," I say, "I'm hot, hot, hot."

Luce knows I have a reputation as being exactly that with the boys in the school. Right now she's getting hot standing in my presence. Her cheeks are pulsating and I can tell her heart is hammering. I have her in my thrall. "Ready to run?" I say, pinioning her with my stare. She nods and pushes open the door, and the two of us bolt it down the stairs, past Mother's bulk as she tries to block the door but finds two hurtling teenagers too much for her. "Oh, my poor heart," she says, gasping, grabbing at her humongous bosom as the two of us fly past, laughing so loudly it seems we might combust. "You're my knight in shining armor," I say to Luce. I know she likes that one.

We burst outside into the limp sunlight that does little to heat the expanse of my bare goose-pimply skin. We run fast, past all the other identical white semi-Ds with their neatly tarmacked drives and their 4x4s, past the scrawny newly planted trees, past Spar, past Murtagh's pharmacy (purveyors of Xanax and Lexotan to the stressed-out mothers of terrible teenagers), past Café Zefferelli's, past Butler's Pantry, and further on—to the Holy Grail, the all-important booze emporium. "Where do you think you're going?" Luce says to my back as I disappear into the offy, where Mother has won "Customer of the Year Award" the last five years straight.

Inside, the boy with the pimples who doesn't look old enough to be serving alcohol looks me up and down, running his gaze over my legs. *As if.* I know this game. I pick a naggin of vodka off the shelf.

"ID," the guy manages. The sound comes out all muffled. He's having a hard time swallowing.

"Do I look like I'm too young?" I say.

"Sorry, no can do. If the boss sees me selling booze to you, I'm out of a job," he says, warming to his theme of power and guardianship.

"Tell your boss to come on out here." The guy is silent. I didn't think so. "Come on, just let us buy the booze and I'll make it worth your while." I frown at him. The frown says more than a smile in this instance. It says: I will, you know, I'm serious. I'll do anything you want me to do, if you'll sell me this booze.

"Come on, Sam, let's go," Luce says. "I'm starving."

"You go if you want to. I'll follow you when I'm good and ready." I know she won't leave me here. The guy is staring. I can hear the voices warring in his head. If he won't sell it to me, I'll take it anyway. He knows it, I know it, Luce knows it. The boy crumbles, asks for my number. I smile and give him Luce's.

"Great. Now I'm going to have Creepo calling me all times of the day and night, obsessed." She knows what she's talking about.

We walk out of the shop with a bottle of clear liquid in a brown paper bag, and I turn to her. "Now, let's go get off our heads."

"I'm starving," she says.

"Good, good. It's better that way. Works faster, burns the fuck out of your stomach and swims into the bloodstream directly." She's probably wondering why I'd want to be like Mother. Sometimes I ask myself this question and it's complicated, 'cause obviously I don't want to be . . . but . . . sometimes . . . getting off your head is the only response: it's like sleeping without the nightmares. I need to numb now, and quick.

"I'm getting us some pizza first," she says.

"Knock yourself out." She goes into the Spar that serves heated pizza slices. She must have some other money her dad gave her. He's always giving her spondoolas. She comes back with two slices of margherita, another with mushrooms and ham, and a bottle of water. Go Luce. I'm sitting on a high wall opposite, swinging my legs, wedges dangling around my ankles.

"Are you okay?" she asks. "Your eyes look all bruised underneath."

"It's only that shit new Maybelline mascara. It runs like hell," I tell her. "Come on, Luce, race ya," and I jump off the wall, wincing as one of my ankles turns sideways. I take off the shoes and leg it.

Her breath is close behind me, both of us running like loopers until we reach the gates of the convent garden. Heels dangling in one hand, the brown paper bag in the other, I scramble over the top of the spiked gate, landing in a tangled heap on the other side, screeching.

"You sound like a demented baby hyena." That's pretty original, coming from her. She hands the bag with the pizzas and the water through the bars and starts to climb. She's terrified of falling on a spike, impaling herself there. I grab her on the other side and we roll, limbs entangled, breath shared and caught, hysterical. She falls onto her back and I sit on top of her, pinning her arms to the ground. "Now swallow," I say, pushing the bottle of vodka to her lips. She has no ability to say no to me, ever.

The burning liquid gushes down her throat and bloats her stomach. I can see it blowing up in front of my eyes, like a little helium balloon. She's not hungry now, either. She has no desire to do anything except lie here, me astride her, the cloudy sky above us. I glug, like a greedy baby with a bottle of formula.

"Hey," she says, "slow down."

I collapse onto the grass beside her and we both stare up at the sky.

"Look at that cloud. It's like a great big cock." Luce doesn't see what I see. I bet all she sees are gray billowy things. The whole sky is different shades of gray. "Hey, lezzie, I know you want to. Why not?" And I do what she dreams of me doing: I grab her tight, push my mouth onto hers. She tries to stop me, to stop herself, to be my protector, yet here she is, no better than any of the others. I can hear her thoughts clearer than I hear my own.

She pushes me off her eventually. "What if a nun sees us?"

I laugh. "They're at it every night of the week anyway."

We lie on our backs on the damp yellowing grass.

"Back to school in five days," she says.

"I'm not going back."

"Don't be such an eejit, of course you are. What else would you do?"

"I have to get a job."

"Who's going to give you a job? You're only fifteen."

"Would you stay in that house?"

"You don't have to. Come home with me."

"Your mother can't stand me."

"Not all mothers are psycho like yours."

I turn my back on her.

"Oh, shit. I'm sorry, Sam. I didn't mean that."

That's for me to say, not you, Luce. It's getting cold. She takes off her hoodie and lays it over me. I roll onto my back, staring up at the almost-night sky, snuggled deep under her fleece. My eyes close. I know she's watching the rise and fall of my chest; I know she wants to lay her head there. She doesn't move. I allow myself to go under, my guardian angel watching over me, but then I feel a shadow crossing my body and I raise my spikes. The machine is going to flatten me, but still I don my armor. It's futile, gonna happen anyway. I can smell her boozy breath. I push her off me. No. No. No. No. No.

"Sammy, it's okay," a voice whispers. I open my eyes and flow back down inside my body. The sky above is navy-black now and pricked with tiny stars. I'm on the grass, with my friend beside me, and although we are far from that house, the reverberations are still inside me: *maximum exposure.* I look down at my long, stick-like legs and red, scuffed knees.

"Come on, let's get you home," she says.

"Are you insane? Insane in the membrane?" I'm singing and wide awake now. "I told you I wouldn't spend another night under that stinking roof."

"I know. I know. I meant my home. Let's get you back there."

"Your parents will be furious, and they'll blame me." I give her my phone. "Look, it's one in the morning and not a call. Mine probably don't even notice. Check yours, I bet there's zillions of missed calls. I bet they'll have called out the cavalry."

I'm stomping on the damp grass in my bare feet. "Do you honestly think we can just go on back there now and get hugs and food and warm beds and snuggle up close to each other and have sweet dreams?"

"No way I'm leaving you here alone."

"No way I'm going back to your gaff with you now. We both stink of booze."

"No way I'm going without you."

This is the moment inspiration hits. Heat rises in me and the hair on my arms spikes upwards. I start riffing on a theme, feeling like I'm Ireland's answer to the king of Beat Boys: Guys and girls and damage done / Guys hurt girls / Hurt girls = concerned parents = attention diverted from pissed wayward friend. This is genius. This is why I get As in English when I pretty much fail everything else. "You have a powerful imagination," Miss White would say as she'd hand me back my pages topped with a gold star. "Powerful." And now the ideas are coming, in a torrent, like what I imagine King Em experiences as he floods the pages with his scorching rage. I can see the picture forming: me dripping in blood, clothes torn, sobbing, distraught, in need of care and medical attention. I've always liked the fact that Luce's dad is a doc, some top-notch consultant saving lives, whereas mine is some guy with a suit and a briefcase, selling stuff. So, there I am—hurt, really hurt, and Luce's parents are too concerned to be angry, even though I'm well aware of what they think of me. Particularly Mrs. O'D. She practically wrinkles her nose every time she sees me. "That girl has trouble written all over her." Well, tonight, Mrs. O'D, I'm going to prove you spectacularly right.

"What's going through your mind?" Luce says, crashing in on my buzz.

"We could do it to ourselves." I point to the bottle. "We can do a lot of damage with that."

"Don't be such an idiot. My parents are not going to go mental if we go home now. We can tell them the truth, tell them about your awful row with your mother and you needing to get out of the house and needing air and headspace."

"Do we also tell them about their daughter comforting me?"

"Sammy . . . don't," she says.

Pacing, my heart is pounding and the blood is pulsing faster than it's ever done. I can feel it thumping in my ears. This is like the time I took poppers and couldn't stop dancing and couldn't slow my heart down for days after. This is like that time, and then some. The train has left the station now, Lucy Lou, and you laying yourself out on the tracks ain't going to stop it, so you better just get out of its way. I can hear her twittering on, telling me to "calm down" and "think clearly," but I'm not listening with the force and speed of the thoughts tumbling around in here. I lift the empty bottle and suck down the last few dregs, then sit back on the grass, and watch.

I witness my hand moving of its own accord, or according to the yank of some giant puppet master in the sky. Whatever; I have no control over the hand that places the bottle between my legs, and pushes it hard, ramming it, so I tear. Luce screams, then goes quiet, whispering, "Oh, Sammy, Sammy," over and over. She sounds muffled, as if we are both underwater.

A voice comes out of me, high and giddy. "It's not like it wasn't broken before." Lucy's whispers taper off, and she falls silent. The silence envelops the moment, stilling it, distilling it.

We are both captured in a perfect freeze-frame. I'm calm, hyper, shocked, elated by this thing that my hand has done. I'm sore, and that feels right. The demented ventriloquist speaks though me, "Now I'm all smashed up. Now someone might take notice." My body spasms with horror and ecstasy at what I have done, or what *it* has done. Yep, Mother, I'm a crazy possessed child, all right.

3

Nico

When I stretch my arms to their widest span, my fingertips hit against slimy moss-covered walls. The freezing water is at my chest and creeping its way higher. I hold my breath while telling myself that no one really dies in their dreams. Even when I open my eyes, pinch myself, and let the bedside lamp cast its glare around the room, I feel as though I'm deep down under and there is a cover blocking out all the light. I did not meet a white rabbit, nor did I tumble—I was pushed, by Sergiu and Victor, with Papa looking on. Mama taught me to twist the skin on my arm, hard, to scatter the ghosts that have entered my imagination. My forearm is mottled pink and purple, my lungs filled with well water.

Maria likes to tell me of her dreams, which involve boys, and those spitting men. I bet Luca is in some of them. I tell her about the ones where I'm climbing trees, or swimming in a river, or sometimes in a sea that is like swimming in the sky, or about winning first prize in the essay competition. I don't mention any of the other visitations that have Mama running to my bed and slapping me, pinching me hard. I never remember these after, just the sense of having been invaded. This is different. I hit myself on both cheeks to shake the memory, which is as alive as this moment I am living.

Outside, a strange bird sounds. I think back to nature class and try to remember—jay, song thrush, blackbird, woodlark? Placing my feet on the patch of worn carpet beside my bed, I stand and stretch, pull back the tattered lace window dressings, turn off the light, and allow my eyes to adjust to the darkness outside. Through the grimy glass, I can make out the shape of the small tree with its carpet of shed helicopters, the rusted wire of the sleeping chicken coops, and the silhouette of the dog, tethered to a post, curled in on itself, its body rising and falling. I want to go outside and bring it back to my bed, but Papa would never allow it: "Filthy flea-ridden thing." I listen to the sound, which is thin and distant. Maybe it's not a bird at all. Maybe it's the cry of a baby acorn being taken too soon. Red squirrels live in the forests around here, although nobody I know has ever seen one, except Papa, who claims they are like "giant rats with fluffy tails and razor-sharp teeth."

When I turn back towards the bed, I see a staining on the sheets: berry red and glistening. Did this happen in my dream? Was I hurt when I fell into the well? I look down at my body and there is blood between my legs. The water should have washed me clean. Maybe I punctured myself climbing the tree. The Virgin Mary, in her gilded picture frame above my bed, glints at me and smiles. I want to go to Mama but am too afraid to wake Papa, who was late coming back from the village for dinner and had taken too much Rachiu. His eyes were shining overbrightly and two spots of purple appeared high on his cheeks, crisscrossed with veins, like bruised plums. I could feel his gaze on me. Mama and I were careful not to get too close, not to look at him directly, and not to say anything that might make him laugh, or cry, or swear, or punch a hole in the wall.

"You two are much too silent," he said. "What are you plotting?"

When we assured him, "Nothing, nothing at all," he kicked at the already unsteady leg of the stool, buckling it. He roared and bucked, declaring it was all our fault, all our fault, all of it, before he slumped back on his armchair, falling unconscious immediately, making soothing snoring sounds that signaled it was safe to lift him into bed.

I pull the sheets off my bed, go to the kitchen to fetch the bucket with the well water, and submerge the stain into the cold clear water, which turns pink as I scrub. I don't dare put the water on to boil. I scrub, rubbing my knuckles against each other until they are red and raw. Mama would not want me to use the soap for this purpose. The staining won't disappear; it changes from red to rust to brown. I must get to Mama first thing in the morning, before Papa or my brothers hear that I have hurt myself climbing trees.

After I've cleaned myself, changed my clothes, padded my underwear with tissue and hid the bucket under the bed, I sit on the sill of my bedroom window and open it wide. Hues of dawn are leaking into the corners of the black screen of night. I wonder if the sandman could still appear. Papa always said that if you didn't close your eyes late at night, a man would come and fill them with sand. When I was tiny, I asked Papa what this would feel like. "Stingy like salt, dirty like grit from the backyard, and sore like an attack by stinging flies," he said. Although I didn't really believe him, I made sure to close my eyes after midnight. So, we will see, Papa. No wonder Mama throws her eyes towards heaven when he speaks, or sometimes she blesses herself when she thinks no one's looking.

My body feels charged with electric energy, so sleep will not come. I take out my notepad: *My Summer Holidays*, by Nicoleta Zanesti. I write about strange images of spiky branches that pierce me and the river running red as I swim through it. I want to wash myself clean, from the inside out. My cheeks are blushing at what has just happened. My body feels like it doesn't belong to me; there is a dragging sensation deep inside. I'm not sure who is writing this thing that seems to whisper and cackle in my ear, flowing to my hand, the pen, the page. Miss Iliescu would not recognize these words, these secret words of shame, as mine.

Mama rises with the first cockerel's cries coming from the Petran's farm next door. Our own died a long time ago. We do not expect a replacement. I am careful to dress in long trousers and brush my hair and tidy it back in a ponytail before I go to her. "Mama?" I say to her back as she bustles about the kitchen.

"Nico, we must go to the well straight away. The water's gone." She turns to look at me and sees the bundle under my arms. "It means you are a woman now." A fiery heat blasts through my body. She points at the sheets. "Quick, before the others wake. We'll boil those. Go get the bucket."

"But the water is stained."

"Just do it."

I return with the rose-colored water, which Mama pours into the pot over the fire. She stirs it impatiently.

"Mama?"

Her body stiffens. "Just what I said, young lady."

I want to ask if this has happened to her; I want to run to Maria to find out if she's also a woman now, but I know not to ask Mama any more questions when her face is set like this. I think of the whisperings of the older girls in school, which would stop any time I came near. Irina would say, "Definitely not, she doesn't even have to wear a bra," and Petra and the rest of them would laugh and the skin on my face and chest would become hot and blotchy.

Mama pours the boiling pink water back into the bucket, submerges the sheet into bleach, and we take it to the shed where it's left hidden for the morning. I untie the dog, whose tail thumps loudly on the ground when it sees us, and we walk single file on the narrow path through the yellowed grass to the well, one empty container in each hand. The pale sun is creeping steadily higher, irritating my already hot skin. My insides feel twisted and raw. Mama expects me to gather the water as I normally would, but when I lean over the wall I feel as if I might fall into the black mouth, which looks like it will swallow me whole. Mama waits, saying nothing, then stretches over and fills both pails, scooping the water sideways, which makes a greedy glugging sound as it rushes in. I want to tell her about my dream, but my throat narrows and stops my voice. The thing I want to say gets pushed back down and lodges in my stomach like a stone. We walk, the only sound the water sloshing about inside the buckets, the metal brushing against our bare legs.

When we get home, Luca is in the yard feeding what's left of the chickens, and the others are still in bed. "Race you?" Luca says when he sees me.

"Your sister will not be climbing trees today, Luca. She needs to rest." I feel like running and climbing and swimming, but maybe Mama knows more than I do about what it means to be a woman. "You go on, Luca," Mama says. "Did you eat your breakfast?"

Luca nods and looks from me to her. "Are you okay, sis?" Mama tells him to go find some boys of his own age to climb trees with.

"Can I just go and sit in the shade of the tree?" I ask.

"No, Nico. Today you will stay with me in the house."

Luca scuffs his shoe, then bends to tie his laces. "Off you go," Mama says, shooing him with her hand. He shrugs, sticks his hands in his pockets and walks slowly down the lane, sneaking a backwards look when he thinks Mama has gone inside. She is standing there still, one hand gripping my shoulder, narrowing her eyes at her youngest son. The dog doesn't know what to do. It chases Luca, then comes back to me, barking. "Come on," it's saying, "it is time to run." I look at it and turn the palms of my hands towards the sky, as if to say there's nothing to be done, dog—today is a new day, with a new set of rules, and I am as much in the dark as you are. Mama tells it to shush, and she looks at me like she might hit me or hug me.

Papa has a sore head when he wakes and does not pay much attention to me, although Sergiu and Victor are sniffing around. "What is wrong with her?" they ask Mama and each other, with sly smiles. "Get out of here, you good for nothing layabouts," Mama says. I have never heard her speak this way. I'm not sure what is expected of me today. She told Luca I was to stay in the house and rest, but I have never seen her sit for more than the length of time it takes her to gulp back a steaming mug of tea. How she does not scald herself I do not know. Am I meant to sit and watch her as she sweeps and chops and dusts, and serves the men of the house their lunch of pickled cabbage soup and dark bread?

"Here," she says as she passes me the ladle to dole out the broth to the boys.

After lunch, Sergiu and Victor scratch their full bellies and belch. Do they hang around Mama all day? As soon as it's late enough to be served alcohol, they wander slowly up the lane towards the village, where Papa had gone to do "business" with a man from another village just after breakfast. I could see Mama bite down on her cheek as he informed her of his day's plans. What would his new venture entail? Would it be scrawny chickens that arrived with a disease, or a rotting tomato plant that had no hothouse in which to grow, or a goat that frothed at the mouth if you walked anywhere near it?

When the boys have disappeared from the lane, Mama and I breathe out at the same time, and without saying anything, we go to the shed to check up on the sheets. They have washed clean. We hang them on the line under the high blue sky, where they flap gently in the breeze, the dog growling at them from the shade. It did not go with Luca, without me.

Just as I wonder if Maria and Luca are swimming in the river, I see her running down the path towards the house. I have to stop myself from sprinting to her and throwing myself into her arms. The strange energy that visited me in the night charges me with restlessness and tears. Perhaps the sandman did come after all; my eyes are scratchy and my skin sore to the touch. Mama is watching me carefully, so I smooth back my hair and nod at Maria coolly.

"Are you okay?" She is breathless. "Luca said you were sick."

Mama asks her if she would like some compote. I look at her, surprised. The last time we had this treat was my twelfth birthday, almost a year ago. "You two sit down out here under the tree and I'll bring you some juice."

"Thank you, Mama Zanesti. I can't stay long. Papa will be worried." When Mama can no longer hear us, Maria tells me her papa has forbidden her to come to my home. It is not a safe house for a young woman; it is a house of too many men.

"But you have two brothers," I say.

She shrugs. "Not the Zanesti brothers."

I have heard this whispered in the schoolyard before.

"Did you go swimming with Luca?"

She shakes her head. "I was too worried about you."

Mama comes outside with a jug of water mixed with apples, sour cherries, and sugar. She leaves it on the crooked wall beside us and goes back into the house. I catch the jug before it topples and pour the sweet, cloudy liquid into the chipped glasses. I want to tell Maria about the dream and the sheets and the bleeding, but she is strangely quiet today and looks off into the distance, as if she would rather be anywhere but here. She jumps up suddenly, "Gross." There is a battalion of tiny black ants marching across her hand.

I laugh. "They don't bite."

She stands and brushes them off her skirt. "Ugh, where did they think they were going?" We both giggle as she flicks a few fellows intent on climbing up her inner thigh.

"I better go, Nico. I don't want Papa finding out I came here."

"Will you come again tomorrow?"

"I'd better not . . ."

A long silence stretches between us, and then, as she goes to leave, she whispers, "I know what has happened to you, Nico. Maybe now your papa will start to look for a husband for you too." She is looking at the sheets drying in the hot sun. "Now you're like all the other girls in class."

I double over. It's as if the stone in my stomach has

splintered into tiny shards that catch in my throat. "I'm too young."

She squeezes me quickly. "I know, dreamer. Don't worry—our papas are only starting to look. We all have to finish school first, and anyway, you're our star pupil!" She blows a kiss as she hurries away down the lane. I look upwards and notice that I can't see any shapes in the clouds. They are just streaks of dirt across a hard, polished blue surface.

4

Sammy

I am right: Mr. and Mrs. O'D *have* called in the cavalry and the troops are swarming the gaff, devising a plan, every light on inside so it's lit up like the White House. The garden is floodlit, sprinklers on full blast, the spray caught in the beams, dancing. I fucking love this house. Luce rings the discreet singsong bell, and her mum, Mr. O'D, her auntie Bryony, and uncle Bob crowd behind the door, all red-wine boozy, goblets of the stuff gripped in their hands. The remnants of a dinner party are sitting on the dining-room table; the smell of garlic, onions, and oozy steak makes me want to heave.

"What the hell?" says her mum when she sees me in Luce's arms. "I should have known it had something to do with this girl."

Right on cue, Mrs. O'D.

And then her dad's voice, calmer, soothing, "Is she all right, Lucy? What happened? Are you all right? Come in, come in."

As we step into the brightly lit hallway, I can see blood trickling down my legs, which is a good move as far as this pantomime is concerned.

They all take a step back and I'm sure I can hear a shared intake of breath. Mrs. O'D will be sorry now for what she said. She looks pretty pale and takes a big, comforting glug from her chalice, checking to see that the carpets are okay. Mr. O'D is the first to speak. He orders Mrs. O'D to get blankets and hot drinks for both of us, then he puts his arm around me and tells me to lean on him. Bryony is suddenly full of the questions. "Are you okay, dear? What happened? What happened?"

I can't speak. Tears cascade down my cheeks, although I'm not sure if they're real or for show.

"Did anything happen to you?" Mrs. O'D asks Luce as she bundles her in a blanket and leads her to the couch as if she's one of her priceless porcelain figurines. Bryony rushes back in with two steaming cups of microwaved milk with gray old person's skin on the surface. I gag.

Mrs. O'D leans in closer and sniffs like a bloodhound on the scent. "There was booze involved, right? Were there men?"

Luce nods. So, she's going along with it.

Mrs. O'D's voice is rising to hysteria. "How many? Did they touch you?"

Luce shakes her head.

Mrs. O'D looks at her brother and sister and whispers,

audibly, "Jesus, I always said that girl has trouble with a capital T written all over her."

I can't believe she'd take that line with me standing there all smashed up. Bryony is outraged (although she doesn't know what Mrs. O'D knows about me: the cutting and the cannabis, and that's only half of it, and I'm pretty sure Mrs. O'D knows this too). "You can't go blaming the girl, Katherine, she's still only a child. No one asks for that kind of trouble."

Mrs. O'D stands up straight and rubs her back, staring at me, her words tumbling out and tripping over themselves. "Oh, I know, I know, but I guarantee you, this would not have happened if Lucy had been hanging out with any of her other friends."

She's right about that, but she's kinda making a fool out of herself, spittle spraying in my direction. It seems she can't control herself; it seems I have that maddening effect on her, like with my own mother. Bryony and Bob look incredulously at each other, and I realize she's playing right into my ploy for the sympathy vote.

She continues like a mad hag, her voice scratchy, "Were you attacked by strangers, or someone you know?"

I mumble that I don't know. I couldn't see clearly in the dark.

"Why were you dressed like that, Samantha? What were you doing drinking spirits outside in the dark, dressed like that?"

In answer, Luce pukes the hot milk all over her blanket.

"That's enough, Kate," Mr. O'D says to his wife. "Samantha may need stitches. I'm taking her to the hospital."

"What about the police? Shouldn't we call them straight away?" good ole uncle Bob chimes in.

Mrs. and Mr. O'D exchange a knowing glance, like maybe the police wouldn't be the best idea right now. Thank fuck.

"Let's get the girls sorted first, have a chat, before we involve the police. That procedure can be invasive and quite traumatic. I'll take her to the hospital first."

"What about Lucy?" Mrs. O'D asks, hovering over her like a giant hippo protecting her baby from a predator, like maybe a lion, or a cheetah, or a fully grown hyena.

"Come here, love." He extends an arm towards his daughter. "Did anyone touch you?

She shakes her head.

"Did you see what happened?"

Luce looks to me for prompting and I nod. She mirrors me.

"Kate, you stay with Lucy while she has some rest," he says, in a stop-with-your-nonsense-wife voice.

I wish Dad would pull that tone on Mother once in a while, instead of his wheedling Mr. Nice Guy act, which usually ends with her shouting at him, him giving her money for her supplies, and then leaving.

"Samantha needs to be looked at," Mr. O'D continues in that commanding way that makes my knees shake.

"What about her parents? Won't they be worried?" Mrs. O'D says, not looking at me, trying to put on a veneer of concern.

"My parents don't care."

There is a silence, and then Mr. O'D cuts through it. "I'm sure that's not true. You're overwrought."

"Well go on then, try calling them." I hand him my mobile, challenging him, which I bet no one in this house does, and which I think he's enjoying, maybe just as much as me. "You could ring and ring and no one will pick up, they don't even know I'm not there."

He calls, and sure enough no one answers. He gives up after three tries and leaves a message. "This is Dr. O'Donoghue. We have Sam here with us. She is going to be admitted to hospital following an incident. Don't worry, she's going to be fine. Call me as soon as you get this message."

"Incident"—that's a funny one. And "worry"—that's even funnier.

"I'm not letting Sam go alone," Luce says.

"I'm fine. I'm not alone, I'm with your dad." *The doc extraordinaire.*

I lean in closer to him and my boob rubs accidentally against his arm. I can feel Mrs. O'D's hyperfocused gaze on me.

"It's okay, love, you get some rest. The police might want to question you later, but first let's get Sam sorted," Doc O'D says to his daughter in his professional medicine-man voice as he ushers me out the door. I wonder if he will be the one to stop the bleeding.

I realize I'm pretty pissed in the back of the speeding car. Wouldn't do to dirty the pristine interior of his latest BMW.

I imagine Mrs. O'D staring sternly at me, warning me off causing any more "trouble," so I swallow back the stuff that is threatening to erupt.

"You all right back there?"

I mumble something, pretending to be further gone than I really am, deciding on a course of hazy unconsciousness to stave off the questions. Luce and I really need to get our story straight, and anyway, I'm way too traumatized by the events of the night to face any kind of interrogation.

"Don't worry about a thing. You'll be right as rain in no time . . ."

Kind of disappointing, that response, under the circumstances. That's the kind of platitude my ineffectual dad spews and it achieves precisely NOTHING. I lie back against the cream leather interior, inhaling the smell of wax and musky aftershave.

The vodka really kicks in when we get inside. Doc O'D switches into high-commanding mode, corralling me through the endless maze of corridors, greeting the nurses with their clipboards clutched tightly to their heaving bosoms. The intense bright lights pierce my eyelids and the stench of antiseptic gets stuck in my craw, tickling, threatening tears and a violent eruption. Hands steer me into a cubicle, and as soon as a nurse arrives with a kidney-shaped dish, I let it all out. I congratulate myself on my self-control until that point. Then Doc O'D's voice, indistinct, blurry, ". . . check for the level of damage first before we go down that route . . . my daughter's friend, might have been an accident . . . not sure what happened, fairly intoxicated . . ." I think I'm being saved from some pretty bad shit. "She has hurt herself before . . ."

I'm wheeled on a trolley into an even brighter room, more voices mumble, "Local or general?"

Oh, just knock me out, please . . .

"Too much booze . . . risky . . . stitches."

Then I hear a soft female voice say, "Open your legs. This won't take long."

It doesn't hurt, just a sting, then a swab, then a tugging sensation. They did a good job of numbing me first. Okay, really. It's okay. Worth it? Was it worth it, Mrs. O'D? You seem to still think all of this is my own fault. I'm not to blame. I'm not the one to blame.

I'm steered back into a cubicle where curtains are drawn around me and I fall into a deep and woozy sleep, like a blackout without the nightmares.

When I wake, Doc O'D is standing over me, gently prodding me. "All over now, Sam. You're coming home with me." He winks, like the two of us are in this thing together. My tongue has swollen to twice its size. I don't even bother asking him if my parents have called. A nurse has brought a glass of water and my clothes. Doc O'D holds the glass to my lips. "Little sips."

He bundles up my clothes and tells me I can stay in the gown, then wraps a blanket around my shoulders and holds me under my arm, supporting me. I feel so loose and floppy I lean right into him, so he's forced to kind of carry me. I want to curl up in his arms. The car is right outside the entrance with its flashers on; one of the perks of being a hot-shot consultant. He helps me into the back, the gown flapping open so bits of my tummy and thigh are exposed. I lie down flat as he pulls the gown tight around me, and I drift off to the notes of musk and leather, and the sound of a purring engine and a deep voice, humming. Lucky Luce with a dad like this.

When we get back to the house, there's no sign of the troops; the lights are off and the washing up is done, the smell of lemon Fairy Liquid floating in the air. Lucy Lou is sitting at the kitchen table in the dark.

"Jesus, Lucy. What are you doing up? It's almost six o'clock," Mr. O'D says as he switches on the overhead light, plunging the marble-topped, island-in-the-middle, high-tech kitchen into startling brightness.

"Couldn't sleep."

She looks like a panda with her white face and black-ringed eyes, which almost starts me off.

"How is she?" she says to her dad, who seems pretty pissed to see her. And then to me, "How are you, Sammy?"

She's wearing that look of concern that I've seen so many times before: when she caught me behind the bicycle sheds smoking dope, or when she couldn't stop me stealing the Lycra pants in Topshop, or when I told her I had gone all the way with David, and Stu, and Brian (though not the others, not that). Poor old Luce.

"How many stitches, Dad?"

Mr. O'D rubs his forehead and stares out the window at

the silhouettes of spiky branches in the night sky, making me think of the shadow-finger games I used to play with Dad on the bedroom wall.

"Not many. It wasn't me that did them, obviously."

I can see Luce is relieved by this.

"Now, you two better get some sleep. It's almost dawn. We may have to make a statement to the police about the nature of this attack tomorrow."

By the way he says the word, I can tell he doesn't really believe it either. Do they think I'd do this to myself? Do they really think I'm that kind of girl?

Then Luce says something mad. "Surely we should go straight to the police station now so we can report the crime and make sure those bastards are caught?"

Jesus, she's really getting caught up in this.

Her dad starts scratching the back of his neck over and over. "The hospital tests showed it didn't conclusively look like an attack by a male," he says, almost in a whisper, almost apologetically, not wanting to admit that I'm a pathological liar.

"That's 'cause they used a bottle." Luce is shouting now, high on her lies.

"Okay, okay." Mr. O'D seems out of his depth with this new hysterical version of his usually calm daughter. "We'll discuss it in the morning. You're both exhausted . . . come on . . ."

She starts to sob and Mr. O'D goes to rub her back, then pulls away as she convulses. He stares incomprehensibly at all this teenage angst. Stop, Luce, it's only a game. It's worked . . .

look . . . your dad was lovely to me, and I'm allowed to stay the night. This is what we wanted. I suddenly feel stone-cold sober.

"Bastards," she says, shaking her head, "bastards." This is not like her.

Maybe I pushed it all a bit too far. Shit, Luce, I'm sorry. I have a weird desire to get down on my knees and confess it all. Mother is standing over me, kissing the top of my head. "It's okay, darling," she's saying. "It's okay. Don't worry about a thing. I love you no matter what, you know that." I shake my head to stop the tears from falling, and this time they're real. I look at Mr. O'D, who looks gray and suddenly old and has started scratching that spot on the back of his neck again. I want to reach out and take his hand and tell him everything. Dear confessor. But I can't risk it, can't risk his hatred too. Look at how he's looking at his daughter; he's worried for her. He's right to be, with a friend like me.

5

Nico

Miss Iliescu will be gathering our essays about summer at the beginning of the day and we'll find out in a week who has won. I'm fairly certain it'll be me again, but there's always a possibility of doubt, and it's this doubt that catches in my heart and makes it beat twice as fast. Papa won't look at me this morning—he hasn't looked at me since the day of the staining, although how he knows, I don't know. Mama's face is hard and the boys are chomping loudly, except for Luca, who hasn't touched his porridge.

When the others have finished eating, Papa wipes his face with the back of his hand and speaks loudly into the air. "You won't be going to school today."

I look around to see who he's talking to, presuming it's to Sergiu, who doesn't go anyway. "You'll be staying at home with your mama to do the chores."

The room is spinning beneath my feet. Although he hasn't

looked directly at me, I know this could only be addressed to the girl of the house.

"What about my essay?" I say, my voice sounding small, as if it's coming from far away.

Victor laughs. "The only one with an ounce of a brain in the house. Too bad you were born a girl."

Papa speaks low. "A woman now."

The boys look back down at their empty bowls, Sergiu having polished off all of Luca's, and start to push their chairs away from the table. As they leave, Luca turns to me and says, "I'll give your essay to Miss Iliescu."

I don't trust myself to stand, so Mama takes the papers gently from my hand and gives them to Luca. "Good son," she says. "Now go."

I look out at the sky, which is heavy and low to the ground, the thin sunlight diluted by the polluted haze. There are rumbles of thunder in the distance. "What's going on, Mama?" She seems distracted, then angry, like I've done something wrong. She offers me more bread with butter and apple jelly.

"Need to make sure you're not too scrawny."

"Too scrawny for what?"

"No man likes a scrawny girl and, with all your tree climbing, you are sinew and bone."

I wonder why there is this talk of pleasing a man all of a sudden. "But Mama . . . ?"

"Now, none of your cheek, young woman."

I am only warming up for a question that I can't put words to. The gap at the top of the well is closing in.

"More bread?" she asks.

The dog slinks around the kitchen with its tail between its legs and its ears flattened, whining, or "begging" as Mama says. She grabs the brush from me and whacks the creature on its behind.

"Don't, Mama."

She's not usually so violent with the dog. But then, it doesn't normally come into the kitchen; it's usually running free, digging, chasing rabbits, or us. I look at it, poor thing, hunting its tail and biting down hard on it, an act that surprises it each time so that it yelps in pain. I ask Mama if I can go out for a walk with the dog, and she says that the man will be along soon and I'm not to mess up my hair or dirty my clothes.

"What man?"

"Stop with the cheek."

"Who is this man?"

"Stop asking questions, you'll find out soon enough."

There's a stretched, strained silence, broken only by the dog's incessant twirling and yelping.

"More tea?" Mama asks.

I push the chair away from the table, the bockety leg trailing on the ground, screeching. Mama winces as I go to the door and open it, breathing in gulpfuls of thick, stagnant air. Speed builds up inside of me until I find I have pushed off the ball of my right foot and burst into a run. The dog follows, and Mama's voice follows still, "Come back, Nico. He is a nice man, you will see."

I race to our tree and stop only long enough to press my body against the old fellow's reassuring trunk, fingertips reaching a third of the way around. The familiar smell of tobacco and leather envelop me, reminding me of when I was small and used to sit on Papa's lap, my smooth cheek against his whiskery one. My heart is thumping against the wood, reverberating in my mouth and ears. The wind rustles the leaves so it sounds as if they're whispering to me, telling me to run further into the forest where the trees are closer together and the branches lower to the ground. The air is getting thin and cool, the leaves forming a canopy above my head so no sky is visible.

We run and run until the hound flops onto the forest floor. I stretch out beside it, and all I can hear is our jagged breaths, at times together, at times apart. "Good dog," I say, as it stretches out a paw towards me. It sleeps easily as I lie awake staring up at the dense green cover above me. Was this how it was for Mama? Is this why she is so angry?

I think of Maria and wonder if maybe her papa is introducing her to a man now too. Is this how it works? Why so early? I am not to get married for at least another four years, possibly six, if I can go all the way at school. Is this man to wait that long for me? Will he allow me to become a teacher? I want to see Maria, talk to her, but then I think of her papa and the spitting men, and his comment about the Zanesti brothers and my home of too many men. An image of my cousin Katerina comes to my mind. The man they chose to be her husband was old and heavy and not from around here. We have not seen or heard from her since she left, two days after her eighteenth birthday. When I asked about her a few weeks later, an icy wind seemed to blow into the room, and Papa pressed a finger against his lips.

The dog is licking my face and I push it off me. Its ears are pinned back and it snarls at me, tail wagging still. I know enough not to look an animal in the eye when it's feeling threatened.

The light is fading and it's difficult to tell if this is dusk or just a thickening of the cloud cover, which settles over our heads on still, musty days like these. Papa says it's from the factories that belch out big black clouds of ash in Chişinău. Although you never know with Papa.

The man may have come and gone, or the man may still be there—I must have been gone for hours now. I look around me at the forest floor and know that I wouldn't stand a chance out here: I haven't a clue what would poison and what would feed, or how cold it gets at night. My stomach feels bloated from too many hours of not eating.

The walk home is not as long as I wish it would be. I debate whether to run back into the forest, run to Maria's house, run to the town, run anywhere but towards this man, when I find myself at the old fellow's side. I wait a moment, hoping for whispers in the wind, some direction to take, some call to action, invocation. The sky reveals itself in yellow patches as daytime still, casting its eerie light through his feathery branches, but no instructions are issued. I find my feet taking off in the direction of our house. What other choice? What, dog? It cocks its head to one side and barks gustily.

We reach the clearing of the forest when I see Mama hanging out washing. She notices me, turns her back, and returns inside the house. I push against the door and there she is—busy as ever, making tea, blowing on the embers to keep the fire alight. It's smoky and silent, and unbearably hot.

"Sorry, Mama, I got lost."

She has her back to me, and I notice her shoulders are moving up and down jerkily, like her whole body is hiccupping.

"Sit down, Mama, I'm all right now. Let me make you tea."

She turns towards me, her jaw set, and she wipes away the wet on her face. "You sit down. I'll make you a drop of warmth."

My insides are boiling. Can't you see this, Mama?

"Did the man come?"

"Not yet."

She comes over and wraps her arms around me, pressing my face against her soft bosom so I can barely breathe. The dog is whinnying now. Mama kisses the top of my head over and over, so much I think she might rub away my hair. "You're the best girl, good girl, good girl . . ." The dog thinks she's praising it, and does something I've never seen before—it rolls onto its back, paws in the air. I see that it's a girl and I am glad. I rub her tummy. Mama joins in and says, "Filthy thing," and we both laugh until we sense a shadow in the doorway.

Papa is hovering, blocking all the light. "Are you going to clean yourself up?" he says, still without looking directly at me.

"Put on your pretty dress," Mama says.

I go to my room and open my window wide, sit on the

ledge and try to drink in air, although the sky is sitting on the ground and there's not even a whisper of wind. I think of Maria and wonder did she go to Luca at break and ask where I was, or would she be happy now that it's only the two of them?

"Hurry up in there," I hear Mama's voice with a new crack in it. "You don't want to be late."

I open the wardrobe and take out my best blue dress. It's tight under the arms, pinching me, and too warm for weather like this.

When I return, I see that Mama has put on her Sunday-best headscarf, the one she would normally only wear to church. The pretty green flowers cast a sickly sheen on the high, wide planes of her face, accentuating the bulrush color of her eyes. She brushes my hair hard and scrapes it back with a new blue suede ribbon, which matches my dress. I wish I could loosen the pull on my scalp and stick my head under cold running water. Papa is outside in the yard, smoking.

Luca arrives back from school and stands in the doorway, staring at me. I want to ask him all about Miss Iliescu and my essay and Maria, but he speaks first. "Where is he going to take you?" His voice is angry. I look at Mama, who shakes her head. "It better not be the same place as Nina."

I hear these words but try to pretend to myself I have not. Mama bangs things around the kitchen. Luca goes to the kitchen table and drags a chair heavily out from under it and sits, like an old man.

"Your father would never let that happen to Nico. And anyway, Nina was old enough to look after herself."

How I wish Luca had not said her name. An icy breath haws on my neck.

"He has been telling the men in the village how pretty she is."

"Enough, Luca. Please . . . Nina had no parents to look out for her."

Nina's family were too ashamed to talk about what happened to her, although her brothers bought more chickens for the farm after she left.

Papa comes back into the kitchen, which feels too small for us all. He tells me how lovely I look, that my eyes are the color of the sea in this dress. My eyes are blue, not black, Papa.

Luca tightens his hand into a fist and punches down onto his thigh. "She's too young," he says.

Something I have never felt before lands in me.

"Your mother was the same age when I married her," Papa says.

"That's not true," Mama says. "It happened to her very early."

"Well, it's a sign isn't it? If it's not a sign that she's ready, then what is?"

"She's too clever not to finish school."

"This man has promised she can continue her education."

"She is too young, Nicolae, you know this. This is not allowed. What will the school say?"

"She is my daughter and I say what is allowed."

"Papa, I am at the top of my class. I must finish school first."

"You will go to a better school, Nico. I only want what's best for you."

I want to say I am afraid but am too afraid to say the words.

"I don't think it's right, Papa. I don't want her to go," Luca says.

"Want her all to yourself, do you, BOY?"

I wish I could throw my arms around Luca and say, "Yes, let me stay, you can protect me," but Papa has put something poisonous into the air that hangs there between us all, and I know Luca has to act like he doesn't care.

6

Sammy

I'm lying with my head on the pillow and Luce's feet beside me, top to tail. She's wriggling her toes and tickling mine. I hate my feet being touched. Mother likes to rub her calloused ones against mine. "Don't, Luce." Then she burrows down in the bed, reaches out towards my hips and circles me with her arms, her face pressing against my belly. I draw back the quilt so she can breathe. She flips her body back right side up so her head is lying beside mine on the pillow and she strokes my hair.

"I really don't know what I'd do without you," she says, which is exactly the kind of thing Mother says when she's in one of her gooey rheumy-eyed moods. Luce snuggles in close, her breath in my nostrils, my own getting tangled in her rhythms. She falls asleep again, her forehead pressed against mine. I move my head away so I can see her more clearly. She has a crease between her eyes that makes her look so much older than fifteen, yet her long gangly body is like a child's that has bits attached to it that do not belong. I look down at my own and poke my knobbly knees.

At breakfast, Mrs. O'D serves us an assortment of mini cereal packs, her eyes puffy and vague, not focusing on either of us. Weirdly, I'm starving. We both choose Frosties. Luce eats hers while they are still crispy, but I like mine all soggy.

"Did you sleep okay?" Mrs. O'D asks, genuine concern in her voice despite herself.

"Greeeeeeaaaaat . . . ," I say, which makes her turn her back and stiffen.

"No news from your parents yet, Sam. I wonder, is everything all right?" She's looking out the window at that sickly tree with those scabby branches, which even in daylight look like nighttime shadows.

"Mother won't have woken up yet, and Dad is probably away on 'business.'"

Her brow furrows, as if she is worried, which I really hate. I prefer my version of her as she was last night: just another mother who doesn't give a shit about me. "So, have you got your story straight this morning? I hear the events of the evening were confused last night."

I chomp so loudly that my jaw clicks.

"I don't remember exactly. It was a bit of a blur, to be honest. Waaaay too much wodka."

"And I suppose you don't remember either, Lucy, do you?"

"You saw how drunk I was . . ."

"I see. So what is the point of making this statement if all we have is two drunken witnesses who can remember nothing about what happened?"

"My thoughts exactly, Mrs. O'D."

Mrs. O'D turns around to face us directly, her hands gripping the countertop. "Do you feel the same way, Lucy?"

"I didn't see anything. It was too dark."

She seems to have come to her senses this morning, back to her normal dreary self, not a whiff of the hysteria of last night about her.

"And yet, you were made to watch," Mrs. O'D presses on.

I can't help it, but a big laugh erupts out of me. Luce shoots a warning glance at me. She must've been pretty pissed or knackered last night to have been acting like a Technicolor version of me.

"I see," says Mrs. O'D, with a huge effort to contain herself. "Now you can take yourself out of here, young lady. Time to go home."

"You can't do that, Mum. She's hurt," Luce says.

"And how exactly did that happen, Samantha?" She turns to face me directly.

God, she's like a dog with a bone this morning. "As I say, it was like a dream, or a nightmare, a hallucination. It was dark and they just pounced."

"Who did? The bogeymen? Was there more than one?"

"Yes. Three. They were speaking in a foreign language."

Oh, Jesus, stop it now.

"Enough, Samantha. Enough. That's enough. I think you should go home now."

She's right, of course. Sometimes I can't stop the lies tumbling out. This is enough. I get up from the table and thank Mrs. O'D politely for her hospitality. If there's one thing Mother taught me, it's good manners: don't chew with your mouth full, don't lean your elbows on the table when eating, and always say please and thank you. Such a well-bred young girl.

"Well, I'd better be off, so. Mother will be out of her mind. Probably had to down a bottle of Pinot for breakfast to stave off the worry." I'm wearing Luce's tracksuit bottoms that are falling down around my hips so I hold them up with one hand. I'm amazed that I'm not sorer. Luce follows me to the door.

"Bye, girl Friday," I say, blowing her a kiss. Mrs. O'D is clearing the dishes loudly, clattering them on the countertop.

"You can't let her go like this, Mum."

"No, no, of course not." She takes a big breath, battling with a maternal instinct that doesn't know what to do. "Wait there, Samantha, and I'll drive you home."

"You're okay, Mrs. O'D. I'll walk. Thanks though. I fancy a bit of fresh air."

"I'll walk with you," Luce says.

"You will go nowhere," Mrs. O'D says. "You're grounded."

Ah, the inevitable. Not sure it will work though. I reckon Luce will find a way to come to the rescue. "Don't worry, Luce. I'll go on home."

She turns on her mum then in a fury. "Are you really going to let her walk back to that alchie bitch like that, in the cold?"

"Don't dare use that language around me."

"But you have no idea. Her mother is deranged."

"If you know what's good for you, you'll stay away from that girl . . ." The warning bursts out of her, and she looks appalled by her own words. "I'm sorry, Samantha, I'm sorry. That was way out of line." She's shaking her head as if to rid herself of the viciousness I inspire in her.

"As I said earlier, thanks for the hospitality, Mrs. O'D." All sweetness and light, and I pull the front door closed politely behind me. I'm curious to see how Luce navigates this one, so I walk around the side passage and listen.

"She needs help," Luce says.

That is so patronizing, and I've a good mind to run in there and tell her.

"You may be right, but you're not the kind of help she needs. I've called the principal, explained the situation. He'll make sure she sees a counselor."

"Mum, she's not going to go back to school."

"Well, what can we do about it, Lucy? We can't force her. We're not her legal guardians."

"Mum, she's fifteen, she's all alone in the world with an alcoholic mother."

"I don't know what to do, Lucy. Should I call the guards? I called the school . . . what else can I do?" She sounds desperate.

"You really shouldn't have let her go like that."

Mrs. O'D obviously has a change of heart, a major attack of the guilts, as I hear her sigh, really loudly, a big tired one, then she scrapes her chair along the floor, grabs her keys, and slams the front door. I run around to the front of the passage, making sure I'm not seen, and watch Mrs. O'D shift the car into gear and screech down the road. I debate going back inside to Luce and finishing my soggy Frosties, only problem is: I'm pissed with her, and I want to be alone right now. I wish I hadn't put on Luce's Converse. They're a whole size too small and pinching my toes. I didn't have time to collect the wedges and gear from last night, and anyway, I didn't think turning up to breakfast dressed like that would do anything to help further my cause. Wouldn't have made a jot of difference the way it turned out. I wonder what Mrs. O'D reckons she would do if she found me, although there's no way I'm going to let her. No way I'm going into the "care" system or the central mental hospital, as my mother threatened so many times. No way are the guards getting involved.

The sky is high and blue with wisps of cloud floating. I look up to see if I can see any shapes. Nada. The convent materializes at the end of the yellow-brick road, must be I have a calling—the gates are open, beckoning me in. There are a few aul dears shuffling in their habits, muttering prayers, Rosary beads rolling between thumbs and forefingers. The youngest looks to be about eighty. Are they really at it at night, under cover of darkness in their gray domain? Are they atoning for their sins now? I feel a bubble of laughter rising in my stomach, fizzy. I think of the three nuns that still teach in our school, the last ones standing. They're so ancient their skin looks like it might crumble off their faces with the slightest touch. Poor old Sr. Wendy in religious instruction class has a thing about "tongues" and the holy spirit flowing into her. She wishes. The laughter erupts, and one of the nuns doing the rounds turns her shrewd eyes in my direction.

What I see there is worry, or is it pity? I despise pity. "Are you okay, dear?" she asks and I wish she hadn't. I shun her concern and run away.

I'll have to go home, have to change, nick a few notes from Mother's purse, take some "special" food from the fridge that's only for her: prawns and pink dips and the posh dark choccy labeled "DO NOT TOUCH." Mother goes to a lot of trouble putting different-colored stickers on jars of pickles and jams, cartons of juices, and boxes of wine. I remember Luce calling over one day and staring into the fridge. "What the fuck are you meant to eat?"

I pointed at cheap, store-brand processed cheese and ham, packets with reduced-price stickers on them, and milk. "She's very thoughtful, really. Wouldn't want me to get scurvy." I'll never forget the look on Luce's face. Murderous—isn't that what they say? I've seen it.

Once I start on this track, I can't stop. I know it's not good for me, storing up the memories, taking them out, spitting on them, polishing them so they are as vivid as the moment I'm meant to be living. I'm reliving the exact moment now and can hear Mother's footsteps coming up the stairs: I'm twelve, it's late, maybe two or three in the morning, and she has been drinking all night, alone (she just found out that day that her own dad had died, the man she hadn't spoken to in over twenty years, the bastard who left when she was a child, so I've no idea why she was so mad-sad looper about the whole thing). The door to my room is pushed open and I pretend to be asleep. I've learned at this stage that there is no point talking to her or trying to reason with her when she's like this. She walks over to the bed and sits down heavily on the side of it, starts to stroke my hair with her hand. "Beautiful girl," she is slurring. Then I feel a tugging, not unlike the sensation of the stitches earlier, and the mad cow is cutting my hair, in the dark. I don't move. The following morning, she tells Dad that I did it; look what a state I had made of myself. By this stage I know enough not to take her on; I never win. Dad just ducks out of it and tells me not to "rile her up." He takes me to the hairdressers and I have to get a pixie cut, before they were trendy: code for a short, short mess. Not such a beautiful girl now.

At the parent-teacher meeting that year, Mother turned up alone and explained to the teachers that I had done it to myself and that I was disturbed because my father was never there. Mr. O'Grady called me into the office and asked if everything was okay at home and if I had anything I wanted to tell him. "Yup, my mother is a crazy psycho bitch." I was suspended and sent home to that woman.

I find myself walking in the direction of that house. It's midday and all the curtains are still drawn—Dad must be away on one of his trips. I open the door and tiptoe in, careful not to wake the sleeping beauty. She'll probably be out for the count till well past five, when it's permissible for her to start the booze again. That's a pretty decent hour, really. She's good at keeping up appearances; it amazes me how well she can scrub up when she has to, although I wonder whether the madness has inhabited all of her by now—it's all I can see of her, in her eyes, which are yellowed and watery, shot through with little pink veins. Maybe strangers don't look that closely.

I go to my room, change out of Luce's oversize sweats and undersize Converse, and take down my purple-spotted luggage case from the top of the wardrobe, the one on wheels that Dad picked up on his last trip. I also get my rucksack, go to the fridge, open the door, and take all the stuff that is labeled "DO NOT TOUCH." I stuff the backpack full to bulging. Even if I don't like a lot of this shit, it's the principle of the thing. Her handbag is sitting on the kitchen table and I empty its contents and lift her cards, lipstick, mascara, and 300 euros: Dad's guilt-induced presents. He'd never buy the booze for her, that way he's not really complicit. Not really.

Just before I leave, for what will probably be the last time, I have a momentary pang of conscience. Who'll put a blanket over her after she's collapsed on the floor? Who'll check up to see she hasn't swallowed her own vomit? Who'll listen to see if she's still breathing? Who'll put a warm facecloth on her forehead when she wakes with a banging headache, and bring her sweet milky tea and toast in bed? Who'll climb into bed beside her and snuggle her when she's out cold, her body jerking in one of its recurring nightmares?

And then I think: who'll take her ranting rages now? Not

me, no siree. I'm outta here. Had enough of feeling winded from the force of her words slamming me against the walls. Had enough of lying in the dark, coiled, waiting for the door to open, the bedsprings to creak, her hand reaching out, not knowing what's coming.

Still, old habits die hard, so I creep to her door, which is half open, and listen to her strangled snores.

I wonder where Dad is now, who he's with. He couldn't handle this house of women. Poor old Dad, always trying to keep the peace, deny the truth. Well, maybe now I'd smack him around the mouth with it: she is your wife, your responsibility, not mine, never was, Pops. I walk into the room carefully so as not to creak any floorboards and look at her bloated face creased against the pillow, her hair lank and limp, graying at the roots. The pictures of her when she was younger show a tall, dark-haired, dark-eyed girl, with plump lips and cheeks, not unlike me today. What happened, Mum? I try on the word for size and it sits like a lump of raw liver in my mouth. Mother. That's what you are: Mother.

I lean in closer and am hit by a wave of stale booze. I wonder if I smell like that this morning. I kiss her on her forehead and push her hair back off her face. The rhythm of her snoring changes and she makes a contented sound, like how the dog up the street does when you rub its tummy, until he starts his humping. For a moment I stand there at her side of the bed, paralyzed. I'm sure none of this is her fault either. I have to give myself a little shake to dislodge the lump in my gullet.

I kiss her again and walk slowly down the stairs and lift the bag. Maybe I shouldn't have nicked all her food and cash, but then I'm hit by an image of Luce's face full of murderous intent. That food should always have been my food. I won't have to defy you again, Mother.

When I open the door, Lucy Lou is sitting on the wall. She smiles. "I didn't want to ring the doorbell, for obvious reasons."

There's no escaping her. "What are you doing here, Nurse Nightingale? I thought you were grounded."

She hands me a plastic bag with my wedges and gear and tells me that after I left, her mum screeched off to look for me. I don't tell her I know this. I don't tell her that I heard the conversation between the two of them. I'm still sore from the whole "I just can't bear to have her around you" comment.

"Do you not think we should call the Guards?"

"And say what?"

"Report the violence in your home."

"It's not violence, Luce. Let's not go getting all dramatic here. Do you see any broken bones, any marks on me that I haven't done to myself?"

"It's unacceptable the way she treats you."

"Ah, it's not so bad. The poor old bird is comatose up there now. Better than your one, always sticking her nose into things and making judgements on people she doesn't even know."

Luce goes silent.

"And anyway, you don't want me being taken into custody, do you? We might never see each other again. . . . I have some cash, let's go to a posh hotel now, before anyone realizes what's happened," I say.

"Don't you need your passport to book a room?"

"Everywhere?" Shit. I'm gonna have to rethink this plan 'cause Dad keeps all our passports in a top-secret file somewhere. "Do all those Eastern European girls have passports? I hear some of them are imported and given false IDs. I could pose as one of those." My stomach tumbles; I feel the edge of exhilaration as a plan starts to form, as inspiration takes hold. "I saw a documentary about it. They're young. I could be one of those girls."

"Yeah, what a genius idea! Go find yourself a violent pimp and go work for him for nothing."

"Nah, I'm not so stupid as all that. I need to earn some money. Brian taught me a trick or two."

This idea, once aired, hangs in the air between us and gains solidity until it feels like a hard wall has been erected between us.

"Brian's such an asshole," she says, trying to smash through it. "Big thicko. Kept back two years. I don't know why you let him anywhere near you."

I ignore this. We both know all the girls in class fancy him. Except for Luce. And she's jealous.

"My name is Natasha," I say, giddy.

"I won't stand by and watch you do this," she says.

What, like you didn't stand by and watch me last night, or in Topshop when I lifted the goodies, or in the offy the other day, or behind the bicycle sheds? I don't say anything but start to walk in the direction of this dodgy place where Brian took me, my wheelie bag jolting over every bump in the road.

"Where do you think you're going?" Luce asks.

"I really think it's time you went home. Your mum'll have a fit if she sees you're gone. And you know who she'll blame. I don't fancy being at the sharp end of her tongue again."

"I can't let you do this."

"You really don't have any choice in the matter. It's my life, Lucy Lou."

She's still following, so I decide I have to be cruel now to be kind. The first cut is the deepest and all that, so I turn to her and say, "Fuck off home, Lucy Poo. I've had enough of your puppy-dog face following me wherever I go. Sandra's right. You *are* obsessed . . ."

This is the single worst thing I could ever say to her. Sandra is a toxic cow who tells everyone Luce is a lezzie who has a crush on me, and she makes up all these stories about Luce following me and writing poetry about me and wanting to suck me out. I've seen Luce crying her eyes out over this, and here I am throwing it in her face.

"Hey, at least I'll get paid for it now," I say, which is pretty high up there on the scale of completely alienating my best friend. I'm not even sure if I'm just saying this to make her hate me, or if I mean it. Brian had arranged payment once before, behind the bicycle sheds with four of them whose names I don't remember, not that I remember much after downing almost a whole naggin. He only told me after that's what he had done. I vowed never to speak to him again, although really it wasn't such a big deal. I'd probably have done it anyway. And I did continue to speak to him, of course, and sleep with him.

Luce's face is a mask of disbelief, which crumples into hurt and tears. She wipes them away roughly, turns her back, pulls her shoulders high to her ears and walks away.

7

Nico

The man arrives at the front door and seems to suck all the air from the room. He stands in the exact place Luca had been, his feet planted wide apart, his shoulders squared, head nearly touching the doorframe.

Papa says, "Come in, Petre, come in, sit down, sit down," and gets off his chair and offers it to him. No one has ever sat in Papa's chair before.

The man walks in, his heavy boots trailing dirt after him. He sits on the good chair, which creaks beneath his weight, then he leans back and looks around the room. He has not yet regarded me.

"Would you like some of Nicolae's homemade wine? It's particularly sweet this season," Mama asks.

He nods curtly, without any please or thank you.

Luca stands. "Go out and feed the chickens," Papa says.

"I will when I'm good and ready," Luca says, staring at the

man, defying Papa for the first time. “So, this is the man who is to marry my sister.” He extends an arm that could be a punch, but which turns into a stiff handshake instead. Both men grip hard. I can see the skin turn red on Luca’s fingers, and white after, when the man releases his hand.

I look at Luca and try to smile at him, but Papa glares at him in such a way that he cannot look at me or smile back. He stands stiff and tall, puffing out his chest, the way he does when Sergiu tells him to strip and get into the barrel that he and Victor would roll down the hill. Luca only cried once. It was going to happen anyway.

The man swallows the wine in one gulp.

“What strange weather,” Papa says. “A storm has been threatening all day.” He looks out the window at the low dusty-yellow sky and then down at the glass in his hand, blowing on it absentmindedly, as if he’s about to drink from a cup of hot tea. The man makes no attempt to join in the conversation. I move from the fire towards Mama. I want her to wrap me in her arms and pull me close. She moves away. She is busy cleaning. I stand beside her and try to get a sense of this man who is to be my husband. He has a brown mark on his cheek, a sign from God that he is touched. He thinks he’s better than us—I can see it from the way he coldly scans the room, my papa, and Luca, and the fact that he has not once looked at Mama or me.

He speaks, and his voice rumbles like the thunder that has been bursting to sound all day. “Thursday?”

"Yes," Papa says. "She is to your liking then?"

Mama clatters the dishes in the sink, Luca puffs out his chest even further, I pinch the skin on my forearm. The man nods.

"Where are you taking her?" Luca asks.

"Now, none of your cheek, son," Papa says.

The man puts his empty glass down on the table and leaves. He does not thank Mama; he does not speak to me. What is it about me that makes him want to claim me as his wife? We have not even exchanged a glance. He does not know the color of my eyes.

He is not so old, or fat, not like Katerina's husband. He is tall and has good shoulders.

Mama says to Papa, "No, I will not allow it."

"Who asked you, woman?" Papa says, and then he goes to her and puts his arms around her. This is the first time I have seen him do this. She slumps against him. "He has money. He will look after her, and us. She will have better opportunities than we could ever give her."

I walk to the door and inhale deeply, feeling as if all the factory smoke is clogging my lungs, filling them with burning ash.

"It will be okay," Papa says to my back. "He will buy you nice things and bring you to nice places. I have made sure he is a good man."

An image of the goat frothing at the mouth comes to mind. His voice wavers slightly as he tries to convince himself that he is doing the right thing, being the responsible father, and that this is, after all, the best fate for a girl like me. I turn to look at him, to challenge the lie in his eyes, but he looks away.

His voice is full of Rachiu as he says, "You are a lucky girl, Nico . . . you will see the sea. I have always wanted to see the sea."

8

Sammy

I look at Luce's back walking away down the road and know what I've done. I'm not sure we can ever come back from this, even as I tell myself it's for the best, in her best interests, anyway—she has parents who adore her and she'll get on much better in school without me around. What I didn't think about was how bad it would make me feel. I really didn't think at all. It just happened, like last night just happened; things just happen in my life and I'm powerless to stop them. When that mad feeling takes hold, I can't think straight, I just do whatever it tells me to do—it's like I have that demon puppet master living inside me. I'm not so unlike Mother after all. When that switch has been activated in her, that's when the crazy shit happens. What I just said to Luce is exactly the kind of poison Mother spews at me, especially after consuming a bottle plus of Chardonnay.

The B&B is on a side street, up a back alley, in behind a big swanky office building, all glass and chrome, with a fountain out front, none of which I'd noticed before, as Brian and I had come in the night, off our heads. The door is painted a matte black and looks fairly innocuous. I knock, then push on into the hallway, which is dark and dank, and I feel ice-cold the moment I step through. I go to the desk and wait. There is no bell or buzzer or anything, so I shout as politely as I can, "Helloo, anybody there?"

A woman passes me by, wearing dark sunglasses, skinny jeans, and high heels, her long dark hair swaying down her back, the skin on her scrawny arms loose and saggy and tattooed, jangling bangles from her elbows to her wrists. She turns to me. "What you looking for?"

I tell her I'm looking for a room.

"Jesus, they're getting younger by the day," she says to no one in particular. "Go home, young one. Get out of here before it's too late." She looks as if she's talking to herself, or a younger version of herself.

A young guy appears from the back, the same one as the last time. He's mates with Brian. At first glance, he appears like a preppy, reassuring college kid with his collar turned up and his navy-blue wool jumper slung over his shoulders. In other circumstances I might have considered it.

I introduce myself as Brian's friend, and he nods absently, as if this is not the first time he's heard that particular line. He doesn't remember me, says there are plenty of others who looked just like me. That doesn't happen to me often.

He looks blankly at me and asks how I propose to pay for the room. I flash the card at him.

"How long will that work, kiddo, before they find out?"

Kiddo. He's only a couple of years older. Okay, maybe sev-enish. Still, not enough of an edge to take that tone with me, although the closer I look at him, the less sure I am about everything to do with him: his age, the college-kid act, the whole "reassuring" bit.

"Are you sure that's what you want? You know they can trace you here if we use it."

"I wasn't planning on staying long."

"Oh no, and where were you planning on moving on to? There aren't many establishments like us, you know, the no-questions-asked kind."

"How much for a few weeks?"

"I'm sure we can work something out," the guy says, picking at his teeth, which are brownish-yellow at the tops where they meet the gums. "Did anyone follow you here? Anyone know your whereabouts, apart from Brian?"

"Nope, and I haven't even told him I'm here."

"Good."

"I have a couple of hundred cash."

"That'll give you a bit of breathing space. Then you'll have to earn your keep," he says, checking out my knees.

"I'm a pro in the kitchen," I say, "well trained."

"I'm sure you are." He wipes his wet fat lips with the back of his hand. "Okay, let me show you to your new abode."

As he stands, I notice his trousers are hanging off him. He's as skinny as a lanky streak of bacon with the fat trimmed off—one of Granny Mona's favorite expressions, which brings her to mind, and with her, a faint thrum of foreboding.

He tells me to go on ahead as we climb a narrow staircase with trippy, brown-patterned carpets and peeling, bubbled wallpaper on the walls. The stitches start to itch and I try to walk with my legs really close together. I wish he wasn't so close behind me. The house is tall and has zillions of little warren-like rooms, some with the doors half open. There are sounds of loud breathing, snoring, music playing, and other noises that I try to blank out. It smells of mildew and sour milk, thickly disguised with incense.

"Some of the 'residents' like to burn those brown sticks. Sickening," he says, as we pass by a room where the aroma is particularly pungent. I inhale deeply. It's calming.

"Here you go," he says, as he pushes open a door that leads into a dark low-ceilinged room with no window.

"Do you have any rooms with a window?" I ask, feeling like I might pass out.

"You looking for a room with a view?" he says, sniggering like a little girl.

"Yes. I can pay."

"Sorry, no can do, this is all we have available at the moment, but if anything else comes up, I'll upgrade you."

"How much?"

"Thirty-five a night."

"For this shithole?"

"Be my guest," he says, holding the door open. "No one's forcing you. You can earn a whack of a lot more than that in one evening here."

"Just want somewhere to stay, is all."

"You hiding from someone?"

"Look, just take the money," and I take a wad of tens and count them out. "There's seventy. That's enough for two nights, right?"

"I can't guarantee this room will be free in two nights' time. It's a very popular establishment, you know."

"I'm sure it is," I say. "Thank you for showing me to my room. Can I have a key?"

He drops a heavy wooden keyring with a tiny, rusted key into my hand.

"Is this the only one?"

"Of course not. The establishment has to have a spare in case you lose it."

"Can I pay extra for the spare?"

His eyes narrow and he seems to chew on his tongue as he sucks in air. The impression of Preppy Boy has completely disappeared and been replaced by something darker, older, more menacing. "I don't want anyone following you here. If I see anyone looking for you, there'll be a much bigger price to pay."

He closes the door. I lock the door and pick up the rickety fake-mahogany chair sitting in the corner of the room and jam it underneath the handle. I'm a dab hand at this particular maneuver. I lie back on the bed and stare at the maze of cracks crisscrossing the ceiling.

The bedcover is nylon and, as I pull it back, I see the sheets are the same, the same scratchy sweaty stuff, and they're stained. I jump off the bed, feeling tainted. I must go to the shops and do some damage on that card before it's stopped, buy some of those incense sticks, booze, food, sheets. This is no different from home, I've been doing this for years, only difference is I won't have her screaming shit at me and staring at me in that way.

I go back to the same offy to stack up. The skinny geek is there, and as soon as he sees me, he shakes his head in warning. I notice a guard talking on her phone in the corner, and I back out, sitting on the same wall as yesterday. As soon as she leaves, I hoist my skirt up even higher, bite down hard on my lips, pinch my cheeks, and go back in. "That was a close one," I say laughing.

"You'd better go. The guards are everywhere. Clamping down on underage drinking."

"You'd think they'd have better things to be doing with their time, like catching the real criminals."

"It's weird, all right. They're crawling all over this place these days. She wanted to see my ID, make sure I wasn't underage."

"And you're not?"

He shakes his head.

"Me neither."

"I can't take your word for it, I have to see ID. I could lose my job and be fined, or imprisoned, or both."

I decide to play along with his little game. I run outside, looking up and down the street. "The coast is clear."

"See that?" the guy says, pointing at a camera lens.

I nod. "Those things don't record sound, and I can show you something from my wallet with my back to the camera. That way you're covered. The quality is shit."

"Nope, I said no."

"Oh, did you? I'm sorry, I hadn't heard you."

"Look, you'd better go before the boss walks in."

"I really could make it worth your while, you know . . ."

"What's that, young lady? Are you trying to bribe one of my employees?" A guy in his forties, slim, buffed, manicured nails, flashes of silverfish in his hair, walks in. He smiles broadly at me.

I bend one knee, try on a smile, and lean into my hip. "Have you got a job?"

"That depends, what kind of a job?"

"Any."

"How old are you?"

"Eighteen."

"ID?"

"No, I've already told your man here that I don't carry ID."

"Well, you should."

"Do I look like I'm too young?"

The man tells the young pimply guy, whose name is Tommy, to go out back and close the door after him, then he turns to me. "I can't have you working here. The guards come in regularly asking my kids for their ID. Where do you live?"

"Nowhere, right now."

"Fight at home?"

"You could say that."

Shit, I wonder if he knows Mother, but even if he did, he couldn't have any idea I was her daughter. Still, the mention of "home" so close to that house, is making everything speedy inside. My leg starts to jangle.

He stares at my spastic jerky leg. "Where you staying tonight?"

I tell him the address of the B&B, before I realize I shouldn't have.

"So, working already?"

I pretend to look surprised. Of course he knows about that place.

He considers his next sentence carefully, weighing up whether to pursue this line of inquiry. "You still at school?"

"No." I take out Mother's Visa, wondering whether to risk it. "This is good for another few hours."

He shakes his head. "Pick what you like. We'll put it on your tab. And if that place gets too much for you, here's my card. Don't go wasting your wares on idiots like Tommy here, and don't go putting out in that shithole you're staying in."

What is it about me that men like him know?

He looks me up and down. "I could get you some new threads too someday."

The tremors in my leg have passed into my stomach, which

is jumping about like a scalded monkey. I saw that once in a video: asshole trainers in India, or somewhere like that, making the poor little guys walk on burning coals. Dance, monkey, dance.

I need to be cool here. "Thanks for the booze, mister."

"Any time, you know that."

I walk away, all fake "I couldn't give a shit about any of it." Funny how the more you pretend not to feel something, the more that pretending becomes real. I could walk this way after a session behind the bicycle sheds. I really could.

A voice from behind me: "Be careful of him." I turn around; it's Tommy and he's looking at me in a way I'm not used to: as if I were his baby sister. "Stay away from him, do you hear? He's beyond shady . . ."

He looks behind him, then reluctantly goes back inside.

9

Nico

Papa goes to Mama, takes her head in his hands, and kisses her softly on the forehead. "She's my daughter too, you must trust me. This man can give her a better life." Mama collapses against him. "I've asked him to pay for you to go to school, Nico."

I hear his words and try to tell myself they are true. Mama scrubs the tears from her face. "But where? Where will she go to school?"

"In England," Papa says, and Mama drops to the ground like a stone. Papa looks at me helplessly, as if to say this is all your fault. And then he leaves.

Luca runs to Mama's side and holds her head, while I move in a trance to the bucket of water and dip a cup in and hold it to her lips. She takes one sip and waves us away. She lies on the cold concrete floor, staring at the ceiling, then gets up like she's sleepwalking, takes the broom and a chair, climbs onto it and reaches to the corner of the ceiling with the head of the brush. She swipes at a cobweb. "What a monster of a thing. How did I miss that?" And she swipes and swipes, brushing the air, sweeping the space above her head, long after the web has disintegrated onto the floor. The dog sticks her nose into the drifts of dirt, then Mama turns on her and whacks her flanks. The poor creature yelps.

"Mama, don't," I say.

"Who asked you?" She steps down off the chair, advancing on me with the broom. I back away and cover my face with my hands.

"Mama!" Luca cries. And then she turns on him, lashing out, hitting him hard across the face, the body. He tries to fend off the blows and grabs hold of the bristles. They have a tug-of-war until the brush falls from Mama's hands and she is on her hands and knees, weeping. I feel cold inside. Luca goes to her and wraps his arms around her. This is only the second time I have seen Mama being held by any of the men in her life.

After a moment, she pulls away and stands. "Now go feed the chickens, son."

He looks at me, I nod at him. "Yes, Mama," he says as he goes into the yard, although the chickens don't need feeding at this time. I bend to stroke the dog on her head. She wags her tail half-heartedly and I lean in to kiss her on that soft spot between her eyes.

"Don't do that, Nico, she probably has fleas."

"Are you okay, Mama?"

"Fine," she says, her voice full of bustle. "He's a good-looking man, Nico. We must get you some clothes for England."

Has she really given in that easily, or is she trying to convince herself that she can trust Papa, in spite of everything?

"There is no fighting with fate," she says, more to herself than to me.

But Mama, England, without you? My voice gets pushed down somewhere deep inside me.

She falls silent and then says softly, "I've been lucky . . . I have you for a daughter."

Not for much longer, I think.

"You might have a beautiful girl of your own one day. You'll be a lovely mama," she says.

What would it be like to be a mama without my own around? A silent, heavy cry builds in my chest.

Mama nods her head, coaching herself. "Your father has decided and he knows best." Her voice is high and false from the effort of trying to contain the lie. Not for the first time, I wonder what kind of a world it is that Papa gets to make all the decisions over Mama.

A sound leaks out of me then, and it doesn't sound like my voice, it's young and unformed, like a five-year-old's. "Don't let me go, Mama, please don't let me go . . ." I want to wrap myself around her, hide under her skirts like I used to.

She moves away, her back tall and stiff. "Your Papa is a stubborn mule, Nico. It will be for the best, in the long run . . . yes . . . for the best . . ."

There is no arguing with Papa. Once he has made his mind up about something, it will come to pass, like the overly sweet wine that no one wants to buy, or the rotting plants or sick animals that he kicks about like stones. Our house is a world where Papa's word goes. I will not be allowed to go back to school, and I am to be married to this man. Mama learned, and he no longer has to hit her.

I think of the poor dog and how she will be treated after I leave, and somehow this forces my voice back to the surface. "Can I bring the dog?"

"Now don't be a silly girl. You'll be going on an airplane. How do you think that dumb animal would like that?"

The dog's helplessness makes me feel strong. Her silence allows me to continue to speak. "She won't like being left here without me. And I don't like the idea of flying through the clouds away from my country."

Mama's face has turned hard and rigid, and she pretends she hasn't heard me as she begins to hum a tune I've never heard, off-key and wobbly. She always said someone would have to kill her before getting her up there in one of those containers in the sky, those "metal tin cans with wings." I decide now is not the best time to remind of her this. Maria would love to fly away from here, but not even Maria would want to go away with a man whose eyes have never sought hers. My throat feels raw, cut on the shards of stone as I try to swallow.

Mama's voice has a new, high-pitched, singsong tone to it. "Maybe your new husband will get you a puppy. That would be nice. Company for you while he is out at work, until you have your first baby, then you'll be so busy you won't notice that you're alone all day."

I'd make sure the puppy was a girl and I'd call her Silvia. "What does he do, Mama?"

"Your Papa says he is a very rich man. He'll wear suits every day and you'll have a lovely house, with carpets and heaters on the walls. I've seen pictures of these houses in England. There will be pink and purple flowers in your garden, and your papa is right: you will get to see the sea."

"And you will come someday, Mama, and we can go together?"

We are both playing this lying game.

She grabs her purse from the container that is hidden behind the jars of pickled beets and cabbage under the sink.

"Where are you off to, Mama?"

"Ask me no questions . . . ," she says, trying to crack a smile. "Can you peel the potatoes and carrots and put them on to boil in about an hour? I should be back by the time they're soft."

She leaves, without looking back at me. Mama never leaves the house alone, and as I look out the window, I can see Luca following her as she walks down the lane from the house towards the village. She turns on him and shoos him away, like she's herding the chickens back into their henhouse, then she turns her back, arms swinging ferociously by her sides, as if propelling herself forward. I see her stumble on a loose rock, shake her head, and keep on going.

10

Sammy

Options: it's always good to have options. Today, there's a new pep to my step. In Tesco, I stock up on six-packs of Monster Munch and Heatwave Doritos, a bag of apples (for general good health), a few sandwiches, cans of 7Up and Coke, and some crackers and Laughing Cow cheese. Even though I have the rucksack full of Mother's forbidden foods, I'd better maximize this credit card today, now, before the thirsty one awakes. The first thing she'll notice is the stolen money. I can hear her yowls of outrage from here.

Outside, I hail a taxi, which is driven by a shriveled angry Irish aul fella, who asks me if I would ever get into a cab with one of those foreigners. I say I don't care either way, I just want to be dropped off at my destination.

"You should care . . . young one like yourself . . . you never know what those strangers are capable of."

I look at his face in the rearview mirror and see it's scorch-marked by hatred, red lines crisscrossing his nose. I bet he has a favorite poison, and I play my guessing game, knowing the answer immediately: whiskey—Paddy's. That stuff'd turn anyone mean. I open the window and stick my head out, breathing in the fumy air.

"Hey, close that window, young one," he says, all cranky.

I suddenly want to get out of this car. "Pull over," I say.

"Not there yet."

I tell him I might puke. He pulls over. "That'll be eighteen euros."

I hand him twenty. I walk the rest of the way with the bags full of food banging against my legs.

When I get into Arnotts, I go straight to the homeware section, buy three separate sets of the most expensive duvet covers, and throw a few smelly candles in there too. I can't find any of those incense sticks, must ask the girls where they procure them. I'm exhausted, suddenly. It's weird, going shopping and not having to steal anything. I consider sticking some lacy undies in my pockets but just don't have the energy. I put my hand in my pocket to check up on my phone: blankety blank. Not even a Facebook message from Luce, but then, her phone has probably been confiscated. Sonya's put up a stupid bikini shot on Snapchat. Pathetic. That girl is so desperate for attention. Brian told me it was never a good idea to post shit like that around: "Lowers the value of the stock," or something like that.

I haven't been gone that long, so no need to panic, just yet. But then . . . just who will panic? Mother will have a fit when she realizes she's been stolen from, then she'll relish that call to Dad. "See, William, see! What trouble we've raised? It's all your fault for never being home. A girl needs her father . . ."

I go outside, looking up and down at the taxi drivers' faces. I'm going to make a statement against the racist assholes that make up most of this country. Because I won't get into the car at the front of the queue, all sorts of angry honking starts. Look, Mother: another commotion, and I'm the cause of it. Spectacular! It turns out that number one in the queue is Irish, from the middle of nowhere, what we call a "culchie." He gets out and starts shouting what I can only imagine are colorful expletives at me, shaking his fist. Oh okay, mister, whatever you say, mister, of course I'll get in the car with you, I'm sorry for upsetting you, mister. Not likely. What is wrong with these guys? That kind of approach is hardly going to generate any new business. I store that nugget, for later.

I walk, staring in the windows, brazenly appraising the wares, until I find what I'm looking for. Number eight in the queue—a man who looks like he's a movie star with gorgeous sun-kissed skin and hair, definitely not a pale and ugly Celt. He's unaware of the stir I've caused and is looking down, quietly reading as I knock on the window. He looks up, rolls down the window, and I tell him where I want to go, mentioning the office block by the canal with the fountain out front, not the actual establishment, obviously. He shakes his head, points to the top of the queue and goes back to reading. I knock again. You don't understand, mister, I'm showing you a bit of solidarity here. I tell him I've chosen him out of all the other taxis. He looks at me, like everyone in my life ultimately looks at me, and tells me to go to the top of the queue. I'm disappointed in him. I feel like he's let his fellow countrymen down. This was supposed to be a statement. I'm not going anywhere near the top of this angry swarm of mosquitoes. I walk away, deciding to flag down the next cab I see. I won't even look in the window, I'll just take what I'm given.

It turns out what I'm given is some kind of wannabe priest/counselor dude. His first words to me are: "What's a young one like you doing out all alone? What's a young one like you doing going to a place like that? What's a young one like you doing with all those bags? It won't fill the emptiness inside, believe me, I know. Only Jesus will"—all to a soundtrack of some classic FM shite, complete with squealing violins. "You look like you could do with a friend, and He'll never let you down."

I zone him out. Blaaaah.

We're stuck in traffic, about five minutes from my new abode, when I tell the guy I'd like to get out, pay up, if you don't mind. He says he couldn't possibly let me out in the middle of all this traffic, and puts the child lock on. I'm sure there's a rule against this kind of thing. I look at the door and can't even see a button that I could press.

"I won't charge you, just want to make sure you get back safely. Too much traffic out there."

I can't get an image out of my head of me lying squished under him, reciting his Our Father; I'd much rather be squashed by the traffic any day. If he comes too close, I'll bite, scream, hit, tear him apart with my teeth. I wouldn't let his greasy head anywhere near me. I'm getting all worked up inside. "Control yourself," Mother used to say as she'd stand over me during some outburst, knowing that those very words would make me want to bust a gut.

The traffic crawls along as I try to tune out his monologue. "Is there anyone you'd like me to call? Do your parents know where you are? I sense the need in your life for guidance, a big black hole in the center of you where all sorts of evil could worm its way in." *Twisted-ass mind, got a pretzel for a brain.* Eminem provides the perfect soundtrack. These nonbeats and angry lyrics do much more to soothe me than any classical baloney. Dad likes his Bach, his Mendelssohn, his Mozart. The sound of that soaring screeching makes my head clang and my teeth sing.

"Are you okay back there?"

"Unlock these doors and let me out now. I have your license number. I'll report you for harassing a minor. Let me out, you perv." Maybe I have gone a little overboard now. He's turned pale and sweaty.

"Calm down, young lady," he says, which makes my insides boil. I can feel my cheeks puff up, and I bet they're purple. I start to wave at people in cars beside me but can't find the button to wind down the window. This car is like a coffin. I continue to bang on the glass.

"Stop that right now," he says. "I'm pulling in as soon as I can." He starts to weave his way through the traffic, horns blaring. I might just cause a pileup, for real, this time.

I throw three tens at him. "Keep the change, asshole."

The doors unlock. He leans out the window. Tries to give me back the money. Turns out he wasn't such a creep after all.

"I'll pray for you," he sounds sad, like he really means it.

I mooch along the canal, those heavy bags banging against my leg again, and think about the first week back at school. Would Miss White and Ms. Prendergast miss me? What about the rest of them? I think of Jess and Karen, the only other girls in my class I've heard talking about "going all the way," and they both said it was "delicious," like all the best things in life packed into one tingling moment. "Orgasmic." That word. Although I made all the necessary noises (I know what's expected of me after watching hard-core porn with Brian and his mates), I really didn't feel a thing. It wasn't terrible or anything, just not really anything. But I guess I don't have a great store of life's "delicious" moments to draw from, and I was always pissed. Even on my own, in my room, I never really got the hang of it. The last time I tried, Mother snuck in on me and stood in the doorway watching for fuck knows how long. That kind of killed any fun to be had twiddling around down there. That was also the moment I decided to push a chair under the door handle, which resulted in the chair disappearing from the room the next day. The weirdest thing about it was that she said nothing, just chilled me with her silence.

I feel I'm being watched; then again maybe it's my overactive imagination playing tricks on me, because according to the school counselor (sorry, Mrs. O'D, I've already had a few appointments and it hasn't made one iota of difference), I have "paranoid tendencies." When I step inside the building, I see a suited young fella coming down the stairs. He looks really happy to see me. "What room?"

I don't know why I do this but I tell him number 12, which is nowhere near mine.

"Tomorrow, lunchtime?" he says.

Jesus, this guy's got an appetite, and a wallet. I wonder how many of the clients have a daily habit, like going to the gym. He probably tells his colleagues that's where he's at. I bet "the gym" is code.

I go back to my box and decide to have a picnic. The first thing I do—which is, in hindsight, a mistake—is open the bottle of vodka and drink. I don't glug though; I'm careful just to take little sips. It doesn't take long for my stomach to burn and my head to settle. My body softens and I lie flat out, surveying the cracks. All appetite gone now. I'm exhausted, knackered, cream-crackered.

I drift in and out of woozy consciousness. There go her spikes, and there she lies, under the tires. SPLAT. Resistance. Is. At. This. Stage. Futile. I wake to the sound of my own voice, gurgling. The new sheets are soaked in sweat. I'm dying to pee, so I pad along the swirling carpet in my bare feet. There's a window in the loo, and when I look out, I see that it's dusky outside and hard rain is falling like splinters from the sky. Someone must have tried calling me by now, someone must be worried, but there's no little envelope on the screen. Just a matter of time and then I'll have to chuck the phone, well, the SIM anyway, 'cause when they do decide to come looking for me, this would be the easiest way to track me down. I like that image: the police and my loved ones, in a cell, heads huddled together, on my trail, on a tracking device. Dad is pale and supporting Mother, who's sober and has realized the error of her ways. She's beating herself up over this big time. Ah now, Mother, don't go blaming yourself. You know you're not to blame. We are none of us to blame.

I tune in to the noises of the B&B and wish I hadn't. It's all there: the creaking, banging (I guess headboards against walls), men's voices—it's funny 'cause I can't hear any female ones—and there's even the odd grunt and snore. Lullaby sounds. I have to get out of here. On my way down, I get stared at, solicited by two men together. They could be father and son, and I get told off by another. "Go home," this man says. "You're far too young to be in a place like this."

I run out onto the street, cross the road, and sit on a bench. A shadow crosses me from behind: just two girls on a night out, arms linked, laughing brightly. The moon is a tiny inverted C, peeking out from behind the clouds. It throws its meek shafts of light on the murky canal water, which appears lacquered black. I have a weird desire to wade in, not in a dramatic I-want-to-die way, but just to submerge. I lie on my back on the damp grass, imagining I'm floating, staring at the flashes of the lunar C as the clouds move across its surface. I close my eyes for a moment, and then they jolt open on reflex. It's a furtive place here, among the trees and the benches, the looming long-necked swans. There are shadowy men walking. I stand tall, all spiky elbows and taut body, and go for a walk, swinging my arms, fists clenched. I need to pump my muscles, fill my lungs with air. The rain starts up again, softly at first, but then it pelts down, and still I walk on.

Twenty minutes later, drenched as a water rat, I notice a figure lying on the ground on the pavement in front of me. I start to cross the road to avoid any trouble, but when I look back I see that it's a girl and she's in bad shape. As I draw nearer, I notice she's shaking and jerking and her eyes are rolling in her head, her jeans pulled down to her hips.

"Are you okay?"

She tries to open her eyes and focus on me, but can only manage a nod.

"What's your name?"

"Natasha," she says.

Christ. "Where do you live?"

She manages to mumble something along the lines of "Take me anywhere you like . . ." and then she blacks out again. I kneel on the ground beside her, put her head on my lap, take off my wet jumper, and lay it on her chest. I do my best to pull her skintight jeans back up over her hips. She wriggles and makes a practiced moaning sound. She looks like a child. A car slows down, and a man leans out the window. "Fuck off, can't you see this girl needs help?"

The car speeds away, and another one slows down, but as soon as this guy sees me and what's going on, he's gone. I dial 999. "Emergency," I say, "girl unconscious." I don't know exactly where I am but I describe the building and the canal bank. The voice says she knows where I mean, that I'm to hold tight and they'll be there as soon as possible. Twenty minutes pass and the girl falls in and out of consciousness, at one point opening her eyes and reaching towards my zipper. I gently push her hand away and turn her on her side, in case she chokes.

What kind of treatment has she received to make her act this way? She looks like an abused puppy who keeps going back for more, hoping, always hoping, that this time there'll be a scrap of kindness. I imagine her owners, circling her, and wonder if she's being watched now.

A crappy Ford-type Garda car eventually arrives, and a man and woman step out. Why didn't they send an ambulance?

"Okay?" the female guard says. "Was it you who called?"

I nod.

"What have we here?" The two of them look down at the girl, then at each other, and without speaking, the man lifts the girl, who's light as air, and places her gently in the back seat. The woman hands me back my jumper.

"Is this yours? What are you doing out this late at night?"

I tell them I'm just on my way home from a party.

"On your own? At this hour? What are you doing walking around this area anyway?" She gestures to the sleeping girl in the back, her black, lacy push-up bra visible beneath her flimsy top.

"Can you get a blanket for her?" I ask the man, who carefully covers her with a scratchy-looking tartan blanket that is lying on the back seat.

"Hop in, we're bringing you home," he says.

I tell them I'm fine, fancy a bit of air, had a row with the boyfriend, need to clear the head.

"Where do you live?" the woman asks. I give them an address that isn't mine. "We're dropping you back there now, and we want to speak to your parents, make sure you're safe."

"Look, I'm fine, okay? It's this girl you need to be worried about. She looks like she's been attacked or taken an overdose or something."

Both of them look at her through the window.

"Do you know her?" I ask.

"'Fraid so," the man says.

"She looks very young."

"So do you, missy. Now, where do you *really* live?"

I'm confused why they're not bringing the girl straight to the hospital.

"What'll will happen to her?" I ask.

"Don't you worry about her. Worry about yourself."

I thank them kindly for their concern, and leg it. No one comes chasing after me. Even I can see that this is kind of prophetic; a loaded not-so-coded message from yer woman above. But things will never get that bad for me.

I am, after all, a girl used to getting herself into and out of some ugly scrapes.

11

Nico

I'm wearing the new dress that Mama bought for me the day she went to the village. It's navy blue with polka dots and long sleeves. My hair is tied up in the same ribbon as on the day I was presented to my new husband. I am outside of myself looking in, dizzy from holding my breath.

All the men of the house are there, sitting around the table, drinking tea, talking about the fat clouds, the fact that rain is on its way, and about time too. The rabbits and chickens are dehydrated, they're too scrawny and need to be fattened up, Papa says. Like me. A good soaking will do the ground good and put some moisture back into the fowl. Mama is bustling about. She has baked a cake with flour, sugar, eggs, crushed walnuts, and sour cream borrowed from the Petrans. I wonder how Mama is going to pay them back; she must have spent every penny in her secret jar on this new dress for me.

She managed to get me a suitcase that doesn't close properly, so Papa tied the handle with string. My black patent school shoes were polished by Mama this morning with her spit and a cloth. They were given to me by my cousin Olga at the beginning of school last year and pinch my toes badly now. Inside the case, there is one other pair of shoes: an old pair of Mama's that are two sizes too big for me, as well as a jumble of trousers and jumpers all either falling off me or too tight. Mama says it might be colder in England, she couldn't be sure, but not to worry because as soon as I get there my new rich husband will buy me lovely clothes. There is grit in her voice.

"How will I change and clean my dressings when I'm there?" I asked Mama in private that morning as she pulled my hair back into a high ponytail, her tongue sticking through her teeth in deep concentration. She told me the bleeding would happen again, every month, until I was with baby.

"You'll just have to be careful not to let your husband see."

I told her I wanted to see Maria, to say goodbye, and she couldn't stop the cloud from passing over her face as she said, "We cannot let anyone know. The school might try to stop your papa."

So this is why the whole thing has happened so fast.

The dog is sitting on my feet, nuzzling her head into my skirt. "Get that filthy thing out of here," Papa says. "We don't want you smelling of dog and we don't want Petre to think you're dirty." He kicks her, and instead of slinking away like she normally does, she bares her teeth and growls. This makes Papa kick her even harder.

"Stop, Papa, stop, she's old."

"A useless old bitch then," Papa says, and Victor and Sergiu laugh.

I take the dog gently by the rope around her neck and lead her into the yard, tickling her behind her ears, as she lies down and offers me her belly. I sense the man coming towards the house, see his boots advancing, and I straighten up, trying to arrange my face into a smile. I rub my hands against my skirt. The dog snarls and bares her teeth again. Papa comes out, ties her tightly to the skinny tree trunk, and nods a welcome to the man. The thin twine is pulling on her soft neck and she starts to whimper. I go to loosen the bind when Papa tells me to go inside and wash my hands. The impulse to resist the men is huge, but then I look at the dog straining and see spots of sore erupt on her skinny neck.

"Ssshhhh," I call out to her, "ssshhhh," as I go into the house, abandoning her to her struggle.

My three brothers all stand when the man enters, and they offer him their hands, Luca shaking limply this time, his chest puffed. The other two are making a big show of being friendly, talking weather and crops, and asking him if he had a pleasant journey.

"What's England like anyway?" asks Luca.

"England? Who said anything about England?" The man laughs, Sergiu and Victor joining in. The pressure inside my chest eases a little and I breathe out for what feels like the first time in days. Maybe we would be staying in our country after all, maybe we would be staying close to Mama and Maria and Luca and the dog, and I could come visit them.

"Which village are you headed to then?" Luca speaks up again.

"Now don't be rude, son," Papa says.

How is it rude to ask where your only sister is going to?

Papa and the man look at each other and nod. They go outside and we strain to hear what they're saying. Through the kitchen window, we see the man taking a roll of notes out of his pocket and counting it in front of Papa, who takes the offering palm to palm, pumping the man's hand in a vigorous handshake.

"Why is he giving Papa money?" Luca's voice is hoarse.

Mama looks like she might have one of her strange fits again, when Sergiu speaks up. "Don't act like you don't know, fuckwit."

I want to cover my ears with my hands to block the noise that word makes.

A silence follows, except for the mumbles of the two men outside and the whimpers of the dog. She has not yet learned that it's better not to struggle.

My held-breath moment lasts too long, the lid closes down, everything falls dark, and I crash to the bottom of the well. When I hit the ground, I curl up on my side. The air is liquid and I drink it in, drowning.

My eyes are shocked open, and I sit up, fending Papa off with my hands as he throws water on my face. Luca is trying to pull him away from me. Where is Mama? I see her through a blurry lens, slumped on a chair, staring at the man with a look that is full of poisonous arrows.

The man says, "Is she sick? I will not take her if she is sick."

Mama jumps off the chair and goes to pummel Papa on his shoulders. "Of course the child is sick, why else do you think this man is getting rid of her? His own daughter?"

Papa turns on Mama, grabs her hands and tells her to quieten down, staring into her eyes. It's as if she is mesmerized: her shoulders slump forward, her body seems to lose its substance, its fight, its desire to draw breath even, as she stills to an empty silhouette, an outline of the woman of flesh and blood of a moment before. Mama has disappeared, the struggle over. She knows what will happen if she continues to fight.

The rest of the leave-taking happens as if behind a gauze: woozy and out of focus. Mama is so still, it's as if she has been turned to stone. Where is Papa? Papa? I cannot see him. The boys? Luca is there, at the door, his emotions swirling and visible to me, almost too big to be contained by his skin. Almost. He lets me go without a fight. They all let me go.

A wail follows on the air, which could be the dog or Mama, or a fairy cap being ripped from its branch too soon.

The suitcase is banging against my ankles, its useless contents bulging against the piece of string that looks like it might snap. The man doesn't slow down, even though his legs are twice as long as mine, and he watches me struggle with the case. Maybe Papa will change his mind and claim me back as his? Luca? I have to trot to keep up with the man. "Where are we going?" I ask after some time. There is no sign of anyone coming after me. My question is answered by silence and a quickening of the man's stride. I follow, not knowing why I follow, head down, feet tripping in my too-tight shoes, the red dust clinging to the polish and the spit. The man tells me to hurry, that a car is waiting for us. My heart is banging so wildly it feels like it might crash through my ribcage.

The car is at the back entrance to my school and I wonder if Miss Iliescu is inside—can anybody see me with my new husband and my new dress? I stick my chest out like Luca does, before he has to get into the barrel, hoping to simulate whatever feelings he generates to get him through the dark tumbling. It's easier to breathe with my ribs jutting forward, a space to draw breath into, and I play that game of holding air inside for ten, then twenty, then thirty, forty seconds. The need to let go is too great, and I don't get anywhere near my personal best of sixty-one.

The blinds are pulled down, covering the windows in school so no light can get through, like eyelids sewn shut. I've never seen the tiny concrete building empty before, and it's weird, sad somehow: an abandoned bomb shelter. A familiar smell of sweaty feet and musty chalk leaks through the bunker-like walls. Do memories play tricks, tantalizing the senses? Already this place is playing out like the past, all of it witnessed as if from a distant point.

The engine of the car is idling and I see a figure in the driving seat. The walls of my heart thicken in an attempt to protect myself from this future. Now. The car is a metallic blue, rusted, with the back left door hanging off its hinges. As we draw nearer, the figure in the front reveals itself to be a woman. The man sits in beside her, gesturing for me to climb in the back through the half-open door. The seats are plastic, my thighs sticking to them.

The woman half turns her head, her glossy black hair falling over one eye, and introduces herself as Petre's wife. How many wives does one man need?

"Hungry?" the woman asks as she turns the key in the ignition, revving the engine, not waiting for an answer. I look at her in the chipped windscreen mirror and see only her painted lips, cherry red and shining. I want to ask where we're going but no sound will form through my cracked lips. I long to lie down at the edge of the well and scoop the cold clear water into my parched mouth. Sometimes, if I feel the longing deep enough, I can make it happen. I open my mouth and draw the liquid in, swallowing long deep mouthfuls. The car starts to move and I close my eyes, not wanting to see the familiar slip by.

"Tired?" the woman says.

I nod, not opening my eyes, letting the thrum of the engine vibrate in my body—a new experience, my first time in a car.

When my eyes flicker open, they meet the woman's as she stares at me in the rearview mirror.

"I'm Magda, by the way."

I nod, not wanting to say my name. The silence yawns wide and rude, so I force myself to speak. "Are you from around here?"

"I was, a long time ago. I live in Italy now."

I try to remember what I know about Italy: it's shaped like

a high-heeled boot and is surrounded by the sea and gets very hot in the summers.

"Will I get to see the sea?" I ask.

"If you like."

"Is it blue or black?"

She looks puzzled. "The sea is always blue."

So, Papa.

"Can I continue to go to school?"

"You'll receive an education, all right," the woman called Magda says, and the man laughs.

"I'm one of the best in my class."

"I'm sure you'll be a quick learner," she says.

"Can I get a puppy?" I say, an image of my dog tethered to her post causing my eyes to flood with tears.

Magda is silent, she looks down, then at her husband and whispers, "How old is she really? I know what the father told you, but I don't believe it for an instant. She's no more than a child."

The man replies, "Good, there'll be more demand for her."

"That is not our thing."

I hear them but not really, my own head whooshing with tumbling thoughts, blocking out what their words could mean.

The car stops on the outskirts of another village, about an hour's drive from my own, and two girls are standing by the roadside, two guys about Sergiu's age on either side of them, holding their hands.

The man opens the door, gets out, slips the men the same cash handshake he gave Papa. I'm sure these girls don't think they are going to marry Petre. They jump into the back seat beside me, excitement leaking off them, an electric charge in the air.

"Quick," they say, "before our papas hear we have gone."

They are older than me by a few years and they seem as if they've known each other a long time. I think of Maria. My throat hurts as I try to swallow. The car drives away and the girls ask why the boys aren't coming.

"Not enough room in the car," the man says. "They'll be joining us later."

They girls look back at the boys' retreating figures. Did they notice the money?

The car builds up speed, its tires throwing up clouds of dirt against the already grimy windows so all I can see are streaks of trees, electricity poles, flashes of green and silver against the backdrop of a bank of heavy yellow sky. The landscape is flat and dry, parched, like my tongue. The girls giggle and whisper amongst themselves, ignoring me, pretending I'm not part of their picture.

"You're very quiet, little one," Magda says suddenly.

I nod, squeezing back fear.

We pull up outside a bar with a swinging neon sign outside, like in one of those sawdust-and-spit places in the cowboy films. The sign creaks in the windless night, as if disturbed by ghosts. We don't have a bar like this in our village, but I imagine Sergiu, Victor, and Papa would come, if there was one. The five of us go inside and it's dark and dusty, wet stains on the concrete floor and walls. Loud music is pumping into the beer-soaked air, and half-dressed women are dancing around silver sticks stuck into the ground. Some of them are wearing only underwear, and some of them have no tops on. I look away. I've never seen a woman naked before. Mama taught me it's rude to stare so I look down at my dust-flecked shoes.

Magda asks if we'd like Coca Cola and chips. I nod. I've never had either but have seen them on the TV in Maria's house. Everyone in America wears lots of makeup and very little clothes and drinks Coca Cola and eats chips. I feel like I'm on the flickering screen, caught in the TV box. My eyes can't focus properly in the gloom and, anyway, they're not sure what they're seeing, like the game of trickery the boys used to play when I was little, blindfolding me and making me stick my finger into disgusting things, and then eat them. The other girls have gone very quiet.

"Would you like to do that?" the man asks, gesturing to the women dancing. "It's better than working in a factory, or cleaning tables, no?"

I rub my eyes, which feel like they're being attacked by stinging flies. I can't dance. I'm the worst dancer in the village. Everyone knows that.

"I can't dance," I tell him. "No rhythm."

The taller girl bursts out laughing, clapping her hands.

The man looks at them both. "Can you dance?"

The same girl laughs harshly as her friend tells her how happy Ivan would be to see her dance.

"Go on, show us how it's done," the man says, before leaving to go to the bar.

Magda takes the laughing girl by the hands and moves her

hips in time to the music, twirling her around in circles. "Very good."

I can see the girl is pleased and she takes her friend's hands and they dance together. Magda starts to take off her blouse. "Copy me," she says to the girls.

They both stop; my cheeks are flaming.

The man returns with the black, fizzing drinks in long, clinking glasses. "Put your clothes on, plenty of time for that later," he says to his wife, who puts her blouse back on and sits with us at the table.

"I'll teach you to dance, little one," she says to me, suddenly looking very sad.

"No thank you," I say, as politely as I can. "I'm very good at cleaning and sweeping."

"That's boring," she says. "I'll teach you to do other work, where you'll earn much more money and get to look like me." She seems as if she is trying to convince herself more than me.

The other girls are happy about this and discuss what color lipstick they would like to wear and how they would like to style their hair. I wonder what their boyfriends told them they were going to do. I swirl the drink in my hand, the ice clinking against the sides of the glass, tiny bubbles floating upwards. Maybe I should go to the toilet and climb out the window, but where would I go? The fizzy syrup is delicious and cool against the sides of my throat. I start to feel sleepy and worry I might fall into the well again. Gripping onto the sides of the table, I hear Magda say, "It's okay, girls, it's just time for a nap. You've got a long journey ahead of you."

12

Sammy

After a bad night tossing and turning in my cupboard (the wet cotton-wool balls I stuck in my ears to drown out the noise kept falling out each time I moved, and the dreams of Prickles and the Machine pierced me each time I fell asleep for even a millisecond), I get up and get out. I need air and a juice. In the landing outside, there is a girl in glasses and a baseball cap. So not so paranoid after all.

"Cool pad."

God, she's persistent, I have to hand it to her. She pushes on past me into my room.

"Where's the window?" she asks.

"There isn't one."

"Oh."

The two of us face each other.

"Nice sheets," she says. "What a spread." She takes in the

mess of "delicacies" jumbled about on the covers. "From your fridge?"

No shit, Sherlock. The labels are still on them. I can see she approves of my act of defiance. I'm not in the mood to bring Mother into this conversation though, so I ask, "How the hell did you find me?"

"Not so hard, really, I just called Brian."

I wonder how she got his number. He probably thought she was hitting on him.

"He took me here once," I say.

"Romantic," she says. "When was the last time you ate?" She flops onto the bed. We both hear a muffled wheezing sound coming from the room next door and a rhythmic thumping. Usually this kind of thing would send us into spasms of laughter, but today we both pretend it isn't happening. She cracks a crap joke about me turning all Desperate Housewife-y with my candles and posh Egyptian cotton sheets. She makes a big show of eating some crap tuna sandwich, saying it's delicious, when in actual fact the bread is curling up at the edges. She asks again where the window is.

"Do you see any window, dummy?"

"I didn't know places like this exist. It feels like a storage cupboard."

"Seriously, Luce. I want you to get the fuck out of here. You don't belong here."

"Neither do you," she says.

I tell her that I feel right at home here and am fitting in just fine, that I've met some of the other girls here and they're cool. I know it's ridiculous, under the circumstances, but I think Luce is jealous of these other girls. She's been excluded from joining the gang again. I always had the edge there.

"You can't stay here. This place is a shithole," she says. I laugh. She tries a different tactic. "Come on, let's go outside and have a picnic. We can sit by the canal. It's gorgeous out there."

I'm still shattered and not in the mood to be sociable but reckon the path of least resistance is the right fork in the road, for now. And I owe her a picnic at the very least, after the way I treated her last time. What's wrong with her that she just keeps coming back for more?

In the daylight, that spot where I met the girl last night is all businesslike, busy guys and some women, but mainly men in their suits, on their phones. I wonder, was it one of these important-looking dudes who curb-crawled us last night? The guy from last night spoke with a posh voice and surely could have afforded to do some "wooing"—*if* that was what he was after.

I take the naggin out of my pocket and take delicate sips, Lucy muttering her disapproval: it's too early, you need to eat something, you need to start looking after yourself, you don't want to turn out like your mother.

Fuck that, Lucy Poo, not in the mood for a lecture.

My stomach burns and I feel a lovely sense of floating ease. I lie down on my back on the damp sweet-smelling grass and stare up at the warm blue sky. The sun doesn't normally shine like this, and I don't feel like me, and that feels great. I'm in the driving seat now. I look over at Luce in her stupid disguise. She's destined to be a passenger, which is, of course, much more dangerous, especially if the driver is freewheeling and off her head.

"Aren't you going to get in big trouble if you're found out breaking your parole?"

"Dad's in the hospital and Mum's at Meals on Wheels for another half hour or so. I can't stay long. Just needed to see you're okay." She hands me twenty euros. "I can get you some more in a day or two; Dad's always losing track of what he's given me."

A guy in a suit sits down on a bench beside us and looks at me sideways. He's a little younger than Mr. O'D, with a pouch where his chin should be. I doubt he has much luck with the ladies. I climb on top of Luce—this will have the desired effect. He's gripping the sides of the bench. He turns his head sideways, makes a kind of backward nod of his head as if to say, Where?

"Haven't you got some work to do?" Luce says to him directly. That does it. He scurries away, pretending he never saw us.

"What a class-A creep," she says.

Oh I don't know, Luce, I've seen worse. I reckon he'd be an easy first-timer, going solo, without Brian there to orchestrate proceedings. "You'd better go now before your mum finds out you're gone," I say.

She nods but seems incapable of moving.

"Luce, you're not going to do either of us any favors by being found out."

She seems to agree with this, and stands, shaking herself out. "See you tomorrow. Don't do anything stupid, okay?"

"I'm hardly in a fit state, now am I?"

She smiles grimly. "No, you're not." And she walks away, looking back every few steps, her head whizzing with plans about how to rescue her very-best best friend.

The same guy that scampered off when Luce challenged him scuttles back when he sees she has vamoosed. I pick a blade of grass and suck on it, looking at him from under my lashes. He leans towards me and in a strangled whisper says, "How much?"

I pretend I don't hear him and roll back onto the damp earth. When he gets up to leave, I hear my voice tell him the address and room number. There's that demented ventriloquist in the sky again, speaking through me, wanting to land me in some deep shit, although really, what's the difference? Brian or Niall or Tom or Kev, Stu, or any of the rest of them? At least this time the money I make will be mine.

I'm lying on the bed when he knocks, and I wonder about the whole open-door policy. Is it a safety thing? I decide I'd prefer to leave it open a crack—it's what the other girls do, and even if skeleton-man downstairs gets off on it, at least it's better than being locked in this sweaty cupboard with a stranger.

The guy seems older, his face shiny, wet patches under his

arms. I tell him what I'm prepared to do and what I won't, in a professional-sounding voice, imparted to me from above. Although the biggest part of me wants him gone, wants to tell him to fuck right off, in fact, my strings are being jerked and I'm way outside my own control. I've never done this kind of thing almost-sober before, and it's feeling way too real.

He nods, like he's in a trance, staring at my legs and knees, especially my knees, as he begins to undo his belt. Before I know what's happening he has pushed the door closed behind him and turned the key in the lock, then puts the key in his pocket.

"Hey," I say.

"Privacy," he says, as he pulls his clothes off, except for his socks, and he stands there in all his fat-suit glory.

My hand reaches out and does what it has to do.

"No," he murmurs, and pushes my head down.

I do what Brian taught me. It'll be over quicker this way.

He strokes the back of my head. "Good girl, good girl," he says. "How old are you, anyway?" He pulls my hair hard and yanks my face to look at him.

"Eighteen," I say.

"Sure you are, girlie. Now swallow."

That wasn't in the plan but I do as he says. I want him gone.

When he's finished, he insists on lying on the bed, pulling me close.

"Time's up, mister," I say after what I consider to be a polite amount of time.

"I'll say when time is up. I'm the one paying." And he draws me even closer, his bulges of flesh pressing into me.

"Don't you have to be back at work?"

"You're a cheeky young one," he says, all delighted with himself. He gets up, dresses slowly, carefully rearranging his tie, then he throws ten euros on the bed, unlocks the door, and leaves with the key still in his pocket.

"Hey," I shout after him, "it's fifty. And I want my key back." I think back to the "how much" moment and realize I didn't name my price. I wonder if it would have made any difference anyway.

I let the asshole go and light a candle, White Linen, and wave it around the room, then rip the sheets off and snuggle into the new duvet cover, wrapping it tightly around me. I cover my head, inhaling the smell of clean cotton, until I have to come up for air. My hand reaches for the naggin on the bedside table and I swallow, erasing the sensation of what went before. The fiery liquid purifies and numbs. Those lines zigzagging across the ceiling begin to look like giant zips, all ready for the opening. Laughter erupts out of me, harsh, teary, uncontrollable. My stomach spasms. I hear footsteps on the stairs stop outside my room, and then a female voice. "Everything okay in there?"

Hohohohoho. I hold my sides, splutter, choke.

The woman's head pops around the door. "I thought you were being strangled."

Hahahahahaha.

"Are you okay?"

I can't speak.

"Did he hurt you?"

I shake my head from side to side, side to side like the head-banger that I am. The woman walks over to the bed, puts her hand on my arm and looks at me. She has washed-out blue eyes.

"Stop that now," she says, like she's speaking to a toddler. My stomach is heaving and the tears are pushing. I wonder, has anyone died from laughing? Next thing I know, she's slapping me on the face.

"Hey," I say, which seems like such a ridiculous thing to say under the circumstances that it starts me off all over again.

This time she leaves the room and returns a moment later with a glass full of water, which she throws on my face.

"Bitch."

"Calm down," the woman says. "Shhhhhhh."

I reach out to hit her, but she grabs me firmly by the wrist and sits on the bed. I wriggle up so I'm sitting on a level with her.

"What happened, love? Are you going to tell me? Did he hurt you?"

I start to shake my head again and she grabs it between her hands. "How old are you?"

This woman is fine-boned and tiny, dried-out with dyed-blonde hair, and looks about as old as Luce's mum.

"How old are you?" I say back.

She grins. "Wiseass. If you're not careful, in a few years you'll look like me." She gestures to the vodka. "That stuff will wreck you."

As soon as she smiles her face opens and softens, and she seems so much younger. She settles herself on my bed, sitting back against the pillows.

"Nice threads," she says, fingering the duvet cover.

"A leaving present from home," I say.

She considers me very carefully. "Is there no going back?"

Mother's bloated face floats before me. She's got so much worse in recent years; there's not even a trace of the woman who used to love to dress me up in pretty clothes and braid my hair into a French plait, who smiled when people would say, "What a beautiful daughter you have." I think back to our "pink-party days" when she'd buy me my favorite food—anything pink, like strawberry jam, plums, marshmallows. We'd go to the shopping center and order two Mister Whippys with sticky raspberry sauce. But now, she scowls if someone calls me pretty, taking it as a direct slur on her own waning looks. Now, she has special pink food, like prawns and taramosalata, just for herself in the fridge. Now, she spits and hisses and acts possessed, although she likes to tell me I am. Now she visits me in the night and I don't know whether I'm going to be hugged, or cried on, or cut, or stared at, or touched, like that last night, the night she crossed the line. No, there is no going back. I shake my head, once, forcibly.

"I know what it can be like, love, but there has to be another way. Have you been to social services?"

I don't think this woman has a clue who she's dealing with. No way am I going to be put into a reform school or foster care with some other mad fucking family telling me what to do. Anyway, no one would believe me when they met the so-called abusive parents, from a perfectly respectable family home on the south side.

"Not going to happen."

"If I could do it again another way, I would."

"You're not me."

"Right, try to get some sleep and let's talk tomorrow. I may be able to hook you up with someone who'll look after you."

"Thanks, but no thanks. I can look after myself."

"Is that why you were hysterical?"

"It was funny."

She looks at me in a way that says, it's anything but funny, but doesn't patronize me by saying it. She gets up and pats my arm before she leaves the room, leaving the door ajar. "I'm on the floor above," she says from the doorway.

After she leaves I want to curl up in her arms.

13

Nico

When I wake, my tongue is twice its normal size, the ground is moving beneath me, and my eyelids are heavy and can't open fully. I wonder if the sandman came. I lie in the dark and try to calm myself, count backwards, imagine the dog is lying beside me, protecting me. I reach out to touch her tummy and my fingers brush against a warm human body. It stirs and shouts in its sleep—a female voice, one of the girls from the car. There is a low humming noise, a vibration, movement, but not like in the car, here everything is rolling and swaying. I need to go to the toilet so I swing my legs to the side of the bed and stand. The room is so narrow I can reach out and touch both walls with my fingertips, hitting against cold plastic—no slimy moss here. On the bed I can make out two bodies, breathing jerkily.

I grope along the wall towards the door and push against it, feeling for a handle, but can't find anything, so I press against the door with my shoulder, and then I knock, timidly at first, so as not to wake the other girls, and then as the need to get to the toilet becomes unbearable, I start to bang on the door loudly with my fists, shouting, "Hello, anybody there?" There are whispers first, then mumbles, then, as the other girls slowly adjust to the dark and narrow space, they too begin to shout.

The door falls in and there behind it is Magda, her long hair framed in a halo of light. "Shut up," she hisses, "just shut up if you know what's good for you."

My chest is heaving and I fall out the door against her. She holds me still as I try to calm my breathing and the other girls' screams still to a stifled sobbing. "I need the toilet." She points to a bucket in the corner of the room and I shake my head so hard it feels as though my brain hits against the side of my skull.

The woman puts her hand on my arm and says, "Okay, little one, it's okay, come with me and we'll find a toilet." She closes the door behind us and I can hear the latch click.

The other girls shout louder, and Magda speaks through a crack. "Don't make another sound." The girls fall silent immediately.

Her voice changes register as she speaks to me, softer, almost like a mama would to her child. "They'll be okay, they have each other." There are small circular windows along the corridor, peepholes to a dark night sky. Magda points through the glass. "There's the sea. You said you wanted to see the sea. Well, we are on it."

I wonder which sea, although I do not ask. I am afraid to know. How far did we travel from my village before getting on this boat? My head feels stuffed with cotton. I press my face against the glass and see only a black screen. Maybe Papa was right, after all. The ground beneath me swells and I fall to my knees, yellowish-brown liquid pouring out of my mouth. Magda cleans the mess with tissues and says briskly, "You must stop now. You mustn't let Petre see you like this," and she pulls me to my feet and hurries me along the corridor to another door, which opens into a bathroom. She tells me to stand and put my hands in the air, then pulls the dress, which has yellow bits all over it, over my head. My best dress. "Don't worry about that. I have bought you much prettier dresses. Come on, now," she says as she guides me into the shower, holding me steady, one hand on my hip, the other on the small of my back. "Try to relax."

I think of my dog straining against her rope and close my eyes and allow my body to go limp as she rubs soap on me and washes my hair with foamy bubbles.

At the back of this bathroom is another door, which leads into a bedroom, lit from above with harsh lights. Magda hands me white underwear, smelling of spring flowers, and the prettiest green dress I've ever seen, with puff sleeves and a swing skirt, then she turns her back to me and looks in the mirror, brushing out her long shiny hair. "My mother taught me to brush it a hundred strokes twice a day," she says. She tells me to stand in front of the mirror while she brushes my hair, which looks brown and lank when it's wet, but is blonde and full of bounce when dry.

She puts her hands on my hips and turns me to face her. "Just do as they say. It will be over quicker that way."

I nod. I don't know who "they" are or what they will say, but I know she knows something I don't. "Shall I go and get some food?" I shake my head. She pours a glass of clear liquid from a green plastic 7UP bottle and tells me to drink up. Even though I know what happened the last time I drank in front of this woman, I grab the glass and gulp. My mouth is craving this cool liquid and I like the feel of the bubbles as they slide down. Falling into darkness wouldn't be the worst thing right now.

She tells me to lie down on the bed and that she'll be back soon. I wonder why she dressed me in such pretty clothes when I'm about to go to bed. I ask about the other girls.

"Don't worry about them. They are older than you and they have each other," she says, again.

The rocking and swelling is soothing, and the smell of clean comforts me.

"I won't be long," she says as she closes the door behind her and turns a key.

I lie still, holding my breath, hoping to go under.

When she returns later that night, Petre is with her. He bangs into the room loudly and suddenly it's plunged into piercing brightness.

"Shhhh, you'll wake her," Magda says.

"What's she doing in here?"

She tells him that I was very sick and could have choked and died. "You don't want that after all the money you paid, do you?"

Petre goes silent for a moment. "And the other two?"

"I guess I'd better go check on them."

No, don't leave me here, with him. I curl up into a ball and screw my eyes shut. I can feel him sit on the edge of the bed. He reaches out to touch me when I hear Magda's voice at the door. "Don't, she's not ready yet. I'll teach her and make sure she's ready."

He laughs and calls her a "lesbian." When Magda leaves, Petre pulls the covers away from me and lifts my dress above my head. He sits and looks at me, pushes my knees out of the way, reaches out to touch a breast, grunts, then falls silent, before getting up to go to the bathroom. I can hear the water falling. I'm lying with the dress pulled above my head, too scared to move in case he knows I'm awake, and I do not want to be awake.

When Magda comes back into the room, she pulls the dress down and covers me with the sheets, then gets in beside me and lies on her back. "God help you, little one, if you were mine I wouldn't have let you go with a stranger."

I wonder if the same thing happened to her. I can smell cigarette smoke. Petre returns, and I screw my eyes tighter. Soon there is a creaking sound from the bed, which moves beneath me. After, I can hear snoring and think back to the same sounds coming from Papa.

The night passes and I do not sleep, my nails digging deep into my palms, my teeth clamped tight. In the morning, Petre says to Magda, "It's time. Remember what I told you?" The door slams. I open my eyes a crack to see Magda staring at me. "We're going to get in a big car now and there'll be other girls, okay?" I nod. She plumps the pillows behind my back and helps me sit. "I want you to eat something," and she hands me a dry biscuit, which I nibble and swallow slowly. "Here," she says, handing me a glass of water. It burns when I swallow.

"We have to hurry," she says, as she helps me out of the bed and into the bathroom. She gets a toothbrush and tells me to open wide. She squirts a minty paste into my mouth that tingles, in a different way from the baking-soda solution Mama makes at home, and brushes it against my teeth. She asks me to open wider and scrapes down my tongue. I am loose and floppy.

"Now, we are all going to be very quiet today and there is to be no repeating of the screaming yesterday. Always remember: it's easier if you go with it. Over quicker that way. Do you understand?"

I think of Mama's words about there being no fighting with fate, I think of the dog's sore neck, and Luca's chest, heaving—and I nod.

We leave the room, and she is pulling a big pink suitcase on wheels. I ask her where my bag is, and she says, "Probably in the sea. You didn't want to wear those awful clothes, did you?"

My notebook is floating around in the sea. I wonder if it has sunk or if it's on its way somewhere. My cheeks flare—I don't want anyone reading those words. I feel stupid now in daylight dressed in this party frock, like a toddler. We walk along the corridor, and this time when I look out the round windows, I can see blue. Maybe the sea changes color depending on the sky above.

We get to a staircase, and at the top, I can see Petre and the two girls, who look filthy and pale, flattened, not at all like the girls that jumped into the car yesterday full of fizz. They notice me at the bottom of the stairs. Petre looks at them and puts a finger to his lips.

The movement stops, and I can feel the hum ebb away. It's strange when the noise is no longer buzzing in my ears. Magda squeezes my hand; hers is wet, and I wish she would let me go. "Welcome to Italy," she whispers.

As we get to the top of the steps, I see Petre give papers to some men in uniform who nod at him and wave him on. Then it's our turn. Magda speaks to one of the men in an overly familiar way. The officer doesn't respond, just stares at me. Magda's voice goes higher and she speaks fast and loose. She brushes specks of invisible dirt off her top. The man looks disapproving but waves us on.

We walk until the first corner and then turn right. A loud cracking sound as Petre whacks Magda on the side of the head. "What have I said about drawing attention to yourself? Only ever answer questions you are asked."

Magda looks at the ground and says, "Yes, sorry, I forgot, sorry."

"The van is waiting," Petre says.

The van is huge and dirty-silver and has tinted windows. The sun is beating down on us, and Magda says the windows are to keep us all cool. She looks at the girls and asks them if they are thirsty.

"Let's hit the road," Petre says.

In the van there is another man who greets Petre, handing him a can of cola, but he ignores Magda and us, pretending we do not exist. There are three other girls in the back. Petre turns around to look at us all. "Not a peep."

There is barely breath drawn and the van is filled with strained silence, until the man turns on the radio and loud, harsh music pours into the space. One of the girls beside me covers her ears with her hands. I want to, but I think of what Magda said, "Don't resist, it's easier that way," and I allow my head to adjust to the loud thumping. I let it flow through me, like liquid, until I have calmed down.

We drive for hours as the van gets choked with smoke and thumping noise, and Magda's head lolls against the window. None of the girls make a sound. I want to turn around and look at them; I want to ask them their names. Some invisible force stops me. I wonder if a man came and asked to marry them too. Suddenly the van stops, and when the doors open, we see it's dark outside and we are in a car park, with cars and trucks, and in front of us is a brightly lit sign, swinging. Again, I wonder at the ghosts that disturb these signs, making them swing, when there's not even the tiniest breeze.

Inside, the music is so loud it seems to bounce off the walls and burrow down inside our bodies. There are girls and women with no tops on again, serving drinks, and five shiny metal sticks in the center of the room with naked female bodies rubbing themselves against them. We are brought into a quieter, cooler room and are served cola and chips and chicken covered in bread. I stuff the food in my mouth while the other girls stare silently. There's a hole inside of me that feels as if it might never be filled. Mama always taught me that a full belly will soothe a rising fear.

"Eat," says Petre, and the girls obediently try to swallow.

The driver of the van points at me and laughs. "Greedy little cow. Looks like we have a natural!"

Magda says, "Not yet. She's still only a girl. Her father lied."

The man shrugs. "Many will want that."

"That's not our thing. That's a whole other world."

Petre eats a mouthful of chips. "Who's to know?"

"We know, and that is enough."

"Who asked you, woman? You'd do well to keep your trap shut."

She smiles sweetly. "Okay, but just give me some time with her. She cost too much money to make her work before she's ready."

The two men speak amongst themselves in a hacking language I don't understand. They sound as if they are clearing their throats, ready to spit on the ground. Magda speaks back to them in the same tongue, then I hear her say in our language, "She is worth more to us alive. You could kill her by getting her to do things too soon. There are men who will pay top money for a girl still intact and this place will only cheapen her value."

I try not to think of what she has just said, even though the words are echoing in my brain. The men just laugh.

When we finish eating, the men tell the girls to take their

clothes off. This is when some of the girls make the mistake of screaming. I know better. I take my clothes off, looking straight ahead, imagining I'm about to step into the warm, soapy bathtub Mama has prepared for me. We are all standing naked, some of the girls are shivering, one of them shouts and is hit hard. Then, one by one, the girls are taken away into separate rooms. The two friends cling to one another. They are torn apart. I think of the baby acorns. When all the other girls have gone, there is just Magda and me left.

She says in a cold voice, "Put your clothes back on," and she hands me another glass of cola. I wonder, is she going to put me to sleep for what is about to happen?

I don't fall asleep and instead I sit in the room with Magda—waiting. Neither of us looks at the other, and neither of us speaks. I swallow the cola slowly, holding a sip in my mouth until the liquid goes warm and the bubbles are dead. The room is cold and bare, just six metal chairs and a long oval table, a lone bulb swinging from the center of the ceiling. The concrete floor is tattooed with boot marks. The girls return. I try not to look at them to save them from shame—my own and theirs, but I am drawn. Some of them dress carefully, with dignity, striving to act as if nothing just happened. Their faces are in the shadows. Some of them are shaking so much they can't put their legs back into their trousers and the best they can do is hold their clothes against their bodies, like a flimsy shield. No one makes a sound. We are all taken to a room at the back of the bar. There are mattresses on the floor, a jug of water, and a bucket. It's as black as the well, and the room in the boat.

A tall, dark-haired man steps into the room and speaks in a thick accent. "Magda here will explain the business end of our arrangement. Once you've paid off your debt to me, you're free to go. Until then, you work for me." He leaves.

"What Bardhok says is true," Magda says. "I'll be here for the first few days, show you the ropes. Remember, do as they say. That way it'll be over quicker." She throws a bunch of bras and panties in the middle of the floor and tells the girls to find their size and get dressed. They know what is expected of them now, she says, it's not so hard. The air fills with whimpers, like the puppies Papa tied in a bag before taking them to the river. I wonder if those nightmares will visit me again. Magda looks directly at me and gestures to follow her.

I am brought to a bedroom with a proper bed and told that although I will have to work, I won't have to do what the other girls will have to. I will have to "pleasure" the men in other ways, she says. "I think I can get you out of here. I think the men in suits will want to pay good money to be with you, but in the meantime you too have a debt that has to be paid." I nod, already having decided to hand my fate over to this woman. What choice do I have? The alternative is in the other room.

"Good girl."

14

Sammy

The walls of this house shake and conduct noise and smells. Thoughts of the girl in the back of the Garda car are wrecking my head, so a social visit is on the cards. Distraction technique. The woman from earlier seemed like the kind type, and not one given over to dramatics. I put on my comfy socks and climb the steep, narrow staircase to the landing. She said she was in the room above me, so I turn left off the main corridor. There are four doors on this side, all of them open a crack. I listen to see if I can hear her voice, but there's never a sound from the women, not even a peep. I sit in the landing and wait for the men to leave.

The first guy passes me by a few minutes later. "Hello, you," he says, as if he were addressing one of his daughter's school friends he just happened to bump into in the canned-fruit-and-veggies aisle in Tesco. He seems fine, normal, okay-looking, polite, mannerly—and married. He hasn't bothered taking his ring off. I get up off the brown, swirling-patterned carpet and knock. There's no answer, so I curl my head around the door.

"Fuck off," a woman's voice says. She's sucking powder up her nose. "Not enough to go around," she says apologetically when she sees me.

"That's okay, I was just looking for someone," I say, backing out of the room.

"Are you looking for your mam? I think she might be in room 422. Don't burst in there without knocking though, okay?"

I tell her I'm terribly sorry and she laughs, saying I have beautiful manners, and I'm just as Zoe described me. Zoe. She turns back to her snorting.

Brian told me we would do cocaine one day; he said it made everything sharper, more intense. I think I'd rather something to knock the edges off a bit, not sharpen them.

Another guy comes out of one of the rooms; this one is young, skinny, and greasy, and he nods at me. "That old yoke's getting a bit past it now. This place needs a new filly like you," he says.

"Mum?" I say, the word slipping out of me for maximum effect, as I poke my head around the door. I look back at Slimy Boy, who can't seem to process what just came out of my mouth. He legs it down the stairs. The woman inside is sitting on the bed, smoking. She looks at me closely. "You've lost me a perfectly good customer, you know. That little stick insect liked to talk rough but he was as puny as a fly. He'll never come back now that he has heard the word 'mum' and me in the same sentence."

"Sorry," I say, a weird yelping laugh escaping from me.

"Oh, I think I know your ma. Room 522, the other side of the corridor."

I walk to her door and listen outside; there's no sound at all, so I knock.

"Come in," she says.

When I push the door open I see the same blonde woman from last night lying on the bed in a blue silk nightie.

"I'm expecting someone. Everything okay?"

"Are you a mother?"

"Are you judging me?"

"No, no, just surprised, is all."

She shrugs. "Have to earn the schoolbooks . . ."

I sense a shadow hovering in the door behind me. The woman's tone changes to a higher register and she says in a tight, practiced voice. "Well, hello . . . David . . . is it?" And then to me, "Go on back to your room, love."

"What room's that then?" a sly voice says.

"The girl isn't working," she says.

The man walks into the middle of the room, closing the door behind him. Does he think this is part of the act?

"I'd like to see you both naked," he says, abruptly, so full of entitlement, sounding so much like Doc O'D, that I almost do his bidding. Jeepers, not much foreplay going down here. That thought aggravates the back of my throat, ticklish.

"I'm sorry, that's not on the menu."

His face turns cartoon-angry, like a sullen eight-year-old whose sister won't play doctors and nurses.

I feel like I'm going to explode with laughter, belch it right out of me. It's bubbling up and I have to work hard to push it back down.

"What's wrong with her?" the man asks, pointing at me as I swallow and swallow the mounting hysteria, which is making all my limbs shake with the force of it.

"Sorry 'bout this, but it's kind of an emergency and we have to go," the woman says.

"I'll be complaining to management about this," he says.

"I *am* the manager," the woman says. "You responded to my advertisement. What exactly is the nature of your complaint?"

"What kind of a game is this?" he says.

I gag, not knowing if I'm putting on an act or if the bile rising in me is real.

"No game. Sorry for the inconvenience, but I have to get this girl home. She's not well, as you can see. How about you come back in a couple of hours?"

The man's face suddenly bloats and turns bright red as he goes to grab the woman by the hair. All the air has been sucked from the room; it shrinks and the walls close in. "Next time, I just want the young one," he says.

The woman nods, playing along now. "That's fine," she says.

He looks pleased with this response and lets the woman go. "I'll teach you a few tricks," he says, standing too close to me, his breath full of rotting meat. Such an ugly man with his soft middle and yellowing eyes. I don't think I could, even for a thousand euros. I think I might puke, so I put my hand over my mouth.

"You have my number," the woman says, looking at me.

"Yeah, and I also know where to find you."

The door slams and rattles in its frame.

The laughter that was threatening to explode has evaporated, leaving a flat, dead feeling in its place.

"You okay?" the woman says.

I nod and sit on the edge of the bed.

"Time to call it a night," the woman says, getting up to take off her nightie and put on jeans and a sweatshirt. "I'm going to go home."

What does she mean, "home"?

"I don't live here, love. I just rent the room for the night. And I'm going to give this place a wide berth for a while. You should too. That guy is gunning for trouble. He isn't going to leave it there."

I feel like that time with Brian when I swallowed the worm at the bottom of the empty bottle of tequila. Days of wriggling, niggling, black thoughts followed that one: memories of hands, tongues, blanked-out faces, sore spots, black spots, blank spots, and Brian looming large over the spectacle, directing it all.

"You really better get out of here," she says, "that eejit downstairs will tell him your room number."

"Could I not work with you?"

The woman looks at me with something like pity. "Tonight

didn't exactly go well, did it? I don't work for, or with, anyone anymore."

I ask her could I meet her again some time. She tells me she never meets anyone from these places outside of these places, ever. "Guys like that one are everywhere in this game . . . Actually, we got away lightly in there. He could've got really ugly and I think he will, once he's regrouped."

She has changed her clothes and her hair is pulled back in a ponytail. She seems tiny.

"Do you have a husband?"

"Just me and the kids. Believe me, I wouldn't do this if I didn't have to." She takes me by the shoulders and turns me to look at her straight in the eyes. "You wouldn't get a job stacking shelves or something? This is no place for a girl like you to do her growing up."

The wall whooshes tall and thick in an instant. I push her off me and say, "What the fuck do you know about a girl like me?"

"More than you might imagine," the woman says. "If you hand yourself in to the guards and tell them about the stuff that's going on at home, social services will get you somewhere else to live and you'll be able to finish school, go to college and all."

How does she know anything about what's going on at home? No one has believed my stories before. My parents would persuade the world of my madness. Sometimes I think they're right: that I am mad, that I've made the whole thing up, that the lovely woman with the powdery-soft voice and scent, the one who presents herself at parent-teacher meetings, is the real woman, and the other one—the raging, spitting, nighttime one—is a figment of my "overvivid" imagination. Luce knows the truth of it (although not all of it, I wouldn't tell her that), but even her parents won't acknowledge there is a problem. As far as they're concerned, I am the problem. The woman is looking at me as all these thoughts tumble about my head, rattling around so loud I reckon she must be able to hear them.

"Is there really no way of surviving home, at least until you finish school?" This is a desperate measure on her part, and she knows it. "Have you no one you can talk to? No auntie or anything?"

I think of Dad's spinster sister, Marge, with her perfectly coiffed hair and her nails, her manicured house and life. Imagine if I told her? The little madam is telling lies again.

The woman is studying me forensically and I feel like I'm one of those rare butterflies Doc O'D has displayed in his study, pinned and laid bare. After some moments, she sighs. "Okay so, here . . ." She scribbles something on a piece of paper. "Call this woman, she'll look out for you. Tell her Sandra recommended you."

Sandra. How many other women are mothers here? I nod and thank her. The fist I swallowed earlier has settled in my stomach and is punching its weight in there. It lands a thump and I feel cold anger settle in me and with it, a strange growing power. I can do this.

I get up slowly and stand tall, legs planted, to counteract the juddering.

"Here, take this," the woman says, and she hands me a few twenties. I shake my head. "Take it," she pushes the cash into my palm, "and make sure you leave here as soon as possible. That guy will be back. I know his type."

When the door closes behind her, I slump on the bed and do what I haven't done since I found Mother collapsed on the kitchen floor surrounded by bottles of pills. "It's all your fault. You don't love me," she said that day, before Dad came home to find her lying there, comatose. "Why didn't you call an ambulance? You stupid girl," he shouted at me, "or go to the neighbor's house?"

He'd have gone ballistic if I'd let the neighbors see her like that; the neighbors were not meant to know, no one was meant to know, because it wasn't real. It was all in my imagination, even the ambulance and the sirens. None of it was real. Neither were the tears that dropped down my cheeks. Dad wiped them away and said, "Be a big girl now. Your mother needs you to be a big, strong girl. Big girls don't cry."

No, they don't. And I swore I would never let this happen again. I rub the pathetic tears away, licking the salt off the back of my hand.

I stride into the corridor, wishing I wasn't wearing my granny socks. Now I want to feel the sharpness of it, now I want to give myself the edge. I have the cash Sandra gave me, which, when I count it, comes to eighty euros. My eyes water.

No more. I never want to feel the vulnerability of those tears again, and in my hurry to get to the stuff, I forget to wait and I forget to knock, and just barge on in there. The woman is on all fours on the ground facing the door, facing me, with a blank expression on her face as a man stands behind her, grinding himself in and out of her, slamming against her. I've seen this on the screen many, many times, but never let it happen to me, even when I was off my head, not for want of Brian trying. The women in the flicks don't seem real, but this woman's dead eyes lock on to mine and when she registers me, flickers of pain and shame and recognition pass through them. There is a moment when I see her, really see her, and I realize this is worse than I ever imagined it could be.

I run out of the room and downstairs to the cupboard. I push the back of the chair against the door, light all five candles at once: White Linen, Vanilla, Lemon Balm, Lavender, and Geranium, and waft them into the air. I open the second bottle of vodka and gulp down mouthfuls of the stuff until I have sucked the teat dry, until I feel a tearing sensation in my neck and stomach and a numbness in my mind. My mind has stopped chattering, my heart has stopped hammering, I'm lying in a hammock in the wind, the sun is shining on my face, my skin is tanned, the birds are singing, and I can hear the sea, cresting and crashing. I turn on my side and rock in the wind.

Suddenly, buffeted by a big gust, I'm on all fours and vomiting all over my new sheets. It comes and comes, waves and waves of it. When it finishes, I lie on my side, feeling the wind tracing my face with its fingertips, except now, the sky is covering me in rain and I try to open my eyes and put my hands up to shield them.

"You all right there?" I can just about make out a shape standing above me. "Sit up," a female voice says as she lifts me by the shoulders. As she comes into focus I see that there are bruises, not tattoos, on her skinny, bangle-laden arms. I wonder how she got in here, and look at the door and see that the chair has toppled to the floor. "That won't keep anyone out," she says, nodding at the chair. "You new here?"

I try to nod but it feels as if my brain has expanded to twice its size and might leak through my nose if I make any movement.

"What were you looking for when you came to my room? You should always knock, always wait." Yeah, says the woman who barged in here unannounced. I can't believe this woman who is standing here talking to me is the same woman who was on her knees. I can't believe she's not smashed to smithereens.

"You have to get away from here," she says.

Yes, I do, but not now, now I need to just curl up and sleep and feel the wind stroking my hair, my face. I try to lie back down.

"No, you don't," the woman says. "Come on, I'm taking you to the hospital."

You're taking me to the hospital, but surely you're the one who is broken in two. I choke back some liquid that is threatening to erupt from every part of me.

"Come on now. I heard you from above. The whole place heard you. You sounded like you were dying."

You looked like you were already dead.

She heaves me to my feet and there is more mess, then she puts one arm around my shoulder and another around my waist and carries me downstairs, and outside.

15

Nico

After Petre leaves, I feel Magda curl in close behind me, her breath rising and falling in my ear. "Some of us have to work," she says after a while, her voice a different register, hard and high. "Have to make sure those little cats are doing their job." She gets out of the bed, talking to herself in hoarse whispers, and I think I hear her say, "Stupid little bitch, could get me killed . . ."

I don't know if it's me she's referring to, or another girl. The door slams.

I pull back the sheet, lie on the cool covers and stare at the crumbling wall. The paint is bubbled and peeling, and when I reach out to press a swelling with my fingers, it disintegrates beneath my touch. I think of Mama swiping the cobweb that settled into drifts of dirt on the ground. I screw my eyes shut and see Papa and Victor and Sergiu shaking their heads at me in shame. They turn their backs one by one and walk farther and farther away until all I can see of them are specks of dust.

I bang my head against the wall, over and over, hitting against the same sore spot until I feel warm liquid oozing out. It releases the pressure and stops the swirling strangeness inside. I drift.

Some time later, a voice shouts, "What has happened? What have you done? What have you done you stupid, stupid girl?" Magda slaps me on the cheek. "Open your eyes. I can't let Petre see you like this." She lifts me up so I'm sitting with my back against the peeling wall. "Drink this," and she holds a glass of cola in front of my mouth. I swallow. She goes to the bathroom and runs the water. I think she's going to hold me under it again, but instead she comes back with a wet cloth and presses it to the back of my head. "Shit, the sheets," and she hurries out and returns with new ones. I would help her but I can't move. She lifts me onto a chair before she changes the sheets. The ground is tumbling beneath my feet. At least my head is still.

Magda doesn't look at me, but leaves me sitting there, dazed. "Do you have a death wish? Do you know what would happen if Petre saw you do that?"

All I can think, through the dreamy haze of release, is why on earth would he give a damn?

"Come on," she says harshly, "stand," and she hauls me to my feet, then hits me, hard, on both cheeks and tells me to follow her.

I walk down the corridor, reeling and numbed, to the same

room where the men ordered us to take off our clothes. The girls are sitting there, silent and shrunken, bowls of broth with chicken and vegetables, and warm bread, potatoes, and cola in front of them. "You must eat," Magda says. "Keep your strength up." She goes to the door and looks into the corridor, and when she's certain no one can hear her, she says, "They won't come near you now."

I can tell the girls don't know whether to trust her, and they're finding it hard to swallow, but the soup is good. Magda is telling the truth: this place is only alive with men after dark.

"Girls," she says. They tense, shoulders high to their ears, legs crossed, arms in front of their breasts. "You will have to pay Bardhok back. Five euros each time a man does what he wants with you. You can start counting."

"How long?" a girl, who seems to be older than the rest, says to Magda. "Can we start counting from last night?"

"Yes," Magda says. "You started last night."

"Ten men on the first night," the girl says, startling herself by laughing, "how many nights is that?"

One of the girls from the car speaks. "How will he know how many men we are with? He can't know where we all are."

Magda looks at her closely. "That man knows everything that goes on in here," she says. "You will buy your freedom. I know."

"Five euros. Fuck, that's cheap," the older girl says. "How much exactly do we owe?"

"Whatever you were sold for, and interest."

The room is silent as the other girls try to understand what ten men a night will mean for however long it will take to get to however much they owe. They look at Magda and think: she is alive, she looks no different from anyone else, she wears pretty clothes and has a husband; they look at Magda and tell themselves it will be over soon; they look at Magda and they hate her and they envy her; they look at Magda and they want to bury their heads against her chest; they look at Magda and they want to scream at her and hit her; they look at Magda and they wonder how many of them will be her. She stands and claps her hands, gestures at us to follow her, leading us to the back room. I try to catch her eye, but she looks away as she closes the door behind her, locking us in.

"Why didn't you come with us last night?" the older girl says. "Where did that woman take you?"

I shrug. "Same as you," I say, not knowing why I'm lying. "Ten men."

"Have you even started bleeding?" she asks.

I look down at the ground.

"You look like a child," she says.

I tell her I'm a woman now and that's why my papa found a husband for me. He couldn't have known where I was going, he must have believed it was to a better life. Yes, my papa only wanted the best for me. I am nodding furiously, like Mama sometimes did as she walked around the house talking to herself, trying to convince herself about one of his harebrained ideas. It works—this repetitive upward, downward movement of the head, it fills me with a determined yes, yes, yes. Of course my papa only wanted the best for me. Mama?

"Are you okay?" the same girl asks.

I continue to nod. Yes.

"My boyfriend told me I would be working in a bar as a waitress and the tips would be huge," she tells me.

Then other girls start to tell some of their stories, in whispers. Two sisters say it was their mama that sold them. She told them they would be working in a rich lady's house and they would earn good money, that they could go to school and get good jobs.

"Did she know?" one of them asks the other.

Other girls were also told they were going to be waitresses; one of them knew she was going to a place full of men where she thought she would dance for a living. She was not told what she would have to do; she was not told she had to pay off a debt. Neither of the girls who came in the car with me says a word. Can they accept that their boyfriends sold them, like ponies?

The girl who had her head thumped is beginning to bruise around the eye. If we are really worth so much money, then why would they hurt her in this way? The older girl tells us her name is Ana. She wants to know everyone's favorite color, and why. Mine is blue because it's the color of the sky sometimes, the sea sometimes, and Luca's eyes, always.

"Where are we?" a pale girl with pudgy, childlike hands asks.

"Italy," I say.

"Where is that?"

"Not too far from our country by boat. It's surrounded by the sea, shaped like a boot."

"Ah, yes. I remember. Mussolini."

"They grow grapes there," another girl says.

There is a thud outside the door.

"Five minutes. Put these on." A man throws black panties and bras and belts into the room.

"Come on now," Ana says, "ten more, we can do this, we can count down." As she says this, she goes to the pile of underclothes and holds a tiny pair of pants against her. She is trembling so badly she lets them fall. "Come on now," she says as much to herself as to the rest of the room. "The sooner we start, the sooner it finishes." She rips her clothes off and puts on the tiny black bits. "Magda did it. We can too."

The girl with the black eye undresses as if in a trance. I tell myself to go with it, that way it will be over quicker. I think of the dog's neck straining and the sore spots. The girls are looking at me as I put a bra on. There's nothing to fill it.

Magda comes in, tells us all to get in a straight line, and says, "If the men offer you a drink, you can accept. It makes it easier."

They all file down past her, but she puts her hand on my shoulder, as if to say, Not you.

Ana looks back at me as they leave.

16

Sammy

"What the hell?"

I hear a man's voice. The woman is holding me and trying to hail a taxi. "None of those assholes will stop here," she says, as she half carries, half drags my body a few feet down the road. Eventually a car stops and I'm bundled in. I hear the woman's voice tell the taxi driver to take us to the nearest Accident and Emergency, and fast. My head feels like it might float away; my neck is too spindly to support it.

"You mighta called an ambulance," the driver says.

"I never thought of that . . . ," the woman says, sounding surprised by the suggestion. She has her hand over my mouth in case there's an accident.

The woman shows him a wad of cash and he agrees to drive us.

"Is the girl all right?" the driver says, like he's just allowed himself to look at us. "She's way too young to be so out of it."

"Don't I know it?" the woman says as she brushes a stray strand of hair off my face.

When we arrive the woman asks the driver if he will see me in, and she offers him more cash, before scampering off.

"Lean on me," he says, refusing the money. He escorts me inside and says to the receptionist. "Bit of an emergency here. This girl needs to be seen immediately."

A nurse appears, and the man says, "I have to go now. You're in good hands."

I try to mumble thank you as he puts an arm on mine. "You take better care of yourself, now."

I'm put on a trolley and wheeled into a room with those laser-sharp white lights that land on my skin like needles. Déjà vu. Strong hands hold me as I'm told to lie still and a tube is forced down my neck. The sound of a vacuum, and then my body surrenders to whatever is happening. I go under and in spite of the heat and the noise and the light, I sleep like a baby sucking on a whiskey-soaked pacifier. The smell of antiseptic and the bustle of the nurses is weirdly familiar and comforting.

When I wake, there's a needle in my arm attached to a drip, and there are scrappy geraniums by the bed. Mother's favorite; my least. A male nurse comes in with tea, OJ, toast, and cornflakes. Seriously? My throat feels like it had sandpaper rubbed inside and rammed down it. My stomach could be ripped. This guy looks like he's dancing to a tune only he can hear.

"Sleep well?"

I nod, and point to my throat, making an "ouchy" face. He looks at my chart at the bottom of the bed. "I'll get you some jelly and ice cream as a special treat."

He has left the glass of OJ by the bed and I try to suck some down but it just comes straight back up. I lie back, curled on my side, staring at the white wall, blanked out. Tiredness is a great antidote to thinking too much. I store that one away for later use.

Someone coughs and says, "Mind if I sit down?" It sounds like Doc O'D. Fuck.

"Go ahead," I say, still facing the wall, biting down on my lips to get the blood flowing, to make them red and pouty. I have great lips. Every guy I've ever been with has said that to me; David called me Ms. Blowjob Lips.

"Do you think you can turn to look at me?"

I roll over and try to sit up.

The man stands and plumps up the pillows behind my back. "How are you feeling?" It's not Doc O'D, but a small, muscular man, like a jockey, with a paunch. He wouldn't look out of place in that hovel I just came from. The corners of my mouth curl into a smirk.

"I'm Doctor Maloney, in-house psychiatrist here, and I wonder if you'd like to have a talk with me about what happened?"

I point to my throat to signify it's too sore to speak.

He goes to the bedside locker and pours me some water. "Here."

I try to swallow. It's like knives in there now.

"Is there anything you'd like to talk about? Something going on at home?"

I look at this man—would he believe me? The last one didn't. What difference would it make? Where would I be sent if it was deemed "unsafe" at home? I'd be some foster-care girl, some ward of the state. Oh, the shame I'd heap on poor Mother's head. I smile, a full-on, both-sides-involved kind of number.

"Something funny?"

"Just some boyfriend trouble. Silly breakup."

He stares at me hard, and not in the way men normally do. It's as if this ugly little man has a probe attached to his retinas and it's in there now, rooting around in my thoughts, which are serenely still.

"I wonder if there might be some parental problems?"

Again, I smile. "I'm fifteen. Who doesn't hate their parents at my age?"

The probe is going deeper, into the membrane, the cerebral cortex—I think I remember that from biology. "Hate is a strong word, Samantha. Is there something going on that you'd like to tell me about?"

Is there?

"Would you rather speak to a woman? Would that be better? I can arrange that for you?"

Ah, so he thinks it's some kind of "male" problem, probably some sort of twiddling at the hands of my father. Nobody ever suspects that the maternal instinct can be so thwarted. Not so clever is he, this little man with the big credentials and the probing lens. I don't have the energy for this. I don't have the energy to go into battle with that woman, and I don't fancy being called a liar again.

"There is no problem at home," I say.

"How did it happen?"

I think he's referring to the vodka overdose. "Well . . . I drank a whole bottle of the clear stuff, straight up, on an empty stomach."

He studies me. "And the other? The scars?"

"Oh, years old. Just a cry for attention. You know how it goes with hormones and stuff . . ."

"And the stitches? They look fairly recent."

Oh God, don't tell me he was rooting around down below. I have the good grace to look down, like, oh no, that is far too traumatic for words.

"Did you inflict these injuries yourself?"

So, the probes are working. There is a long silence. Is he getting off on this?

"That is a very violent assault on your body."

That's an interesting concept, and I let it hang there.

"Samantha, are you too tired to talk now? We can postpone this until tomorrow."

How does he know my name? The way he says it, without demands or threats—the first time I have ever really heard anyone, apart from Luce, say my name in that way—softens something inside. There is kindness in his voice, and something real. I almost break and I almost tell him everything, but Mother's voice mingles with his, drowning his out. Her private ranting and her public sweetness. Her loving me, and her hating me, her obsession with my body. Who's the liar then? I have never been believed before. Brian's voice chimes in: "C'mon, Samaanthaa . . . you know you want to, a dirty little slut like you . . . Good girl, you know I was only lying. Have some of this, it'll make you feel better . . . I love you, you know that." A hardness builds up in me again, and I feel the wall whoosh back up, and it's cool to know no one can climb over it. Barricaded and secure.

"Your friend Lucy is very concerned about you."

Ah, so that's how he knows who I am; the bloodhound tracked me down through Doc O'D's impressive connections.

"That girl is a compulsive liar, she has a major crush on me, and wants to control me in some way," vomits out of my mouth.

"I didn't get the sense this was the case."

"Is it protocol to speak to members outside the family?"

He tells me in a calm, contained voice—as if he were speaking to a dog full of fear-aggression, about to bite—that my friend is very concerned, she thinks there may be abuse at home, and that I might be in a very vulnerable situation if no one steps in. She spoke to one of the nurses in confidence. Good ole Luce.

"I'm grand. Do I look like the vulnerable type to you?"

"With tubes in your arms, lying in this hospital bed, yes, I'm afraid you do."

Does he think that's funny? "There is no problem at home," I repeat, almost convincing myself this is the truth. I turn my face to the wall. "I'm tired now. I want to sleep."

The man doesn't leave for quite some time, just sits there making scratching sounds with his pen, like a little mouse scurrying between two floors.

"Are you sure there's nothing you'd like to tell me?"

"Not up to talking right now."

"Your parents have been informed you're here. Would you like someone to be present when they come?"

This might be the perfect opportunity to thrash some things out. Surely these trained counselor dudes would see through her act. I'm just about to say yes when the deranged voice speaks through me in a harsh, biting tone, "Can you tell that girl Lucy that I never want to see her again."

He pushes the chair back so it squeaks on the ground. "It might be better if you tell her yourself," he says. Rude little mouse. "I'll be back tomorrow. We can talk more then. Try to rest up."

I hear the door close, and voices mumbling in the corridor.

The nurse glides back in. He places a tray with the vanilla ice cream and luminous pink jelly on my knees and perches himself on the side of the bed. I let him lift the spoon to my mouth and the cold softness slides down.

There's a timid rap on the door and I hear Luce's voice. "Sammy, it's me, Luce."

She walks in with a massive bunch of purple-dyed tulips and Mrs. O'D by her side. What's this? Some kind of intervention or something? Didn't that psych listen to a word I said? I want to fling the wibbly-wobbly jelly against the wall and see if it sticks, and watch it slide down.

The nurse says, "Ten minutes. She's very tired," before he leaves.

Mrs. O'D comes to the side of the bed and looks at me in a different way than she normally does, as if this time she's really seeing me, not just a projection of the me she carries: a lying nympho. "I really am sorry for what I said the other day, Samantha. I was stressed and the wrong thing came out of my mouth. I hope you know I didn't mean that we don't want you around . . . ," she says. This is hard for her. I think of my own mother and try to imagine those same words coming out of her dried-up, smoker's-lined slit of a mouth.

"Thanks," I manage.

"I'll leave you two here to have a good chat," she says. "I'll be in the waiting room."

Luce sits at the side of the bed. "What happened?"

Something about the way she's looking at me, so full of pity and love and some other condescending I'm-so-concerned-about-you look makes me want to kick her off the bed.

She places her hand on my forehead. "You're clammy," she says.

It's her hand that is clammy. I move my head away so my cheek is pressed into the pillow and I present her with only one eye, a demented cyclops.

"Have your parents been in?"

I grunt.

She gets up, all angry and righteous, and starts pacing up and down by the bed. "I heard Mum and Dad speak about it last night when they thought I was asleep. They said you were obviously very troubled, and perhaps things were not so good at home, but that your parents are your legal guardians and there's nothing anyone can do about this unless there is factual evidence of abuse . . ."

On and on she rants, breathless, basically saying what I knew everybody would say. I would have to go home. I'm not covered in bruises or burns or broken bones, or any marks I haven't made myself—I'm just a highly strung, disturbed teenager, along with the rest of them. And I have lying tendencies, or so the last hospital psych seemed to believe anyway as she waved me goodbye after my pathetic attempt on my wrists and ushered me back into the bosom of my loving family. I was twelve, and prone to self-dramatizing and hyperimagining—something Mother liked to tell me over and over following the assessment.

Luce's grating voice continues, "I got up and joined them and pleaded with them to let us take you in. They said they couldn't do that until you turn eighteen, unless your parents gave their permission. Do you think they'd do that? Give you away? I mean, they really don't want you around, do they?"

Of course they wouldn't "give me up," how could Luce be so fucking stupid? What would Mother do if she didn't have me to torment?

"Sorry," Luce bangs on, "I just want you to know that we're all here for you, and even if you have to go home, you can come and have sleepovers any night of the week. They agreed to that. Sure your parents never have a clue where you are. It has to be better than being in that place where you were last night . . ." She stops for breath and sits down on the bed heavily, grabs my hand and squeezes it tight, crushing my fingers. I want to remove it, and then she's kissing my knuckles.

My new pal shimmies back in, looks at me and says to Luce, "Maybe you could leave your friend to rest now, dear? She looks exhausted."

"I'm Sammy's oldest friend, and I think I know what's best for her," Luce says. "I'll just stay with her for a while, if you don't mind. This is kind of an emergency, you know, and I'm the one best placed to deal with it." Her voice is all high and mighty.

"Best placed"—where did that come from? I think she's getting off on all this, this drama, this "I'm the most important person in her life" crusade. I wonder, is she going to go hysterical, all *Crucible*-witchy on me, like she did that night after the bottle episode?

I turn on my side and groan. I pretend to retch and the nurse says in a tight, official voice, "You'd better leave now."

She gets up and I can feel her backing away. "Are you okay, Sammy?" she speaks to my back. "I won't be far. I'll be outside in the waiting room. I'm not going anywhere."

He ushers her to the door. I can hear her sob as she leaves the room. Who'd have thought? Good old Luce who never got more than a line in the chorus in the school play, executes a perfectly judged dramatic exit. Claps all around.

My stomach hurts I'm laughing so much and there are tears streaming down my cheeks and the room starts spinning and the lights are flashing and we are dancing, dancing, manically dancing.

"Hey!"

I can see his face swimming in front of me and I try to smile but I have no control over my body and nothing moves. An alarm goes off and people rush into my room. I can feel my nose grow long and I'm back in that recurring nightmare from when I was a child. "Liar, liar, your pants are on fire." Mother is standing over me. "You know what happens to lying little girls, don't you? They're turned to wood and their noses grow long and they get swallowed up by the whale's mouth and they live inside his belly forever, being eaten up by stomach acid." I'm so hot. I've been swallowed whole and I'm never getting out.

More vacuums down the throat, more needles probing my eyes, more insides coming up and up. Okay, I get it. No more lying. No more. It stops, and I don't know what's left of me. I try to remember my name, my date of birth, address. Nothing. Where am I? Nowhere. Sweet relief. Slate wiped clean. The whale has shit me out of him and I am floating free. I spiral further down into the water's clean, clear, calm, and it's beautiful here in the shifting blue. I don't ever want to come up, but the need to breathe is too strong, so I'm propelled back to the harsh, bright light, and gulp in mouthfuls of dry, cutting air. My eyes fly open and there's a white roof above me; I turn my head to the right and see that I'm hooked up to a bag of clear liquid that's dripping its contents inside me. And then, in a rush, I remember: last night, and the man ramming into the coked, bruised, skinny woman, and this time I see in her eyes that it doesn't hurt anymore, nothing hurts anymore. And then a flash of me at nine: on my knees, scrubbing a pink spot on the linoleum on the kitchen floor over and over, Mother standing above me. I had spilt Ribena, which soaked deeper and deeper the more I scrubbed.

17

Nico

"Where is this place that will pay so much for the girl-child then?" Petre asks.

I pretend to be asleep, body rigid and angled, at the furthest point on the mattress away from him.

"In London," Magda replies. "I can take her there personally and get a very high price for her, enough for a house deposit."

"Why would I believe a no-good whore like you?"

"Because this whore knows what she's talking about," she says. "I've been in this game a lot longer than you."

"Old slut," Petre agrees.

"And if it's not true, you can put me to work again and I'll personally make all that money for you."

Petre sits down heavily on the side of the bed and looks at me. "What will I tell Bardhok? He was asking about her the other day."

"Tell him she is very sick with syphilis and can't be treated. Tell him she's highly contagious and is as good as dead."

"Jesus, woman, the lies you spin. Sick . . . Now. Come on. We need you to work your slippery magic on one of the new lot. Won't do her job, in spite of some coercion."

"Why didn't you tell me sooner? They could kill her."

"Did I ask you your opinion, woman? How many times?" His voice, cold and sharp, cuts through the air.

"I forgot. Sorry. I forgot."

Their footsteps cross the bedroom and leave, door slamming behind.

The room is cold and it is hot. It spins around me and closes in on me. I can hear the walls breathing, and crying. There is a rustling sound and I think it might be squirrels, monster squirrels the size of dogs with pointy teeth and tails. I wrap the sheet around my body, over my head, under my feet. The room's cries are louder now and they speak in a bruised, belligerent voice. "I won't do it. Kill me, but I won't let you do it." The girl with the thumped head is screaming in my head, and her voice becomes my voice. Scuttling shadows fall across my body and the sheets are tangled and wet.

A hand is pressed on my forehead. "Okay. Just a dream. A bad dream."

I sit up and twist the skin on my forearm. I pinch even harder as my breath settles back down into my body and the ghosts evaporate.

"Please help that girl," I say.

Magda sits heavily on the edge of the bed. "Don't do that," she says, as she brushes my pinching fingers away.

"Stop the men from using her. She can't do it."

"I saw that," she says, and slumps, head in her hands, fingers caressing her temples. "It happens sometimes. I told the men I was giving her a sedative . . . ," Magda continues in a loud, harsh voice, as if justifying her actions to a jury. "She was as good as dead anyway . . . worse than dead."

The cold sweat on my skin makes me shiver.

"She begged me to."

I close my eyes again and feel myself falling into the well. Luca throws down a stepladder, which ends just above my fingertips. Even when I stand on my tippy-tip toes, my hand swipes, and misses. Over and over. The ladder dangles, just there beyond my reach. "Jump, Nico. Jump."

Why won't he climb down and save me?

"She just went into a deep sleep. That girl could not adapt, would never have survived."

I wonder, has Magda played the role of ministering angel before? As she sits there I see her sprout wings, and horns. I see the girl flying away from this place through the clouds and above.

"It was a pill, just a pill . . . ," she says, trying to convince me, God, herself, the imaginary sea of faces: a judge and jury.

I am glad; the girl would not have survived. Anyone could see that.

"What will the men say?"

"I told them she was very sick and weak, and probably had a brain hemorrhage after they hit her so hard. That shut them up."

The veins on her neck are purple, luminous, and raised. "Now, we have to get out of here as soon as possible."

I touch her arm and whisper, "My name is Nico."

She lets out a big breath with a cough that could be a sob.

The door opens suddenly and Petre says, "Did you have anything to do with that girl's death?"

It sounds as if he's growling. Magda stands and gestures at me to get off the bed. I quickly get down on the floor, and sit, pulling my knees towards me, trying to make myself disappear.

"Of course not," Magda says, drawing herself taller. "Why would I do anything that stupid?"

Petre grabs her by the hair and pulls her to kneeling, slamming her head against the side of the bed. He holds her head very close to his and stares into her eyes, as if he's boring himself into her.

"I only care about the money, the money that we need to buy our big house and our car. The money for the life we will live . . . I only care about you . . . ," she says.

This seems to quiet him down and he lets her hair go.

"I don't know if I can trust you anymore," he says.

Now she is speaking to him like he is a child, soothing him in a low, soft voice. "We are going to buy our beautiful house, remember?"

"Are you going to be my wife?"

"Yes," she says softly, "and we can have our own children."

She takes his hands and holds them in her own and turns him to look at me. "But is this what you would want for one of your daughters?"

He pulls his hands from hers, gets up and kicks me in the stomach, a sharp explosion of pain. "Don't be a fool, woman, no child of mine would belong in a place like this."

I curl tightly into a ball, wanting to roll under the bed.

"She is somebody's daughter too."

He laughs. "Her father sold her like a dog. She is worth nothing to nobody."

I sing the happy tune in my head Mama used to whistle as she baked the bread.

"Maybe he had to."

"No, he knew she was meant to be a dirty whore like you," and he whacks her hard on her cheek again so she falls to the ground.

"I wouldn't want to have a daughter with you," he wheezes with checked laughter, "because she would have your dirt on her. If I give you a child, it will be a boy," and he slams the door so hard the room shakes after he leaves.

We both lie on the ground, in silence, curved in on ourselves, until I say, "I thought you were married already."

She pushes herself to sitting, propping her back against the bed frame. I sit, doubled over, holding my stomach.

"It's just something I tell the new girls to make them feel less afraid."

She rubs my back.

"Are you really going to marry that man?"

She rolls onto her back, staring at the ceiling. "It's that, or a pill. And he looks out for me, in a way. He loves me, in his way."

I think about the shape and color of a love like that. It's nothing like the romantic love Maria and the girls speak of. It is darker and heavier than Papa's for Mama, and has a black, purplish hue.

"What about when we go to London?" I ask.

"There are others in London, like him."

I wonder, will it really be any better there?

"I'll take you to a place where there are beautiful rooms with soft carpets and big lights made from crystal hanging from the ceiling, where the men are rich and educated, where they will not want to hurt you so much as pleasure you. It will be easier than here, but you have a debt that has to be repaid, you understand?"

I wonder how much my debt will be by the time I am sold in London.

"You're a clever, beautiful girl, Nico, never forget that. It's a pity your father is such a pig."

I think of Papa grunting in the room where he and Mama sleep and then I think of him tickling me and throwing me high into the air. "Look at the little monkey-girl," and my own squeals sound in my ears.

Magda closes her eyes, exhausted, and within minutes, her chest is rising, falling, in an even, rhythmic beat. She can sleep; she has lived like this so long she can sleep.

But then she mumbles, more to herself than to me, "I can persuade that man of anything—he doesn't know this, he must never know this, but we will get you out of here, and we will go to London. Are you ready to fly through the clouds? I couldn't bear another girl like that one on my conscience, and you wouldn't make it here."

I see Mama pointing at an airplane and shaking her head over and over. "How does it not drop from the sky? God did not make us birds." She is stomping on the ground in her rain boots, laughing. "You'd never get me up there, in that tin can with wings, not in a million years."

18

Sammy

My nurse walks back in, feet firmly on the ground now; he's not dancing and he's not smiling.

"How're you doing?" he says. "You have visitors."

As my eyes begin to adjust to the light, I can make out blurry figures, undeniably familiar. The shape of my father is sitting on a chair beside the bed and my mother's back is to the window. I thought I told that psych I didn't want to see them. He probably met them and decided there's no threat there, believed their stories about my hyperactive imagination, heard all about my history.

Dad notices that I'm awake, and his big warm hand reaches out to hold mine, cradling it like it's a small bird. I try to smile at him, reassuringly, though I'm sure it comes out more like a smirk. He clears his throat as if to say something, but just increases the pressure of his thumb instead.

I can hear my mother start to sob. My nurse goes to comfort her, patting her on the back. "There, there, there, there . . ." as if to a child.

I pull my hand from my father's, not able to bear the feelings that his touch brings up, then turn my back and face the wall. He sits on the edge of the bed and pulls all the sheets with him, so I'm left with one shoulder bare. "It's never as bad as all that. Come on now, love, whatever it is, it will pass, and things will be brighter tomorrow . . . ," he says, trailing off, realizing, I guess, how stupid his own words sound.

"She needs professional help. We can't handle her anymore," Mother's convincingly distraught voice says.

I can hear Dad: "That's not true, Margaret, you're overwrought, you don't know what you're saying. She'll be fine, just needs to come home and rest for a bit, eat one of your lovely dinners."

I almost laugh, but mother's sobs take up the space instead.

"She'll be properly assessed later on today," my pal, the turncoat, says.

"Are we to be part of that assessment?" Dad asks, his voice tight.

"I believe the doctor would like to talk to Samantha on her own first," the nurse answers.

"She has a propensity for storytelling and tends to make things up," Mother whispers, her hand reaching out to touch me. I shrug it off.

"Now, Margaret," Dad says.

Both of them fall silent before Dad suggests they go home and come back later. "Nothing to be done now." He gets up and places his hand on my bare shoulder for a moment before removing it as if he's had an electric shock, then he pats my lower back through the gown, rhythmically, like he's soothing a colicky baby.

"That's probably a good idea," the nurse says. "She could do with resting a little more."

"We'll see you later, so," Dad says, swallowing hard, his Adam's apple bobbing.

"Don't go making things up now," Mother says as they leave.

"Now, Margaret . . ." I can hear Dad's pleading in the corridor.

"Is there anything you'd like to tell us?" the nurse says.

I shake my head.

"Have you tried anything like this before?" he says, looking pointedly at my wrists.

"Just a nick!" I say, batting it away. "And it was years ago now."

I want to say that my mother has tried, and I found her, but some force is pressing on my chest and my ribs are so constricted I can't speak.

Mother's hysterical high-pitched voice pings its way into this echoing room, grabbing all the attention she can get, pretending she loves me, oh, how she loves me, but how impossible I am to love. Her voice rises to a wail. She doesn't like not being the center of attention. I can picture Dad fussing over her when they get home: bringing her a glass of chilled Sauvignon with clinking ice cubes (knowing enough not to pour the Chardonnay), and placing a cool, wet face cloth on her forehead. He might even massage her bunioned feet until she has passed out and then he can leave again, a note beside her bed. "Sorry, had to go. Urgent business," alongside a roll of cash with "Treat yourself to something nice" attached to it. Somehow I don't think he'll stick around to see how this particular crisis plays out. He's not able, and I'm more like him than I realize, 'cause I'm not able either. I get it, Dad, why you keep leaving, but don't expect me to stay in your place, soaking up all her hurt and rage.

The nurse doesn't look at me as he says, "Can I get you anything?"

I shake my head, wanting him to leave so I can enact my new plan.

As soon as he's pulled the door behind him, I yank the needle out, which jabs me with a scudding pain like the time that idiot dentist scraped against a nerve. I press down on my arm to stop the bleeding. When I stand, the floor is moving. I take a step and it's dizzying—kind of cool, being this off-balance, off-center, and it reminds me of trying to walk after an hour of being tossed about in a wave-machine pool in Majorca. I get my clothes and bag out of the bedside locker (good of that coked woman to think to pick it up for me, and she didn't touch any of the cash Sandra gave me). I go to the loo where I manage to dress myself in spite of feeling piss-drunk. I couldn't do this in the public wards. Good man, Dad. I'm freezing in my mini and T-shirt, and a bit conspicuous it has to be said, so I put the hospital gown back on over them. Super surprised Luce didn't bring me PJs all covered in her kisses and her scent. I'd better get the hell out of here now before she comes barging back in, or that Maloney guy, or my specially appointed Mr. Jelly nurse.

I think I see Mother at the end of the corridor, a nurse beside her, arm around her, comforting her. "She's a wicked creature all right, your daughter, you were unlucky there, all right, make no mistake about it."

As my eyes start to focus, I realize it's not her at all, but a woman really crying. I walk by, nodding at the nurse who looks up absently and says, "Where are you off to?"

"Just getting some air."

"That mightn't be a good idea. Go back to your room and I'll get someone to accompany you."

I obey my orders, well, I pretend to anyway, as I've scoped out the other end of the corridor and it's empty.

I go back to the room, close the door, wait for a beat of ten, stick my head out the door and leg it, in my bare feet, heels in hand. I get to a lift and my fairy godmother must be sprinkling me with extra sparkles today 'cause she provides an empty one where I pull off my gown, put on my wedges, and present my legs in their best possible light. The security guy checks me out, his eyes bulbous, not doing his job. I walk nonchalantly to the gates and wait on a bus. Don't feel like getting up close and cozy with a taxi driver right now.

The light outside is white and stabbing, and my eyes feel like they're being jabbed. When the bus stops, I get on and try to count out the fare but my fingers and thumbs are all thick and swollen. I keep dropping the money till some little aul wan behind me pipes up, "Can I help you, deary?"

She counts out the change, handing me back the rest. She probably thinks I'm off my head. My eyes water. I rub them roughly. That's enough "deary." No more room for being a drip. I put my hand in my bag to get my phone only to discover I left it behind. Probably for the best; time to cut the cord.

"Would you mind if I borrowed your phone? I could pay you? I've lost mine and it's an emergency." My voice is slurry and thick, and I point to her phone and make the call sign. I offer her a ten. She hands me the phone, refusing the money. The line connects and I try to make my voice distinct, but all that comes out is a mumble.

The woman on the other end says, "I don't do business with junkies. Get yourself clean and call me back."

The line goes dead. I hand the phone back to the aul dear, who asks if everything is okay. She's staring at my arm where the needle point is bleeding through. I smile at her and nod. I don't press the stop button till the last minute; don't want her following me.

I get off the bus in the center of town, go to a chemist, and stick three Band-Aids on, then go to McDonald's and get myself a chocolate shake. It goes down well, all cool and smooth and sugary. I feel a bit better after, although the ground is still roiling beneath my feet, and I kind of surf myself along the shifting surface, using the wall to balance. Outside, I walk unaided. "Look, Dad, no hands! Wheeee." I go into Topshop and buy myself a pair of huge shades, then I pick up a pair of skinny jeans, a long-sleeved fleecy top, and a big woolly jumper. There's a dress on the sale rack with no security tag on it, which is a bit of an oversight, so in it goes, into my bag, stuffed underneath my bundled-up hospital gown. Must chuck that, and pronto. Next, I go into the mobile phone shop, buy one of those pay-as-you-go yokes, and boom, I'm a new woman, with a new number and new threads. The shop assistants are looking at me funny, elbowing each other and pouring delighted gossip into each other's ears. My hair must be like a mad yoke's. It gets all matted easily, probably has puke in it too.

I push open the door of a hair salon a few doors down, and the smell of cheap peach shampoo smacks me in the face, the fluorescent light dances on my eyelids so I have to close them, and the music is so loud the floor seems to vibrate. I can see my jelly nurse—the "raver" version—doing his thing in here. When I open my eyes, there are three of them behind the desk, giving me the goggle-eyes. They all have that cheap white bleach and short crop going on.

"Just a blow-dry," I say.

They look at each other, not knowing what to say. Have they never had to wash ganky hair before? Oh, come on, guys, surely it isn't as bad as giving head. A filthy, tiring occupational hazard. My own head is coming back to its usual thrum and throttle of thoughts, jumbling and tossing around in there, and I'm quite enjoying it now.

"I'm sorry, I'm afraid we're very busy, fully booked."

I look around at the near-empty room. "I'll wait." I sit

myself down on the shiny plastic couch and pick up a three-month-old copy of *Heat* magazine.

A helium voice, that could be male or female, speaks. "I can do you in five."

Do I imagine it or do the hands lathering my head have plastic gloves on them? I can't see, but it's a different kind of tug at the root, a kind of a pinch and pull on the hair shaft. I close my eyes and inhale peach. My hair is wrapped in a turban and I'm led to a chair squished in between two others who are both at the blow-dry stage. Why do they do this when the rest of the salon is empty? My head is banging from the heat and the noise and the musak on a loop: ". . . clap along if you know what happiness is to you . . ."

A pixie-guy glides his way across to me and smiles at me with an overly familiar, arch kind of friendliness. I'm not in the mood to make chitchat and I know where this one would lead: Do you have a boyfriend, where do you go clubbing, you're *how* old? No way, have you ever thought of modeling? Oh, but no, of course you're too short. And homeless, mister. I can sense he feels dissed by my insistence on reading the latest "celebs with cellulite" snaps instead, and he pulls my hair a little too roughly. I pretend not to notice.

"Straight or with bounce?" he asks.

"Straight." And I look back down at the page. Nicole Kidman is covered in the stuff, but then she is pretty ancient.

"All done," he says when he's finished, "and don't you look a picture?"

I have to concede that I look a billion times better than

when I walked in. I press a five into his girly hand. He wasn't expecting that. That feels good. Paying someone off, having the power, and no one saying no to my demands.

As I leave, I catch a glimpse of myself in the mirror and clock a twenty-something guy with a rugby shirt and a buzz cut checking me out at the same time. Our eyes meet. Not this time, maybe when I'm all set up, mate. I toss my new sleek hair down my back and walk on out into the fading light, looking back over my shoulder once, to see him sucking me in.

It takes about fifty minutes to get to the offy on foot. Pimply Tommy is inside.

I pick a naggin of vodka, wondering if this is a good idea, and tell him his boss said I could have whatever I liked, on a tab.

"He around?"

The guy shakes his head. "Don't do that. Don't get caught in his debt." I wave the bottle at him and go outside and sit on the wall to wait, hoping no one sees me. How long after a girl busts out of the hospital do they put out a search party? Adrenaline spikes and scenarios play out, with me as the starring role in all of them.

19

Nico

Petre tells me to stand in the center of the room and shines a flashlight into my face, so bright that I have to close my eyes.

"Open," he says.

I do.

"What is your name?"

"Nicoleta," I say.

"Have you not taught this stupid girl anything?" he says to Magda, who speaks to me in her new harsh voice. "Your name is Natasha. Remember?"

I don't remember, but I say, "Sorry, yes, my name is Natasha."

"Where are you from?"

I realize I must not be the real me now, so I look at Magda, who snaps, "Romania, remember?"

I know they speak the same language there. I nod.

"Is she mute?" another man laughs. And then into my face, "Cat got your tongue?"

I stammer, "No, sir."

He likes that. "Sir . . . Very good! Now take off your clothes."

Magda stiffens. "Why now? We've washed and we need to get going."

The men look at one another. "Are you answering back, woman?" Petre says.

"No."

I start to pull the dress over my head when Petre says, "Enough. It's time you were going. You'll do as Igor says, *Natasha*, is that clear?"

I nod.

"What's that?" the man called Igor says, his feet planted further apart than his shoulders, giving him the impression of a bull carrying something very heavy between his legs.

"Yes, sir," I say and Igor laughs so hard his face turns red and water comes to the surface of his eyes.

"As for you, woman," Petre says, as he moves towards Magda, looming black and large out of his skin. "Come straight back, you hear?"

Magda nods.

"She is to be my wife, remember?" he says to Igor.

"Don't worry. I know she's out of bounds." Igor's voice and body shrink.

Petre stoops towards Magda and cradles the small of her back with an arm, drawing her in close. They kiss and it looks real—their lips cling to each other and Magda softens beneath him. He hugs her to him and speaks into her hair. "Mind yourself, woman, and come back to me soon." Then he pushes her off him and nods at Igor.

We go outside and it's cool and fresh after days and nights in dark, fear-soaked rooms. The waning moon is huge and lemon yellow—is this a harvest moon, Papa? The sun is just beginning to push through the still star-flecked sky. A big car is waiting, its engine pouring fumes into the clean dawn air. Another man opens the boot and takes our luggage. Magda and I slide into the back seat and I push my nose against the window, but the panes are dark. My whole body aches to see the sun climb and settle in the unfolding blue sky. In the car, the two men talk to each other in that hacking tongue that sounds like the devil's language.

Magda starts to speak to me urgently. She has papers in her hands and tells me I must listen very closely and repeat after her. If we're stopped at any time, I have to remember what to say.

I have a very good memory and I nod, repeating after her, "My name is Natasha Popescu, I am fifteen years old, my country is Romania and these are my parents, Diana and Marius Popescu."

"We're going on holiday to visit your uncle, Dr. Popescu. I'll remember the address. Don't worry. They won't expect you to know the address."

My name is Natasha Popescu from Romania. I am fifteen years old.

"The village in Romania where you come from is Fântânele."

Magda falls silent. And then, "I wonder why they chose that place."

Although I don't ask, I can see this is worrying her. I wonder what kind of a trick they are playing on her. A freezing-cold finger pokes through my stomach even though it's hot in this car, with the windows tight shut.

From the front, Igor's voice speaks, "Are we excited about our little holiday, my girl?" Magda pushes her elbow into my ribs.

"Yes, sir," I say.

"I think Papa would be more appropriate."

Magda nods at me.

"Yes, Papa."

The two men laugh so hard it feels as if the car's shaking. Magda takes my hand in hers and squeezes it tightly.

"Good girl," Igor says, then turns to us. "Ready?"

We both nod.

"What is your name?"

"My name is Natasha Popescu. I am fifteen years old. I am from Fântânele in Romania. We have been on holiday in Italy. These are my parents," I gesture to Igor and Magda, "and we are visiting my uncle, Dr. Popescu in London."

"Fuck's sake, don't parrot it like that. It sounds like a speech, a practiced lie. Only answer what they ask you. Understood? When I ask your name, you say your name, no more." His face is bright red, veins on his cheeks pushing to the surface, like Papa in one of his rages.

"Yes, Papa," I say.

The car comes to a stop outside a big building that is pure glass. There's no time to dawdle, the driver tells us, as Magda and I step outside, raising our faces to the sun and breathing in gulps of air, stretching.

"Don't want to make us late, cats." Igor goes to push against the glass entrance, which opens sideways as he approaches, making him stumble and almost fall. "Cunt," he swears at the door. Magda throws her eyes to heaven and presses her mouth thin. He licks the palm of his hand and then rakes it through his already sleeked-back hair. A cowlick springs loose and he pushes it back. I imagine his mother taming her young son's unruly hair, using her spittle to keep it in place, like Mama with Luca. Or more likely, he never had a mama, or he had one who only raised her hand to him in anger.

Everything inside me has become slow and still. I'm doing that old trick of holding my breath and wonder, has anyone ever drowned out of water?

Inside it's loud and hot and bright and there are more people milling about in one place than I've ever seen. We join a long line of men, women, and children, all ages, with shiny luggage and faces, clutching small leather-bound books and pieces of crumpled or folded paper. Igor's huge shoulders have hunched and his muscles look balled, like wire string. The light-blue shirt he's wearing has dark stains under the arms. I wonder if my dress is wet under there too.

When we get to the top of the queue, there's a woman with lots of paint on her face. Her lips are drawn to seem bigger than they are, making me think of a sad clown I once saw in a raggedy traveling circus in our village. I couldn't sleep for weeks after thinking of the brown bear with the balding fur locked in a tiny cage. I shake my head to try to stop this sadness climbing back inside me. The woman doesn't look at us but takes the suitcases and puts a sticker on them and sends them on a moving belt.

She says something to Magda, who nods and gestures at us to follow her. Igor breathes out into my face as we leave, his breath smelling of stale alcohol. He stands for a moment, looking lost, his body coiled, ready to pounce.

Magda leads us to another line of people who shuffle slowly around corners, speaking loud and fast, clack-clacking, and then we climb aboard a moving staircase made of silver. I grip the plastic sides of the climbing stairs, my body lifted higher and higher, while my feet in my too-tight shoes are trying to get a grip on the unsteady ground. I trip over the lip when the movement stops and the level floor rises to meet us. Magda reaches out to steady me, Igor sniggers. Metal machines wink at us at the top, and Magda puts her handbag on a belt and Igor puts down his mobile phone, which moves through the tunnel with cameras. We are waved under an archway, where men and women in blue uniforms with badges on their chests and plastic gloves on their hands stand waiting at the other side. As Magda goes through, a loud beeping starts and she is made to stand with her legs apart as a woman runs a black device all over her body. I am scared they are going to take her into a room and make her undress, although the woman waves her on, then turns and motions at me to walk through the same arch. My heart is so loud in my ears I mistake it for the machine's beeps, and I'm sure the woman can hear. She studies me for longer than anyone else. Igor is staring and pacing at the other end. As soon as I'm let go, Magda collects her handbag, Igor puts his phone back in his pocket and he grabs hold of me by the arm.

They walk towards a screen with the times of the airplane departures and letters that form words of places I don't recognize. The letters blur and slide off the screen, although not before I see the word "Londra" forming. London.

"This way," Igor says.

We walk down a long, brightly lit corridor and there are shops on either side, shops that sell hats, swimming clothes, scarves, sandwiches, chocolate, crisps, cola.

"Naughty," Igor, says, tut-tutting when he sees me reaching out to touch a pink scarf, bringing to mind Mama scolding one of the boys. How she would love this soft-as-a-petal scarf.

We keep on walking until we get to a place, a holding room, where there are orange plastic chairs all glued together and full of people.

"We have fifteen minutes," Magda says. "Shall we buy some sandwiches?"

Igor tells her to shut up, loudly, and an older woman with steel-gray hair, blue powder on her wrinkled eyelids, and thick gold jewelry turns sharply to stare at him, heavy earrings dangling.

"I'll get the sandwiches," he says, and stalks away. He doesn't ask what we'd like to eat. When he returns he hands me one with egg inside. It smells too strong, but I swallow, and use the cola to help push it down. There are potato crisps, which are salty and crunchy.

Another train of people forms as they get off their chairs—this one is very slow and people start to sigh and raise their voices, and some of the children cry. High-pitched bells and crackling voices speak from the air.

"The flight's delayed," Magda says.

Igor's leg is twitching and he takes out his mobile.

"Not here," Magda says.

He glares at her but does as she says. He taps in a number and listens to a voice on the other end, then puts the phone back in his pocket. When I look at him in this bright light, I realize he's much younger than I thought, maybe only Victor's age. Magda's not so old either. Beside all these other people with their children and their tiredness and their suits, she looks very pretty in her blue skirt and tight-fitting blouse. I see that some of the men look at her, and at me.

The queue starts to move and Igor says, "About bloody time." His voice is much louder and harsher than the other men's voices, his shoes are sharp and pointed, so shiny you can see your reflection in them, his face is flushed, eyes over-bright. The other men look at him sideways and the women look away, apart from the older woman from before who is studying him through her hooded, owl-like eyes.

"What's that old wagon looking at?" Igor mumbles at us.

When it's our turn to show our papers, the man in uniform looks very closely at Igor, and a muscle in Igor's jaw starts to twitch as he clamps down with his teeth. I think of what Magda whispered to me in the car about being careful of him, as he would always want to be the first to "break in" the new girls. Why would Petre want him to come with us? The man studies our papers far longer than any of the other people in the queue, and calls one of his colleagues over. Mother Mary, please let them see into him. The men talk to each other in low, hushed voices, a deep ridge appearing on the younger man's face, right between his eyes. He looks at me closely, then at Magda, who manages to smile reassuringly at him, and takes my hand. The two confer again and then inexplicably wave us on. No, please, help us, do something, stop this kind of a man doing this kind of a thing. Or maybe these men avail of his services. Our services: Magda's and mine.

We follow the line of people into a low tunnel that leads to some steps. My legs feel hollow and spindly as I climb to the doorway of the metal flying machine. I think of Mama stamping in her rain boots. "How can something so huge get off the ground and how does it not drop from the sky when it's up there?" I start to shake my head from side to side to clear the jumbling thoughts when Magda turns to me and holds my chin steady in her hand and looks into my eyes. "Don't do that in public."

I feel Igor poke me in the back of the leg with his pointed shoe.

Again Magda whispers, "Not in public. People do not like cruelty to children."

He pretends it was a joke, a jokey kick. Then he pats me

on the shoulder, "Okay, kid. Excited?" he says, in loud broken English, for show.

I nod along. I know my job is to pretend, but right now I feel vomit rising in my mouth as we walk down a row of seats, so many bodies and stressed faces, so many mouths breathing in the small amount of air in this tight space. I pretend I have gills and can breathe in liquid when all the oxygen has been used up.

I'm told to sit in the middle seat, between Igor and Magda. I wish I were on the outside and Magda was beside me so I wouldn't have to feel Igor's thigh rubbing against mine. He's sitting there, legs splayed, taking up all the space, his elbow jutting above the armrest that separates our two seats. I make myself smaller and angle my body towards Magda. She leans across me and ties me into my seat with a black belt that has a metal sliding lock.

The airplane drives on wheels first, gathering in speed and force, revving itself the way I do just before I run—until it builds enough momentum to lift itself off the ground, vibrating with sound. I cover my ears with my hands and Igor points at me and laughs, and I screw my eyes shut. The airplane shudders and lifts into the air. My ears feel like they might explode. There's so much pressure as the machine climbs higher and higher, and over Igor's shoulder, I can see the clouds, which look like floating strips of cotton until we go so high they merge together and cover the airplane in one large sheet of billowing white. As we climb higher, we leave the clouds behind and then there's only space. I can breathe easier here and the pressing weight on the bones of my face lightens. It's as if we are gliding, like that day Luca and I went to the lake that had frozen over and slid across the surface on Mama's tin tray.

Another woman with too much paint on her lips walks up the central passage, as if she's sleepwalking, pushing a metal container on wheels with drinks and food. Magda asks Igor if he would like anything. I tell her I'd like some 7UP. It comes in a small plastic cup with clinking balls of ice at the bottom. I pour and it fizzes over.

"Stupid girl," Igor says as Magda wipes up the wet with a piece of tissue.

"Not to worry," Magda says, staring at Igor. She leans across me and whispers in his ear something about him meant to be acting like my father, and when we're in public he should pretend to be like a real papa. "You don't want to draw attention to yourself," she says. He does not like being told what to do, especially by a woman, and he turns his back and squashes his nose against the window.

The hum of the engine and the soaring sensation lull me into a kind of a stupor. I feel safe with Magda beside me out in public. It's been so many nights where I haven't slept that my body twitches as I fall. Once I've landed in that dark space where I feel held, I breathe easy.

I wake to the sound of a voice on the air, the smell of crisps and stale sweat, and look at Magda, who is lying with her head awkwardly on her shoulder. A loud bell sounds and her eyes fly open as she jolts upright. There are marks on her cheek and her face is puffy and red. Bending down, she retrieves her handbag from underneath the seat in front. Opening it, she reaches for a tiny mirror and looks at herself and me in the reflection, crosses her eyes and touches her nose with her tongue. A Zanesti thing. I miss Luca so much in that instant, I feel I might evaporate from longing. Magda rubs lipstick on her mouth and brushes powder on her face, then pouts at me. I try to pout back.

"Hello, cats," Igor says. "Getting yourselves ready for the night ahead?"

She puts the mirror away and snaps the bag shut. "When we arrive, we'll all be resting," she says.

"We'll see," Igor says.

Another journey: I wonder if it'll be a boat or a car with black windows. I imagine I'm on the highest branch of the highest tree in the forest and a soft breeze is tickling my nostrils. The clouds are dancing around my head and I reach out and grab one and burrow down into its feathery folds. The airplane starts to descend and the pressure builds, pushing against my cheekbones so hard I fear they might break.

Magda nudges me. "Do this." She holds her nose and blows hard, turns bright red, and looks as if she might explode. When I swallow, my ears pop and I yawn. I try to tell her she doesn't have to push so hard, but she can't hear me. Igor is rooting around in his ears with his fingertips and his forehead is bunched. I hope his brains erupt through his ears.

When the plane hits the ground, the wheels bounce and the engine makes the loudest noise I've ever heard. People on the airplane clap and cheer.

20

Sammy

After about twenty minutes Mr. Manicure arrives, dapper in chinos and a blazer. He's delighted to see me and is super-duper false-friendly. "Well, look who's here . . . wasn't sure you'd turn up again, wasn't sure I'd ever see you again . . ." Something about the tone of his voice, which is patronizing and overfamiliar, and the way he's looking at me, like I'm a couch he's considering buying, makes me think of Brian. My spikes rise. There's still time to rethink this plan.

"Still at that place?" he says, doing that fake-concerned thing with his face.

"Actually, I thought you might be able to recommend somewhere else." I'm not slurring; my words are crisp and precise.

He looks around him and says in a hushed voice, "Come inside and we can go out back and have a proper chat, in private."

My eyes fixate on his unbuttoned shirt and I imagine his gray, clipped chest hair rubbing against me like a Brillo pad, and my leg starts to do its spastic thing again.

"What's up with that?" he says, staring at the shaking leg.

I shrug. "Just been to the hospital. Hurt my ankle."

"You sure it wasn't another failed attempt?" he says, looking pointedly at my wrist.

The scars are so faded no one normally notices them. I pull my sleeves right down. "If I'd meant anything by that, I'd have cut vertically, not horizontally," I say, trying on a jaunty tone, even though his observation has made me feel shitty and exposed. I know I should go now; I know this man shouldn't be speaking to me in this way, yet neither of my legs seem capable of movement.

"Your mother's a regular in here," he says, hoping for some kind of a reaction from me. I'm too stunned. How has he made the connection? She never brought me here, never—hoping, I think, to keep the fantasy alive that it wasn't as bad as all that, that *she* wasn't as bad as all that. "Just a glass or two of an evening, William, that's all," in spite of me telling Dad she fell on her way to the bathroom, wet herself, or couldn't speak her tongue was so thick, or that she hit me, breaking the wooden spoon over my legs in one of her rages. There eventually came a time when I stopped telling him anything; it felt too bad to be disbelieved, or dismissed.

The boss man tries on his fake-concerned voice again and says, "Couldn't blame you for running away. Can't be fun having to contend with *that*." This is the tone Brian used with me when he was gaining my trust: make her think you care, and then she's putty in your hands. She's so starving for love, that one. And I fell for it. Not this time, mister. "I'm sure you must need someone to talk to . . ." Yup, this is the spiel, all right.

"Come on in and we can have a nice cup of tea—discuss your options . . ."

I almost go with him, out of habit, out of a lack of care, or a taste for danger, or some equally thick reason, but Tommy's voice is ringing in my ears: Don't get caught in his debt. He sounded like he knew what he was talking about. I could call Brian, of course. He'd sort me out. Which is worse? Not which is better, but which is worse? A girl'd want to be a complete gobshite to fall for that, and then to see, and then to fall for it again, and then to see, and then . . . I may be an adrenaline junkie, but I have my limits. That knocking sensation hits me deep in the guts. This is the same feeling I'd get lying in bed at night listening to Mother's footsteps climbing the stairs towards my room.

"Thank you for your time," I say, "but I've changed my mind."

He laughs. "Probably don't have a clue what you're thinking. Teenage girls are like that."

I nod, thinking how best to withdraw from this situation. "That woman you think is my mother . . . I don't think so," I say. "My mother is dead."

He stares hard at me. "Funny little thing."

He might as well just pat me on the head while he's at it. Anyway. "I'll see you around . . ." Come on, legs, don't fail me now. One foot in front of the other. Can't be that hard.

“Aw, now. You came to me for a good reason. You know I can help . . . I’m well connected.”

“I’ve decided to go home. Thanks for the advice.” And then my muscles are pumping me away from him, legs and heart, propelling me as fast as I can go.

“Anytime . . . you know that. You know where I am . . . ,” his voice chases me down the road. “You’ve no idea how bad it can get out there for a girl like you.” He sounds like he’s salivating as he considers this. “No clue.”

I run like a maniac, going over on my ankle in the platform sandals. It burns, but I sprint on anyway. I slow down as I get to the convent walls. Should I go in and ask for help? Should I find Luce? Doc O’D? The guards? Should I go back to school? As soon as these thoughts cross my mind I know it’s impossible. I’d be sent back to that house and that woman. And I’m not able anymore, Dad. It’s over. I place my hand inside my pocket and finger the piece of paper with the woman’s number on it. I take out my new pay-as-you-go yoke, and fully galvanized by my little chat with myself, I dial.

~

The woman standing beside the drama society bulletin board under the arch in Trinity College doesn’t look like what I imagine a madam, a female pimp, brothel owner, procurer of women, whatever, to look like. She’s a mumsy librarian with glasses, short, dark, sensible hair cut in a neat bob, comfortable flats, sans makeup, somewhere in her forties. Maybe she’s wearing lacy suspenders underneath her pencil skirt, although that's about as likely as Sister Rita wearing them. She nods at me as I approach, and we walk in silence along the back of Dame Street.

"I'm Sammy," I say after a while, just for something to say. She doesn't return the pleasantry, and I realize that the piece of paper Sandra gave me didn't have a name on it, just a number and a blank where the name should be. I guess that's right. An anonymous setup.

"How old are you?" she asks, after a while.

"Fifteen," I say, all delighted with myself, expecting her to clap her hands in glee, what joy, a schoolgirl.

She looks at me sideways. "Is there anyone looking for you?"

"Nah," I say. "My da's dead and my mam's a junkie, doesn't have a clue what's going on, won't even notice I'm not there," which is stretching the truth to beyond taut, so that it might snap back at me. Even to my ears I sound like a raging liar. Rein in it, Sammy—the wide-boy act.

She studies me sideways. "Friends?"

I shake my head. "Free as a bird."

"What about your school?"

I hadn't thought of that one, but no thinking required really. "I started mitching three years ago, when Mam turned really psycho. No one's tried to contact me in months. They've given up." Mam. Where did that come from? And the accent. Is she falling for it?

"That easily?" she asks.

A silence descends that I wouldn't exactly describe as

companionable as we continue to walk up lanes and alleys that are unfamiliar to me. We arrive at a tall Georgian building with the biggest door and the biggest knocker I've ever seen. Fee-faw-fo-fum. There's no number outside.

"I'll show you to a room. You can have a bath and some food and then come downstairs and we'll have a chat. You'll find me in here," she points to a room just inside the front door. "The kitchen's down there," she gestures to stairs leading down the back, off the main corridor. "I'll leave you a plate."

I nod, and rub my stomach, which is fizzing. This is strangely without drama, and for that reason, is making me uneasy. She tells me to go to floor 3, room number 36.

I climb the threadbare stairwell, which looks like it's seen a lot of traffic. A musty smell climbs into my mouth, coating my tongue. It's weirdly silent. I push the door open and the first thing I notice is the window, which looks out onto a car park where there's a car below, belching black fumes. Here's my room with a view! There's a sink in the corner and a bed, of course. A light is hanging from the center of the ceiling, with a cream Home Store + More shade, shaped liked a hat. Where are my chandeliers? There's a bedside table in heavy fake wood, and when I pull open the drawer, I see it's crammed with condoms. I sit on the bed, which doesn't make a sound. I couldn't bear if it squeaked. When I lie back, I roll into the groove in the middle.

I go to the sink, wash my hands in the antiseptic green slime, and throw some cold water on my face, checking myself out in the mirror on the wall above. When I yank the pulley cord, the light that explodes is mega wattage, throwing a harsh fluorescence on my face. I don't think I'd want to be looking in this too often, although it's probably handy for putting on the war paint. Wugawuga. I stick my tongue out and see that it's all furry and coated in white slime, so I do what I used to see Mother do after a hard night: I take out my toothbrush and scrape it down.

I walk back downstairs and go into the kitchen, where the grub, a ready-meal chicken curry, pale and anemic looking, is sitting beside the microwave, with instructions laid out to heat on high for three minutes. The kitchen is nothing special: just some linoleum on the floor and white plastic cupboards and cheap countertops, pretty similar to the one at home. I pour a glass of tap water and swallow slowly. It's still fairly raw in there. I cut the dried-out chicken into tiny pieces and blow, and chew and chew. It goes down okay. I listen to my stomach's gurgles, hoping to fuck none of it comes back up. After a while of sitting, staring at nothing, I walk to the door the woman showed me and knock.

"Come in."

She's sitting at a desk with a paper pad in front of her.

"Sit," she says as she gestures to a hard, high-back chair on the other side of the desk. My bony bum would greatly appreciate a cushion right now. I push my back against the chair, noticing the sensation of the stitches for the first time, and try to remember when I'm supposed to get them taken out. I wonder if my name is down on every hospital register: Samantha Harvey, girl missing from hospital, high risk. Is my face on the news yet, in the papers, on posters in doctors' offices, lampposts, on the side of milk cartons (which I particularly like the idea of, although I think that only happens in the US of A)?

The madame has a form in front of her, which she reads from in a monotone voice, barely looking at me. "First period? Any terminations? Any diseases?"

I hadn't even thought of that last one, and think of Brian.

"I'd like to take some swabs, check out your general health, make sure you're not pregnant, okay?"

She's going to stick things inside me? Now?

"Right, perhaps you could lie on this table?" (First time I've noticed it. It's there all right, tucked discreetly away in the darkest corner of the room.) "I have medical training," she says.

A doctor madame?

"I'm a nurse," she says. That all seems suspiciously convenient, and creepy.

"Probably not a good idea right now," I say.

She looks at me, but not really. What's she imagining? HIV, syphilis, chlamydia . . .

"I had an accident," I say. "Fell on a spike climbing over a wall and hurt myself down below."

She almost barks, "Is that the truth?"

I think she's pressing me for some kind of a rape story, but I'm not going back into that one. "Seriously, I know it sounds mad but I was drinking outside the other night in the grounds of a convent and had to climb over these tricky spikes, and I fell. I've been to the hospital and I'm all sewed up."

She gives me a look over her glasses, like, Are you fucking with me?

I'm not, missus. Glad you're qualified to take the stitches out.

"Are you on penicillin?" she asks. "Did they give you a tetanus?"

I think they did. They certainly gave me a few jabs. I don't tell her about my vodka fiasco and the stomach pumping. Figure that might just put her off the new merchandise.

"Anytime it gets too much, you can get up and leave." Isn't that what Brian said? Only problem is that by the time I felt that, it was too late and the worst had already happened.

21

Nico

Having collected our luggage from the moving belt, Igor notices the gray-haired woman taking out her phone and pointing it in our direction.

"Does that old bitch think she's going to take a picture of us?" he says to no one in particular as he strides towards her, anger in every bunched muscle.

"Don't draw attention to yourself." Magda grabs hold of him by the arm. "Let's just turn our backs and walk away."

The struggle inside Igor at that moment reminds me of watching Maria's dad's young colt buck and rear, being made to canter in circles, tethered, while every part of its body was crying out to gallop across the fields. Retreat, surrender, a gracious acceptance, is not Igor's way.

"Not in public," Magda whispers to him again, a refrain for the day, one which makes me wonder what will be allowed in private.

He seems to snap out of it then as he shrugs Magda's arm off him. "Come on, woman . . . they'll be waiting," as if he came to the decision himself. We join yet another long queue and Igor's color is high, his leg twitchy, jaw clamped, mouth moving from side to side. I imagine his teeth worn down to his gums, and feel the corners of my face move into a tight smile.

Magda whispers to me as we near the front of the line, "Remember, don't say anything except to answer a question directly." She stops to think. "Actually, don't say anything at all. Let me do the talking."

"What if I am taken into a room on my own?" I ask.

"That won't happen." She smooths her skirt down over her hips. "If it does, you just remember what I told you. Never tell them more than they ask." There's an angry silence before she says, "Don't think like that. You can make bad things happen by thinking about them." She makes a tiny sign of the cross: forehead, breastbone, shoulder to shoulder, making it seem as if she is brushing dust off her suit jacket. And then I wonder why she wouldn't want us to tell these people who Igor really is.

A loud whooshing sound fills my ears, as if I'm on the airplane again, and the ground beneath me begins to vibrate. We're at the front of the line now, and I don't know if we're all meant to go together, but I see a real family go ahead as one group. I thank God that Igor is not my true papa, as we move as one small circle.

In the cubicle, a man in uniform, a man with pale eyes and skin and hair, sits behind a sheet of glass. Again, this man studies our documents far longer than any of the other people that went before, and glances at us every so often, his eyes flickering up, down, up, up, down, up, like a machine tracking a pattern. I pray this man sees the truth of what is standing in front of him. Magda squeezes my hand so hard it feels as if the bones in my fingers might break. She's wearing a bright smile that doesn't stretch to her eyes, and I can see how tired she looks beneath that smile.

The man looks up and asks Magda a question in English. "How long are you staying?" I understand his question. My mind whirls around like that spinning top the boys and I were given one Christmas, and I can't hear Magda's answer, as the whirring inside my head is too loud.

My name is Nico. I am thirteen in two weeks and two days. I come from Moldova. My country is shaped like a bunch of grapes and no sea touches it. I shake my head. No. No. No—my name is Natasha Popescu, I am fifteen years old, from a village in Romania whose name I've forgotten. That's okay. The country, the country is all they are interested in. Only answer the exact question you're asked. The back of my throat tickles as I attempt to swallow and my eyes feel like they're bulging from the effort of trying not to cough. I'm on holidays with my mama and papa. Uncle . . . a doctor . . . I can't remember his name. What does Romania look like? It is next to my country and people there speak the same language as at home. Does Romania touch the Black Sea? Will the man ask me about the black salty water? I try to remember what England looks like. There are no other countries around it—it's floating in the sea. I wonder how it doesn't sink and then

I remember it's because the water is salty. I would like to run into a body of water and put my head under and wash out my head.

The man looks at me. "Is this your first time in England?"

I nod.

He nods back at me and waves us on. Again, they do not see the truth. Igor did not understand a word of what was said. He did not go to school, or if he did, he sat at the back and yanked the girls' pigtails and pulled up their skirts, like Sergiu. We walk on, faster now, free of the slow-moving lines of people. No one speaks. Igor cannot read the signs and so is hurrying us in the wrong direction.

Magda stops him. "This way," she says.

He frowns but follows.

As we walk through the sliding glass doors into white light and gray drizzle, Luca is standing there, leaning lazily against a car door, his tongue poking out through his teeth. He gestures at me to follow him. Igor is smoking a cigarette and talking on the phone in the same devil's language they spoke in that dark place. When I hear it, my whole body starts to shake.

I whisper to Magda, "My brother has come to rescue us. Come with me."

"How would your brother know where we are?"

As she says it, I see that the man I thought was Luca is putting his arms around three little children. He walks away, one of them wrapped around him like a baby monkey and the other two holding a hand each. One, two, three, wheeee.

An invisible hand in the sky pushes its way down my throat, gagging me and squeezing my heart.

"Are you okay?" Magda says as she takes off her cream jacket and puts it around my shoulders. The shaking is deep inside and won't stop.

Igor turns to Magda. "What's wrong with the girl? I heard a rumor . . . does she have a disease? We won't get paid if she's sick."

Magda pulls me to her. "She's frightened."

"Of what? The bogeyman? Boo-hoo." Igor finds himself hilarious and doubles over he's laughing so much.

Again, she touches head, heart, side to side, in miniature, so no one but me would notice.

"Can we go for a walk?" I ask.

A black, shiny car pulls up; a man rolls down the window and pokes his head through. "Igor Alexandrescu?"

Igor nods, opens the boot, throws our cases in, and roughly pushes Magda and me into the back seat.

"Not in public, remember? People might notice and call the police."

Igor is back to the way he was before he walked into the airport; his shoulders have settled back into the sharp, straight lines of before, making him seem so much bigger.

"We're not in public now," he says, as the car door bangs shut, and he presses a button that makes the now-familiar harsh, banging type of music flood the car. The sound of it hits against the inside of the doors. I close my eyes. I'm on top of the tree and the only sound is the wind in the leaves.

Igor and the man are smoking, the windows are tight shut and I feel as if I might get sick. Magda notices and rolls down a window in the back.

"Did I say you could do that?" Igor asks. He is sore from having to follow her in the airport.

"If you want her vomiting all over the car, then fine, I will roll the window back up."

He takes a deep pull on his cigarette and turns to us, blowing smoke in our faces. We cough, and I lean out the window. "Why are we bringing the girl here again? Did you tell Petre she was worth a lot of money?"

Magda settles back against the seat and closes her eyes. "Yes," she says, "men will pay a lot more for a body like hers."

Igor speaks into the small mirror in front of his head, where we can see him magnified and looming. "Why would they like little girls with no titties? Call themselves men." He rolls down his window, throws the butt of the cigarette out, and spits onto the road. The car behind us sounds its horn loudly and Igor puts his two fingers in the mirror, then leans out the window and sticks up one finger at the woman in the driving seat.

I cross my legs tightly. "When are we stopping?" Magda asks the driver. The man makes the car go faster.

"You'll just have to hold it till we say," Igor says. "Good for you, make it tight." The man behind the wheel laughs. I wish I could hit them both over the head with a bottle and see the blood gushing down their heads. I wish Magda and me could take over the car and drive into the sea and hold their bloodied heads under, watching them until no more bubbles come out of their mouths. Then we would swim to the surface and float on the salty water.

We drive for hours. The heavy, gray sky sits low over everything and there is a damp mist of rain encircling the car. The light is brighter at home at this time of year. I think of my school friends sitting on the benches, staring at the map, and Miss Iliescu telling them I have gone to England, like Petra's dad and Liliana's mum, and Ivan's sister. They're all thinking how lucky I am, especially Maria, who would love to have been one of the chosen ones: a handsome husband and a big house and car. Lucky, lucky you.

The pressure in my stomach is building and I squeeze hard. After some time, Magda speaks. "Where are we going, Igor?"

"Shut up, woman."

"This is not the way. We have gone too far from London."

There is a silence, then the two man start to talk, raising their voices to shouting. Magda tenses. "Can I speak to Petre?" she asks.

Igor ignores her and the two men go back to their shouting. I squeeze harder. Magda looks exhausted as the car speeds on.

"Aren't you hungry?" she asks the men.

The driver speaks in our language, in a heavy accent. "I have to be somewhere in an hour. There's no time for stopping."

Another hour. The loud music is still banging against the insides of the car, the smoke is still wafting. I look at Magda, who has her eyes closed. Her lips are moving.

The car eventually comes to a stop in a deserted place. It's dark outside. I get out, the ground spinning sickly beneath my feet, and I hold my stomach as everything inside me comes up. I can feel pee trickling down the inside of my leg. Magda is holding my hair off my face and rubbing my back. Igor waves a hand in front of his nose and then pinches his nostrils. "What's wrong with her? Is there something you're not telling us. Is she with child?" Am I? Could Petre have put a baby in me when I was not looking? What if it's a girl?

"She just needs some water and air. We need a break," Magda says.

Igor speaks to the man, who shrugs. I look around me and can make out a dark field with low hedges and silhouettes of tall, shedding trees, their branches beckoning. I want to run to one of them and put my arms around its girth, feel its solidity, hear it whispering to me. I want to press my body to its old, leathery skin and climb. The headlights of a van sweep over us before it pulls up beside us, and two men and more girls get out.

"I want to speak to Petre," Magda says to Igor. "He'll kill you when he finds out what you have done."

Igor comes close to her, sticks his face in hers, their noses touching, and says, "If Petre gave a damn, he would be here with you now. I don't think he cares for old mutton anymore."

Magda makes a sound like Mama made when Papa told her I was going to go away to England, for an education.

"Now shut up, woman, and get in."

There are seven girls and three of them have the most beautiful skin I have ever seen, like a dark winter's night without a moon. A ghost passes through my body and I have to pinch myself hard. They're making noises like they're talking gibberish and one of them is banging her hands against the pane of glass. I think the men might stop and hit her, but they only laugh and turn the music up louder. I wish the gibbering girls would be quiet; I wish the men would tell them to shut up. I want to scream at them to shut up.

Again, we drive. The rain intensifies, big fat drops smashing from the sky, bouncing against the roof and the windshield. The van slows down and the driver curses loudly, and the other two men speak low. I look around me at the girls' faces, all so young, and I want to play a game of Chinese Whispers; I want to send a whisper around, pour into their ears that there are eight of us and three of them and we can bite, hit, hurt, push the men out the doors. We can do something, anything, instead of sitting here waiting for them to do things to us. The waiting, the not knowing, is the worst of all. But we don't speak the same language, and we are all too tired, too frightened. Even Magda has shrunk back inside herself.

The van stops after hours of moving slowly through the pounding rain. The men jump out and go to the toilet in the grass, and gesture at us to do the same. The girls try to find a private spot, somewhere to hide, but it's a big open field. As my eyes adjust to the darkness, I can see the outline of a small boat with no roof. Must be moored near a river, or a lake, or the sea. The man who was driving herds us towards it, like we are stupid sheep—we are stupid sheep. I look at Igor, who is checking his phone. Magda is wet through, her hair sticking to her head, making her seem vulnerable and very young.

The boat is waiting at the mucky, sandy shore and we all step in one at a time, no helping hand to guide us. Our feet are wet and slippery and we sit, clutching the low sides of the plastic floating tub, which doesn't seem big enough to hold us all. It rocks and sways each time another body enters. Two of the men push it deeper into the water then jump in, the boat almost capsizing. Everyone is soaked with rain, everyone is cold; no one seems to know what they are doing. The driver of the van gets a phone call and speaks to the other men, and one of them pulls a string and a chugging sound starts up. It gets louder until it has revved up enough power to motor. I hold on to the side and look down at the water. Is this the sea, Papa?

One of the girls stands and rocks the boat, clawing at the sky. A man shouts and pulls her back to sit. She moves from side to side, trying to turn the boat over. I join in, although I try to make it seem as if I'm doing nothing at all. Come on, girls, I will them to make it happen: let's topple this floating bathtub and swim away, far away, anywhere is better than here. The man slaps the screaming girl on the face, but this doesn't stop her, just makes her scream louder. She stands again and the man pushes her so she topples over the side. Igor and the other man make angry sounds and gestures with their hands. They are thinking: someone paid something for her, somewhere.

She's trying to swim away from the boat, and before we can

attempt to get her back, one of the men pulls out a gun from under his arm and aims at her. He shoots and he hits. Bubbles float up from her and across the surface of the water. I imagine they are crimson red, seeping into the black.

The man makes a shrugging movement with his shoulders to the other two: What was I supposed to do? The mad bitch might have escaped. The mad bitch might have spoken. The mad bitch needed to be taught a lesson. A type of fear creeps into our hearts, encasing them in ice. Magda is crumpled and tiny. Even Igor's body is deflated, like someone took a pin to him and all the air has leaked out.

I'm glad of the rain; I'm glad of the wind that is making the water swirl. I open my mouth wide and drink it in. I can taste salt on the air, against my lips, on my tongue. Look, Papa! The air is fresh and clean. I look up and there are flashes of moon and stars, a cover of clouds scudding across the sky, full bellied, swollen with rain. Out here there is no need for tears.

Lights from another boat are moving towards us, a hulking animal looming bigger and bigger as it gets close, growling in its guts. It casts its shadow over us and I wonder if it will open its jaws and swallow us whole, the way the whale swallowed Jonah. One of the men stands and the beast sticks its tongue out, which has rungs on it, like a ladder. The man pulls it towards us and sees me watching him. He looks me in the eye and gestures for me to stand. I do. I want to feel my arms pulling, my feet pushing; I want to root and dangle in the air.

He barks. I climb. The wind is making the wooden tongue sway. I'm holding close to the trunk. You won't knock me off,

Luca, not this time, not ever. I hear him laughing. A hand reaches out towards mine. I reach towards it and hold on as it pulls. I'm suspended in the air for a moment until the hand yanks and I'm thrown onto hard ground.

"Are you all right?" a man's voice asks.

It is kind, the voice, and speaks English. I nod. Is this inside the belly of the beast, the end of it all, or is this just another part of the journey, another beginning? Everything goes black and I go under. The lid closes down.

22

Sammy

"They're dissolvable." Nurse-Madame is referring to the stitches. This woman doesn't even know my name.

"I'll wait to get the results of your swabs and then we'll be good to go in a few days. Now, how can we tell there won't be a nationwide search for you?"

I'm not sure there won't, to be honest, with Luce at the fore, rallying the troops: we must save her from herself. I don't tell nurse this. Ratchet, Hatchet . . . can't remember the name of that psychotic one from *Cuckoo's Nest.* I decide on Hatchet. *What worries me, Billy . . . is how your mother is going to take it . . .* I feel a hysterical pressure building, and I can't help myself, I burst with laughter, rude with laughter, blowing out my nose, my arse, my pursed lips. *You seem to forget, Miss Flinn, that this is an institute for the insane . . .*

She stares coldly beyond my eyes, her gaze resting on the tip of my right ear, which burns. "Are you quite finished?"

"Yes, sorry, sorry," I say, wiping my eyes. "Honestly, I've spent more nights away from that house than in it. Ma wouldn't notice anything different." Oops, first slip. Mam, Sammy, *Mam.*

She picks up a sheet of paper, looks down, scribbles some notes on it in silence. "I think it would be safer if we moved you on."

Maybe this is it, maybe this is my chance to travel, go to exotic places, feel the sun on my face, lie under chandeliers. "Cool by me," and I tell her I want to be operating in an exclusive place where the men wear suits, smell nice, and are stinking rich.

"Doesn't everyone. But in your case, this may just be arranged."

That's 'cause my knees stop traffic. Pity I'm not a few inches taller or I could storm into one of those modeling agencies that I've read about, except I'd need to have parental consent. No consent needed for where I'm about to go, what I'm about to do. No height restrictions necessary. "Being flippant," that counselor said, "is a way of deflecting from the real feelings . . . a coping mechanism." I knew what she meant, even though I laughed straight into her face, spraying her with spittle.

"There are certain things I won't do," I say, trying to assert myself. "Not from behind, not on my knees . . ."

"We can give them the menu, tell them what is allowed, but there are hazards involved once you're alone."

I think back to sex education class with Sister Wendy: "Men are wild beasts when they're aroused." I choke on a laugh that is pushing back fear. That's okay, I can manage them, find a way to tame the beast. I think of the guy from the bench and know I have a ways to go yet; I'll have to develop strategies.

"Because of your age," Hatchet goes on, "I'm sending you to a place that is more tightly controlled than others. The clients are vetted and known, on the whole. Although as I said, there is no telling what can happen behind closed doors."

I imagine a line of pom-poms, faceless cheerleaders, a chorus of high-kicking legs, bravura voices: "Go, Sammy, go." What does it mean to be a "vetted" client: swabbed? I doubt it. Police checked? Even more unlikely. This is a risky venture, no doubt, but then, I haven't exactly been risk averse till now. I have to remember it's just until I'm eighteen and then I can go work legit. Doing what? Luce is always telling me what a great actress I'd be. By then I'll have a world of experience. I'll be able to buy my own place, get an agent. Yup. I congratulate myself on a workable four-year plan. Mr. Kelly, the career guidance teacher, would be proud of my forward thinking. I crack up, rivers of tears and snot flowing.

Hatchet sits and looks until the storm has passed. "You sure you're up for this? There are other ways, you know."

"What do you get out of this?" I ask, when I can speak again.

"A one-off sum," she says. "And the woman who runs the house will get a percentage of your earnings."

"That's a whole load of moola for doing nothing."

"Count yourself lucky," she says. "Some of the girls from overseas are sold by family members or friends and spend their lives paying back their owners, earning nothing. Most of them never get out."

I think of that girl I met in the street, and of my joke to Luce about calling myself Natasha, and it's as if an ice-cold lump of metal is slowly forcing its way down my gullet. "How is that allowed to happen?"

The woman shrugs and looks down. Conversation closed.

"How much is your fee?" I ask her.

"I'll work that out with the owner of the house. Don't worry about that."

But in spite of the noise ringing in my ears, the fecking glaring alarm bells doing their mad GONG thing, in spite of this, I tell myself . . . in two and a half years . . . thirty months, I'll be done . . . and I'll have a nice wad of cash saved up.

Hatchet tells me to rest up, not to go outside, to eat and build up my strength. I spend the next two days and nights in the house with the Home Store + More lighting and the drawers full of condoms. Condoms and me get up close and personal in the next few days. They're strong little buggers; my fingers can't break them. "No way," Brian used to say, "can't feel anything." I like the idea of a barrier between some guy's bits and my insides.

I hate waiting—waiting is the worst kind of torture. I'd rather be there now, doing it, getting into the swing of things. I veer wildly between wanting to run and wanting to stay. It's this or home I tell myself over and over, on a loop, replaying the worst of Mother, cranking up the images so she's caricature and grotesque. I'm like Dorothy in *The Wizard of Oz*, clacking my heels together, except instead of saying "There's no place like home," I chant, "Any place is better than home, any place is better than that place, any place has to be better . . . ," out loud, over and over on a loop. I make up elaborate stories about the generous, loaded men I'm about to meet, men who'll want to show me a good time, and who'll be proud to be seen in public with me on their arm. I'll be wearing beautiful couture outfits and they'll be falling at my feet.

The day of departure finally arrives. Hatchet shakes my hand formally at the door. "Good luck," she says, which ignites a flicker of fear in my belly. Her eyes meet mine for the first time, and I never noticed (maybe because she hasn't given me direct eye contact until now) that they're milky blue, almost transparent, a thin film over them blocking any light. Her hand, as it brushes against mine, is dry as that tiny salamander I once touched on holidays in Majorca, then stamped underfoot. Adios, dead lady.

A car waits for me outside. It's not swanky or long with tinted windows, it's actually pretty normal: silver, sevenish years old, a Cortina or a Nissan or something, a daddy's car. "Are we going to the airport then?" I ask the driver. All I can see of him are his bulges of angry neck flesh hanging over his too-tight collar.

"Something they haven't told me?"

I don't have a passport or a bikini, but well, all that can be arranged. "Not heading to the sun then, mister?"

He shakes his head, the fat wobbling, chuckling. Oh, this is a funny one, to be sure. "Am I on the news yet?" What started off so promisingly then becomes a bore; the guy won't tell me a thing. "Where are we going then?" He turns the music up louder and some moonshine shit fills the space: 108.3 FM in that phony English voice. Some crooner is singing about love in a broken voice. You'd think they'd learn.

"Can we stop for a loo break?" I ask, after an hour or so.

"We'll be there soon," he says.

Sure enough, half an hour later we pull up at a semi-D in a housing estate in the middle of nowhere. This place is shit-ugly: unfinished, bits of builders' stuff left behind. Hardly Las Vegas.

"What are we doing here?" I ask.

"Your new home."

You're shitting me. A woman comes out, this one looking more like a tart, with her over-done face and short skirt. She's young and speaks in a weird accent.

"I think there's been a mistake," I say to the driver. "This isn't the right place."

He ignores me and talks in a low voice to the woman. The man leaves, and she takes my rucksack, hoists it on her back like she's used to carrying extra weight on her body. "Are you coming?" she says.

I stand in the doorway. "This is a mistake."

The woman does not acknowledge me.

"Uhh, excuse me . . . there's been a mix-up." We're standing in a kitchen, all Jeyes-lemon-cream smell, gingham tablecloth, and dead carnations in a fat-bottomed IKEA vase. Fucking carnations.

"No, no mistake. Kathleen sent you here."

Hatchet?

I'm allergic to these places, these estates, like where I live, only ten times worse. Fields all around. Concrete. Nothing: no pubs, no restaurants, no shops, no peeps, no churches even. Zombie towns. Who the hell would come out here? Where the feck is this dump anyway?

"Sit," the woman says, "eat."

She places a sandwich with economy white bread lathered in easy-spread butter and cut-price ham in front of me. Mother would approve. This is not where I'm supposed to be.

As if reading my mind, she says in staccato English, "You are in the right place, the girls are young here." She looks me up and down. "Nothing happens in this house here. You will be going to hotels with the men." Right. Maybe then I'll get my chandeliers.

You can leave at any time, Sammy. Just take it step by step, and if it gets too much for you, get up and go. Remember that.

I don't eat a bite; the woman looks on. After a few minutes of silent protest, I'm shown to my bedroom: a twin room, with valance sheets with scalloped edges hanging low from the two single beds. There are swirly quilt covers, purples and pinks, and shell-pink walls. The light that hangs from the ceiling is a darker pink and stenciled with flowers: an upside-down flowerpot. Not exactly a man's room then. This is like being in boarding school, except it's not quite Enid Blyton land. Where are the rolling green fields, the vaulted ceilings, the posh uniforms, and the girls who speak with marbles in their mouths? My new madame, who I pretend is French and is called Solange, tells me the other girls are all asleep and it might be a good idea to get some rest. Kathleen had told her I was ready.

"Tonight you will work, yes?"

This is beyond surreal.

"Help yourself to anything you need in the kitchen," she says, as she moves towards the door.

"What about my roomie?" I gesture to the empty bed.

"Someone new will be arriving in the next few days," she says, before disappearing through the door.

My brain is buzzing and banging, and I'm desperate to go outside, get some air, move my legs around. As I walk to the front door, the woman appears—like vapor, so soundless it's spooky—and asks where I'm going.

"For a walk," I tell her.

She shakes her head. "That won't be possible."

"Why the hell not, there's no one around here, surely?"

"There are some families here," she says.

"Oh, come on . . . I can't stay here and not be allowed go out."

These are the rules, she tells me.

"So what happens if I decide I want to leave?"

She looks directly at me. "You owe a debt to Kathleen and to me, and I will tell you when that is paid off."

You've got to be kidding me. Fuck Hatchet, fuck this one standing in front of me, it's my body and if I choose to sell it, it's my money, and I tell her this.

"You will do well," she says. "You will earn well here. Out there, it is ugly."

She looks like she knows what she's talking about. In spite of my little alien doing his kung-fu thing inside, I tell myself that maybe I *am* better off here, in a tightly controlled environment where the clients are vetted, as "Kathleen" said. It can't be that hard to just walk away anyway. Haven't seen any bars on windows or anything. I'll give it a go and see what the pay is like, see what kind of client I have tonight. "One day at a time, sweet Jesus," Dad used to say when my mind would be buzzing with worry. "Nothing's ever as bad as you think it's going to be, my little catastrophist."

Any place but home, I chant silently.

Calm the head, Sammy. Breathe in, breathe out. "When exactly will the money I earn be mine?" I ask.

"Tomorrow," she says. "I will organize payment, take my cut, pay Kathleen her fee, and then give you yours."

I'm impressed with how good her English is. Suddenly I see a flash of me at fifty: preserved, stinking rich, and with a gaggle of young ones, all working for me. I wonder if that's how Kathleen got where she is; there's no way she worked her way through the ranks with a face like that, or maybe the face really doesn't come into it all. I look closely at this one in front of me and see that, beneath all that caked makeup, she's pretty, and pretty young still, maybe midtwenties. And already she's graduated.

My body feels like it's one of those fizzy sherbet dips that Granny Mona used to bring me, the ones you dip the licorice in, the powder bursting in your mouth. I could do with some of the clear stuff to calm me down. I need to lie on the grass, see the sky, stare at the clouds, and trip out, seeing shapes where there are none. As I make my way back to the bedroom a small, black-haired Asian girl comes out of a room, wearing spiky heels, a crop top, and tight mini: the requisite uniform. Brian got it right, all right. She has a far-off look in her eyes and her body kind of flows. She smiles and I see that her eyes are out of focus; she seems like she's floating above or beside herself. She manages a wave.

"I'm Ling," she says.

"Sam."

"Off to work I go!"

"Heigh-ho, heigh-ho," I say.

She looks at me funny. Maybe she doesn't share the same cultural references. I wonder what fairy tales she grew up with, if any. She sways towards the door, and when she opens it, there will be a man waiting on the other side to whisk her away to his castle.

I go back into the bedroom and push against the window, which only opens a crack. I had been planning on sitting there, on the ledge, drinking in the sky. I just want to breathe the outside in, so I crouch beneath the sill, being careful not to let my knees touch the ground, and stick my nose into the airstream. A sweet little breeze tickles my nostrils. I turn onto my front and place my body in a plank, hands beneath my shoulders, back straight, and bend my elbows, out to the sides, up and down. I push up and down forty-eight times until my arms are shaking and my heart is pounding, then I collapse onto the ground on my back and stare at the ceiling. My legs fly in the air and start doing the bicycle. I'm riding fast, feeling the wind whipping my face, the sun warming my cheeks, and now I'm pedaling all on my own without stabilizers.

I can hear Dad clapping behind me. "Wheeeeee, what a star. Look at you go, Sammy." I pump my legs even faster. "Slow down, Samantha, you're going to fall . . . ," and then Mother's voice, "Let her. It's the only way she'll learn. A few tumbles will knock sense into her."

I pedal faster, and topple and crash to the side, landing with my arm folded beneath me. There's a crunching noise and the sound of my own voice, high and disembodied, in my ears.

"That'll teach her," Mother says.

Dad is breathless and his face is pale as he picks me off the ground and bundles me into the car. We speed to the hospital. Nothing broken, the doctor tells Dad. He looks so relieved I'm scared he's going to cry. Mother tells him he's a wuss; all that blabbing over nothing. "Man up," she says. "It's what kids do . . . they fall over . . ."

I rub my arm and pedal the air faster. Dad's face is swimming in the air, looking down on me. "Your mother's overwrought, she doesn't know what she's saying. Don't take it personally."

I can't remember when Dad stopped hugging me. There came a point where she wouldn't allow it anymore. "It's unnatural," she said.

23

Nico

My eyes are open and staring, full of salt and grit, and there are blurry shapes and muffled sounds moving around me. I'm lying on my back, pinned. I don't know if it's a person, the sandman, a dream, broken bones, but I can't sit up. Count backwards, breathe. I rub my cheek against the rough bark and press my body into the branch, hugging its undersides. It will pass.

Magda's voice pierces through the swirl. "Nico?" This is the first time she has called me by my name. "Can you move?"

I try to nod but nothing is working. I wonder where Igor and the men who speak in the devil's tongue are, and just as if she can read my thoughts, she says, "They have gone . . . their job was to deliver us."

To deliver us from evil . . . I try to remember how the rest of that sentence goes, but it blurs at the edges and moves away from me.

"We're going to another country, beside England, another island," she says. All my life lived on the same patch of ground between home and school and forest and river, then in days, weeks, months—I don't know, I've no idea how much time has passed, although I think it may only be days, maybe tens of them—I'm transported on boats, in airplanes, in cars, the ground moving beneath my feet, my feet having no say over where they go. I wonder if my birthday's come and gone—if I'm thirteen yet.

I think back to the kingdom of our tree and the fairy caps. Luca brought bad luck when he pulled them before they were ready to let go. Are he and Maria happy together now, swimming in the watering hole, climbing the old fellow, without me there? Is Luca teasing Maria about being able to see up her dress? Is Mama being kind to the old dog? Maybe she managed to break her binds and run away; maybe she's running loose under the canopy of trees, maybe she knows now what would poison, and what would feed. Maybe.

Magda is lying on the bed beside me, cradling my head in her hands. "Can you sit up?" She puts one hand behind my shoulders and lifts me so I'm sitting, and holds a glass of water to my lips. "Little sips," she says. "What is it, little one? What are you staring at?"

I cannot speak.

"There's nothing there. It's okay, there's nothing there," and then she pours water into her hands and cups her wet palms over my eyes. She tells me that we can stay together. She has made them promise her that.

Slowly, my eyes start to blink and clear themselves of the stinging grit. Magda leans in and kisses me on the forehead, over and over, the way Mama did the day before I left. As I come to, I realize there's no movement, the ground beneath this place is not going anywhere. I don't think I can face another voyage, confined in another small space. Of all, the worst was the van with the music, the harsh tongues, the smell of fear from the other girls, their crying, their silence, the smoke, the cursing, the lack of air, the rain drumming down on the roof, like pounding hands. Of all, that was the worst. I can't do that again.

A man walks in. "How is she? Can she walk?"

I understand this. I want to walk, I want to run. I try to move my legs but they feel as if they are encased in cement. My heart starts to sound very loudly behind my eyes and I can feel my eyelids pulsing.

"I think it might be shock," Magda says.

He nods. "Well, we've arrived. We might have to lift her."

I don't want to be carried, I don't want to be touched, and as if just by thinking these thoughts, my body goes into revolt. It seems to jolt itself into action, and my legs kick hard, smashing the concrete shell.

"It's time to go," the man says.

Magda's eyes look huge and hunted, and something inside me hardens. That giant hand that has pushed down inside me is protecting my heart, putting a barrier between me and anything that hurts. "Come on," I say, swinging my body to sitting position.

"Be careful, Nico."

But it's as though a God-like force is galvanizing me, and my muscles are pumping and strong. Magda moves slowly, like she's pushing against an invisible weight, and stands, arms dangling down beside her, palms facing forwards, in worship, or supplication. I tell her to come on again, a new power flooding and moving through me as I stand and walk tall through the door.

A man is waiting at the top of the corridor and waves at us to follow him. Magda reaches out for my hand and we climb narrow stairs into the dark, wet night. The man is watching me but says nothing. He leads us out onto a large, black, concrete field, where I see a huddle of soaked girls and a figure standing near them, an umbrella protecting only their own head. Behind them, I can make out a van. No. No. No. As soon as my feet touch the solid surface, I walk in circles, slowly first, pacing, making sure my muscles are working, then I build up my speed inside and push off the ball of my right foot. Magda screams at me to stop, to come back, but I'm running on pure instinct, like the blood is up. I'm the hunter, not the hunted. My blood is pounding, my heart is pumping and I am free, for a moment free, until I feel hands grabbing onto my clothes, pulling me to the ground. This is the moment the rabbits freeze, when they pretend they're dead. I won't give these hands the satisfaction of feeling me go limp, so I hold myself hard and make my body into harsh angles.

Go on: hit me, scream, shout, pull a trigger. I am ready. Instead, two pairs of hands lift me and carry me back to the van. My body is stiff and I have vacated it, watching the men hauling it. They open the back door and push me in beside five other girls.

"Magda?"

No one answers.

"Where is Magda?" I ask.

A female voice from the front of the van speaks. "She's gone in another car."

"What car? Where? They promised we could stay together."

"They don't tell me anything," the woman answers.

I shake my head and bite down on the inside of my cheek until I taste metal. I know enough not to scream or bang my hands or head against the windowpane. I know enough to say nothing.

Maybe Petre has come and rescued Magda, and they will marry and have a baby boy. Or maybe she's speeding away in a van towards a room like the one we just left. Please, Mother Mary, don't let anything bad happen to Magda because of me.

"Not long now, girls," the woman who is driving says. "I'm sure you must be starving. We'll have a nice hot meal and bath when you arrive."

I hear sniffing and I want to thump the sniveling girl.

The van drives on. It is still night and the sky continues its weeping.

24

Sammy

I'm wearing the new gear Brian got for me, the gear I wore the first time behind the bicycle sheds, and the night with the bottle, and the day I busted out of hospital. My lucky garb. I look at my image in the full-length mirror and give myself a proper wolf whistle. I'm hot, hot, hot in my wedges and mini and T. The woman comes in and nods approvingly. She has a bag full of tricks: condoms, makeup, some kind of painkiller I don't recognize, lube jelly, and curling irons. The painkiller and the lube fills my head with some pretty gross stuff so I do what I do best—I break out laughing, tears sloshing down my cheeks. The woman leaves and returns with a glass of water and a pill.

"To calm," she says.

I pop it and swallow. Then she tells me to splash water on my face.

I go into the bathroom and drench my face in freezing cold water. It feels so good, I fill the sink and stick my head under, ducking and holding my breath for longer each time. There's a knock on the door.

"Your taxi will be here in ten minutes," the woman's voice says, "you need to fix up your face."

I pull the plug and watch the water gurgling away down the drain. I start to have these floaty thoughts and think: fuck, that pill is good—straight into the bloodstream.

Back in my room, the woman is sitting in front of the mirror with her makeup things spread out on the dresser—expensive shit, no Maybelline muck here. I close my eyes and offer my face to her, letting her slide her fingertips on my skin, spreading foundation, patting blush, and smearing on lip gloss. Then she curls my eyelashes with one of those metal contraption things and gets the mascara wand and brushes downwards, then upwards, telling me to look up, then down. She brushes out my hair and takes the curling tongs. I hope she doesn't give me a Shirley Temple do. The laughter that is bubbling won't come up and out, the floaty shit she fed me is doing the trick, making everything vague and smudgy. There are three of me in the mirror.

"Have some more water," she says. "Now stand."

I weave to standing.

"You will do as you are told, yes?"

I try to tell her that there are certain things I won't do, like getting on my knees. "When will I be paid?" I ask her again, my voice thick and foggy.

She holds me firmly by the elbow, ignoring the question, and walks me to the door. "Don't drink too much alcohol."

I'm hanging on to her shoulder. The taxi arrives and the driver is the same fat fella from earlier. I wonder, does he get a cut of my earnings too, or maybe he gets his kicks this way, or maybe he's paid in kind? Hatchet said the men would be rich and wear suits. As I walk down the path towards the car, I fall over on an ankle.

"How much did you give her?" the man asks.

"Just one."

"She must be allergic or something. She's wrecked."

"She'll be okay in an hour. Make sure she gets some fresh air and water before you bring her in . . . Samantha? Is that your real name? Samantha? Tonight you are called Natasha. And tonight you must smile."

Did I hear her correctly, or am I hallucinating? Mr. Taxi helps me into the back of the car.

"Don't puke in there," he says. "Tell me to stop, if you need to," and he hands me a half-empty bottle of lukewarm water.

My new knight in shining armor! Luce's face appears before me—a mask of horror. Too late now, Luce.

"It's all happening exactly as it's supposed to with hidden blessings we will soon understand." Granny Mona's refrain echoes in the chambers of my brain, deep in the membrane.

We drive, and I loll, accompanied by flashbacks of Luce's dad, protecting me, supporting me. Oh, Mrs. O'D this is exactly as you would imagine it would pan out for a girl like me. Mother, you said it—you knew it, even before I did.

The car slows down in a brightly lit street, which seems

pretty swanky: posh bars and bistro-type French places, a whole strip of them. People are queuing, and bouncers with tough, appraising faces look the line up and down, letting only the good-looking girls in, only the youngest.

Mr. Charmer opens my car door. "You okay? Need some air?"

I shake my head. I'm cold in my getup and can feel people's eyes on my goosepimply flesh. "Let's go inside."

He shakes his head. "This is where I leave you. Go straight in, sit by the bar. A guy called Mark will come find you."

So, Mark, hey? I think of my cousin, who's a pretty decent guy and a primary school teacher. Wouldn't it be a scream if it was him? Oh, such a scream.

I teeter past the bouncer, who I swear licks his lips as I pass him.

"Why is she going on through? We've been here for ages . . . ," I hear one of the women at the top of the queue whine. Because, love, in all seriousness, you need to knock a few pounds off, a few years off, and a few layers of threads off. The bubble of funny is beginning to form. I can walk in a straight line. No one is immune to my charms. The whole room is a sea of craning necks, and not just the men, the women's eyes burn into me. I have never felt so visible, or exposed. Jesus, it's not like I'm doing a Gaga on it, wearing only a thong and black, lacy push-up bra. I wonder if any of them have seen my face staring out at them from the page or the screen. Obviously not, or I wouldn't have been sent somewhere so public, or maybe they're just bargaining on the fact that no one would recognize me in this gear, or maybe in places like this, people know not to ask questions.

I sit at the bar, open the cream patent handbag the woman handed me as I was leaving and see the bottle of lube glinting at me. I push it to the bottom of the bag. She's also stocked it with a mirror, lipstick, brush, mascara, condoms, blush, those painkillers, baby wipes (gross), and a new phone. Oh, and fresh undies. She thinks of everything, that one. Except she didn't tell me when it was time to go home.

Did yer man in the taxi say something when I was out of it? There were no instructions like: 3 a.m. at the front door. I don't even know where that house in the ghost estate is. The phone rings.

"Has he arrived yet?" The woman's voice sounds more foreign coming over the phone.

"No."

"Good, drink lots of water and smile. He's a very important client."

"What time am I being picked up?"

"The client will decide what time he is finished. Don't worry, he knows how this works. You will be brought back here when he is finished with you."

"Only one tonight then?"

"Yes."

I guess this is what they call "breaking her in lightly."

"He has paid already."

The phone goes dead. A hand touches my shoulder. "Natasha?"

I turn to face "Mark." He's about fifty or so, hard to tell when they're gray like that—his skin and his hair and his stubble. He's wearing a shiny black leather jacket, a pressed shirt with the collar starched, and high-waisted jeans. His shoes are brown leather, pointed. Obviously he has no woman in his life to dress him. His skin is florid and flaccid, one of those pasty-faced Irish men gone to seed. Would he look any better in a suit?

"The eagle has landed!" he says.

I force my face into something resembling a smile, but it feels cracked, like I'm slathered in a dried mud mask. Maybe this is what that expensive foundation shit does to your face—mummifies it? Am I pretty, sir? Am I pleasing? The crack is where the light gets in.

"What can I get you?"

I can hear the woman's voice say, "Not too much alcohol," just as I hear my own say, "Double vodka, please."

He chuckles to himself. Glad I'm amusing you, sir. We sit at the bar, gulp back a few, make some polite chitchat bullshit. He seems surprised that I'm Irish, though it doesn't faze him, just makes him more excited.

"Your real name's not Natasha, is it?"

Brilliant. I'm dying to ask him if he's married. Does he have any daughters? Does he do this often? There is nothing about his demeanor that suggests he's embarrassed. He's getting redder and puffier in the face from the double measures of gin he's downing, and louder, drawing glances from the people around us.

I could still walk away from this. I could.

We're in a lift going to the sixth floor when he pushes his bulk against me and sticks his tongue down my mouth. Did I ask for that, mister? The lift stops and he gets out. I follow, even though the kicking sensation has started deep in my stomach. He opens the door to room number 606 and I notice there's a bucket with champers in it and a big, fake chandelier hanging from the center of the ceiling. I watch how the light plays on the bedsheets beneath it, turning everything into a dappled display of pyrotechnic wizardry: disco balls, fireworks.

I keep my eyes on the light as he undresses me, licking as he goes, groaning, grabbing my thighs and sticking his head down there. The lights are dancing, dancing. Then I'm on top of the bed and he is on top of me. It's like the moment with the bottle: blurred, slo-mo, and sped up all at the same time, except this time it's yer man that is pulling my strings, not some crazy lady in the sky. The same feeling of powerlessness applies here. I hear myself saying, "Condom," and try to open my bag, but he's holding my arms down.

"I'm fine," he says. "Clean." And in he goes, filling me up with him.

When he's finished, he goes to the champers, makes a big show of opening it and pours bubbles into my glass and his, clinking the two together. Cheers. Thank you, kind sir. I swallow fast. The bubbles explode in my mouth, the fizz burns a hole in the lining of my stomach. I can see it tearing away in there and I glug.

"Hey, slow down. You're a greedy little one," he says, as he drinks in my body with his thread-veined eyes.

I wrap myself up in the sheets. Can I go now? Is it over yet? Evidently not, as he pries the sheet from me and starts his sucking thing again. I drink and drink and stare directly into the light, which makes black circles swirl in front of my eyes. I try to count them. They float up and swim away before I can get a grasp. He bites me on my inner arm, then under my arm, then on my breast. The guy is biting me.

"Hey," I say.

"Don't like that?"

I decide not to say anything further, guessing that he would probably bite harder if I did.

It would be easier having to do a load of them in one evening; I reckon I could handle that better than this—this one-on-one intimacy. He's fooled himself into thinking we're engaged in some sort of reciprocal situation. And then my mind gets all tangled up in its own tripping thoughts, 'cause, really, I am here because I want to be. No one is forcing me, are they? No one is holding a gun to my head, are they? No, Sammy, you chose this for yourself, and it's this thought that lands and punches me in the gut; it's this thought that makes the tears come when the guy is asleep, snoring, his arm draped over me, spooning me to him, like we're cozy lovers.

I try to twist from under him without waking him and reach for the bag and the phone. I'll hook up to the net and see how the world is getting on. Imagine a selfie here now? Imagine Luce's face if I sent her a video? I wonder, can they trace you by making updates, posting shit?

I track that thought to its furthest edge but it kind of slips away from me. I just want to let Luce know I'm okay. Am I okay? You're fine, kiddo. This is it: the good life, the chandeliers, the champers, the middle-aged rich guy. I have to remind myself I never liked it anyway. Love is for suckers. Then Eminem's lyrics are bouncing around my head: *I just don't give a fuck*. Hello, Emmy, my old friend. Mr. Em is my soul mate; I reckon he'd have done exactly the same thing if he'd been a girl and hadn't become a huge star. Imagine the inside of his head? Maybe I should start writing it all down. I think of Miss White's words: "Powerful, Samantha," the page topped with a gold star, "where *does* your imagination come from?"

The phone is a dud and it won't hook up to the internet. I tap in a random number and it doesn't connect, and I try another. The phone is for incoming calls only, for them to keep a track on me. I dial 999. Nada. Have they not got a hotline to someone, in case there's an emergency, like in case one of these guys decided to get too kinky, like maybe strangle me or something? But then if there were big hands around my neck, I wouldn't be able to move to get the phone, to make a call. I can feel the acid rising in me, alongside a harsh sort of laughter.

I'm a bit sore, it has to be said. I wonder was it all too soon, although Hatchet did clear me for business, and she should know, being a nurse and all. I slip out of the bed. Yer man is snoring away goodo, so I glug on the remnants of the champers and pull back the curtains, peering out the crack. There are lots of peeps milling around out there. Good windows, must be triple glazed or something, can't hear a thing from outside; it's like watching a film with the sound turned off: so many drunk girls out there, in their high heels and little skirts. I wonder how many of them will go home with some guy they've just met. How many of them will really want it? How many of them will wake up in the morning not knowing where they are? At least I'm being paid. *Any place but home.*

I turn to look at the man who looks like a big baby blowing bubbles through his little O-shaped mouth. Pudgy cherub. The laughter has grabbed hold of me now and there's no pushing it back down. Up and out it comes. I hold my nose and knock back the dregs of the bubbles. It's funny, the more I drink, the more sober I feel. The hysteria is rattling about against my ribs, shaking me. The baby opens one eye. A pudgy hand gestures for me to join him in the bed.

"Mama, Mama . . . ," he seems to be saying, "feed me." And his little plump lips are latched to me again. I look down at his head and pray he doesn't bite.

After he's had his fill, he looks at me, really looks at me, seeing me, now his appetite has been sated.

"Are you okay?" he says. "Your whole body is shuddering."

Shuddering. What a funny word.

"Fine," I say. "Would it be okay if I had a shower?"

"Sure," he says, playing coy, head to one side. "We can have one together."

I've completely decided there's no way this dude ever got

any woman to marry him or carry his child. Aw, fuck. He didn't use protection. I'll have to go to the doc and get a morning-after. Last time I took one of those, I was so sick for days after. They're ferocious, those tiny pills, flooding the body with crazy-ass hormones. I cried nonstop too.

We go to the bathroom and he adjusts the taps, doesn't even ask me if the temperature's okay. It's a bit scalding. He likes it hot. Then he rubs me down with soap and washes my hair. I'm screaming inside, a fucking giant's roar. I can't believe I'm managing to stay silent, the fist knocking against my ribs, working its way upwards, so I think it might get lodged in my throat and gag me, from the inside.

He's being all gooey. "You're so beautiful. Oh, oh . . . ," and on, "oh."

25

Nico

After some time, the van begins to slow in the middle of a maze of streets where all the houses look the same: box-like, with two windows on top and two on either side of the white, plastic-looking door. We're told to stay very, very quiet, any sound and there will be trouble. Some of the girls don't understand, so a man goes to them and puts a finger to their lips, his hand slicing across their necks as they step out of the car, blinking under the yellow flickering streetlamp. Now they understand.

This place is a home, like the one Mama described when she said I was to be a wife in England. There are soft carpets and electric lights and heaters on the walls, which, when I slide my fingertips over them, are warm to the touch. We're brought to a kitchen and told to sit and eat. The hole inside of me is crying out to be filled and I eat sandwich after sandwich until my belly is round, while the others look on. I don't care if there is poison in the sandwiches, which are made from white bread, ham, and cheese. There are flowers on the table, not purple and pink roses like Mama said, but pink and white scraggy things, their petals drooping. They smell like a musty dishcloth. A long, white light is fixed into the ceiling, which illuminates the face of the woman of the house, who looks like she could be Magda's sister—the same flecked-green eyes with long eyelashes, the same svelte body, her face molded from the same hard, shiny stone.

She speaks directly to me in my language. "I will show you to your room."

"Do you know Magda?" I say.

She looks blankly at me.

We all stand at once and she gestures with her hand for the other girls to stay, and tells them to use the toilet, as they'll be getting back in the van. There are a few scared sounds of protest, like kittens squealing when they are first handled. I remember Sergiu and Victor roughly handling a wild cat's litter this way. Their cries fill my ears. I have not really allowed myself to look at these other faces. I follow the woman out of the room, without looking back.

She seems to glide, her feet hovering along the corridor, which has four rooms coming off it, and a staircase leading up to another level. The carpets are soft and bouncy, the same creamy color as the walls, the lights too bright for anything furtive to happen here.

She pushes open a door and says, "Do you understand me?"

I nod. Her accent is familiar. "Moldovan?" I ask.

Her face closes down. The door opens into a bedroom, which is soft and pink. It doesn't feel like any man has ever set foot in here. There are two beds, both draped in sheets that are hanging over the edges, with fluffed-up pillows and plump, soft quilts. I want to run and dive under the covers and burrow deep and never come out. The room smells of sickly flowers, like a stale scent has been sprayed in the air.

"The toilet is over there," the woman says. I put my hand out and tell her my name is Nicoleta, Nico, although I almost say "Natasha."

I can see her hesitating, wondering whether to tell me her real name.

"Irina," she says.

Once inside the bathroom, I lock the door, open the taps, and pour soapy liquid into the running water, which makes bubbles pop and hiss. I take my dress off, which is sticky as I pull it over my head, and step into the foaming hot water. When I think I cannot stand it any longer, I can. I sit, then lie, submerging my head. There is rose-colored shampoo at the side of the bath, which is thick like honey when I squeeze it into my hand. I can feel its sweetness and stickiness soaking into my scalp as I lie back down under the water and hold my breath. An image of me waving at Luca and Maria: "Look at me," as I pretend I've been under for sixty-six seconds.

I pray to the Madonna who lived above my bed, for the first time since that night, when her smile glinted at me—was she mocking me?—from inside her gilded frame. Praying blocks out other sounds and pictures in my head, although the people I want to pray for are the people I need to forget. Magda's face fills the picture frame. Static builds up between my ears and I have to shake my head violently. I try to make sense of what I saw between her and Petre. How can someone love and hate so much at the same time? I paint an image in my head of the two of them together, her safe inside his arms, but a shadow falls over it.

I concentrate on rinsing my hair, imagining the bad thoughts are flowing down the plughole with the suds. I remember Miss Iliescu telling us that in some big cities they have pipes where wastewater flows underground, all the way to the sea, and then it is pumped back into toilets and showers and taps. I turn on the showerhead and let scalding water pound on my shoulders, imagining this is the sea pouring over me, salty and clean. I step onto the bath towel and dry myself off roughly when there's a knock on the door.

Irina's voice: "Everything okay in there?"

I don't feel like speaking, so I open the door a crack with the towel wrapped tightly around me. She looks at me closely, and then walks soundlessly away down the hallway.

Back in the bedroom, I find freshly washed nightclothes on the bed. I step into the soft, long-sleeved top and loose bottoms and feel glad to be covered up. Beside the bed, there's a table with a drawer, which has a pen and small notebook inside. I take it out and try to write something down. So,

Miss Iliescu, what do I write about here? I don't even know what country I'm in. I know it's next to England and there is sea between it and this. I go to the window and pull back the curtain. It's dark, although not pitch-black, and there's a light drizzle falling from the sky. The front door opens and bangs shut, and I hear the revving of the engine of the van. The girls are on the move again.

I get into bed and snuggle deep, close my eyes, and let my head rock from side to side rhythmically, which stops the swirling of jagged thoughts. In my dream I'm at the bottom of the well, and when I look up, Papa, Victor, and Sergiu are at the top staring down at me. "Too bad you were born a girl," Sergiu says. "A woman now," Papa says, and then Petre appears behind him. I bolt upright in the bed, sweating and cold, turn on the bedside light, twist the skin on my arm and take out the pen and open the notebook. I try to write something: My name is Natasha. I am fifteen years old. I like to climb trees although I am too old.

The door opens. Maybe it is my new roommate. "I saw your light on," Irina says. She's holding out a glass of water and a pill. "To help you relax." I take it and swallow, drinking the whole glass of water in one go. "You should sleep soon," she says, as she closes the door softly behind her. I wonder if this is one of those pills Magda gave to the girl in the room, not caring either way. I begin to float up out of my body and can see myself lying on the plump bed, then I continue on up through the ceiling and out into the soft rain. Hovering above

God's breath, I settle into myself, falling down into the cushion of the cloud.

The next morning, I wake to sunlight seeping through the rim of the curtains. I hear a bird singing: it sounds like the song of a blackbird from home. I rub my eyes and stretch my body long, pointing my toes. This must be Sunday; it's the only day Mama doesn't get out of bed before sunrise. I swing my legs over the side of the bed, holding on tightly to the sheets. The world is spinning again. I look around and see a shape in the bed beside me, long dark hair spilling out over the back of the quilt. She's making light singing sounds. I go to the window and pull back the curtains a little. The girl in the bed stirs and mumbles. I can smell the weak sunshine and think I see green leaves rustling in the breeze.

I find the kitchen, where there are cardboard boxes laid out on the table. One of the boxes says cornflakes and there's a picture on the back of a jug pouring milk. After I've eaten three bowls, moist with milk, I walk to the front door and try to pull back the bolt.

Irina appears at the top of the stairs. "It is locked. We cannot have the neighbors see you."

I wonder about these neighbors. Are they families, or men who will use us? It seemed very empty and quiet last night; there were no lights on in the houses.

"It's a residential area," she says. "Too risky."

I'm not sure what she means exactly—risky for whom?—but she has that set to her face that Mama used to wear when she was angry, and I know not to ask any questions.

"Did you eat breakfast?" I nod. I am craving fresh air. "Cat got your tongue?"

My tongue feels like it doesn't belong to me, neither do my limbs, my head, my hair, my fingers, my nails. Every part of me feels like it might float away.

"Don't worry about it," she says. "Just the sleepers."

A shaft of sunlight burns through a small window in the hall, and lands in a puddle at my feet. I move my right foot into the light, and then my whole body. I let it flow through me, warming every part of me. My eyes close.

"You'll build tolerance, you'll see," Irina says, speaking harshly in English, sounding like she's someone else, before she turns on her barefooted heel and is gone.

I'm left standing, swaying in the light, wondering about the word "tolerance." Even though I don't fully understand it, I'm not sure it's something I would want to build.

I follow the light from puddle to puddle, imagining I'm splashing about in my rain boots at home, until I hear a door creak and a girl appears.

"Sleep good?" she asks in staccato English. Her hair is long and dark, eyes curious like a cat's. I wonder if this is the girl who was in the bed next to me. She is tiny. I sway towards her, following her back into the kitchen.

She laughs at me as I try to speak. "I see Ana give you sleepy-time tablets."

Ana? Who is Ana? She pulls up her sleeves to pour the milk and I can see marks, like grips or burns.

She notices me looking and says, "Handcuffs." She turns her

arms over for me to inspect her wrists. "Game the man likes." She traces the marks with her fingertips before pulling her sleeves down abruptly, as if she's suddenly ashamed by what she sees. I try to block the thoughts that her voice brings, and focus on the bird that is still singing, faintly, in the distance.

26

Sammy

It finishes, like all things eventually finish, but Jesus, this is, without doubt, the longest night of my life. After he rubs me down in a towel, he dresses me, brushes my hair, dries it with a hairdryer, and tells me I'm a "splendid specimen," and that I am even more beautiful barefaced. I got the measure of him—Mr. Bareback Rider. He kisses my face, then picks up his mobile and walks me into the lift, his hand on the base of my spine.

It's weird, but I've kinda gone all floppy, like I'm a rag doll, or this guy's Muppet. It's like there's nothing of me inside. Even when he pushes his tongue down my gob again, I feel nothing: not hard, not spiky, just nothing.

He walks me through the empty bar downstairs and out into the soft pink almost-morning. The street is splattered with puke, but the sky is high and mighty and the birds are tweeting away. Mark squeezes me one more time and kisses me long and deep. I think he's cast himself as the hero in some romantic war-era film, where he's about to leave the love of his life for what may be the very last time. I wonder what his real life consists of. Is he going home to sleep, tasting me on him for the day? How long will that sustain his greedy little "O"?

"Have a good night?" Mr. Taxi asks after the door has shut on Mark. I let my head fall against the window and shut my eyes.

When we get to the house, everyone is asleep. I open the door to the bedroom and see that my roomie has arrived. She's out cold, so I don't turn on the light, just throw myself on my bed, fully clothed, facing her. She has thick blonde hair, looks natural, and seems very small bundled under the quilt. I close my eyes and let her sleep drift into me as I breathe with her. I wonder how much I'll get paid. I hope it's by the millisecond.

The next morning, Roomie's up and left, and I wake to the sound of a chirpy little fella tweeting away outside the window. I lie on my back, staring at the freshly painted ceiling. No cracks here. Any time any thought of Mother, or Luce, or that woman on her knees, or the jerk from the canal, or matinee-idol Mark, or anything shitty pops into my head, I'll smash it down, like Punch does to Judy's head. I could never understand the drips that cried every time Punch threw one. I credit those shows with developing my advanced sense of humor. When other girls were crying with sadness, I was crying with something else, something giddy and harsh. I can feel it rising in me now.

I go into the kitchen and Ling is there, and the new girl,

sitting in silence. They both look up. My stomach is cranky this morning, loud and bloated. *Sugar-coated flakes of golden corn*; this is what I'm thinking as I take in the newbie. Her skin is creamy, the sunlight catches in her hair, and her body is small and compact, like a gymnast. She looks like one of those Eastern European Olympians that twist and tumble high in the air and make the crowd gasp.

"Hi," I say, pouring myself a bowl of cornflakes. "I'm your new roomie."

"Neekoh," she says, extending her hand formally. Her accent is Russian or something, her voice slurred.

I doubt she's one of those Natashas—she looks way too good. Then again, I doubt she'd have chosen to be here. She looks very young. And dazed. I look at Ling for a moment; she's also younger than me, but she's tough, she's seen things, and I bet she knows, like me, what it is to be steamrolled in her sleep. Stories rush into my head, stories I don't want to be told. The girl in the back of the Garda car opens her eyes and stares at me, opening her mouth to speak. I shake my head.

The three of us sit, Ling and I spooning mouthful after mouthful of cereal into our gobs, as Nico delicately sips her juice. She's like something out of the pages of a fairy tale. Will she be rescued by a kind and handsome prince? I think of Mark and her in the same bed and feel sick. No doubt, Ling and I'd be thrown in cages and gobbled up. No one says a word, the tension thick, until I can bear it no longer and I belch, a really loud one. A party trick of mine. Ling giggles, but Nico pushes back her chair, and says, "Excuse me," in a tight voice before leaving the room. Ling is falling around the place she's laughing so loudly. There's a manic light in her eyes fed by years of adrenaline.

Another girl walks in. Stunning and so sad. I can't stop staring. For a girl from white middle-class suburbia, this place sure is multicultural.

"Morning!" I say. She scowls at me, at the air, at life in general. "I'm Sammy."

She pretends she doesn't hear me and goes towards the cereal boxes, studying them closely, then pours and eats fistfuls, dry. Then another girl comes in. They look so alike they must be sisters, but they don't even register each other. Just munch, munch, silently. Ling throws her eyes up to heaven and giggles. The girls don't react.

I try again, with the second girl. "Hi, I'm Sammy," and put my hand out, but she looks as if she might bite it off, so I quickly drop it. Ling's giggles are mounting in intensity and I can feel the tickle in the back of my throat.

"Have you been here long?" I ask.

The girls don't answer, just continue to focus on eating. Their eyes are blank. They're pretty far gone, probably been fed too many of those pills. The expression on their faces sort of worms its way inside me, and I feel like I might topple into the abyss with them. Fuck this, I'm outta here. "See you later, so," I say, trying to breathe some warmth into them, some life, with my forced cheeriness. They don't look up. I reckon they don't understand a word of what is being said. For a moment I'm inside their heads and it's terrifying: an upside-down, inside-out world where nothing makes any sense. Maybe people being nice to them signals some kind of a threat. They can't even find comfort in each other.

Ling has stopped giggling. The only sound is of a bird, just outside the kitchen window. It's delicate and pretty, high and thin. I bet it's a girl. The music fills the kitchen, and for a moment, no one moves. The girls stop eating and listen, their eyes glistening. The notes fill me with something I don't want to feel.

I go the bathroom, turn on the shower and step into it, letting it all flow out of me, until every part of me is wet.

27

Nico

A tall girl with stretched limbs and long dark hair and eyes that dart all round—searching for something—stands at the kitchen door. The air around her seems to crackle with some kind of energy, electricity, excitement.

Ling lights up when she sees her. Instantly, I feel excluded from their secret world, which consists of giggling about nothing at all. I have not felt like laughing since before the day of the sheets and the staining. The girl tells me she is my roomie, which I take to mean she is sharing my room. I tell her my name is Nico.

"Hello, Neekoh!" she says. "That's an unlikely name for a girly girl like you."

I nod, not knowing exactly what she means—she speaks so fast, and in a strange voice with its own tune.

A bird sounds outside, but I strain to hear it through the noise Sammy's jaw makes chomping on the dried flakes of corn. A question seems to hover in the air around us, in the song outside the window, in the silence between the bites . . . as if in answer, Sammy belches, pretending to be a man, rubbing her belly the way Sergiu and Victor would after dinner. Ling thinks this is hilarious, and for a moment, these two have become my elder brothers, egging each other on. I feel myself shrinking around this girl as she fills all the corners of the room and sucks up all the air. I get up to go and brush against the flowers with my elbow. A withered pink petal falls onto the table.

I go back to the bedroom and sit on a sill beneath the window, which I open as far as it will go, only a crack. Outside, there are lots of houses, all the same, all concrete, most of them unfinished and empty, with builders' tools lying about, including one of those round cement mixers that Maria's papa had hired to build an extension that never got finished. There is the beginning of a playground, with a ladder and a slide made of mirrors, and two swings that look like no one has ever sat on them. I think of our swinging tires, suspended between two maple trees in the field across from the house, and the hours we used to spend screeching through the air. These trees are saplings, newly planted and skinny. None of them are big enough to climb, or to support the weight of a body, swinging. The sunshine of the early morning has given way to gray cloud, and the sky is low and heavy.

I take out the pen and notebook and stare at it. *My Summer Holidays* by Nicoleta Zanesti. Those days are gone. I write "Day 1 in the Cream House" on the first blank page and think of Magda telling the girls to keep count. How much am I even worth? I stare at the whiteness of the paper and worry that by writing it down, it will only make it more real, so I close the pages, close my eyes, and try very hard to think of nothing at all.

"Hiya, Roomie, what ya doing?" She doesn't even bother knocking; she is wrapped in a towel, her hair soaking and dripping onto the carpet. She repeats herself loudly and slowly, "What are you doing?"

I understood her the first time. "No thing," I say, speaking low, hoping my tone will influence hers, the way Mama used to speak around Papa when his energy was loud and vexed, after having drunk too much Rachiu. She bangs around the room and dries herself off in front of me, fully naked. I turn my back and stare out at the gray.

"Where are you from?" she says.

"Romania," I say, the practiced lie slipping out of me.

"Cool. Never been there. What's it like?"

"It is no thing special." I surprise myself again with how good my English is. Miss Smith would be proud. I see her smiling face and bite down hard on the inside of my cheek.

"Ever been to good ole Dub before?"

I think back to geography. Where is "good ole Dub"? Dub. I shake my head.

"Bit of a shithole," she says, laughing again. "Never stops raining." She looks out the window. "Yup, those clouds are going to burst their skin any moment now."

I wonder why everything is a joke with this girl. Is rain really that funny?

"Have you been anywhere else? This place is seriously weird. Could be anywhere."

I think she is saying this place is like any other place and this is true. There is no character to the landscape here.

"We must mitch off out of here one day. I'll show you the sights!"

Mitch. I must have looked blankly at her because she explains, "We must go on a trip, into town one day, see the shops. I'm sure we can do a lot of damage with our considerable earnings."

I think I understand something about shops, which doesn't make sense, as I'm sure we would not be allowed to leave, and also why would anyone want to go shopping with no money?

I ask, "Are we near to sea?"

"I haven't a clue, to be honest. But on this little island, you're never more than a couple of hours from the sea."

She starts to skip around the room half-dressed. The air around her fizzes, and although I don't want to look, my eyes are drawn.

"That's a great idea," she says. "Let's go on an outing to the seaside. I bet Ling would like it too. We'll all go skinny-dipping in the rain. So exhilarating."

I understand she means swimming in the rain. I shiver. Does she really believe it would be that easy to leave this place? I think of Irina's soundless footfall and know that although this house is warm and bright, it's still a container of sorts, and I have no doubt that the lid is firmly closed. I can hear Magda's voice: "You have a debt and it needs to be paid." To whom do I owe the money now?

"What's the sea in your country like?" she asks.

"Is black."

"Coooelle. I've read about that: the Black Sea. Didn't know it was really black though. How weird—like swimming in squid ink."

I nod, possessed by Papa and his giant squirrels, his sandman, his stinging flies, and his inky Black Sea.

"I wonder if they have a telly," she says. "TV."

I wonder if they show cowboy-and-Indian films here.

"I'm going to go explore," she says. She's wearing loose trousers that look like sleeping clothes; they are so big she has to hold them up with one hand. "Catch you later, Miss Romania."

She slams the door so loudly behind her that the ledge beneath me shakes, and for a moment, I have a feeling of movement again. A vehicle is spinning its wheels beneath me, driving me, away from home, propelling me onwards.

I am parched, so I go back into the kitchen, where I see two girls from far away with faraway expressions; so lost, so cold. They look like they belong in the sunshine. I quickly pour a cold glass of orange juice and think of Mama's apple-and-cherry compote, and try not to.

I follow the sound of loud voices to a room where the curtains are drawn and there are flickering lights playing on the walls. The picture is so much brighter and clearer than on Maria's papa's television. I stand and watch from the doorway as the people on the screen shout, hit, hiss, kiss, and cry. Sammy sees me and gestures for me to come in, to sit beside her on the couch. Two women's lips meet and they pull each other close, sighing and rubbing against each other. The icon on my bedroom wall appears and frowns, and I turn my back, closing the door.

Irina drifts down the corridor towards me like smoke. I ask her in our language whether there are any books to read in this place. I suddenly need to lose myself in the words of someone else, set someplace else, telling any other story but this one.

"Have you found the TV?" she asks, looking at me like I've left my mind somewhere else.

"Yes, but I was wondering if you might have any books from home?"

Bitterness bites into her voice. "Didn't exactly think I was coming on holidays when I came here."

I can see in her face she's thinking reading is the last thing anyone in this place should ever feel like doing. I'm a queer duck all right. Maria appears, laughing, and I swat her away.

"There might be some English shit lying around in the kitchen drawers that a driver left there," she says, before floating back upstairs.

In the kitchen, the two dark girls are still there, motionless, locked deep inside themselves. I sniff the air and don't detect anything, other than the musty dead-flower scent, disguised with bleach, then I hold my breath as I open every cupboard, rummage through cutlery, tea towels, plates, pots and pans, until eventually I see the books, hidden at the back of a drawer full of plastic folders of papers with lists of names on them. I grab them, desperate to lose myself in them. On the front of one is a picture of a long corridor and a figure running down it, on the other is an image of a barred window and a single cloud floating.

The rain has started outside, but it's so light it makes no sound. The dark girls are staring through the window beyond the watery sky to other worlds—worlds that only exist in their minds. My own mind won't let me fully enter this thought, blocked as it is by Papa and the boys' words, and I suddenly need to get as far away from these sad girls as possible.

I'm relieved to find Sammy is not in the bedroom, so I open the book with the person running on the front, hoping to be led on an adventure far from here. The print is large, and although I don't understand every word, I get the sense of the story: a pretty schoolteacher is taken by a murderer who kills time and time again, and the police can't track him down. The woman is kidnapped by the man when she is walking home late one night and bundled in a van. He places her in a dark room below ground and ties her to the wall with silver metal cuffs. I think of the marks on that girl Ling's wrists. Maria and the other girls in school would love this book. Time passes, and my mind is filled only with this woman and her killer, my own situation receded to a background hum, until Sammy flings open the door.

"Didn't see you at lunch."

I hadn't realized it was past lunch yet.

"You'd better go eat something before the shenanigans of the night start."

Sometimes it's as if this girl speaks in riddles.

"There's a chicken curry in the fridge. I wonder who cooks for the inmates. Doubt it's that woman, ghostie. She doesn't look like the type to chop vegetables."

I nod, even though I don't have a clue what she's speaking about, and I'm still in the world of the woman tied in the cellar.

"Hey, it's nearly seven o'clock. You'd really better eat."

I think of Mama's words about food soothing fear, although right now I don't feel anything, just numb. I look up and out the window and see that the light is draining from the sky. I turn the page down at the corner, on page eighty-eight.

Sammy picks it up. "Did you read all this today?"

I nod.

"Looks like a pile of crap."

I understand from her tone she means stupid. Yes, it is stupid, but not as stupid as life in this house where we pretend everything is normal—where we eat, watch television, read, talk, move freely inside, waiting for the night to come, waiting for the men to come and do with us what they want. Magda said it would be easier than that place of ten men a night. Anything has to be easier than that.

At least the woman in the cellar is straining at her ties.

28

Sammy

Roomie has her head stuck all day in a shit slasher-type book with the biggest print I've ever seen. Her huge, far-apart, alien eyes have almost dissolved into the pages, and when I speak to her, she looks really pissed, like I've interrupted her from studying Shakespeare the night before an important exam or something. Just my luck to be paired with this one, and then I think of the girls in the kitchen, and vow to make a huge effort in case she complains to management, and I'm moved on and out.

A documentary comes to mind, the one with the posh blonde dude who goes to live with weirdo tribes and takes their drugs and summons up spirits—and puke. There were masses of naked women's shriveled breasts, usually with a baby attached, and the witch doctors wore loincloths and carried spears. Imagine if those girls came from somewhere like that. Maybe they've been voodooed. I've read about girls like that, girls who have been cursed and cast out.

The day passes watching daytime soaps from all over the world. The best is from Russia: all the women are such beautiful, cold bitches, smothered in makeup, hitting or kissing each other, everything said in a sigh. The Americans and Aussies have fake baloobas that don't jiggle when they run. I'm pretty sure this isn't straight UPC or Sky; I reckon Irina, or whatever her name is, got this multicultural TV thing going on so that all her little charges would feel right at home.

Time drags so slowly, it's like the day is clogged with sticky viscous stuff, and yet at 6 p.m.—I can't believe it's 6 p.m.—the rituals for the night of subterfuge are about to begin, and it's time to don my disguise in the form of makeup, curling-tonged tresses, and maximum-exposure gear. I must get some time alone with Irina to get paid, and to tell her about Mark's "mishap." That morning-after pill has to be swallowed within seventy-two hours of the incident, and I'll have to get tested. Been there before, and I really don't fancy having to do that every few days—I'd be sick as that dude in the jungle after he swallowed some liquid of the gods. I remember thinking at the time that it was their gods he was drinking down and they might not like it, and sure enough, angry eruptions poured out of him. Mark is not anyone's god, to be sure, and his liquid has no place inside of me.

How do you insist on them wearing one? There should be a training manual and video: how to use coercive charm to make a client put a lid on it! I couldn't even get the guys in school to wear one, so what hope do I have if the guy is paying? When he's paying he *is* a god—I'll have to work on strategies for that one. I wonder why they don't put us on the pill and pump antibiotics into our system.

Roomie doesn't look like she's moved since the morning, glued as she is to the bondage book. I wonder if she's preparing herself for the worst, learning some tricks of the trade. I tell her there's chicken curry in the fridge, full of veggies and home-made goodness. Someone, somewhere, is cooking good, whole-some food for us girls. Important to present a glossy package. She thanks me and closes the door without making a sound. Okay, I get the point, Princess, I'm a bit of a heffalump with my slamming of doors and thumping around—a habit I acquired in the early days, just to get a rise out of Mother. Habits are hard to break, even when getting a rise out of her wasn't necessary anymore—her rage had permanently risen.

Just as Roomie leaves, Irina appears with her bag of tricks. "How was your first night?"

I tell her about him not using a condom, a lid, a cap, a sheath, a protective cover (just so she gets the picture) three times.

She shrugs. "It happens. Here." She hands me a morning-after pill.

"I can't take that now. Last time I took one of those I was sick for two days."

She roots in her bag and takes out another kind of a pill. Hello, Floaty, my old friend.

"Take half now, and half later if you need to . . . You can take the morning-after tomorrow morning. You may need one after tonight, anyway."

I think back to Hatchet telling me that this was a safe place where the clients would be vetted.

"There is no way of making them wear one," Irina says. "The doctor will come in two days and fit you with a diaphragm."

I thought those things were only for baggy women who've had kids.

"He can also check you for disease."

Imagine if it was Doc O'D? His office of good works? I start to chuckle, low and deep in the back of the throat. Irina looks concerned. This particular grade of noise has that effect on people. They think I'm choking.

"When do I get paid?"

She is rifling through her bag of tricks and doesn't look at me as she says, "At the end of the week."

"But yesterday you said it would be today."

"Change of plan." Her face is all harsh angles, her cheekbones pointed, jutting like they could cut through skin—her own, and someone else's, if you got too close.

I decide now is not the best time to push this particular line of inquiry, so I choose to believe her, kind of, although Fisticuffs is knocking her weight about in there. "Hey," she's saying, "wake up, dummy." I've been known to ignore her warnings before, and usually by then it's too late.

I take half the pill (although I have every intention of swallowing the other half just as soon as Irina is gone), then

I succumb to her makeover, her fingers sliding over my face. The war paint acts as a barrier of sorts. Look at me: I'm so pretty, and I'm caked. I snort.

"How is your new roommate?" she asks.

"Keeps herself to herself. She looks way too young to be doing this kind of thing."

The woman is silent.

"I doubt she's done this before." Again, a picture of her in bed beneath Mark grabs me by the throat and rattles me around a bit. "Her English is really good, like yours. I can only speak about three sentences of French. Shitty school system we have here. You guys must be doing something right."

The woman gets out of the chair, gripping onto the side of the table, stands, steadies herself, then leaves, treading heavily this time. She passes Nico, who's coming out of the bathroom, a towel wrapped tightly around her, skin glistening, and says something to her in their own language. Nico nods.

I turn my back to let her get dressed. "Is this going to be your first time?" I ask the wall, which doesn't answer. "Make sure you take one of the pills that knocks the edges off, and just let them get on with it. It'll be over before you know it." I hear a gulping sound, like she's just come up for air. I turn around to face her and she's sitting on the side of the bed, dressed in clothes that are more suited to a slut like me. I watch as her small body is racked with sobs that won't come. She's doing a really good job of battling them.

Then I hear her voice, trying to steady itself as it speaks. "Magda no allow."

I wonder who Magda is, or was, but don't want to get drawn into any conversation that might weaken her for the night ahead; she's going to need all her fight, so I laugh and say, "Whoever the fuck Magda is, she deprived you, big time. You might even find you enjoy it!"

"You are that shape of girl, but that is not I," she says in her crystal-clear Enid-Blyton voice, her English archaic and bookish. Miss High and Mighty is back and I'm glad; she can go some way towards protecting herself that way. Irina comes back into the room with her bag, and in silence, the older woman gestures to the younger to sit on the chair in front of the mirror. I watch as her fingers slide over the wide planes of newbie's face, sweeping powder over her high cheekbones. She applies lip gloss and mascara and asks Nico to stick out her tongue. She then takes a toothbrush from her bag and scrapes it down. Maybe the princess has a bad smell in her mouth, maybe her insides are rotting.

Nico's eyes are open and she is staring blank eyed at the image of herself in the glass, and I wonder if she has managed to erase the outside world. A good trick, that one: eyes open, yet unseeing. The men wouldn't know the difference. They wouldn't like closed eyes; it would remove their power over us, that submission they like to imagine they see as we lie beneath them.

When the makeover is complete, Nico looks almost old enough to be going to work on the night shift. A soundless giggle plays out in my chest. The layer of foundation on her face mutes her natural glow, the powder on top cheapens her and she looks better able to handle the coming night. Irina hands her the pill and a glass of water.

"No, thank you," she says.

Irina tells her she may need it later and puts it into a pouch in the glossy patent-leather handbag, an exact replica of the one she gave to me. The Handbag Girls.

"Do you know how to use one of these?" Irina says, as she holds up a condom still in its wrapper.

Nico looks away. "Yes," she says, "Magda showed me."

I want to shout at her to insist that the men wear them, but I just laugh, loudly. Neither of them look my way.

"It is time."

The two of us follow Irina, who has managed to get her glide back, to the front door where Mr. Taxi stands.

"Joe," Irina says, nodding at him.

So, Taxi Joe. I laugh. He looks at me, checking to see I'm not wrecked again.

"Ladies . . . ," he says, as he walks down the path, gesturing at us to follow him. His gaze rests on Nico's face for a moment, and then he looks away. There's something holy about her—she'd definitely have been cast as Mary in the school nativity play—and I like to imagine he's fighting an impulse to bless himself. We follow, Nico teetering in the high, needle-thin heels. I put my arm out to steady her and she holds on.

In the back of the car, I stare at the fleshy neck in front. Tonight his collar is even tighter, pushing the fat into angry red bulges that seem to be wiggling, like live things, ranting at each other. I dig Nico in the ribs. She doesn't react. We both settle back into the seats, looking out steamed-up windows. I wonder what she sees out there. Rain is drizzling onto the gray concrete. We drive for over an hour out to the countryside, until the car pulls up outside a fuck-off mansion, fields all around. The lawn that surrounds it is floodlit. A blast of ice bombards my body; my skin is hot and sticky.

"Where are we?" I ask Taxi Joe.

He taps the side of his nose as he gets out to open the door.

"Wait," I say, "how will we contact you if anything goes wrong?"

He looks at me like a worried dad, just for a moment, until he remembers what we are. "When they are finished with you, they will call," he says.

My imagination is pumping into overdrive and I see the two of us in a rich man's cellar, handcuffed and flayed. I wish I hadn't picked that stupid book up. "What is this place?"

He decides on the silent treatment.

For a moment I consider running, then I pop another Mr. Floaty (I nicked a few extra when Irina was focusing on Nico's face) and tell myself it'll be fine, just another client, just another night, and I'll have a big, fat paycheck at the end of the week.

Taxi Joe's fat finger presses down on the doorbell.

I look at Nico, who has gone, disappeared, vamoosed. Seriously, I mean she's standing upright and her heart is hammering away, but she's not there, not really. I'm spooking myself even more. I kinda want to give her the kiss of life. A butler dude answers the door, nods at Taxi Joe, doesn't look at us, but gestures to follow him down a long hallway. And here, Miss Samantha Harvey, are the real-deal chandeliers you have been craving. Dadedelahdahadah! We are walking down a red carpet, lines of faces waving at us to get our autographs. Trays of Champagne bob about, held aloft by white-fingered gloved hands. A door closes behind the butler guy, and I notice six glasses and a bottle of Moët & Chandon. Six glasses.

I look around at the dark mahogany-panel walls, roaring fire, dining-room table, and high-backed chairs, like something out of a medieval banquet. Plum velvet curtains are pulled across a window, which is, I'm sure, framing a splendid view of a fountain or a lake, or a pond with golden carp.

I pour two glasses and hand one to Nico. She shakes her head. "Go on," I tell her, "it's deeelicious!" She takes the glass, sniffs it, and sips daintily. I can tell she likes the sensation of the bubbles sliding down her throat. Bubbles are always soothing, in the bath, or in the glass. I try to force out a laugh to warm up the hollow room, but it sounds desperate even to my ears, so I glug silently instead.

A man enters the room, dressed in a suit. His hair is slicked back off his face, not greasy, but perfectly styled. He smells of Paco Rabanne, or Dolce & Gabbana's The One (an educated guess—something pricey and pungent, anyway). He smiles easily at us.

"Good evening, girls," he says. "You're most welcome."

I look at Nico, who is swaying on her feet. God, has the champers had that much effect already, or is she just feeling unsteady on those spiky heels? I try to smile back at him but can only manage to move one side of my mouth. Two floaters and one glass of champers.

"Our guests this evening are important men. I hope you will show them a good time, yes?"

Them.

"One of you is intact?" he asks, staring at Nico.

I splutter. You've got to be kidding me. Others walk into the room: all men in suits, all important-seeming men with big, loud, booming voices. They sound posh, like they went to Oxford or Cambridge or Trinity. Some of them have strange, clipped accents, maybe South African. I'd say the youngest is forty-fiveish. I can see the tabloid headline: "Poshies on Sex Safari in the Arse Hole of Nowhere," and I don't want to imagine the rest of it. Why didn't Irina send more of us? The men sprawl out in the big leather armchairs and gesture for us to sit on the arms. I empty out inside and allow myself to go floppy. Nico is stiff as a board.

29

Nico

My face is covered in makeup by Irina's fingers; I'm disguised so I don't look like myself and I am glad. I'm told to wear dark lace underclothes, and I think of Magda and the girl she put to sleep, and of Ana and the other girls in the room. Sammy is watching closely and I wish she wouldn't. Being witnessed makes this more real. I try to imagine we are characters in a book, or on the screen—someone else is writing this life now.

We're brought to a car by a fat man wearing a too-tight collar. In the back seat, Sammy is laughing silently at his ugly rolls of squashed flesh, and elbows me in the ribs. It's more disgusting than funny, but with this girl, everything is funny. When she thinks I'm not looking, I can see her smirking at me, eyes shining, holding back the laughter that would like to burst out of her. I wonder why she held her arm out to steady me. Would she not have laughed at seeing me fall?

After some time, the car pulls up outside a huge house made of gray bricks, surrounded by flat, silent fields draped in cobwebs of misty rain. The driveway is lined with tall narrow trees I have never seen before, their green branches dense yet feathery. There are bright lights flooding the ground, making it seem like a lake. I try to steady myself on my heels, which catch on the slimy loose stones, and I imagine reeds wrapping around my ankles, trying to drag me down to the depths. The door is black and monstrous, as if from a tale Papa would have told. A bell rings out and a man wearing white gloves answers. He speaks to the driver, pretending he doesn't see us. As I cross the threshold, I bless myself secretively, like Magda did, as if I'm brushing dust off my top.

We are brought to a long, high, empty room with beautiful markings on the ceiling, the corners etched into concrete peaks of whipped cream. Mama would love it here. The chairs are like giants' chairs, tall and straight backed. There is a fire in the center of the room and I watch the flames dance as wind from outside blows down the chimney. Sammy comes up beside me with a glass of clear liquid that sparkles in the reflection of the light hanging from the ceiling. This is where Magda said she would bring me: to a place of crystal lights, soft carpets, and rich men who "will not want to hurt you so much as pleasure you." I can hear her voice wafting on the air.

"Champers," Sammy says. She drinks back a mouthful. "Go on, it'll help take the edge off."

I think of the smell of alcohol on Victor and Sergiu's breath and shake my head, but then Magda's shrieking voice, the last time she called out to me, rings in my ears: "Stop, Nico. Come back." I reach for the glass. I'm the one who is responsible for wherever she might be. The bubbles help soften the sore when I swallow.

Six men walk into the room, all Papa's age, smelling of spice and tobacco and wearing crisp suits and polished shoes. They act as if they do not see us as they talk among themselves, pouring amber and clear alcohol into chiseled glasses, patting each other on the back. Their voices are loud and echoing. Sammy and I have moved to the edge of the room, away from the light. After some time, the men settle themselves into the armchairs and turn their attention to us.

"Well, hello," one of them says. "We didn't see you there, hiding like shadows. Come on out and let us have a good, long look at you."

I wonder why they are lying. "Turn around," the same man says.

We do. There are claps and Sammy starts to bend her body from the waist, like a strange dance. The men clap even more. I stand tall and stiff, like Luca used to before the brothers would put him in the barrel. I think of him standing by the door, watching me leave, his hands tightened into fists, his muscles straining against his clothes.

The men gesture at us to sit on the edge of their chairs and one of them puts his hand on my thigh. I want to kick him off, but I think of Magda's words: "Do not resist, it is easier that way." Mama appears for a moment. There is no fighting with fate. No point. A thin, wailing sound is coming from deep inside her.

The man pulls me down onto his lap, murmuring in my ear, "Oh, beautiful, beautiful . . . have you ever seen anything so beautiful?" He announces to the room, "Finders keepers . . . and I must have. I will pay whatever the price."

The other men make strange sounds like dark animals grunting in the fields as they circle around Sammy. I wonder, was it true when she said, "Maybe you'll enjoy it"?

The man's hand has crept further up my thigh and his fingers are opening me up. I have left my body and am watching from a distance. He stands, takes my hand, and leads me out of the room. I'm surprised my legs have not given way beneath me; they do not feel as if they are made of muscle and bone. There are noises of approval from behind me. I hope Sammy will not have to make the other men utter those sounds.

There is a way of blurring what is in front of you. I allow myself to see only the outline of things: the bed is big and I am small, the man is heavy and old and smells of soap and alcohol. He asks many questions but does not wait to hear my answers. He undresses me slowly, pulling off his own clothes in haste. I feel hair on my skin and his breath on my face. I tear and burn as he breaks me open, invading my body as he leaves his. He is trying to climb deep inside me, filling all my spaces with his everything. I hold my breath for as long as it lasts, feeling as if I'm under water. If I don't breathe I'm not really there, not really. The man does not look at me.

After, when the man lies panting on the bed beside me, he looks down and cries out, "Why didn't you say?"

Say what? I look down at my body and see that my legs

are covered in red. Magda told me it would be so. This is what he wanted. Why is he lying, again lying? Maybe he needs to believe his own lies, telling himself, "I am not that kind of a man," maybe he is asking for my forgiveness, maybe he's feeling guilty after all. I wonder if he has children. I don't want this man seeing this part of me, I don't want this man anywhere near me—blood rushes to my face, belonging only to me. I feel myself flow back down inside myself, although I am altered—my body has taken on a different shape and form and I am not sure I will ever live in it fully again.

His face closes as he gets out of bed and dresses himself. "Thank you, dear. You will be paid richly."

Perhaps it is this thought that allowed him to do this—except, I will not be paid at all.

I am left in the room and look at the wall as if there is a picture of Mother Mary there, but there is none. I sit and stare at the blank spot and wonder, will others come? Then I pull the sheets from the bed and see a few stray hairs from the man's head, which are white and thin. I do not know why I do this but I pick them up and put them in my pocket.

I go the bathroom and find soap and scrub the sheets. It's making it worse, like the night of the staining, so I bundle the sheet into a tight little ball and hide it beneath the bed, then I sit on top of the bedcovers, hunched into the same tight shape, and wait.

After some time, counting backwards from a hundred, thirty times, I risk taking a short shower, although I do not want to be caught naked. I allow the water to spray between my legs, but I do not wish to see. Then I quickly dry myself and put on my clothes and walk down the hallway towards the room where we first came in. There is only the smell of cigar smoke and the lingering sound of Sammy's laughter. I fold myself into one of the big chairs. In my mind, I write the end of the story of the girl in the cellar. I finger the wispy hair in my pocket, feeling sick and feeling strong.

The door opens. "It is time to go now."

I follow the small man with the white gloves to the front door. The taxi driver with the fat neck and fingers is standing outside. As I step through the door, I feel a dark, shadowy presence perched on my shoulder. It is whispering: beautiful, beautiful. I try to shake it off, but it has claws that will not loosen their grip.

The morning sunshine is white and weak. Sammy is in the car, her head against the window.

"Hi, Roomie," she says when she sees me.

I want to ask her, but I know this would be the worst thing, so I try to smile.

"Aha! I knew I could crack one of those," she says, as she turns her back on me and pushes her body tight against the plastic door so she looks tiny. My heart flies up and out of my mouth. It cannot find a way back in, so I sit there with a hole in my chest, as it—a beating, hurting thing—flies aimlessly around the car, looking for somewhere to land.

30

Sammy

Oh, I'm a boozy woozy floozy all right. Woozy, boozy, floozy in the jacuzzi. I'm singing along in my head to my own manic tune. Heigh-ho, heigh-ho, it's off to work we go . . . The old guy with the gray hair is snaking his hand up Nico's skirt. Heigh-ho, heigh-ho. I start to bray loudly. To my own ears I sound like a donkey, okay so, Luce, like a demented baby donkey. Heigh-ho. Ho. Ho. My body is hollow and I am light. Mr. Floaty is doing the trick. I see the man leading Nico out of the room, his veiny hand on her arse. I want to scream, till the world cries out . . . I want to follow her and say to the ole lecher, forget about her, have me, have me . . . but I don't . . . I don't and my insides are hardening, caked. I wonder if the blood flow is obstructed. I drink some more. The faces surrounding me are hazy, their voices muffled. They're all clamoring for my autograph, telling me how beautiful I am, how talented. Superlative—in that role as the whore with no heart. Once Nico has left the room, there is no reason to be afraid. The worst is happening to her right now and I haven't tried to stop it.

Someone keeps filling my glass; there's the sound of clapping as I swallow. I really am a wonderful actress, wonderful. I curtsy and the applause gets louder, ringing in my ears. The sensation of tongues in my mouth, hands on my breasts, inside me, I think. I drink some more. My stomach is burning from the booze. Ah, the wooze. Thank God for the wooze. I get it, Mother: edgy, but with the edges worn off. Black spots swim in front of my eyes. I am led to a room with a bed. Whiteout. Blankety blank. Thank fuck. Whatever is happening to me right now will not be remembered. No consciousness. None. Falling and flying, and laughing. That sound still comes.

I wake and I'm alone, sore and sticky and cold. Gray-white light floods the room. Stabbing sensation in my head. I sit up slowly and puke all over the beautiful cream, soft pile carpet. I get up to go to the toilet and then I'm on my knees, on the cold tiled floor, wave after wave of it coming up and out of me. Please God, no. Not on my knees, never on my knees. I force myself to stand. Please forgive me for what I've done. Who is this God I'm crying out to? What the hell has He ever done for me? When the tidal wave stops, I get a facecloth and soap and try to remove the vomit and the staining. There is a floral-scented room spray, "Spring Bouquet" it says, and I spritz and I spritz. Then I turn on the shower and stand under its scalding spray. This is one of those tropical rainforest showers, the ones that spray you from all directions to make sure you're clean inside and out. Floaters float before my eyes and I give myself a little slap. Wouldn't do to faint and be found naked in a shower. The shame of that, Mother. I step out, dry myself off, put back on the skirt and top, bundling the underwear into the handbag. They need to be put in a plastic bag and drowned.

I have to get out of this room, out of this place, back through that door, that portal. As I walk slowly along the corridor I see there is no red carpet beneath my feet. It's all cream, subdued, and in perfectly good taste. Mr. Butler appears, and I do my best to light him up with my mega-wattage smile that I've been told illuminates me from within. Nothing happens. The batteries are dead. He opens the door and I see that our golden chariot awaits. I hope the slumbering princess is inside, I hope she's okay; the most I can hope for is that she survived. Taxi Joe has a look of disgust on his face as he sees me, barefooted, bare-arsed (although I'm pretty sure he can't tell that), stepping carefully over the gravel. Wouldn't do to get a splinter now, would it?

I climb into the back seat and can hear Dad's voice: "Okay, love, you'll be right as rain in no time. You'll see." Dad of the bland. What does that even mean anyway? What the fuck is right about rain? Sleep is the antidote. Sleep is the thing, to numb, to recuperate, rejuvenate, recharge the batteries. When we wake later today, all this will be a distant memory, although thank fuck I won't have many of those. The head is not working properly yet. That is definitely the way to do it. Wipeout.

I'm relieved to see Nico is in the car already, although I don't like the shadows under her eyes, the shadows that seem to dance in the air about her head. I have to stop looking at her—the things that crash into my mind are too much. I hope next time she'll listen to me and take the helping hand of Mr. Floaty, so at least her body could soften. I worry she might be snapped in two.

I have an image of the two of us swimming in the sea, newly baptized, our sins—and the sins of those inside of us—washed clean. Since she mentioned the sea, I've had this thing in my head: I want to go swimming in the rain. Weird, seeing as I've only ever gone swimming in Ireland once before, and it was so, so bloody cold my whole body broke out in purple spots and I had to down a flagon of whiskey to get the blood flowing again. The Med, on the other hand—Dad, Mother, and I, in Majorca, on a tasteful side of the island, far from the madding crowd (one of Mother's favorites, back in the day, when she could still concentrate enough to read). I'm ten and Mother's pissed at me, at life, at Dad. She's also just pissed. The sun is a perfect yellow disc in the high blue sky and hugs me daily with its warming, soothing rays. Dad and I make sandcastles—even though I'm really too old—and he buries me up to my neck. The best part is running into the crystal sea and washing all the grainy bits away. Mother finds the sun too bright, the light too exposing. She stays indoors until after sundown. I don't mind. I have Dad all to myself.

I curl myself against the hard door, feeling its solidity. The doors are locked, child-locked, in case anyone decides to make a run for it. The white light outside makes me shut my eyes. Maybe I'll live my life in the shade now, always wanting curtains drawn, dark glasses on, blinds down. The car trundles along, a lulling motion beneath me. Taxi Joe stops at a petrol station, fills her up, gets back in, stuffs his mouth full of crisps and coffee. He offers us one—one crisp by hand, like he's feeding animals through a cage. Neither of us takes him up on his fine offer. I catch her eye, which glints—a tear, or a laugh, or both?

The car pulls up outside the house and Nico and I both pad barefoot up the newly tarred driveway. The inky blackness beneath me is swelling and rolling. Is this the Black Sea? Are we walking on water? We are special, all right, the chosen ones. It's weird not finding that funny, the thought just rolls up and out before I have time to laugh. Nico's legs look tiny and frail; all her athleticism seems to have been sucked out of her after the night's sport.

Irina is waiting at the door and her usually blank face wears a look of worry that cuts deep.

"Come in," she says, "you must eat something"—like she's playing the part of a loving mum. We both follow her into the kitchen where some other girls are seated, the sisters and another one who I've never seen before, could be Eastern European, with her wide eyes and face. She's older than the rest of us and plain, in a soft, pudgy, unremarkable way. I doubt any of the guys in school would have given her a ride, I think harshly, appraising her wares, but still I don't laugh. It's super early and that birdie is singing her little heart out. I wish she wouldn't do that; it makes my whole body ache. Winter is coming and soon she'll fly away to sunnier climes, thank fuck. How do they rev up their batteries to that extent, power up their tiny bodies to travel thousands, even hundreds of thousands of miles? It must be the singing that does it, generates that kind of turbo boost. I know that feeling myself, although I can't think of a single song right now, not a single Eminem lyric to inspire. Blankety blank, and into the gaps the songbird tweets.

Nico sips a glass of OJ slowly as she stares out the window, her face blurred at the edges. Granny Mona always wore that rheumy, misty, eyes-full-of-tears look at the end. I used to watch her watch her daughter, when she couldn't speak, and those eyes said it all: How did this happen? What did I do wrong? Poor old Granny Mona always had a soft spot for me, buying me bags of licorice and dipping sticks, which Mother would confiscate the minute we left the stinking old folks' home where Granny'd been left to rot.

"She's the reason I am the way I am," Mother used to say.

Funny that, 'cause I always thought it was because of me.

I pour a long, cold glass of water and sip slowly, scared of the ripping sensation in my throat.

Irina says, "I did not know about last night until after you were gone."

She seems to be pleading for some sort of forgiveness. She's an intermediary between their world and ours, belonging to neither, and that must be shit lonely. Me, on the other hand, I could just get up and walk right out of here, but not until I get paid. Triple pay for that fucking fiasco, thank you very much. I hope the memories don't come crashing in days later like that time I took shrooms with Brian, and a week later, shards of what happened pierced through me. Technicolor memories, accompanied by loud techno music; harsh, strobing memories that assailed me for months after. I couldn't know if any of it was real.

True, false, or imagined, I don't ever want to think of this night.

"You must all get some rest now," Irina says. "What happened was not meant to happen. You will not have to service so many men again."

I can see the other girls shift and squirm. Not one face looks into hers. I wonder what she heard about last night. Is she speaking to the other girls as much as to us? Were they sent to a similar party? I can feel her gaze burning into me. Fuck Irina, this isn't going to help, so I get up and walk out, slamming the door behind me, although why I do that is anyone's guess. It's not going to provoke a reaction, it's not going to recharge or reenergize or re-anything at all. Is there a rewind after tonight? Is there a reframing that can happen? Is there a reworkable title to the thing that took place? Re-re-re-re-re-reeeeeeeee—one of the school counselor's favorite prefixes.

I get into bed, putting on the long-sleeved, long-legged PJs that smell of fresh lavender and burrow into the quilt, inhaling a field of perfumed purples and blues, and I fall into a deep bruise of a sleep.

When I wake, I see Nico sitting in her bed with a notebook on her knees and pen in her mouth, which she's biting down on and rolling between her teeth. I watch her for some time before I can think of a way to lighten the mood.

"Writing a bestseller?" I ask.

She smiles at me out of the corner of her mouth. I try on one myself and it seems to crack the surface of my skin. An engine is revving, cranking itself up, and before I know what I'm doing, I throw the covers off the bed, jump out and do a hoopla dance, a rain dance, a mad-thing-possessed dance. I pull up my sleeves and roll up my bottoms, splashing about in puddles. Something in Nico's face stops me. I look down and see what she sees: my arms are circled, blotched, mottled. Purples, blues, pinks. Dizzy and breathless, I plonk myself at the edge of the bed as my brain somersaults, whacking itself against the fleshy insides. Insane, insane in the membrane. Granny Mona appears beside the bed, stroking my forehead, cooing, and clucking, while Mother is passed out downstairs; then she leaves, she leaves me alone in that house.

31

Nico

Irina looks like a ghost has slipped inside her as she apologizes for what happened tonight. I follow Sammy to our room after she slams out of the kitchen. She has pushed herself down under the duvet and I can see the shape of her, rising and falling. I am scared to go to sleep in case I fall into the well again, so I take out the notebook and pen, and draw squiggles, lines, circles, dots, then I press the pen onto the page and scribble over the whole thing. The ink is blue, making it appear like a jagged whorling sky. I tear the page with the pressure and feel a little better. I bite down on the pen. No words will come. The creature on my shoulder is still there, its whispers quieter now.

After some hours, Sammy's bed moves and groans, as she pops her head out. Her face is puffed and red and her swirly head of hair looks like hedgehogs made their home there. I can't help smiling. She tries one back; it's twisted and hard. She asks me if I'm writing a book, and seems delighted with the idea. She throws her legs over the side of the bed, stands for a moment, then sways and shakes and stamps to some imaginary music. She pulls up her sleeves and her sleeping trousers and I see that her body is covered in marks—handcuffs or hands grabbing at her, encircling her, holding her down. She stops dancing as she sees the reflection in my eyes. I worry she might faint from the shock of seeing their imprint on her, but she just sits, dazed.

There are no bars on the windows, no men with guns, no chains tying us down. The weight of that thought crashes into the room and settles on us both. Without having to speak, I know we are thinking the same thing.

She looks closely at me. "Did he hurt you?"

I shake my head. I knew from what Magda told me that what happened last night would happen, the first time.

A type of silence grows tall and strong, like the beanstalk in Jack's fairy tale. We could climb high and crash through the roof.

In that instant we make a pact, and I imagine us spitting and shaking on it, like the cowboys in the films Maria and I used to watch.

I look out the window and let my eyes soften and blur with the rain. Mama always loved the rain. "So much promise," she used to say, "so much new life . . . as if the pregnant skies above are breaking their waters."

A loud grumbling sound comes from my stomach. Mama's voice still lingers in the air: "Food will help soothe the rising fear." And I am surprised to find that I am hungry, or maybe it is the hole inside of me that is crying out to be filled.

"Sounds like you have the acid monster in there too, eating you from the inside out," Sammy says.

This makes no sense to me, except I understand she means it as a joke. I close the notebook, pressing the man's hairs between the back pages, careful not to let Sammy see—this has to be my secret—and we both go to the kitchen in our sleeping clothes. In the hall we meet Irina, and Sammy asks her when she'll be paid.

"At the end of the week," Irina says, her eyes looking anywhere but at her. They look into mine for a moment and then dart away. Sammy moves towards the door and pushes against it, half-heartedly, not looking at me. She cannot really believe their lies.

We go into the kitchen and see Ling sitting on her own at the table, eating.

"Morning," Sammy sings. "Have a good night?"

Ling doesn't react, just continues to eat, methodically, with great focus.

Being ignored seems to make Sammy angry and her color rises as her words speed up. "How about a trip to the seaside, Ling?"

Ling's eyes look like deep black holes. "We cannot," she says. "I here twelve weeks and no time away."

"What, not even a Sunday?" Sammy says.

Ling rolls her eyes. "The men no care what day of week is."

Sammy breaks a croissant in two, slides butter and dark

pink jam on it, and chews loudly, her jaw clicking, though she doesn't seem to swallow. "I'll organize a day's outing and we can all go swimming."

Ling looks out the window as droplets of rain wriggle down the pane. "In rain?"

"Yes," Sammy says. "In the rain. You'll love it, Ling."

Ling shivers and wraps her arms around her body.

Sammy's voice is getting louder and higher as she paces in circles. "We'll dive under the crashing waves, and let the water tumble us around, head over butt, heel over tit, upside-down inside-out."

Although her words are flowing fast and make no sense, in a strange way they make perfect sense. They conjure images in my mind the way musical notes do, and I can see a vision of us all swimming in the sea, upside-down inside-out, clean.

Ling is scowling at the thought, and this makes Sammy laugh even louder. "I'll kidnap you from your bed when you're sleeping and tie you up, and only let you go when you're in the cold, gray sea!"

"I no swim."

Sammy puts her arms around her neck. "That's okay, old sport, I'll teach you." She sounds and looks like the men in the room last night, her grip tightening around Ling's small neck.

"There's a first time for everything, eh, Roomie?" She looks at me with a cold glint and winks. "Never as bad as all that now, is it?" she says to me, then whispers in Ling's ear, "I'll show you how it's done!" Her voice has lowered and is clipped. For a moment I wonder if those men last night were bats of the night. Maybe this is what is sitting on my shoulder. I shake my head and brush my left shoulder. Ling tells her to stop and hits out at her with her other hand. She seems genuinely afraid. Sammy hits back and then the two of them are slapping, kicking, and screaming. This is no game.

I get a glass of water and pour it over their heads, like Mama did when a stray bitch wandered into our yard and got her teeth stuck into our hound. Both dogs squealed and let go—the girls do the same. Sammy looks at me, grinning wildly, and then picks up the rest of the glass and throws the water in my face, then down Ling's back. Neither of us reacts as Sammy builds herself into a fever. She has that look of cruel glee I used to see in Sergiu and Victor's eyes as they'd pull ponytails, or tails, peals of laughter falling from their mouths.

The door opens and the silent sisters look on, their faces stony. One of them walks in and before I know what I'm doing, my shaking hand is filling a glass with water, and I throw it at her, flinging the whole glass, so it shatters at her feet. Still, not a flicker of emotion in their faces.

"Wake up, zombies," I shout, words that are not mine tumbling out of me, in a voice that does not belong to me, but to my older brothers. The room falls silent, and I am trembling, hot with rage and shame.

The two sisters freeze, their bodies like Mama's at the end, emptied and stiff. They walk out of the room slowly and carefully as if they might break. I want to follow them out and say, "Sorry, I don't know what came over me," but no amount of sorrys will make up for what I've just done.

We are all silent until Sammy puts on the radio and turns up the volume. A voice that could be a man or a woman sings about a lost love: "Won't you stay with me . . . ?"

Sammy calls it "soppy shit" and turns a dial that changes the music. This time it has loud beats and harsh edges, exactly the same noise the men in the van played. My body reverberates sickly as Sammy starts to dance around the wet floor. Her feet stamp and her body rocks, her head banging against the air. I am surprised she would let us see this. I would not want anyone to see me shaking my head, even though it would help me clear the vicious thoughts. I wonder why she is so full of dance. I wonder how her body is able, after last night.

"Come on, ladies," she shouts at the room. "Come on, headbanger," to me, "you know you want to!"

No one moves.

She jumps, twists, shouts, stamps, oblivious.

I feel a strange and strong desire to push her out of her happy place, make her tumble far below, push her in a barrel, and hear her squeal. Maybe those men last night were bats of the night and I was bitten, infected. The cruel voices inside my head do not belong to me.

32

Sammy

Even though I'm sore as hell, I'm possessed by a crazy energy this morning—capable of murdering someone, setting the place on fire, cutting myself to shreds with the kitchen knife, or maybe chopping Taxi Joe into little bits of lard and swirling him around in the pan.

There's a roaring inside me, a relentless revving, like someone put the pedal flat to the floor, in a stationary car. A blurred image from last night is hovering just behind my eyes. Five of them. Dance, monkey, dance.

Nico looks like she hasn't slept a wink. Her stomach is gurgling, which I guess is a good sign; she's hungry, it's all still working in there. "Come on, brekkie?"

We're on our way to the kitchen when we bump into Irina in the hall. That woman is everywhere. I decide on the direct approach, so I tell her I want to get paid and want to leave, just like that. She sucks in her cheeks and says, "Next week," before drifting away to her hidey-hole, her lookout, from where she can observe her kingdom. I go to the front door and try to open it, kind of, 'cause the reality of this place is sinking in, kind of, although it has to be different for me. I'm Irish—I can't just disappear like these other girls. What did Hatchet say? "Count yourself lucky. Some of the girls from overseas . . . earn nothing. Most of them never get out." Not *my* story.

Ling's sad little eyes piss me off when I walk into the kitchen. She's not meant to look like this. Ling, you're meant to be my sidekick, my bratty baby sister, and here you are letting the side down with your sad, tired face. Wipe that look off, or I'll wipe it for you. I put my arm around her neck, to give her a friendly hug, except the pressure against her windpipe makes her eyes go poppy. She hits, hisses, bites. That's more like it, my little firebrand. Then Nico throws water over us like we're rabid dogs. I chuck one back and a full-on water fight starts with me as the only player. Ling looks terrified, and I get a kick.

The sisters enter and Nico throws water at one of them, the glass shooting from her hand, shattering at their feet. Her cheeks flare and roar and she shouts something in her own language, like a bonkers banshee. The girls freeze, their bodies hardening into resigned statues, their response muted, hopeless even, as if this is something they've experienced many, many times before, but not from a girl like Nico. This seems so out of character for her (although what do I know, never been the best judge before), that I put it down to a kind of delayed reaction to trauma, a kind of misdirected anger. We spoke about this in my counseling sessions and although I laughed at the idea then, I can see it play out here. I guess it's always easier to recognize this stuff in someone else. I make some inane comment, not really in the mood to debate the merits (or not) of this line of thought, and pump up the volume, find some house crap, and dance it all out. The world has slipped its axis and I am off my head, out of my brain, no substances taken. Isn't this what they call a natural high?

I get a stool and push it under the kitchen window and climb up, opening the window as far as it'll go, which isn't very far at all, as it turns out, like every other feckin' window in the place. I ram my elbow against the glass, again and again, heat and energy propelling me on as the others stand staring like mute, dumb animals.

"Help me, throw something, come on let's go, now, now, come on, Miss Romania." The glass is impervious to the battering. Nico doesn't move, she seems paralyzed, entranced by her own shitty behavior. I bash my whole body against the glass, a battering ram, until suddenly I stop, aware that someone else has walked into the kitchen and is watching me. A dark, male presence.

Hands pull me down, a voice pours into my ear, stabbing and insistent, jerking around in strange halting English. He grabs the top of my arm, which is covered in bruises, and it's like a metal clamp. None of the girls move. Another man enters and two sets of hands encircle me, and I'm being lifted, carried the length of the hall, into a room where the curtains are drawn. The two men place me on a table, one holding my legs, the other my arms. "Shhhhh, good girl."

I've never felt such rage—like one of those cartoon characters that have smoke pouring out their ears.

I hear mumbling, and snippets of: ". . . good girl . . . over soon . . ." The pricks prick me. There's no fighting with this woozy; it's too strong. All the angry eruptions I've ever heard in my life, and some I've never heard before, pour out of me. I cover you with my curses: I curse you and yours and your unborn babies, I curse the eyes you see with, the tongue you speak with, the skin that encases your body, the bones that hold you up. I curse you with a painful, slow, cancerous death.

When I wake, I'm in the pink bedroom and Nico is at the bedside table in front of the mirror, being daubed and lacquered. She's wearing a teeny twinset of leather skirt and cropped top. Irina is applying touches of gloss, the final sweep of powder. If I could make that woman wither and die by my stare, I would, but then I think of the looks Luce visited on Mother over the years and know that no good will come of them. I mean, if Luce never managed it . . . It's not Irina's fault anyway. We're just tiny pieces in a devil's chess game. There goes his big hairy hand descending from the sky, lifting Irina's tiny hand to apply the powder to the dewy skin of a girl-pawn, in this single-sided game of moves and countermoves.

Are there men hiding behind walls and scrubby trees outside this house, is there an invisible electric fence, or is there simply a wall of evil between all those who enter and all those outside? How do the guards not know about places like this, with the cars coming and going late at night? There are other houses like this on the street, I'm sure of it. I'm bamboozled with all the drugs in my system but something tells me, some hunch, that punch-in-the-guts kind of intuition, that a run for it would definitely end with a blasted body.

Nico notices me staring at her and makes a tiny movement of her head backwards. I nod back. Irina pretends not to notice and tells Nico to "Hup," it's time to go. I hadn't noticed it before, but it's not just Irina who hovers above the ground—all the girls glide in this house, which must come from losing substance, losing a part of themselves. This place is spinning so far out of orbit, gravity doesn't apply.

Whatever sedative they pumped into me is making it hard to hold on to any thought for long. My brain is like a washing machine, all jumbled up and soapy, and my body won't do as it's instructed. The muscles inside seem to be loose and I can't hold on. There goes the devil's hand again, pressing me back against the cold, wet sheets. You chose the wrong girl, horned man. You chose the wrong victim.

He's sitting on my chest now so it's hard to breathe.

33

Nico

Sammy is dancing, dancing, again dancing, banging her head so hard it looks like it might fall off, then she climbs on a stool and throws herself against the window over and over in a frenzy, when I notice a man standing in the doorframe, watching her. This is the first time I've seen a man in the house and it makes my body shake so hard it seems as if parts of me might break off. A second man walks into the kitchen and they both lift her as she flings her body against the glass. She shrieks like a ripped fairy cap in the wind. I cannot move, not believing this is really happening, not believing I am capable of doing what I just did, saying what I just said.

Irina shakes her head at me and puts her fingers to her lips. Silence. Someone taught you that well. Into that silence tumbles all sorts of noises: hissing, buzzing like giant flies, thumping beats, and it goes round and round.

The fat taxi man and others like him are circling this place. There are seeing eyes planted outside.

Irina tells me to follow her to the bedroom and turns a key in the lock when she leaves. Everything changes into something else. I see a younger version of Mama, looking like me, sitting at the end of the bed: "Maybe you'll meet a man who will want to marry you, maybe he'll allow you to become a teacher, maybe the good police will come and free you, *draga mea*, my little chick." Maybe, Mama. She reaches out to touch my hair and disappears. I place my hand at my throat to try to dissolve the lump.

Maybe Mama is right and the police will come. I saw how frightened Igor was of the men in uniforms in the airport—although in this place, this "Dub" of which Sammy speaks, maybe these things are allowed.

The light in the sky is fading from gray to a darker shade of blue. The navy night sky is prettier here than the dreary daytime gray, the clouds seem to lift and the pressure eases, while another sort of pressure builds up inside. The key in the door turns and Irina enters with one of the men from earlier, who lifts Sammy back into her bed. I feel my whole body stiffen. Sammy is floppy like a cloth doll whose stuffing has been pulled out of her. I am happy to see her chest rising and falling, hear her gentle snore-song. Although her energy is high and strong, beneath her laughter and dancing, this girl is more hurt than I can imagine. I don't think she had a favorite tree, or a brother like Luca, or a mama like mine.

Irina is carrying a short skirt, bra, and black underwear

in her arms for me, as well as her bag with its brushes and lipstick and eyelash wand. I dress, sit at the table, and let her fingers draw a new face onto mine.

Sammy stirs and one eye opens. I attempt a smile. Irina pretends not to notice that Sammy is awake, but I can see her looking at her sideways and her jaw relaxes and her lips loosen, making her mouth seem plump, and not tight as it normally looks. She rubs blue powder over my eyes that make them bluer than any shade of blue I have ever seen. I startle myself in the glass, so I bring on the haze. I want to ask how much I owe and to whom I owe the debt, but this is not the right time—this is the time to face forwards and get through. Sammy's eyes are boring into my back as I leave the room.

In the hall, we are given big baggy clothes to put on over our tiny outfits. I'm sent in a car with Ling and the two dark sisters, who hold their bodies like cats under threat from a pack of wild dogs, every sinew straining. Sorry, sorry, sorry, I want to reach out my hands and take theirs, but I'm frozen and know that nothing I say or do will make that moment disappear. Instead, I make sure that Ling gets in the middle so they don't have to sit beside me. The driver is a skinny young boy who whistles as he drives. We pull up outside a tall house made of red bricks, with three stretched, shiny cars outside, and a neat, clipped garden with roses so perfect they don't look real. There's a small watering hole with a statue, its mouth gaping open like a fish, water gushing through. The driver tells Ling and me to get out and continues off down the road with the sisters. A woman in a white uniform answers the door and turns on her heel as if she is disgusted by what she sees. We follow her broad back down a hall with a marble floor and steel rails on the walls.

She brings us to a room with a huge unlit fireplace, tall windows with heavy curtains fully drawn, and oversized couches. There's a wide TV mounted on the wall that's playing very loudly. Ling sits directly in front of it, and I watch as the expression on her face empties out. People on the screen are watching other people on the screen as they shout at each other, their faces full of hatred, and the people watching either cheer or boo. I pull my eyes away from the images and the noise, and get up and walk around the room. This place smells of antiseptic and old people. I remember reading *Treasure Island* to my baba at the end, her freckled hand holding tightly to mine. Her room smelled musty, a mixture of talcum powder and moss, disguised by bleach that used to attack my eyes and make them water. I rub them roughly now. Maybe this is all they want us to do here, yes, maybe we'll be reading to an old person, a sick person, yes, maybe this is why we are covered up. Yes. I am nodding my head, trying to convince myself, the way Mama used to. The nurse returns and clicks her fingers at us to follow her. We shuffle along a brightly lit hall until we reach a door that's ajar, and Ling and I are ushered inside.

A young man in a suit is sitting in a dark wooden chair by an old man's bedside. The old man is dressed in a pink shirt and tie, and is propped up on top of a quilt and cushions. He smiles widely when we enter and makes a purring sound. I think he's calling us cats as he says, "Mmm, pussy, pussy," and the young man laughs loudly, his face red and greedy, chin wobbling underneath.

The young man speaks for the old, "Take off your clothes. It's Pop's ninetieth birthday and I wanted to get him a present he would never forget. Present of a lifetime, eh, old boy?" He sounds angry. Every word lands somewhere deep in my body, making ugly pictures, although I don't know exactly what they mean. The old man makes slobbering noises like a baby feeding. I feel doors inside of me slam shut and worry that I won't be able to do this. The young man begins to undress the old, revealing hairless skin, like putty.

"What are you waiting for, girls?" the younger says.

Ling and I look at each other and she begins to undress first. I copy her until we are standing in our underwear. "Do not resist, it's over quicker that way." Magda is there in the room with us, guiding us through. I feel her squeeze my hand.

"Everything," the man says.

I do not want Ling to see me naked, nor do I want to see her that way, so we continue to look into each other's eyes as we remove the rest of our clothes. The younger man takes us by a hand each and tells us to sit on either side of the old man. The old man's blotched hands shake as he reaches out and grabs hold of each of our thighs and pinches hard, his fingers creeping upwards.

"You, chinkie," the younger man says, "climb on top of him."

The old man's razor-thin lips clamp to Ling's nipple as he sucks and bites, and she winces.

"You, blondie," the man tells me, "play with him, make him hard and then suck."

The younger man watches as the old man's limp bits come to life. I unfocus my eyes so I don't have to see.

I block out his voice. I am sitting on the highest branch of the highest tree in the forest and Ling is there too and we are swaying in the breeze.

When it's over, the nurse woman escorts us back down the hallway so fast we have to run to keep up, then opens the front door a crack, peeps out, and pushes us through. "Straight to the car," she says.

The boy is sitting, waiting, and we set off immediately to pick up the sisters, who are in a similar house in an almost identical street a few minutes' drive away. As we wait outside, my mind curves inside the house, and it sees the sisters and many men having a party, where the girls are the prize. I try to pull my thoughts back inside this car and focus on the driver's head, which is small and shaven, his neck swimming in his shirt, scrawny like a chicken. I think of the fat man's neck and feel a tickle in my throat that might be the beginning of a laugh. Perhaps I have caught Sammy's habit of making a joke of everything.

Ling is exhaling on the window and draws on the condensation with her fingertip. "What are you drawing?" I ask her.

"My boyfriend name," she says, as she adds a heart. "He will come find me."

I can smell Papa's cigarette smoke in the car.

The sisters eventually climb back into the car and I feel as if my heart might burst from seeing their blank eyes, which are permanently fixed on some point as far away from the here and now as possible. Their pain is palpable—it beats in the air like injured birds, trapped.

I try to make them see my words hanging in the air. "You don't deserve what these people do to you, what I did to you . . . you don't deserve any of it." I summon the Madonna to come to them and offer some comfort. My own body is beating to a familiar tune, everything rushing and racing and needing release. The need to run is making me shake in the deepest part of me.

As soon as we arrive back to the house and the car door is opened, I sprint. There is no stopping my body. The boy shouts after me, filthy curses. A man comes out of one of the other houses and chases me, his face purple with exertion and rage when I glance back. Maybe Luca was not pretending after all, maybe I am as fast as a bullet. At the end of the road there is a high wall, too high to climb. The man reaches out to grab my arm and misses. I hear a noise coming out of me that is like the ghost sounds of a chicken squawking after its head has been cut loose from its body.

At the top of the road, the three girls are all staring at me, Ling shouting at me to come back, come back. There's nowhere else to go. We're caught in a road that only goes one way and then loops back on itself. Irina comes to the doorway and watches silently.

The man is shouting, "Stop, you stupid bitch, there is nowhere to run."

I lift my knees as high as they will go and kick my heels high. My muscles are burning, my lungs are screaming and my mind is calm. It's a soft night and the damp, dark sky falls down around my shoulders like a cloak.

When the man sees that I am just sprinting up and down the street, he stops, holds his sides, puffing. "Lunatic."

I look up and see the stars. They are so close I could touch them. I think of Mama telling me to wish upon the brightest star in all the sky. Maybe if I reach up I'll be able to draw one down. The moon is tiny and buttercup yellow. I see flashes of its face as the clouds careen across its surface.

When there is no breath left inside me, when my insides are coming up into my mouth, I slow down and gently jog. Sammy has come to the door to join the others and claps for me, as if cheering me on over a finishing line. I go into the kitchen to pour a glass of water. The man who was chasing me walks in and cracks me on the side of my head with his hand. I fall to the ground and the man walks out, muttering under his breath.

Sammy hunkers beside me. "Hey, looper, you okay?"

I push myself to sitting.

"I know what to get you for Christmas. How about the latest Nike Air? You could be an Olympic runner . . . such talent!"

"What is Nike Air?"

She laughs loudly and I try to join in, before my brain does a flip and hits itself against the side of my head. It goes dark for a few moments and I feel Sammy lift me and carry me back to the bedroom.

"Well, we are a right pair!" Sammy says, when I open my eyes. She's sitting on the edge of my bed, holding a wet face-cloth to the side of my head. "Quite a shiner!"

I push myself onto my elbows and come to sitting. Sammy plumps up the pillows behind my head and holds out a glass of water. I sip.

"How are you? Bad night?" she asks.

"I needed running."

"Know the feeling! They'd have a much happier, more productive team if they let us out for a bit of exercise once in a while. Did no one ever tell them that exercise in the fresh air is good for the morale?"

Her words are pouring out of her, electric, exciting, and I'm getting caught up in them, smelling the old fellow's leathery scent on the wind, feeling the breeze whipping my cheeks.

"I spended many times running," I say.

"Me too," Sammy says, and falls silent.

She gets off the bed and starts pacing the room. "Excuse me, you inspired me!" She gets down on her hands and knees and straightens out her legs, pushing her body up and down by her arms. Her face goes ripe-tomato red. "Push-ups," she says, "exhilaration, followed by exhaustion."

She pushes up and down, up and down, until her eyes look like they might pop out of their sockets, then she rolls onto her back and makes circles in the air with her long legs. Her cheeks are purple now and sweat is covering her skin.

Suddenly, she stops, lies flat on her back, puffing for a few moments. "Rebooting!" she says, before she climbs onto my bed. She offers me her hand and pulls me to standing. "Fuck, that felt good."

I say the word. F-U-C-K. I do not know the direct translation, but it sounds hard and is good to say. Over and over the two of us shout the word, jumping on my mattress.

34

Sammy

Where was that big thumper from? He wasn't Irish, that's for sure, but Taxi Joe is, and so was the boy that drove the girls today. I track back to the moment Hatchet handed me over, and wonder about her reasoning regarding how risky it would be to have a Dublin girl among the ranks here. She must have done her fact-checks. After three days of resting up and no big breaking news story, she took me for an unloved loser, and completely bought my sorry tale. It must have happened before. And anyway, as far as my lot back home are concerned, I have disappeared for days before, always with Brian, and always on weekends. I see Hatchet's dry, lizard-like eyes, staring at me, appraising her new merchandise. Could that woman in the brothel—Sandra?—who gave me Hatchet's number, have known what kind of an organization she was involved with? Brian appears before me and my thoughts jumble and shatter. How much of this is about what happened with him? Naive is not a word I would have ever had attached to me, before now. My body blasts with heat.

How long have I been missing now? Almost a week. Only a week since I left the hospital. How can so much happen in one fecky week? They must all be looking for me by now. There are no newspapers or Irish TV channels here so I can't know, but of course a fifteen-year-old Dublin girl doesn't just vanish off the face of the earth, like these others. Or do they? There *are* unsolved cases. Is this where the missing go?

"Where have you gone to?" Nico's voice interrupts my spinning fantasies. That girl's got more spunk than I gave her credit for—all that crazy-ass running, playing a game of catch-me-if-you-can with the dude from four doors up. She was lucky all she got was a thump, you wouldn't want that big fucker climbing on top of you and teaching you a different kind of a lesson. Funny how wrong first impressions can be. We've just been effing and blinding to our hearts' content, both of us jumping up and down on her bed. She sure can run and she sure can cuss. Her talents are definitely not being put to the best use here.

I was the first to stop. Unheard of, but the juice in my batteries is still running low. Those drugs and that night spent in the wet sheets battling every kind of demon imaginable have left me pretty shaky. "I pissed myself in my sleep last night."

She looks at me and shrugs. "They give you strong medicine. No your fault."

It may not be my fault, but it still happened, I still pissed myself.

"Do you want for me to help wash sheets?" she asks. I nod. The two of us take the sheets off the bed and go to the kitchen, where I open the washing machine, stuff the bedding and a washing capsule into the drum, and close the door. Nico's eyes are huge.

"Never seen one of these before?"

She shakes her head. I wonder how much new stuff she is having to process every day. We sit at the kitchen table and pour glasses of juice, lather soda bread with butter and raspberry jam, and then both of us fall silent, neither of us eating, as we listen to the wind outside, which is fairly whippy this morning and seems to want to get inside—it's rattling the windows that much.

"The man was so old he no get up out of bed," she says quietly, after a while, as if by whispering the words she won't give them any power.

I choke. "I bet he could still get *it* up though, right?" And I mimic my pinkie standing to attention, just in case she doesn't get it.

She sucks air in through her mouth, a swallowed whistling sound. "His son looked us."

"Fu-uh-ck!"

"I thought about Luca and Papa and sick almost was."

"Pity you weren't—all over the two of them! Is Luca your brother?"

She balls up her hands. Putting up a good fight.

"Lucky you! I always wanted a brother . . ."

"I have two eithers. You have them!"

She is rubbing her eyes with her fists. I suddenly have a desire to hug her, weird, but I sit on my hands instead. "I had the maddest dreams last night."

"The medicine," she says.

"I gave birth to a fish boy."

She smiles and frowns at the same time. "Boy who is fish?"

"Or a fish who is a boy, or something like that. A boy's face and a fish's body. The face was one of the men from the party, as a boy."

Nico is tracing the edge of her glass with her fingers.

"What does that mean, do you think?"

"Maybe you worry you are with baby," she says. And then, "The dream telled you that man was one time boy."

My throat hurts like fuck. "What happens to them, do you think?"

Nico falls silent, staring out the window at the almost-bare tree dancing like a crazed skeleton in the wind.

The washing machine beeps loudly and Nico jumps. I go to the machine, turn another knob to set the dryer, and put it on for an hour. "That blows hot air," I tell her.

She nods and shakes her head at the same time.

"Have you finished the book? Did she escape?"

"In book, yes, but in life it is no possible," she says.

"So, in your version you had her die?"

"Yes, chopped tiny. The man ate her."

"Cheery!" I say. "You must be knackered." I yawn.

"Tired?"

"Yes. You must get some beauty sleep."

She scrunches up her face. "Perhaps if I ugly I no be here."

"Perhaps," I say. "But there will be a life after here. And that face will serve you well out there."

"No if we are cutted up first," she says, trying to make a joke.

"Come on. None of that talk. We'll do it. We'll get out of here. Along the way, we'll meet a decent man at one of our soirees. As soon as we do, our eyes will fill with tears and we'll appeal to their masculine macho sides. We'll ask them to rescue us. Or *you'll* ask a man to rescue us. I've been thinking long and hard about this, and it's the only way. I reckon you might just be the girl to make a man like that fall for it."

She is studying me intently, trying to understand "soirees" and "macho," I imagine, and then surprises me by saying, "I do not think a good man would be in company of men that way," in her strangely precocious English.

Wise little owl really, from her backwater barnyard. I need to tell myself being rescued is a possibility, even as I know it's an absurd comedy: a farce, or ridiculous Hollywood happily-ever-after. Although if anyone has the power to stoke compassion in a dead person's heart, it's Nico. I should know.

She gets up, goes over to the dryer, and sticks her nose to the glass, then looks at me, throws her hands in the air in amazement, and leaves the room.

I sit at the table, trying not to listen to the birdsong, which

I can hear over the wind and thrum of the tumble dryer. She's so loud and insistent for such a tiny thing. I know, I know, I get it, birdie, but shut the fuck up, will ya? I'll try again when I have a better plan of action, a clearer course to steer.

Ling walks in, and in silence she pours herself a bowl of Snap, Crackle, and Pop. Down the hatch, then another bowl and another. Where does she put it? She's a teeny, little popsicle herself.

Eventually, she speaks. "Your friend get us killed. She no try run away again."

I tell her Nico was not trying to run away, she just needed to run.

Ling shrugs. "Tell her not do it again. That man . . . he no good."

"I'm not her keeper," I say.

We'll have to set up a track in our bedroom, do a circuit: push-ups, stomach crunches, bicycles, squats, jumping jacks, tuck jumps. I'll have to design a super hard routine for Ms. Olympics. It won't kill the urge to run outside in the elements though. That high is completely different from the one you get from being cooped up inside.

Ping!

Ling drops her spoon, and milk and Krispies go flying into the air.

"It's only the dryer," I say, feeling a hundred years old. The sisters walk in then and watch as I take the sheets out of the machine.

"Pissed myself," I say, grinning, then I squat onto the

ground and make a peeing sound. None of the girls laugh. I look at the clock on the wall: 10 a.m. In less than twelve hours, we'll be doing it all over again.

I'm kicked in the guts and double over. Just what did those bastards do in that room when I was out cold? I haven't let myself admit it before now, but I'm raw inside and there's a dragging sensation deep in my stomach. They inserted something. Ah, so I'm good to go, although it doesn't seem possible; I don't think my body will allow it.

35

Nico

In spite of my terror of falling into the well, I cannot stay awake. I do not know if I dream at all, I'm that tired; I just fall into a blank place. The only sensation is of being covered in darkness.

When I wake, I have no idea of the time, or where I am, or who I am, until I see Sammy sitting by the window reading the "crap" book.

"Hello, Princess," she says, "this is really giving me the creeps."

I push the quilt off me, glad to find that I can move, then I swing my legs around to sit, and place my feet on the soft carpet. My head feels dizzy.

"Take it easy. Looking a bit green around the gills."

Why has she put the color green and a fish in the same sentence? She's talking gibberish and my head hurts.

"Put your head down between your knees," she says. "You've a cracker on the side of your head."

Listening to Sammy, it's as if I've tuned in to a new TV station and the rhythms and meaning have seeped into me, like when Maria and I watched the American programs in her home, in secret. Somehow we knew what was being said, like now—with this girl everything is so visual, it's as if her words are projected on a screen in dizzying, bright colors.

I have only been in this house three days and three nights and already it seems as if three lifetimes have passed. I pinch myself to try to scatter the ghosts, but all I can think of is the old man pinching me hard last night. I did not wake from the shadows then—they crept right inside me.

Sammy pushes my hand away. "Look," she says, pulling the curtains back fully. "Full-on sunshine. Drink that in, Roomie. Not many days like that in the dark winter to come."

I try to focus on the blue sky but my eyes are finding it hard to see.

"You okay? Looking a bit woozy."

I like that word. It sounds exactly as I feel.

"I'll go get you juice. Get some sugar into the bloodstream. Or even better—some booze. I wonder where Irina keeps her stash."

"No, thank you. Juice is good."

She makes a croaking sound like a frog. "Okay, Sandra Dee."

All these names she calls me.

"You look like a movie star," she says, "even with a big bruiser on your cheek."

I put my hand to the side of my head, which is hot and swollen.

"I'll get you some ice too," she says, as she walks through the door.

I stay sitting on the side of the bed, holding tightly to the sheets. A knock on the door sounds, and then it opens a crack. A male voice says, "Hope I'm not disturbing you," and then a body appears in the doorway. I think it's the same dark man who lifted Sammy last night. "I'm a doctor and I'd like to take a look at you."

The icy-cold finger of fear pushes its way deep into my belly. As I try to stand, he crashes through the threshold of our room. Before I have time to react, he pushes me back down on the bed, clamps me with one hand on my chest and says, "Over in no time, now lie back on the bed and open your legs." I see the dog's sore neck and allow my body to go limp. My head turns sideways, and I look out the window where a heavy cloud bank is building in the swirling sky, invading the blue of moments before.

"Bend your knees."

My legs move of their own accord. The man puts something cold and metal inside me, pushing through all the locked doors. He is fast, efficient. "Good girl. Here, take these," and he throws a packet of tiny white pills on the bed.

I feel rather than see Sammy's presence in the doorway, static buzzing from her direction. I'm afraid she's going to say something stupid, and he's going to hit her or put a needle in her arm, but she's frozen, and he smiles and bows to us before he walks out.

Her body is crackling, her unspoken anger ringing loudly in the air.

I pull my pajama bottoms back up. Neither of us moves or speaks for some moments, then her voice bursts through. "Fuck. I'm surprised they haven't branded us with a hot iron."

Her words place unwanted images in my mind, and as I reach out for the glass of cool, cloudy apples, I imagine a hot poker with a number imprinting the skin on my forearm. I can smell the skin burning. Sammy's hand is shaking as she hands me the juice.

I drink long and deep, the cool liquid soothing. Sammy sits beside me and puts a bag of green ice to the place where I was hit.

"Green Giant," she sings. "They're peas," she says, trying to lighten the mood, although there is no part of her that is laughing. I'm burning up inside. We both sit for some time listening to the breeze outside that taps against the window, looking to be let in.

Then a figure appears at the door, as if conjured by the wind. "Dinner is ready."

I look at Irina's mouth, which is again as thin as a slit.

"You must eat." She turns and floats away.

"Think that means we're both cleared for work tonight," Sammy says.

Is it almost that time already?

"Can't believe she's letting you go to work looking like that. Won't there be questions asked?"

What do the men care about a bump on my head? I think of the girl with the black eye and know that nothing will stop this, except one of Magda's pills.

"Come to think of it," Sammy says, "this could work in our favor . . ." She starts to pace, drumming up energy and ideas. "Make them feel sorry for you, make them fall in love with you . . . let your beautiful blue eyes fill with tears . . ."

Does she really believe this, or is she just saying it to make us feel better? I decide to go along with her. "Or one fall with you," I say, copying her words.

"I'm not the falling-in-love-with kind of girl. I'm the other kind. Bad things happen to people who get too close to me."

I wrap my arms around my sides.

"Giving yourself a hug?" Her voice has that hard edge again, like it's a knife slicing the air.

I pick up the pills that the doctor threw on the bed.

"The morning-after pill," she says. "Kills the beginnings of any babies."

I do not want to think of a bad seed taking hold. I swallow one and drink the rest of the juice.

"Now, we'd better eat. Those things are a lot worse on an empty stomach."

When we get to the kitchen, it's full of different girls, and the same driver who brought me here. Irina is talking to the man. I don't allow myself to look at the girls, I don't trust my-self anymore, so I pull my eyes away from the terrified huddle and focus on Sammy, whose energy is rising and becoming agitated and hot.

"More fresh meat?" Sammy says to Irina.

Irina ignores her, but Sammy turns her whole body face on to the man. "I'll remember your face, you asshole," she says.

Her skin is mottled pink and red and a flash rash like a nettle sting creeps from her chest up to her neck. "Where did you take them from?" She is speaking to the driver, who swats her away with his hand.

Irina turns to her. "This man is only the driver."

Sammy starts raving, pacing, and shouts words at Irina. "Like you are only the keeper of the brothel!"

All the other girls look at her in amazement, then look away, terrified by this act of revolt, which should end with a whack, or worse.

"You won't get away with this," Sammy says, words spilling out of her, words which cannot be taken back, words which should be kept inside.

"You would do well to get out of here now," Irina's voice is low and laced with threat.

Sammy curses. Rage, like a ball of fire is building its momentum inside her. The man moves so close that his nose is almost touching the tip of hers. He stands, mirroring her, statue still, dwarfing her with his presence and his shadow.

"You won't get away with this," she says again to the driver, as I pull her away. I can feel the heat coming off her just by standing beside her; her whole body is radiating and vibrating.

As we walk down the hall, I say to her, "You must calm."

"One of them looked about eleven."

"We must be calm if we to get out of here alive." I push the bedroom door open and we go inside.

She breathes in deeply, and as she exhales, her body goes limp. "You're right, Roomie, I have a terrible temper on me. Terrible. Once it takes hold, I'm not in charge."

I understand her emotions have taken her over. I do not think this girl has ever learned anything about how to protect herself. I tell her, "Mama teached me to hide my feelings . . . I was scared of Sergiu and Victor, and she said if they saw it, they eat my fear. They hurt Luca because he could not put it away."

"My mother used to feed on my fear."

She looks like a five-year-old as she says this, biting down hard on her lip.

There's a tune in Sammy's head, which she speaks aloud: *Shit, fuck everything . . .*

As I look at her, saying these raging words with her eyes closed, I wonder how she allows the men do the things they do to her at night; how she does not lose her temper then. I know the answer even as I ask the question—she can only get worked up over other people's pain.

We hear the girls' light footsteps traipse upstairs.

"So," she says, "maximum capacity."

We listen to the creaking floorboards and then the silence. These girls: they come and they go, and no one is stopping them, someone is selling them, their parents, siblings, aunties, uncles, grandparents, boyfriends, friends. What happens to these girls—us—when they are used up?

I touch my forehead, breastbone, shoulder to shoulder, and then place my hand at the base of my neck. "We must eat something," I say, thinking of the pills we have swallowed and Mama's insistence on food being the antidote to any kind of ill. Sammy nods, like she's in a trance.

The driver is standing at the main door when we go back into the hall. He is a goat-man, with his hoofs and his saliva, which lands in a puddle at our feet. As he leaves, he slams the door so hard on its hinges the house rattles. I touch Sammy on the shoulder, and whisper "breathe" into her ear, and her ribcage rises and falls, fast and shallow like a kitten's.

We go into the kitchen and, with shaking fingers, I open the fridge and take the dinner out. It is heavy with layers of pasta, meat, and cheese. Sammy turns the knob on the cooker and puts the bowl in, closing her eyes for a moment. When she opens them again, it is as though the wind outside has blown through her and she has turned back into a version of her former self. Her eyes are glassy as she looks at her watch.

"Are you feeling pukey yet?" she says.

"Pukey?"

She sticks two fingers down her throat. I shake my head at her.

"How's the head?" she says. "We'll be better if we can get food inside us."

We both sit and wait for the bell on the cooker to sound. I

can't hear the bird over the wind, which sounds like it's tearing through the trees. I wonder if she found a sheltered spot to hide, away from the wind's insistent prodding, or maybe she has flown away. I never got to see her, though I imagine a sturdy little thing, two tiny legs and a big proud chest into which she draws air to propel her brave flight away from here. I think of Luca and my eyes fill with water. Sammy takes the dinner out and lifts it onto our plates. It's golden and bubbling with hot cheese. I force a big bowl of it past the stone in my throat, which gets pushed down into the center of me, and my stomach swells.

"Jesus, what is it with you teenies? You can really put it away. You should have seen Ling this morning with her cereal. She ate so much I thought she might explode." On this last word, she blows out her cheeks and makes a sound like thunder.

I think of Ling drawing the heart on the car window—I'm glad she tells herself those kinds of lies.

"Okay so, Roomie. Time to enact our plan. To recap: when you're alone with a man later, let your beautiful blue eyes fill with tears. Can you do that?"

"They don't look to me."

"Well, hook them in, make them look at you, make them really see you."

I cannot imagine any of the men that pay to use us allowing themselves to really see us. They would not be able to do what they do if they did.

Back in our room, we find our nighttime outfits lying on the bed ready for us.

"Nowhere to hide in this gear: *maximum exposure!"* Sammy

laughs, and I catch it. We both start cackling like witches as Irina walks in the door with her bag.

"You two better watch yourselves."

We stare hard at each other, all the while snorting and streaming. This kind of laughter is as much about crying as it is about laughing.

"Snap out of it, girls," Irina says.

"Yes, sir," says Sammy, saluting her.

I swallow back the laughter and let tears stream down my face as I sit down on the chair and offer my face to Irina in the mirror. She wipes away the wet with her fingertips and touches the lump, whistling through her teeth.

"You must never try to run away again. It could have been much, much worse."

I nod. I don't even try to explain that I was not trying to run away, that I only needed to run.

She turns to Sammy. "And you must learn to control your temper."

A tic above Sammy's right eye twitches violently as she nods, silent. I'm glad of the makeup, the mask, as Irina's expert fingers cover me in colors and textures that are not my own. I allow my eyes to snap into focus and really see the girl that is facing her: hardened and hidden. Is this what a man would see if he let himself see, or would he squint and imagine a girl who's enjoying herself as much as him? What I do to the clouds is what these men do to us: create things in the air that do not exist.

36

Sammy

This time there are five of us in the car: Ling, the sisters, and Nico and me. The skinny whistling kid is our chauffeur. The sisters make sure to sit as far from the loopy blonde girl as they can, and I can feel Nico's body tense, her ribcage held high, her breath caught inside. We drive for over an hour. I know I should be trying to lighten the mood but I don't have a joke, or a lyric, or a swipe in me.

We pull up outside a massive hotel, a conference center, a place where businessmen come to do whatever it is they do. It might be one of those joints near the airport where Dad sometimes stays if he has a red-eye the next morning, but I couldn't tell with all the twists and turns the driver took, as well as my overdose of Mr. Floaty. I'm doing that blurry thing with my eyes that Nico taught me, and I intend on getting blankety blank again. The receptionist stands to attention as soon as he sees the party of girls, and I swear to fuck the little shit wrinkles his nose at us, especially the dark sisters. He runs his eyes up and down them apprais- ingly, looking unsure about the quality of the batch sent to him. Better watch out, they might construct a doll of you later, buster! That's inspired. Let's all do that. Let's all make dollies and stick pins in them. Glad to find my sense of humor hasn't totally failed me.

We're corralled together and herded quickly to a big, bright room, all cheap blue carpet and monstrous fake chandeliers. Amazing how quickly the allure wears off. Imagine if one of them were to fall on your head? Kaput, splat. I help myself to an overflowing glass of champers, the cheaper kind, and offer all the girls a glass. They each accept, and they each glug it down. They must have discovered the added numbing proper- ties of booze. The door opens and a clutch of men enter, seven this time: a bit less suited and booted and groomed than the last lot, a bit rougher around the edges. I wonder who's paying for this. I have no doubt we're the luxury line.

The same thing happens as the other night—they act as if we're not there at first, and then they click their fingers and we come to life. Why? Why are we not resisting? Why have I not even tried to slip out to go to the loo? One voice orders us to take all our clothes off; he sounds like he's from the wrong side of the tracks. That voice holds all the power.

Nico hates to be looked at by the other girls, so when she and I are paired up, I stare at my nose, going cross-eyed, and manage to get a tense smile out of her. Again, we're instructed to walk naked in our heels and told to touch each other, kiss each other, then told to watch. The same man who ordered us to get naked chooses one of us: the smaller of the sisters. My heartbeat fades to a whisper, my blood freezes, my veins turn into tiny rivers of ice. I notice one of the men holding back, saying nothing. He goes to the whiskey decanter set up on the baize table at the back of the room, pours himself a large measure, and downs it in one. Then he walks out of the room. A few of the other men look up absently but don't stop what they're doing. They remind me of the boys behind the shed, egging each other on, pats on the back, all the male bonding, clichéd bullshit, except these dudes are middle-aged and the "fun" appears forced, mechanical, and vicious—the shared bonding only seems to aggravate them further.

No one moves, each of us glad in our own selfish way that the sacrificial lamb is not us, and also petrified that we might be next. Everyone seems fixated—us too—and incapable of moving. There are no words to describe the expression on the girl's face. I try not to look, but can't stop staring, and especially can't stop climbing inside her sister's head, who looks as if she's gone, so far removed from this place, this world, that I'm not sure she can ever claw her way back, or whether she'd even want to. I can't let myself imagine the smaller sister's state of mind and can only hope she took enough of Mr. Floaty to make her totally blank out, although her face suggests otherwise. I resolve to glug as much anesthesia as I can get my hands on. Is this why Mother drinks as much as she does? Is she trying to drown some awful memory that lives on and on?

The spectacle finishes, and one by one we are chosen by a man each and led to a room with a minibar (which I'm kindly invited to raid) and a giant bed lit by a massive light, hanging center stage. Apparently I look gorgeous in this light. I'm so out of focus now, I hardly feel any of it; I don't register what the man looks like, his face, his body, his age, any of it. It could be happening to someone else. It is happening to someone else.

After, we are brought back to the room, and we wait. I sit curled up in one of the fake pleather chairs, snoozing. I'm so far removed at this stage, none of it is landing—except for what happened to the sister. I never want to see her again, never want to be reminded, and as I'm thinking this, here she comes, the last to be returned, holding on to a man's arm, as if he's a gentleman helping her cross the road. She doesn't look capable of standing on her own. I stare at my nails, biting them and the skin beneath them till they're pink and glistening. The man deposits the broken girl on a chair with something like tenderness, and the other sister goes to her and holds her under one arm, Ling taking the other. The receptionist gestures, without looking directly at us, to follow him down the hall to the door.

We're bundled in the car, and off we trundle: home sweet home. We walk through the door into the comfortable, cream, centrally heated home; we shower, we eat, the sky is pink tinged, and then we get into bed and go under.

When we wake, we wash again, we eat some more, we watch shite TV, we read the two shite books, and—we wait.

There's no sign of the younger sister, but the elder is wheeled out, all made up, shaky, and stoned. I can't believe Irina is making her do this, but then Irina follows orders from on high. Are they giving the younger one a break, or is she so broken she'll never be good to go again? I'm sure the doc with his bag of tricks will patch her up—she's worth too much not to be worked.

The night comes, and with it another party—this one very young. A twenty-first. This is bad: snooker cues and cigarettes, but it happens at a distance, we survive, we eat, we wash, we sleep, we watch crap TV, read our recycled books, and we don't talk about any of it, and then another night and then another and still no sign of the money, and no sign of the sister. It's better to forget her face, which floats insistently before me, and is accompanied by such a slam of guilt that I am permanently breathless. We watched and let it happen, thankful it wasn't us.

Irina is avoiding me now, having said that payment would be next week, then next month. I guess that's how it works in the real world: monthly paychecks. Since the night of the injection and that particular woozy, I'm not able to hold on to any thought for longer than a few seconds, if even that. There's no thinking in straight lines. Everything jumbles and whirls, fast and confused. Where did both those men materialize from? Haven't seen them since but they're there somewhere, hiding in the walls, the curtains, the fixtures. Their faces accompany me on every outing, and I do what

I'm told, their voices echoing in my ear, the aftershock of the sting of the needle vivid and sore.

The nights stretch, ten, twelve, twenty of them, not a moment off. Time is a shape-shifter, a trickster. It stretches forwards and folds back on itself like an accordion. It's out of tune, out of sync, and there's nothing distinct from the sensation of it passing. I want to scream at it to slow down, to stop, to give us a break, but it pushes on. I feel I'm being played.

As the days go by, Nico doesn't seem to need to run anymore. She has purple shadows under her eyes and sits by the window reading or staring at the clouds. I don't bother looking at myself anymore. The more time slips by the less energy there is for talk of running away, of concocting plans, of life outside, of the future. My sleep is long and deep and low and wide, crazy dreamscapes taking me far away from this place, making it hard to distinguish reality from fantasy (something I was never any good at anyway). I'm not sure if Nico ever goes fully under; she doesn't seem to close her eyes. She's all hard angles and held breath, like if she dares to breathe out she'll fall apart at the seams. Her radiance is gone, her cheeks pale, her hair wispy—like her, which in a weird kind of tragic-heroine way makes her even more beautiful. I can't get my head around how much food she still puts away, although it looks like when she chews, it's being forced down, mechanical and sore. She's reading those two books over and over and must have memorized long passages, her concentration is so intense and consuming. I wish I could sit quietly the way she does. My mind gets louder in the silence and needs the constant hum of the TV to drown out the howling voices. Not even a catastrophist could have dreamed up this reality, Dad.

Nico hasn't met a knight yet. Even her beauty doesn't stir these gents—in their hearts. Ha, I can still make myself laugh. Sometimes.

Some nights we're taken to private homes for parties, some nights to bars with hotels upstairs. I'm never sent to a dirty old man's home—I reckon they know I could bring on a heart attack. We meet many suits and drink much sparkle. I could make a bolt for it, when walking between the taxi and the hotels, but I don't, controlled as I am now by some other invisible master yanking on my strings. I could run and scream, and get the guards on to this place, but I can't seem to do anything. I could tell one of the men who I am, my whole sorry story. Don't they know who I am? That's the weirdest thing about this whole gig—I never tell the men anything about myself. In those rooms with those men, I'm not real, ever, and playing a part is the only way to get through. All we have seen of punishment so far is Nico's whack and my injection, but there's something else at work here, and it's coming from both inside and out. These guys are too good at what they do to carelessly risk a public exposure, but I can't help thinking how come nobody has noticed me in the bars? Am I not a national sensation yet?

Come to think of it, the amount of muck Irina puts on our faces makes us pretty unrecognizable, which, on top of the gear and the curled hair, probably makes me look like someone else entirely. I've seen a few glances in Nico's direction; even with all the daubing and lacquering, she still looks really young. People look, and just as quickly look away.

Most of the trees are bare now, a carpet of dead leaves at their feet, so it must be the tail end of autumn, a whole school term almost over. I never noticed the length of a season before. The air is crisper outside and the nights are drawing in earlier and earlier, which means our start time is earlier too. We never work in daylight hours.

37

Nico

Although this place is cold, this country is cold, my body, hands and feet are cold, I'm boiling up inside and feel as if I'm shape-shifting out of sand. Beneath me, the ground is made of scorched dust, time is like desert sand pouring through a crack in my brain. When I close my eyes, the heat scalds the back of my eyelids and I fight to keep them open. Papa, you were right after all. He came.

I try to keep a note for the days passing: Day 1 in the Cream House, Day 11 in the Cream House, Day 21 in the Cream House, Day 33 in the Cream House—but I still cannot put pen to paper, and I'm not sure these are separate days marked by the sinking and rising of the sun. The sky is so overcast, it's hard to tell day from night, and sometimes it feels as if three minutes have passed when it's been three days, and three nights pass like a shiver of wind through the trees. I can't tell shadows from bodies, voices from spirits. Mama sits at the end of my bed and tut-tuts in her ineffectual way. She reaches out every so often to brush my hair back off my clammy forehead. Luca's face becomes an unknown man's face, me under him, then the man's face becomes Luca's, and I want to reach out and smash it.

Sammy seems permanently fevered although her energy is low, her batteries, as she says, in need of charging. She talks of the sea still, but not of the future, even when I try to make her. I can still see a glimpse of it, sometimes, a halo of light above my head. Somebody might push the lid back and see us, somebody might rescue us, someday. I can see that possibility, sometimes, but, for Sammy, it is too dangerous even to think of. I tell her of my mama, my village, Luca, Maria, the dog, and yet she cannot speak of her home. I think, for her, the future is tied up with the past. Sometimes, she laughs still: big and hard and empty. She sits in front of the TV, which seems to get louder every day, and waits for the nights to come. I have not heard her sing or dance or curse since before we were forced to watch the disappeared sister and the group of men. She has not tried to run away since the day of her injection. I don't know if she swallows much of the food she eats; I see her cough it back into a napkin and put it in her pocket. Maybe she flushes it into the sea.

We have not seen the sister since that night. All I could think, as I was watching, was thank God it's not me. Something bad has taken up space inside me, and I want to turn away from it, and me.

I have read the two books many, many times, so many times I have absorbed the words and they live inside me, although they are mixed up with my own words, which, when I open the pages, are sitting there, sliding and blurring into each other. Now, neither girl escapes, now, the man who imprisoned her holds her forever, so even if she's still feeling a pulse in her veins, she's not really there, she's left herself. Gone. There's a strange comfort in this. I think of the stories Papa used to tell us of the vampires, the living dead, who suck the life force from the living. Sometimes I wonder what would happen if I bit into a man's neck. Could I fill myself with his blood, his essence?

But then, is this not exactly what they do to us?

38

Sammy

On this particular night, a night like any other, after God knows how many of the same have gone before, we're brought to a party in a tall Georgian townhouse, somewhere in the center of town, near Hatchet's house, I think. Well-coiffed and scented men and women are milling around on the stairs, long-stemmed glasses in hand. I notice one of the women registers us as we are pushed into a room and a key is locked in the door. We must have come in the wrong entrance or something. I have a moment of hope. Maybe she'll report what she saw? Nah, she's not going to risk exposing her crew that way, her life, God forbid her man. No. She won't do anything about what she saw. What did she see? Did you notice young working girls being locked in a room at a private member's club? Don't be preposterous. Things like that don't happen in our country, certainly not in our circles. No. I saw nothing.

I'm in full-on head-trip mode when a trio of men walk in the door, voices low and conspiratorial. The room is darkly lit and one of the men is lighting up. Something about the shape of his shoulders and the way he scratches the back of his neck awakens my alien kung fu maestro, who swiftly lands a thump in my stomach. The man turns and scrutinizes the room and the girls with a familiar air of authority. The light must be playing tricks on me, throwing shadows against the walls. He wouldn't use girls like us, he doesn't need to. I hear him clear his throat and speak in a low mumble to one of the other men, and a kick in the guts turns my insides to liquid. I'm back in the car and he is humming, in that deep voice, humming. I have to clench hard to stop my insides from trickling down my legs. Our gazes brush against each other but his is glazed, switched off. He doesn't recognize me at first, and when he does, he pretends not to. I can see the shock register and then the veil of the professional man takes over. He turns his back to me and speaks in that "you will obey me" voice to his cronies. He must be asking specially for me. He must've seen my desperation. He turns back towards the room and the girls, but doesn't look in my direction, instead nods at a different girl, an older one, I am relieved to see. He holds out his hand to her. A perfect gentleman. Maybe he knows it would be too risky to deal with me directly.

Another man, another doctor, one I recognize from my hospital visit with Doc O'D gestures at Nico, nods at her. Surely he has some conscience, some moral compass. His work, after all, is about healing. I try to tell Nico by osmosis this is the man we have been waiting for. Here is a civilized, educated man she can reach. Switch on, Nico, plug back in. She looks at me briefly as she leaves the room and I open my eyes wide. It's all I can manage, but she nods. I think even by the way he offered his arm she knows this is something different. I have to hold myself back, stop myself from screaming at him, at her, as they leave the room: No, don't leave me here.

Oh, Lucy Lou. Should you know this thing about your father? Should I tell you?

I make a snorting noise through my nose and the man who has chosen me to be his for the evening looks at me sideways. Is this little bitch laughing at me? I smile sweetly at him. Not you, kind sir, not you. I'm sitting on an explosion of laughter because I realize that I couldn't tell Luce, even if I wanted to.

However, Doc O'D doesn't know this. Why didn't he ask to speak directly to me? Why didn't he tell me to lean on him and then escort me out of there? Why didn't he leave when he saw me? Why didn't I scream at him, grab him by the coat or fall at his knees, tears streaming down my face? Why? Why? Why? He stands to lose a lot here if he's exposed. What if he thinks this is my secret hobby or something, my secret shame? He's probably able to justify the situation to himself: that one, Samantha Harvey, is well able to handle herself, she's a randy little ticket, and I think back to his wink in the hospital cubicle that night—the wink that said, "We're in this together." We can be the keeper of each other's secrets.

My partner for the evening has his hand on my arse, now under it; his fingers are creeping up inside me. What is it about these men wanting to put on a display in front of each other? He's like a tomcat spraying his territory. I must be a white witch or something, 'cause that's exactly what this dude is into. He empties himself all over me.

"Open wide, darling." Oh what fun, what power, what humiliation. I hate, with all my body, all my soul. I hate so much I become someone else. Tonight you are Linda Bellarusca and then after, you can become yourself again. I would never let this happen to you, Sammy, but Linda, well . . . she's a tough old bird who can handle anything.

After Mr. Tomcat has left, I go into the bathroom as Linda and come out as Sammy.

How the hell is Nico doing with the doctor? It's funny how unshocked I am now that the idea has settled into me. Nothing would surprise me now. Nothing. I'm unflappable—a favorite Miss White expression. I shake my arms like wings and twitch my tail feather. Flap. Flap. Fly away, birdie. Let no birds of worry make their nest in my hair. This was a favorite saying of Mother's, before the booze took her over completely. "The birds of worry are nesting today," she used to say before she'd go to her room and pull the curtains. Safe in the dark, I'd put a warm facecloth on her forehead and stroke her hair.

"There are no nests in there, Mummy." There was a day when I called her Mummy.

Okay, hup now, Samantha. Shake it off, face forward, and forget. Shake and flap. I know now why animals do this. Ever see a dog after a fight? Or a cat after it's been chased? Or a duck after it's been raped? That duck pond in Herbert Park was a revelation. Those randy buggers would sometimes go at one female so hard they'd kill her. If she managed to survive, she'd flap her wings and shake her whole body and swim away. I spent a day there last year, mitching with Brian, smoking doobies under the willow tree, and saw three gangs of ducks go at a single girl duck. I pretended to find it funny, until the last one, where they banged her head so hard against the edge of the pond, her head bled. Then, it didn't seem about desire. Then, even Brian stopped laughing.

39

Nico

This man is different. He looks and he sees, and this makes me afraid. Sammy knows something about this man. I hope he is not her uncle or her father's friend or . . .

When we get to the room, he asks how old I am. I tell him I'm eighteen. He studies me closely, not believing this answer but, I think, happy with what he sees.

"What is your name?"

"Natasha."

"Where are you from?"

"Romania."

"Where in Romania?"

I try to remember the name of the village. I make one up: "Golești."

He nods, as if he knows that place, knows everything there is to know about everything. "Do you mind being here?"

What does he want? He hasn't touched me or taken off his clothes.

"Did someone hurt you?" He gestures to the bruise on my head, which is in its final yellow stages. How many weeks have passed since that night? I sometimes wonder if my birthday has come and gone yet.

"Are you here against your will?"

The answers to these questions get stuck inside. I know I should cry to try and stir his compassion, his rescuing knight tendencies, as Sammy would say—I can see her orchestrating this moment, her hands jerkily drawing out the right notes, her body palpitating with excitement—but I can't squeeze out any sound, it's all dry and caked inside. Can I make this man see without having to say it, the way Mama used to read my thoughts hanging in the air? Even as I think this, I'm waiting for an explosion of colors, a smack on the side of the head, a clap of thunder, ringing bells. I flinch.

"It's okay. I'm not going to hurt you."

I look at the ring on his finger and wonder about his wife. What is this man doing here? I can tell he wants to, with me, but he is battling with this for as long as he allows himself to see me. This is dangerous for him. He looks away out the window at the drops of icy rain that look like smashed crystal, powdered against the pane.

"Always loved the sound of hail against a window, once you're cuddled up inside," he says as he gets up to pull the curtains. "Privacy," he says, without looking at me, and I can feel myself harden.

He sits back against the pillows and pats the space beside him for me to come join him. "Do you smoke?"

I shake my head.

"Mind if I do?" He lights up. "A secret vice of mine. There are so few places where you can smoke indoors these days. Illegal, of course, but well . . ." He inhales deeply. It sounds and smells like Papa. "Is there anything you enjoy doing?" he asks.

Do I tell him about climbing trees and writing essays and running and swimming? I am not that girl anymore. Something about the tone of the question makes me steel myself. "Do you like this?" he says, as he leans in and blows a mouthful of smoke into mine. So, not so different after all.

I start to undress and allow my eyes and mind to soften and blur.

"You're very beautiful," he says, blowing smoke at the ceiling.

I know that line. It's one I have heard many times before. Usually, once they have said these words, they want to empty themselves into me and make their sounds. This man keeps looking. Usually they do not see at all, and after a certain point, I know mine could be any body beneath them. There is a strange comfort in that. This man's eyes bore into me, making this much more intimate than it should be.

"You are cold," he says. "Here, get in," and he holds back the quilt for me to join him in the bed. He is fully dressed and has made no move to undo his belt. Perhaps I am meant to do this for him.

"No, that's okay," he says. "Let me just look at you." And he traces my body with his fingertips. "Has anyone ever given you any pleasure?" he says, not waiting for my answer. He stubs out his cigarette and kisses me all over. "Relax . . ." He blows on my body and uses his fingers and his tongue to moisten me and open me up. "Show me," he says, as he places my hand between my legs.

I do nothing, so he puts his hand over mine and starts to move it in circles. His breath speeds up, and his face goes down.

That thing that could not be said erupts out of me and I choke back a sob.

He stops. "Are you okay?"

The dry tears are stuck at the back of my throat and it feels as if it is closing in. I make a sound like a wheeze.

"Are you asthmatic?" he asks. "Do you need your inhaler?"

I turn on my side, away from him, and vomit.

"Jesus," he says. "Jesus . . . you had better go home, get some rest." He moves fast, handing me my clothes. "Who can I call?"

I'm okay now. Empty.

"I'll go and get some help." He leaves, banging the door hard.

The dark thoughts grow and multiply until there is nothing for it but to rock my head on the pillow. Back and forth, back and forth. I need to dislodge.

The man has returned and is watching me rocking. I do not know how long he is standing there but, when I notice, I hold my head in my hands to stop.

"What is it?" he says.

I curl on my side again, away from him.

"Where do you girls stay?"

I half-turn my body towards him. "I do not know."

He is scratching the back of his neck over and over. "What does it look like?"

I try to describe the place as best I can: the houses that all look alike, the roundabout, the dead-end street, the big wall at the end. He is shaking his head. What did he think when he came here tonight? Something about the way he was with me makes me think he has done this before, many times. But maybe he has never seen a mark of violence on a girl before; maybe he has never met someone as young as me; maybe the other girls were better at acting than I am; maybe no one has ever been sick in his company before. And maybe the fact that he is known to Sammy has brought his other life into the room with him. I slowly sit upright and risk looking him in the eye. I see you. He is the first to look away and closes the door, gently this time.

40

Sammy

Back in the cab, Nico won't tell me what happened, but she looks pale and small, as if she's been squashed and blood-sucked. Was that really Doc O'D and his colleague back there? Family men, top-notch consultants, top-notch, pure, high-grade assholes. This line of thinking is stopped dead by an image of Luce cuddling her dad, his arm around her, kissing the top of her head, his arm around me, supporting me, the way he scratches the back of his neck, his look of concern and worry. Maybe Mrs. O'D knows something is up and that's why she reacts to me so strongly. Maybe she knows her husband has a taste for young girls and me swanning around in there, showing so much flesh, really freaked her out. I feel sorry for her and for a moment I can imagine what it is to be getting old, and no longer fancied by your husband. Is this what happens to all women? Mother too? From where I'm standing, that doesn't sound like too bad a situation to be in.

It is possible that my hyperactive imagination has kicked in and it wasn't him at all—I'm cream-crackered and tanked up on pills and booze. Most of the time I don't know what's real and what's not. Like Linda Bellarusca and the tomcat. Did that happen? Is any of it really happening? I do what I've seen Nico do. I pinch myself hard. She doesn't seem to notice.

"Do you know that man?" she asks, after staring out the window for some time.

"Yes, no, yes . . . I think so . . . Did he hurt you?"

She shakes her head and stares off into the distance.

"Where have you gone to this time?" I ask her.

"Not any place different. I am here," she says, looking sadder than I have ever seen anyone look, even Mother, when the birds of worry were nesting. The other three all have their eyes closed and seem to be dozing, heads lolling. Irina has been increasing our doses of Mr. Floaty, it seems he loses his potency as you build up tolerance. I don't think Nico ever takes them, even though she pretends she does. I saw her spitting one into her hand one time when she thought no one was looking and I bet that wasn't the only time; I bet she feeds them to the sick-looking plant in the hall, whose brown spotted leaves are drooping more every day. I really don't know how she can do this without them.

"What did he say?" I ask.

"I do not know," she says. "It was confused." She's playing with the skin around her fingernails, which has become torn and red. Sometimes she rips it off with her teeth.

"Hey," I say, even though my own nails are bitten to nubs.

". . . was strange," she continues.

When is it ever any other way? But I want to know more, so I don't say anything and wait for her to talk. She checks the driver to see he's not listening. Impossible to tell, but he's engrossed in some shite pop crap, and anyway, he prefers to pretend we don't exist so why would he listen?

"I tell you when we back at room," she whispers.

"Okay," I say, even though I feel like I'm going to combust. The way the doctor offered his arm to Nico makes me think he's practiced at this. Maybe, in the bedroom, he didn't touch her, maybe, only then, did he realize how young she is.

We get to the house and walk—like zombies, puppets, ghosts, dolls, half-dead-alive things—to our various rooms. No one goes into the kitchen this morning. Too tired to eat. It's been a long week.

"So?" I say, when we've closed the door behind us.

She shrugs.

"Was he violent? Did he hurt you?"

She shakes her head.

"Pervy?" Somehow I know she'll understand this word, even though it's probably the first time she's heard it said, in any language.

"Are no they all?" she says, her face tight, hollows below her cheeks and eyes.

I hate to see her look like this. Fuck the whole "I'm a professional man, a man of medicine and a family man" act. How did I not see Doc O'D for who he really is? I guess my danger radar has never been very active. Look at Brian—my first "love." Talk about deluded. I never admitted the half of it, not even to Luce, not even to myself. I thank God that it wasn't Doc O'D himself who took Nico into that room.

"What did he do to you?"

"At the beginning he wanted to just look, and then he wanted me to want it . . ."

"Jesus wept," falls out of my mouth, which almost makes me laugh. It's like something Dad would say.

This isn't usual between us; we don't speak about stuff afterwards, speaking about it only makes it live on. Nico tries to make me talk about what we want to do when we get out of here. I can't see a future for myself anymore—it's like looking into a vat of black boiling tar—it stinks and burns. Only last night, she told me she wanted to be a teacher. I told her she could be a movie star. "And what?" she said. "Be prisoner on screen forever to be look at by any old dirty man?" Such a clever clogs really, Ms. Backwater. She falls silent. I start to change into my PJs, taking the pressure off her.

"He tried stop, I think," she says, after a moment. "He asked me questions but I do not think he want answer. He saw this," she points to the shiner, "and still . . . he tried his 'fun' . . ."

I sit on the side of the bed, heavily. "What kind of fun?"

"Just . . . and . . . he pretend to listen, he pretend to care . . ." Her voice trails off.

My stomach's resident alien is kicking me to shit.

"He come back in room after, and he asked me questions

about where we stay. I could not paint it him. I tried best. Perhaps he knew after he left what he did . . ."

She cannot articulate the exact phrase, and it's not just because she's not speaking in her own language. I know why. There is none. "What the fuck?" might do it, but not really her style. A respectable man, a family man, an upstanding member of our society, a man who makes the sick well, a man at the top of the food chain—what kind of lies could a man like that tell himself about such a transaction?

"Hey," I say, changing the mood, as much for me as for her, "don't think about it anymore. Put it out of your mind. Have you finished that other shite novel?"

She nods. "Many times. It is badder than first one. More bad?"

"Worse."

She nods. "Worse."

"You'd better get writing your own stories then," I say.

"I was first at essay competition in school for five years," she says with some pride.

"I reckon between us we could write a bestseller. I wasn't too shoddy at the old essays either!"

She picks up her PJs and goes to the bathroom. She's had enough chat for the evening. I pop another pill that I nicked out of Irina's bag (although to be honest I reckon she knows—she makes it waaay too easy) and lie down under the duvet, trying to block all thoughts of Doc O'D and Luce. I count backwards from one hundred, and get to three when Nico comes back in. She gets into her bed silently and I count down again, and again, until I'm under and my mind is dark.

The next morning the house is much quieter, even with the new arrivals. Nico and I are having breakfast when Irina walks in.

"Where's Ling?" I ask her.

"Moved on," she says as she pours boiling water onto three teabags.

"Where to?"

She shrugs. I look at Nico, who is chewing her cereal slowly, over and over, as if she's avoiding swallowing, her eyes staring and red.

"Will we be next?" I ask, my voice sounding like a nail dragging on metal, grating, even to my own ears.

Irina shrugs. "Most girls do not stay as long as you have," she says, going to the fridge to get milk. She pours and blows and swallows her witch's brew. I study her. How old is she really? Impossible to tell. She's had the light sucked out of her. Beautiful, yes, with her heart-shaped face, her cat's eyes, and high cheekbones, but dead and ugly too, in a way.

I notice Nico blessing herself, in miniature. She's pretending she's brushing dust off her top, but I can see the shape she's trying to hide. He hasn't done much of a job of protecting her, though, to be fair. Where is He? Thinking of God makes me think of Doc O'D. That man always had that kind of a complex, that kind of an ego that imbued him with power and status, and righteousness. Is that why all these married men come to us? Because they know they can't do it at home? Where do they put their fatherly impulses when they are with us? I think of my dad. Where does he go when he's away on his trips?

I shake my head to interrupt this particularly vicious spiral of thoughts and focus on Nico. She has a weird, stabilizing effect on me.

"Can you make sure that if we're moved on, it will be together?" I ask Irina. I know my survival is linked with Nico's—I can see a future for her, even when I can't see one for myself.

"I have no say, you know that," Irina says.

I want to grab this woman by the neck and shake some life back into her. "You are left in charge of a house full of girls, you must be somebody to these people."

She blows and sips her tea. "I am nobody," she says, before she leaves the room.

Nico is staring out the window. The spinning marbled sky is streaked with fast-moving clouds, which, when I squint, look like cantering horses.

"What are we going to do?" I ask her, hoping to ignite the old-soul guru in her.

"Write our pens on paper."

"And will the doctor be part of our story?"

She looks at me, puzzled.

"That man you were with last night."

"Ah, he is doctor." She stops. "That is sad."

"Yes, yes I guess it is . . ."

We go back to our room and take out our pens and paper, and for the first time, I wonder why they would leave such a thing here. Why have we not written out "Help I am a prisoner" on a piece of paper and handed it to one of the men? I ask Nico this.

"Because they know," she says.

"I'm not so sure," I surprise myself by saying. "I'm not sure at all. I don't think they do know. We look good, we're well-fed, we probably look like 'happy hookers.'"

She looks confused, but obviously understands the sentiment, 'cause she says, "Are there such?"

"They like to tell themselves there are. They probably think we do this for designer bags, or shoes. That's why Irina decks us out in that gear and feeds us well."

"Or, they no think at all . . . ," she says.

"Well, they're certainly not thinking when they're making those faces and noises like bulls and sticking themselves inside us. There's no light on in the brain then, that's for sure."

And then Nico does something seriously weird, for her—she makes a contorted, grotesque face. I mean, I never thought that face could be ugly, but boy, ugly is an understatement, especially when the little weirdo takes out a handful of hairs from the back of her notebook and holds them above her mouth, a fake moustache. She stops her breath, puffs out her cheeks, goes bright red, then pants and grunts and moans. Although I'm totally grossed out by where I imagine the hair has come from, I feel giddy in a way I haven't in weeks. The two of us fall around the place laughing, our own special brand of hysteria. It's a relief to know we're still capable.

When we've calmed down, she places the hair back between

the pages, secretively, as if she's embarrassed I saw her secret stash. I wonder if we could commit some act of voodoo but don't say anything. I can tell by her face not to push it.

We sit on the window seat, pens poised, blank sheets in front of us, and neither of us can scribble a word. I bite my pen so hard the ink seeps all over my mouth and lips.

"You look as vampire!" she says.

I wonder how she knows about vampires, coming from that little village with the green well, where she went to collect water with her mama every day. She has told me more about her life recently, and I can't believe her mother stood by and watched her only daughter being taken away by a man she knew nothing about. And Luca, her brother Luca, the action hero. How did he let it happen? Were they all really so scared of her father, who sounds like a complete eejit. God, if I ever got the chance to meet him . . .

"Of what are you thinking?" she asks.

"Your village."

This is followed by a silence so deep and wide it's as if we have both fallen into that well.

"Sorry, didn't mean to upset you."

"Tell me of your mama," she says.

"Nothing to tell." Enough already. I really don't want to talk about any of that stuff. It does worry me though, that if we get out of here, I would be sent back there. I try on the mantra: *Any place but home*, but it doesn't quite have the same ring as when I first thought it up back in Hatchet's place.

"What have you written, Roomie?"

"No thing. I not write since I leaved, left, my village."

I'm struck by an idea that might get us both going. "Okay, so, let's play the make-up-a-story game that I used to play in drama class. I say one sentence, you say another, and so on . . . until we have finished. You ready? It has to start 'Once upon a time . . .' I'll start: once upon a time there was a house in the middle of nowhere and, in this house, were girls ripped from all corners of the world . . ."

She interrupts insistently, "No, no. This story must be happy one."

"Tragic stories often do have happy endings," I tell her.

"How about this: Once . . . upon . . . a . . . time," she looks at me for approval and I nod, "there were two girls of different countries who become friends and . . ." She stops and gestures at me to continue. Her face is lit up, animated in a way I've never seen before. It's as if she's forgotten where we are, who we are, what we are, and she's back in her school, gathering her gold stars.

"God, this is going to be shite, Miss Twee. And anyway, you can't stop at 'and'—it's got to be a full sentence."

She sighs dramatically, in full-on actress mode, having taken up my mantle, and she starts to babble excitedly. "Okay . . . the two friends broke a window and climbed out to the top of the house . . . roof?" she asks. I nod. "The wind said, 'Giddyup, girls,'" she makes a clucking sound with her tongue, "and when they stood on roof with men climbing at them, the clouds took the space of two big horses, galloping." Then she mimes getting on a horse and waving down at the men, spitting at them.

Is this really the same Nico? I'm getting a glimpse of that girl who liked to run, to climb trees, swim in lakes, and make up stories. The same girl I saw briefly as she bounced up and down on our bed, shouting "FUCK" over and over at the top of her voice.

"This morning, I was playing that cloud game with myself and I saw horses in the sky too . . . but they were cantering, not galloping . . . I swear to my fucking tutu-clad fairy!"

"What is difference—gallop or can-ter?" she says, her voice speedy.

"Well, gallop is faster."

"Then they gallop, no?"

"I think we're both pure fantasists."

"What is 'tutu-clad fairy' and 'fanatist'?" she asks, shaking her head, not really wanting to know the answer.

I pace the floor, hoping to get a blast of inspiration à la King Em. I try to generate heat and excitement but something essential is not working in me: I can't even drum up a lyric. I take out the pad of paper and write HELP in a big scrawl, WE ARE IN DANGER. This is beyond stupid, one of my more "harebrained" ideas, as Dad would say, and I know it, but coming into contact with Doc O'D has thrown this life into sharp relief—seeing him has pierced through this weird fog of denial. He brought my old life, my old self, into the room with him, and I watched this new me from her vantage point, and she said: No fucking way, Sammy, no more. It's time, time to get a grip, time to take some action, time to take your life back, whatever the hell that means. Whatever the hell it means—it means I can't go on numbing out with drugs, booze, and TV; I can't go on pretending to myself that it's only short term, that it's still my choice, that it's not really so bad . . . and that I'll be paid.

The more I think about the possibility of Doc O'D or his colleague being our ticket out of here, the less I'm convinced by it. Doc O'D's paternal impulses are seriously lacking. Neither he nor Mrs. O'D ever did anything to save me from that house, and they knew, Luce told them, and their response was to speak to the school counselor, wash their hands of me, and try to keep their daughter as far away from me as possible. A thump in my stomach tells me to wake up and listen. We need to take matters into our own hands now, no more waiting for Mr. effing Godot (*the* single most boring, pointless play we were forced to sit through by Miss White). We'll end up like those looners talking to themselves, lost in madness, if we don't take action on our behalf. Resolve builds in me as I present Nico with my work of art: HELP WE ARE IN DANGER—big letters on a tiny scrap of paper.

She doesn't look convinced. It's not exactly an original.

"Where you put it?"

"Up my bottom?"

She looks closely at me, hoping I'm trying to be funny. Irina has been known to make us bend over on occasion.

"Under my tongue?" I say. Ridiculous.

"I put pill there, after she cleaned my tongue, and she never notice."

So, I was right.

"But the paper will get wet," she says, after a moment.

I mull that one over. Will the ink smudge? "We can hold our tongues loosely."

"How we speak?"

"You manage with the pill. And anyway, they never really listen to a word we say."

For the first time in a long time I feel the pull of the giant puppet master in the sky. I thought she had left me, but lo, here she is, speaking through me at my darkest hour, and I have to hand it to her, this is the worst dictate she's ever sent, but I'm powerless to resist. I missed her—weirdly, I missed being possessed.

Nico surprises me by saying, "I will do it too," and as she starts to write in beautiful, looped handwriting, she blinks and bites down hard, winning the battle with her tears.

41

Nico

Sammy's plan will never work, and I'm only going along with it to do something, anything, to stop feeling so powerless, which must be why she thought of it in the first place, like the story we made up about climbing onto cloud-horses.

This tiny piece of paper is her call to action, but I feel as if we are being summoned over the top of the trenches, as in the stories of the soldiers Miss Iliescu told us about, some of whom were only young boys. Pointless—but if it helps build morale, then why not try to pretend? And there comes a point where a bullet would be preferable to constant fear, starvation and frostbite, gangrene and rot.

We are in the car and the fat man's bulges are winking at us from behind his collar. We don't speak, as we both have the slips of paper rolled under our tongues, and we're trying not to swallow them, or dissolve them with our saliva. Sammy has instructed me to keep a look out for any landmarks, to give directions should any of the men want to help. Even though she knows this plan will not work, she needs to believe it might.

The driver zigzags to confuse us; every time we take a journey, the car takes us to a big roundabout that you can get to by going left or right at the top of the road, out of the maze of houses. It is never possible to read the signs, as the windows are dusky and smudge the outside, and I'm not even sure it's always the same roundabout. Round we go and out onto a big, fast, flowing road. I notice a tall, narrow building which looks like a spire spiking the sky, and then hedges and road signs, though I can't see any names.

I think of the doctor, lying on his back in that hotel room blowing smoke rings at the ceiling and saying, "There are so few places where you can smoke indoors these days." I imagine a cigarette never tasted so good. These men don't connect our bodies to real, live, breathing ones, certainly not to any daughters they might have. The icy-cold finger pushes its way inside me. This note could be very dangerous if it fell into the wrong hands. It could puncture a dream, and everyone knows it is very dangerous to wake a sleeping beast. But still, I hold it there, loosely, just in case.

The car pulls up in a very busy street with bars and restaurants. Sammy makes a thumbs-up sign at me. The fat taxi man gets out and stands by the front door, on his phone. He's talking urgently to someone.

"Maybe we should give our notes to the barman?" she

whispers thickly, her tongue immobile, trying to hold the paper in place.

I shake my head. "The men who pay for us will see. And the driver," I say, gesturing to him on his mobile, "sees everything."

Sammy laughs at my lisping voice. I notice she has two spots of red color on her cheeks. She has that look that I have seen before, that look she wears when she is about to fling herself headfirst into the shallows. It is reckless and it will hurt. I put my hand on her arm to steady her, and as I look into her eyes, it's like falling into two black holes: her pupils have swum into her irises. I wonder how many pills she has swallowed.

"Be careful," I say, all my excitement from earlier having leaked away. She pokes her tongue out at me, touches her nose, and crosses her eyes, conjuring Luca. I shiver.

"Oops," she says, as she recovers the piece of paper. My throat narrows. "Lighten up, Roomie, tonight is the first night of the rest of our lives. Freedom!" she whispers, giddy and high on her fantasy.

I speak coldly to try to interrupt her hysteria, carefully sorting through my vocabulary to choose the right words. "We must to be careful with who, and if and when, we give these notes."

She laughs. "Yes, Miss Schoolmarm, what beautiful and precise English you speak." Why is this funny?

The driver raps his knuckles against the window and opens the back door. I almost fall out, Sammy clambering after me, and the two of us place our unsteady legs in our thin high heels onto the ground. Sammy stands and sways, drinking in air. I hold on to her as we make ourselves tall, roll our shoulders back and teeter into the bar, where we see the two men smiling at us from under two polished bald heads. I squint and blur my vision but cannot see a rescuing knight no matter how hard I try.

The four of us are seated at the barstools and Sammy's man already has his hand high on her inner thigh. She hasn't even finished her first drink. I see the fat driver sitting at a table nearby and I wonder how many other eyes are trained on us. Sammy's man is the first to take action, his hand on her behind as they go. She turns to look at me briefly, her eyes huge.

My man smiles, almost apologetically, and says, "Well . . . shall we?" He offers his hand and I take it, my insides turning to steel even as my mouth is working itself into a smile. "You're so pretty. Has anyone ever told you how pretty you are?"

This man likes to hold me close and tells me over and over how lovely I am. "Thank you, thank you," he says, and "Sorry," which is not the first time I have heard this word. The piece of paper is still curled under my tongue. I hold that part of me stiff while his invades every part of me. I would not want this person to know anything about me; he needs to remain a stranger. I hope Sammy has some self-protection and she doesn't give that sweating bald man any ammunition. They know, I'm sure of it, and that is part of the thrill for them—the powerlessness of the creature beneath them. I see in their eyes the same manic light that was in Sergiu's as he used to watch the barrel pick up speed with Luca thumping around inside. Roll over. There. Yes. There. No. You're welcome. Nothing has ever been less welcome.

I'm the first back to the bar, where the man insists on sitting with me until my friend reappears. "Wouldn't do to leave you here all alone now, would it?"

Oh no, sir, you never know what might happen to a young girl like me. I can hear Sammy's voice in my head and my thoughts are her thoughts. I sip the glass of sparkling wine slowly, letting the fizz slide down my throat, managing to hold the note in place, clamping my tongue down hard. I try to count the bubbles even though I know it's useless—the bubbles have popped by the time I swallow. I think back to me tasting a fizzy drink for the first time in that bar with Magda and Petre and the two friends from my neighboring village. What has happened to them? What could possibly have happened? I shake my head, not allowing my mind to fill with Magda's face from the last time I saw her.

I start to make a game of counting the flat bubbles, anyway, trying to pretend to myself. Then, on reflex, my tongue loosens and my throat opens wide and I suck the piece of paper down. There you go, sir, a vital piece of information about me, hidden inside me. I can feel it slithering its way down. HELP I AM IN DANGER. But of course this is the sort of man from whom I am most in danger.

42

Sammy

Once I've started on a course of action, there's no stopping me, bar crashing headlong into a wall of sorts. If there's one thing I can count on in myself, it is commitment—particularly once I've handed over the controls to my demon puppeteer. This is the same feeling I got the night of the bottle, and I really hope Nico gets off the tracks so the hurtling train doesn't smash against her, the way my actions have hurt Luce. I can't allow myself to think of Luce now.

I let myself imagine the scene playing out exactly as I described it for Nico: the man will read our plea for help and be moved to tears. The man is an envoy, an angel, dispatched to earth to free us. Yessireee.

Nico is staring at me intently. Somehow I've managed to convince her to keep the piece of paper under her tongue, although she doesn't quite share the same vision (hallucination?) as me.

My brain is a kaleidoscopic whizzing of shapes and colors and speed. It's a weird, wired thing. Tonight I am Ms. Fizzy Sherbert and Mr. Whippy Light. I have a new pluck in my tuck and I have you to thank for that, Doc. I feel as if I've mainlined voltage straight into my highway, as if mania is rushing through me—the way Mother used to get just before an episode of rage followed by a blackout. I guess I'm high.

Nico lays a hand on mine to steady me. I can feel her trying to pull me back down inside of myself. I don't want to land. Tonight I want to fly. I see my knight sitting on a barstool. In place of a shiny, bald head I plant a crop of thick, dark hair. In place of a sickly cigarette-smoke pallor, I paint rugged, sun-kissed skin. In place of slumped shoulders and slack muscles, I create a strong frame and lean sinew. In place of darting pink eyes I see kind, soulful ones.

I'm led to a hotel room where the lights are sparkling, spinning. I am swimming in the lights. The man starts to undress, gesturing at me to do the same, but when he sees my hesitation, he tells me to keep my clothes on. He pats the space beside him on the bed and says, in a deep, honeyed voice, Come now, love. Tell me all your worries. I lift my tongue to release the words that are inscribed on the page, on my heart. He reads them carefully and shakes his head. He reaches out to stroke my hair. Sure, he says, sure. Let's get you out of here. And your little friend. Such beautiful girls. You don't deserve this, any of this.

My eyes fill and he catches the tears.

"What the fuck are you blubbing about?"

I shake my head. That is not part of the script.

"What the hell are you playing at, you slut?"

I replace the smell of booze with fine aftershave. I wash out his mouth with soap.

"Cop on and do what you're paid to do."

My head is spinning even faster now and the lights have broken up into little jagged darts. I wonder if my neck will continue to support my head, which feels hot and inflated, like a balloon.

My body won't do what he's trying to make it do. I wonder how it's been able for the things that have happened to it. As if by giving voice to this thought, it tells me things: it won't allow any more breaking and entering—it has sealed itself tight.

Whack. This is easier. My lip is split. My left eye. Bitch. My nose. Thick warm liquid is leaking from me. My brain zigzags, boxer's brain. Insane, insane in the membrane.

43

Nico

I didn't realize I had you all night," the man says, rubbing his stubble with the palm of his hand, making a scratching sound, like sandpaper. "Maybe we should go back upstairs and finish off what we'd started?"

I'm not capable. I'm not able. I can't. As I say these things over and over in my mind, I see Sammy stumble out of the doorway to the ladies. There is blood on her face and her clothes are ripped.

"Please excuse me," I say as politely as I can. "I must to use the ladies room."

The man looks annoyed. That wasn't part of the arrangement. I'm not supposed to have any needs of my own, not even to use the toilet. I've seen this before. "I must go. I will be back soonest." I should say sorry, or pout, or blow him a kiss to keep the fantasy going, but I can't.

As I get up to leave, he grabs me by the wrist. I tell him I'll come straight back. I can feel his hot gaze branding my back as I walk away.

Sammy steps into the bar, looking dazed, and I shake my head and wave at her to step back inside. She is so outside of herself she doesn't recognize me. I push her back into the toilets and take her into a cubicle and lock the door.

"What the fuck?"

"It is okay, it is me, Nico."

"Ah, Roomie," she says as she slumps against me.

"What happen?"

"The note."

"Oh, Sammy. Why you think it safe to show him?"

"Safe?" she says. "Safe?" as if she's never heard the word before. She spits out some blood.

"We must get you back in car."

"Not sure . . . he is . . . finished with me yet."

"How you leave?"

She shrugs. "I flew . . ."

I unlock the cubicle door and lead her to the sink, where I pour warm water into the palms of my hands and wipe away the blood as best I can. She doesn't seem to notice.

A young girl in spiky heels walks in, looking drunk and overly made up. "Ouchy. Boyfriend trouble?" she says, nodding in Sammy's direction. How old is she? "At least you have one," she says. "I can't seem to keep a hold of any of them. Maybe he was jealous. It's sort of romantic, that kind of thing." She puts red lipstick on her cheeks and lips and pouts. "I'm not all that bad looking, am I?" Then she turns on her high heels and is gone. I look at Sammy, expecting peals of laughter, but she didn't even seem to register the girl.

When we walk back into the bar, the girl with the rouged cheeks and mouth is talking to the man I was with, who sees me and salutes. Something about that curt hand gesture and the set of his jaw tells me that he knows about Sammy and the note. The air has constricted suddenly in the room and it feels as if a poisonous gas is hanging there, coating my skin in a hot, damp sheen. There are a thousand pairs of invisible eyes following our every move, a thousand arrows poised in our direction.

The fat taxi man walks over and motions for us to follow him, and then he makes a minuscule movement, like he's slitting his throat. No one else would know, unless you were studying him very closely, and as I think this, I notice two guys fall silent and turn in our direction. One of them, a serious-looking young man with glasses, is staring right at him.

Our driver must see this as clearly as I do, because his face breaks into a cheery smile and he turns his hand movements into a wave. "Hi there, love. Is your little friend all right?" he asks me, in a strangely kind voice, loud enough to be overheard. "Time to get you both home, okay?"

I hold onto Sammy's arm tightly.

"Come on now, under strict instructions to make sure you get home safely. That's quite enough fun for one evening," he says, gesturing to Sammy with her bloodied face, trying to make light of her injuries. He whispers into my ear, "What happened to your friend shouldn't have happened. Those a-holes know this. You are not punchbags."

I can feel the speed building up inside, which makes my body shake so much I think I can hear my bones rattling.

Sammy is swaying and stumbling, falling against me. I try to hold her up.

The man with the glasses moves towards us. "Is she okay?"

"Fine," the taxi man says, "just a bit of a bust-up with her boyfriend."

"She looks like she could do with an ambulance," the guy continues, as his friend comes to join him, staring at us as if we're animals in a circus. I want to tell them to stop staring, I want to tell them to do something, but the words are stuck.

"Come on now," the taxi man says to me. "Just get your friend into the taxi and we can get her home to her mum."

"Who are you?" the guy asks our driver directly.

"Don't worry. This is a fairly regular occurrence with this little madam. Isn't that right?" he says to me, looking for back up.

No part of me will move.

Just at that moment another man appears. His eyes meet the fat taxi man's, who nods at him, seeming to communicate with him in a secret code. "May I?" the new man says, kindly, offering his arm to Sammy. She slumps against him, slipping from my grasp. He holds her steady and whispers into her ear. She is smiling and nodding, looking up at him in wonder. She is slurring something. Here is her rescuing knight. The man snakes his arm around her back and she falls against him. "Okay, now, one foot in front of the other. Let's get you home."

"He's seen this before," the taxi man says, winking at the guys, who don't wink back.

My blood turns cold and slows down, all my reflexes stilled. I am petrified, frozen. The man holds Sammy up as they walk towards the exit. She has totally succumbed to him. Every part of me wants to run after her, to scream out, but no part of me will move. Is this what happened to Mama when Petre came to take me away?

"Come on now. It's time to get moving," the driver says to me.

My feet are still stuck to the ground. He whispers into my ear, "We will kill your friend if you do anything stupid."

I look outside and I can see that the other man has bundled Sammy into the waiting car. One of the guys takes his phone out of his pocket.

The taxi man notices and grabs hold of me as my legs buckle beneath me. "She's just off her face," he says as he holds me up around my waist. "Have to bring her home. Under orders."

Please, please see my thoughts hanging in the air. Please, please let me not have to say it. Let me not have to speak.

"I don't like this," the guy says.

"She's fine. She's coming with me," the taxi driver says, a new note of panic in his voice.

My head is woozy and spots spin in front of my eyes.

"I'm calling the guards." Now the room is buzzing with voices, people are standing and everyone is staring.

"No need. I'll get her straight home." The taxi man hauls me to my feet. "Come on now, one foot in front of the other, be a good girl."

But I can't walk. I can't be a good girl anymore. I collapse against him and he lifts me with one arm and holds me on his hip, like I'm a sleeping child. My body is slack, a dead weight.

Phones are flashing. "No fucking photos," he says, and pushes against an outstretched arm, the phone crashing to the ground.

"Where do you think you're taking her?" a voice shouts.

"Mind your own fucking business," the taxi man says. He tries to run to the door, me hooked under the crook of his arm, but I fall out of his grip and slip to the floor.

The two guys move in closer. "Leave her, you prick," the man with the glasses says.

The taxi man raises his hand as if he's about to hit the guy, but then he looks around the room at the other peering faces, people on their phones, and looks at me for a moment, unsure what to do, before he races towards the door.

I am lying on the ground, faces staring down at me. "Carefully," a voice says, as hands reach down and lift me onto a chair. A glass of water appears before my lips. I sip, on automatic, and hold the water in my mouth. I can't swallow.

The guy with the glasses is shouting something at his friend, who shrugs and throws his hands in the air. Voices echo across the room, people offering advice—have the guards been called?—heads are shaking, tongues are clucking, futile words of sympathy, anger, outrage flung about, but no one is moving, no one is going after Sammy. There is still time, the car is still there, the taxi man is only just opening the door. The blood is rushing in my ears, a roaring, and my body is suddenly jolted into action. I spit the water out.

"Help her," I say out loud, or at least I think I do, because someone says, "What was that?"

"Help her!" I scream loudly. Those words that I swallowed earlier are erupting out of me. People run out the doors and someone manages to open the door of the taxi, but the driver is behind the wheel and revving the engine. The car begins to inch away as people start banging on the windows and doors. All the speed inside of me propels me through the door, and I launch myself at the car before it has had time to build up any momentum.

Sammy is hunched inside, her body curled into a tiny ball against the door. Sweet Mary, mother of God, please help her, help her.

"Jump, Sammy, jump!" She would be better off hurling herself against the hard ground than anything else that might be in store for her.

I run to the front of the car and stand, blocking it.

The car swerves and screeches, but it doesn't stop. I hear a crunch and feel a snap and I'm on my back, my arm crushed by something huge and heavy.

"Jesus. Jesus."

Voices, voices. I fall into darkness and weave my way into and out of the light, fighting to sit, fighting to run, fighting to breathe. Then I hear a loud wail on the air and hands lift me into another speeding vehicle with flashing lights. I can feel wet, hot tears pouring down my face, gushing, like my dam has finally burst its banks, and I hear myself saying, "You must find her," before a mask is put over my mouth.

Someone is pushing the hair off my face and saying, "It's okay, it's okay, love. All over now."

I am Sammy and she is me and I am sheltering myself from the blows. Then I feel a pinprick or a beesting and my tongue swells up and my body falls down. I am tiny and deep down under and this time there is a white rabbit. "What time is it?" He has pink eyes. It is midnight o'clock and after the bell tolls, the sandman will appear. Look! There he is—all long fingers and trailing shadows. He's stuffing my eyes, my ears, my mouth. "Oh dear," says the rabbit. "That's a mighty fine pickle you've got yourself into. Oh dear, oh dear, oh dear. You're late, you're late, you're late. Oh dear." Then he bunny-hops away. My body is writhing under the weight of the sand, and Mama is standing over me shaking her head: "See what happens when you fight with your fate?" The old dog is yelping and pulling at her thin piece of twine that will not break, no matter how hard she tries. Magda is patting her on her head and trying to soothe her. Papa is telling me how lovely I look, and Luca punches him hard in the mouth. His tooth falls out and a fairy flies in. The fairy has the face of Sammy and she is bleeding and mouthing, "Help me, help me." When I reach out to catch her, she crumbles to dust, like a moth. Oh, what have I done? What have I done? I hear a wailing sound and it is me.

44

Sammy

My knight has deposited me in a getaway car and we're speeding, speeding away down the highway. He came to my rescue, like I said he would.

"See, Nico? I told you he'd come," I say, turning to her. But the figure beside me is my savior. So who is driving? Is Nico in the front? Wavy lines float in front of my face and my eyesight is blurred. I press my knuckles into my eye sockets and rub them. When I open them again, I see that Nico isn't in the car. "Where is she?" I say to the man beside me, who shrugs and stares out the window. "Where is she?" I say again, my voice gathering in volume. "Where . . . is . . . she?"

"Shut up," the man says, in a thick foreign accent.

Panic is building itself into a frenzy. "Turn around," I shout. "This wasn't the plan."

I notice the bulges of the driver's angry neck flesh winking at me, mocking me.

Where is she? Where is she? Screams are ripping out of me. Flashes of her throwing her small body against the car. Did I hear something crack? Without her there to protect, I don't care what happens to me. *'Cause see, they call me a menace and if the shoe fits, I'll wear it.* Welcome back, my king. Rage rears its head and rushes through me, claiming me. I start to bang my hands against the glass, against the roof, kicking out at the seat in front of me. Hands grab on to me, holding me down.

I can hear Taxi Joe cursing at me. "Shut up, you stupid girl." His voice sounds distorted, muffled, and strained, as if he's wearing a muzzle. There's fear in that voice.

Doc O'D is humming in my ear: Samantha Harvey, what a very fine pickle you've got yourself into, and he winks, like we're in this thing together. The night of the bottle flashes across my mind, the night I crossed some invisible line, a psychic boundary, Doc O'D's pissed-off face when he saw Luce in the kitchen—hindsight is a muddied thing, especially as so many of my memories are made up of blurry fragments, remnants of my drinking thinking, and who's to know if what I think happened really happened, or if I imagined it, or if I was lying to myself—always lying to myself?

The car speeds on and I can hear the two men shouting at each other. It's contagious, this rage, and it has spread its angry red rash. I know that eruption. I used to watch it drain away from Mother and take its place in me instead. I saw the power that it gave her. I feel that same power now.

A laugh, more like a gurgle, flies out of me, caught and

stopped in its tracks by the gentleman to my left, who gallantly clamps his hand over my mouth. Seriously? Who's going to hear me inside this speeding car with the rain drumming down? These two are pretty worked up, going at each other and spitting, globules of the stuff spewing from one mouth to the other, tiny shimmering rainbows.

Granny Mona is stroking my forehead and smoothing the wet hair off my face. "Don't mind your mother, she doesn't know what end is up, doesn't know her arse from her elbow." And then her face bloats and goes bright red and she's standing over Mother as a girl, telling her, "It's all your fault, all of it, you're the reason he left." Grandad Stewart was a bolter too. No one could love you enough, Mother. I tried. And now I taste your guilt, your tears, your boozy breath, swollen tongue. I taste your pain.

There's Dad, with his hand on the small of my back, pushing me on my bike with no stabilizers. Go, Sammy. He's clapping me. "Great girl, look at you!" Look at me now, Dad. Maybe if you hadn't been such a "fucking coward"—Mother's gentler term of endearment that she'd hit him with as he backed out the door to go away on another one of his trips—I wouldn't have fallen so far down this stinking rabbit hole, which is lined with shit edging its way higher, climbing into every part of me. Maybe if you had admitted the truth, just once, believed my stories, which I knew you knew were true, instead of dismissing my overactive imagination—"It's never as bad as all that, my little catastrophist"—maybe we could have tackled this thing together, head-on. Well, Dad, look at me now, look at me. It really is as bad as all that. For once in your goddamn life, do something.

I'm whimpering behind the hand, which grips tighter and clamps against my cheekbones so hard they might break. He never listened; he never came to my rescue. He never would. No one would. Something falls away inside, and the hysteria dies, the laughter is swallowed, the king is gone, and I have no fury, no frenzy to shield me.

That wall I built is crashing down, and feelings are invading me, flooding my body, coming up and out through my nose and mouth. The man's voice curses at me. I'm not even sure what language he's speaking, but he's removed his hand and is shaking off my snot and tears, and now he's tying a napkin or something over my face and pulling the knot hard at the back of my head.

Luce, I think you knew I was never in control of myself. I'm not to blame, we are none of us to blame. "Can I write a note to someone?" I say, or I try to say. The man hits me across my gagged mouth and growls, "Shut up," as he ties my hands behind my back with thin string.

Of course they won't get a note to anyone out there. As far as they all know, I'm dead already.

There's a siren ringing in my head. It's a red, flashing, twirling sound and it's burrowing its way into my brain. The accelerator is pressed flat to the floor and the two men fall silent, all held-breath anticipation. The man beside me leans across and pushes the back door open, and Taxi Joe screams like a woman as the man pushes me at full speed, full tilt, onto the hard pavement. My head whacks against the concrete and I hear the car reverse back towards me. Is he going to drive over me? It's as if I'm watching this play out on a screen, except the pain is real, the pain is a climbing plant, like poison ivy, choking me. The car jolts to a stop and a figure gets out, the car spewing fumes into my eyes, my mouth, my nose. Something hot and vital is flowing out of me, something I can't push back inside. A pair of hands picks me up and pulls my mask away. Joe is looking down at me with terrified eyes, shiny and huge; he looks for a moment like he did that time he dropped Nico and I off at our first job—like a concerned dad—until he remembers what I am, what I've done, what I could cost him.

A switch is flicked in him and he steels himself: his gaze visibly hardens, his teeth clamp, a muscle in his jaw twitches, and he sets himself to the task at hand. He hoists my body over a wall and lets it, me, fall into the water below.

I close my eyes and allow my body to go limp; for once in my life I'm not fighting, no kung fu in the old girl left, no laughter, no fizz, no Champagne bubbles, no voices, no song, just flat black water like molasses sucking me down. It's velvet down here, beautiful, all shades of beautiful, and I drink it in.

It's Nico I think of as I go under: I hope she gets her swim in the icy sea, I hope the clouds above are bursting their skin and clean her with their sweet tears, I hope the waves are high and she gets tumbled, head over heel, water flushing through her, making its way inside every crevice until there is nothing left from any of those men and she is clean, squeaky-clean clean and she can be free.

"Once . . . upon . . . a . . . time . . . ," I hear her voice—this story is not over yet—and the puppet master in the sky tears the gag from my mouth and unties my hands and pulls me upwards until I break the surface and the air hurts, everything hurts, but life is living through me and refuses to give up on me, even me, and I look up: written in the gray clouds, blurred by the rain—or is it my tears?—is BREATHE and I suck air in and find I am kicking, swimming, breathing, kicking, swimming, breathing . . .

45

Nico

A cooling breeze blows on my hot cheeks as I climb to the highest branch of the highest tree in the forest. God's breath floats all around. The smells of leather and Papa's tobacco linger in the air. I look upwards and notice that I can't see any shapes in the clouds. They are just streaks of dirt across a hard, polished blue surface. Luca climbs up behind me and starts to shake the branch I'm straddling.

"Stop, I could fall."

He laughs.

I tumble, like a ripped fairy cap in the wind.

A fan is whirring, angled at my face. The light from the window is gray-white. A woman wearing white, with blue shining eyes, is smiling, the light in them glinting at me like the gilded Madonna in my bedroom. My face won't smile back. My body feels like every bone has been smashed and reassembled upside-down and inside-out. She reaches out to touch my arm and I try to move away.

"Okay, dear, it's okay. You're okay. Take it easy," the woman says, smoothing my damp hair off my burning face. "You're okay, healing nicely, just some internal bruising, a few broken ribs and an arm."

How is that possible? She cradles the back of my head and holds a glass of water to my lips. "Little sips. You'll be back to normal in no time." Again, that overbright smile. I don't even bother trying.

The door closes gently and I wriggle my toes and the fingers on my right hand, my left is immobilized in a sling, then I move my head side to side, slowly at first, then faster, rhythmically, until my whole body is involved. I wonder how long before the doctor from the house, or that other man, the doctor Sammy knew, will come looking for me. The door reopens and a hand rests lightly on my good arm, "Okay now, shhhh . . ."

I roll onto my side, then onto my back again. The pain in my ribs is sharp and stabbing, and I turn my head towards the wall and stay there, staring at the white paint, which has streaks of black, like thumb tracks of squashed flies. Victor used to love to make these smears on our kitchen wall, and I can see Mama, her tongue poking through her teeth, scrubbing; all the while tutting and scrubbing.

"Would you like some ice cream?" the voice says. "Vanilla, strawberry, or chocolate?"

Maria and I had strawberry ice cream one time, for her

twelfth birthday. It had slivers of dark pink running through it, and as I tried to swallow, all I could think of was veins. I shake my head.

"Maybe later?" the voice says, and I feel myself slipping into sleep.

I have no idea how long I'm in this place. A lady, whose name is Linda, comes to talk to me every day. She sits on a chair beside the bed and asks how I'm feeling, and I always just nod, like, I'm fine, thank you, now leave me alone.

Then she says, "Do you want to talk about anything?" But staying silent is my only protection against making it real, making it live on again. My head is strangely calm, maybe it's the drugs that are making me woozy, and the counting down from a hundred over and over. I can hold my breath from a hundred back to five now, and longer by the day. Linda gives me my own pad and pen and tells me to write it all out. I do not even lift the pen.

One day, she asks about Mama and Papa. "Do you think your parents know where you are?"

What a stupid question. I see Papa taking the wad of money from Petre, and Mama pummeling him before she is turned to stone. I turn my head away. F-U-C-K. I can hear Sammy's voice.

"I am sorry for asking such a difficult question, Nicoleta. I know this is hard . . ."

Her voice is soft and honey and I feel I may crack. "Is there anything I can get for you?"

My hand reaches for the pen and writes: A book. I need to lose myself in a world far from this one.

"Anything in particular? What do you like to read?"

Treasure Island, I write.

"Sure thing. I'll be back with it tomorrow, and maybe a few others, okay?"

I nod and inside I hear myself saying, Go now, go, just F-U-C-K off and leave me alone to sleep.

"We'll be moving you out of here soon," she says. "Your injuries are healing nicely."

I attempt a smile, which feels forced and tight. For a moment the question crosses my mind: Where? Where are they moving me? Then I realize I don't care. I'm numb and empty and can barely lift my head off the pillow. Let them do what they want to me, I've gone beyond feeling, caring about anything at all.

Days, maybe three, maybe ten, pass in this way, me sleeping and eating jelly and soft toast and drinking tea and trying to read, although the words slip-slide off the page, with Linda at the side of the bed sometimes asking questions and getting no answers, and at other times just sitting there looking out the window at the darkening skies, full of different kinds of rain.

Then the day comes when she says, "Tomorrow. You will be moved tomorrow."

The first night I'm put in a room with four other girls and bunk beds with pink quilts. I would like to be on top because it would be more work for a man to climb up, and I'm sure he wouldn't care which one of us he chose. They won't let me though because of my arm, so I have to lie on the bottom, listening to the creaks in the wood. I hear the other girls tossing off the blankets, murmuring names, sighs, and shouts. I hear quiet crying. I hear one girl banging her head against the wooden frame of the bunk. I never close my eyes or my ears as I lie looking at the wriggling shape in the mattress above me. I hear the door of the bedroom open and feel a presence in the doorway. The person stands for some time, listening, then they gently close the door and walk away. This is the first night in many nights that I'm not awake because of what somebody else is doing to me. This night I'm awake because my mind won't let me rest: images of Sammy curled into a tight ball in the back of the car playing over and over.

The next morning, the girls start chattering in a mixture of Romanian and English. Chitchat: Where are you from? When did you last see your mama? Just how old are you? Have you started bleeding? Do you think these people are kind? I think the women here are very kind. I am so hungry, says one. Me too, says another. I don't feel hungry. A girl called Katya says she is thirteen although she looks to be about seventeen. They seem happy, excited even. One girl starts braiding another girl's hair. They are discussing their favorite dresses: Blue with polka dots, says one. I love stripes, says another.

"What is your favorite color?"

I can't answer.

"Mine is yellow, what is yours?" says the girl who banged her head against the wooden frame. I look at her head to see if there is a lump.

"Why are you looking at me so strangely?" she says.

I look away.

"Cat got your tongue?" says the older girl. "Show us your tongue."

I can feel Irina scraping down my tongue, Sammy watching, and I run out of the room, followed by the girl's whispers: What's wrong with her? I wish she wasn't in our room. She's no fun, no fun at all.

"Create and imagine," a woman says. "I feel like . . . an animal, happy, sad, angry . . . a clown? Happy on the outside, but crying inside?" I think of my sad clown from the traveling circus and then an image of the bear in the cage catches in my mind, playing over and over. I shake my head.

Most of the other girls are pretending to be cats, lions, hyenas, clowns; they are telling each other their feelings. Some of them are mute, like me, and sit on the outside. No one is forcing them to do anything.

"Listen and imagine," the woman continues. "Let's all lie on our backs and close our eyes and relax and imagine we are mermaids." She makes a silly whooshing sound and pretends to splash an imaginary tail about. I try to imagine Sammy here.

"How are you, Nicoleta?" she asks me. "Don't feel like joining in today? That's okay. Do as much or as little as you like, but try to stay in the room with us, if you can."

I stay standing and face the wall, which is buttercup yellow and covered with posters of painted handprints. We are not children.

How does she know my name? No one has called me my

full name, except Papa one time when he came home from the pub in one of his plum-cheeked moods. Her voice is safe, a container. I almost join in but can't bear to feel so young.

The other girls are lying on their backs and some of them are giggling. I wonder how they can lie down so easily. The women here keep trying to make me "draw my feelings," or "write it down, in my own language, for my eyes only." They want me to play, to learn to trust again, a little at a time. They are kind, these women, but I think that would be a very dangerous thing for me to do. I think back to Papa telling me, "I have made sure he is a good man," and see Petre frothing at the mouth.

"This is a safe place," says the woman with very blonde hair. It must come from a bottle because no sunshine strong enough to bleach the landscape or brown the skin or lighten the hair ever gets through the clouds here. She's very pretty with sparkling cheeks and lips and eyes. I don't see any ring on her finger. Why does she wear makeup and dye her hair when there are no men here? I'd like a life without a man, unless it's a man like Luca but more of them are like Victor or Sergiu or Petre . . . or . . . The woman comes to me, she sees, she stands near but not too near.

"Hello, Nicoleta, are you there?" she says gently. Of course I'm here, where else would I be? "You seem to be very far away. Would you like to tell us what you are thinking?"

I look around the room and see that the girls are all sitting in a circle, on cushions on the floor, staring at me. I shake my head at them.

"Would you like to sit down and join the circle?"

I thought she knew what I needed but now she has got it wrong. This feels like a trick, like the time Magda invited us girls to drink cola and we woke in the dark room in the boat. The knock on my head has not totally knocked away all the memories, although they blur and wash indistinctly. My mind is restless, filled with a strong, angry word and with an image of Sammy and me shouting it, over and over, and this memory plays again and again, so it's more real than this moment I'm meant to be living, and no amount of pinching will scatter the ghosts: fuck, fuck, fuck, jumping up and down on the bed, and F-U-C-K, and the laughter.

The woman sees me, again, sees into me. "When you're ready, no pressure . . ."

I nod, ashamed of my anger. She smiles and wipes any shame away.

I am told a week has passed and I still haven't said anything, to anyone. After the group session, where the women gently ask questions and some of the girls cry, or hold each other's hands, or sometimes hug each other, I'm asked by the woman with the bleached hair and sparkling eyes to go with her for a chat. She asks me, do I want a drink. Is it all going to start up again? I shake my head so hard it hurts.

"Now, Nicoleta, is that your real name?" she asks.

I nod. I remember now telling this to the woman in the blue suit who came to visit me in the hospital. Memories are slowly revisiting me, although I'm doing my best to fight them by counting backwards.

"You're from Romania, is that right?"

I nod, the lie so ingrained in me now it feels less dangerous than saying the truth. I cannot find my voice. I swallowed it that moment when Sammy sped away in the car, my last words spoken: "You have to find her," and no one has, and my voice is lodged deep in my stomach, making it impossible to find. My tongue is as paralyzed as my arm. I cross my legs and draw my good arm over my body, looking anywhere but at her.

"Do you know what country you are in?" the woman—who tells me her name is Lou—says.

Dub, Sammy had said.

"You are in Dublin, Ireland," Lou says. She takes out a map and shows me. It is beside England, and it's tiny. It is swimming in the sea. She shows me Romania too, and I notice my country is right beside it. No sea touches it.

"Do you want to go back there?" she asks. "Would it be safe for you to go back there?" I think of the dog's neck straining, and of Mama hitting the ground, and then sitting silently, emptied out, all fight gone in her at the end. I draw in breath and hold it, counting backwards. Sixty-six seconds. Am I impressing you?

The woman touches my hand lightly. "That's okay, dear. No one is ever going to force you to do anything you don't want to again. You do understand me, don't you?"

I nod.

"Would you like to go to school here?" she says. "You are obviously very good at languages," and she smiles, the corners of her eyes crinkling at the sides. "What would you like to be,

Nicoleta? Have you ever thought about what you would like to be when you grow up?"

I stare out the window at the fat drops of rain that stick and slide down the pane like translucent slugs. "Think about it, and if you have any ideas in the next few days, you come to me and tell me."

I prefer to think about this. This woman is not trying to make me talk about the men.

"Have you ever been to the seaside, Nicoleta? Would you like to go?"

I think about the portholes on the first boat, the second boat sitting in the sea, and my heart speeds. Then, I think of Papa's words to me ". . . lucky girl, you will see the sea . . . I have always wanted to see the sea . . ." I think of Sammy's promise about us getting there one day, being tumbled in the waves so fast our brains would be washed clear. We would swim in, and swallow down, the rain.

"There's a bus going this afternoon, and I will be on it. You are welcome to join," Lou says.

Before I leave, I slip a silver pen, like a silver bullet, into my pocket. I think Lou sees but says nothing.

The bus is tall and the windows are foggy. I go upstairs and Lou follows and sits in beside me. I flatten myself against the window so I don't have to feel any part of her touch me.

"Is this very different from your country, Nicoleta?" she asks as she leans across, making sure not to brush against me, and clears a patch on the glass with her shirt sleeve. Not so different. No. The grass is greener and shinier here, and the cows are fat. The sky is almost always overcast though. At home it is constantly changing, high to low, shades of purples, blues and yellow, but then I realize I have only been here for one season, one harvest.

"There it is, look," Lou says. I follow the line of her finger over her shoulder and see a body of gray water.

Papa, the sea is neither black nor blue.

I can hear his voice: "Like the night sky turned upside-down. Imagine that, Nico?" Well, Papa, here it is: a murky daytime sky, fallen to earth. Imagine, swimming in wet clouds.

The bus stops and we get out. We walk towards the edge of the sea, where the water is licking the sand, and Lou takes off her shoes and socks.

I can feel the speed building up inside me. I don't remember ripping off my shoes but I must have, because I'm barefooted, the damp sand rubbing between my toes, and I'm running towards the restless water. I run, the wind pushing against me, salty gusts slapping my face, I run. Here it would be easy. The knot at the back of the sling starts to loosen and I pull it free with my good arm. I run, pushing against the clouds as they gather round me. Mama is calling me on the wind, or is it Lou? "Nicoleta, come back, come back." I wade in, the freezing water lapping at my ankles, my knees, stomach, arms, ribs. I hold my breath and dive down, cradling my arm close, feet towards the sky, tumbling head over heel, tumbling, like I'm in a washing machine, soap-soaked, bubbles rising, dirty thing being washed clean. Sammy's laughter fills my ears, her face floats before me, her hand grabs mine. "Hello, Roomie," she mouths at me, bubbles flying from her mouth. A fish-baby. She squeezes my hand, then drops it, and dives to the depths, waving bossily at me to go back, go back, go back to the light.

The water refuses to let me stay down, and like a giant hand, lifts me up to the surface. Each time I try to go under, it pushes me back up, and so I lie there, floating. I am held by the sea and the clouds, which have dropped from the sky and merged into one. I let go of everything I was clinging to and spread both arms wide. Look: no hands! No pain. A voice is calling me back, full of worry and love and every shade of kindness I have ever known. The sea-sky is piebald-gray on gray and becomes the shape of a horse. I climb on top and I am trotting, then cantering, galloping along the plains.

This time, Sammy, this time.

AUTHOR'S NOTE

Although *Cloud Girls* is a work of fiction, it was inspired by my involvement in the Stop Sex Trafficking of Children and Young People campaign run by The Body Shop, ECPAT International, and the Children's Rights Alliance in Ireland. At the launch of the campaign in 2012, I was invited to read firsthand accounts of some of the girls that had been trafficked for the sex trade.

The stories of the girls I was asked to read that day haunted me. Many sleepless nights followed, and I found myself unable and unwilling to forget. *Cloud Girls* exploded onto the page some years later, when, finally, I could no longer ignore the impetus to give voice to these girls' experiences. The characters of Sammy and Nico are composites of many testimonies I read. I wanted parallel storylines to illustrate the experience of how a young girl can be both domestically and internationally trafficked. The common denominator is vulnerability, youth, and lack of parental and societal protection.

At the time of the campaign there were an estimated 1.2 million children trafficked globally every year, but because of the clandestine nature of the crime, the migrant crisis, and the increasing numbers of unaccompanied minors going missing, it is impossible to know exactly how many young girls (and boys) are exploited in this way. According to statistics offered by the US Department of Justice, an estimated 14,500 to 17,500 foreign nationals are trafficked into the United States annually, with a further 200,000 at risk of domestic trafficking.

This book is my attempt to pay homage to these invisible girls, and to raise awareness of this hidden, flourishing, billion-dollar global trade.

ACKNOWLEDGMENTS

I am indebted to Liliana Rotaru of CCF Moldova for her generous observations on Nico's journey, and to Sarah Benson, CEO of Ruhama, for her careful notes on Sammy's trajectory.

Thank you also to Emma McKinley from the Children's Rights Alliance, and Catriona Graham and Nusha Yonkova from the Immigrant Council of Ireland. To Orla Diffily for helping to make all this possible.

To my early readers, in particular Joanne Hayden, Elizabeth McSkeane, Anthony Glavin, Catherine Dunne, Susanna Jones, Michelle Moran, Emer Conlon, Tom Farrelly, and Hugh O'Conor, you gave me faith to carry on when I needed it.

Special thanks to all at New Island Books in Dublin for publishing the first edition of this work and now to all at HarperVia, in particular Judith Curr and Paul Olsewski for their ongoing support, and to Alexa Frank and Alison Cerri for all their hard work. Huge gratitude to my visionary editor Tara Parsons and to my wonderful agent Clare Alexander.

Here ends Lisa Harding's
Cloud Girls.

The first edition of this book was printed and
bound at Lakeside Book Company in
Harrisonburg, Virginia, in March 2023.

A NOTE ON THE TYPE

The text of this novel was set in Bell MT, a typeface designed by Richard Austin for John Bell's British Type Foundry. Bell is a facsimile of Austin's original typeface, cut in the 1780s. Monotype's Hot Metal Bell font family from 1931 took inspiration from Austin's designs, and the TrueType version, released in 1992, updated the type once again for today's readers. Bell MT is known for its sophisticated, elegant appearance. Its professional and vintage vibes makes it a versatile and effective choice for books, magazines, and various printed matter.

HarperVia

An imprint dedicated to publishing international voices,
offering readers a chance to encounter other lives and other
points of view via the language of the imagination.